Praise for the novels of

JACI BURTON

"Sexy, smart, edge-of-the-seat romance…
Jaci Burton always delivers a great read."
—*New York Times* bestselling author Lara Adrian

"In the hands of the talented Burton,
the characters leap off the page and
the romance sparkles as the sex sizzles."
—*RT Book Reviews* on *The Perfect Play,* Top pick!

"Hot, sexy, romantic suspense at its best!"
—*New York Times* bestselling author Lora Leigh
on *Riding on Instinct*

"Burton continues to display a deft hand
as she combines emotional drama with
plenty of sizzling sex and dangerous action."
—*RT Book Reviews* on *Taken by Sin*

"Burton brings the heat, jazzing her otherworldly
suspense plot with numerous passionate interludes,
without letting the explosive good vs. evil saga flag.
Hot sex, fierce battles and an impending sequel
make this title worth hunting down."
—*Publishers Weekly* on *Hunting the Demon*

D0711438

JACI BURTON

THE HEART OF A
KILLER

MIRA®

ISBN-13: 978-0-7783-1259-8

THE HEART OF A KILLER

Copyright © 2011 by Jaci Burton

For questions and comments about the quality of this book please contact us
at Customer_eCare@Harlequin.ca.

www.Harlequin.com

Printed in U.S.A.

For Charlie, a man whose support is limitless,
whose patience is endless and whose love
keeps me going every day.
Thank you for helping me live this dream.

Prologue

Five minutes till closing time. Anna Pallino scrubbed down the counters at the ice-cream shop while keeping her eye on the clock. They'd be walking in any minute, hoping for free ice cream while she closed up. They always showed. They were predictable. She loved that about them. Her guys. The brothers, though not by blood.

She bent down to put away the cones, when she heard the bell tinkle above the door. She smiled as she stood.

Yup. Always predictable. There they were—Dante, Gabe, Roman and Jeff.

Her heart tripped a beat when she settled her gaze on Dante. He was hers. Her boyfriend, the first guy she'd ever fallen in love with. Tall, with dark brown hair, blue eyes, everything she'd ever dreamed of in a boyfriend.

He grinned and swung into his seat at the counter.

"Rocky Road, please, Miss Pallino."

She gave him a stern look. "I'm sorry, sir, but we're closing."

He rose, leaned over the counter and batted those dark,

sinfully too-long lashes at her. "Aw, come on, baby. Not even for me and my guys?"

She laughed, went around the counter and locked the door, closed the blinds and turned the sign to Closed. "So what kind of mayhem did you guys get into tonight?"

"Best behavior, Anna," Gabe said, leaning his elbow against the counter.

If Anna hadn't fallen madly in love with Dante, she would have with Gabe. What girl wouldn't, with his jet-black hair and mesmerizing sea-green eyes. He was broader than Dante and nearly as tall. He and Dante were the same age, and at nearly eighteen, they were the oldest of all the guys.

But she'd fallen hard for Dante, and after that she'd never even thought about another guy. And with her being just sixteen, Anna was jazzed about having an older boyfriend. She was the envy of all her friends. Though her father wasn't totally thrilled about her choice of boyfriends. But Dante was always on his best behavior around her dad. And with Dante living at George and Ellen Clemons's house, there wasn't much her dad could say. It was a good foster home and they were a stern but loving family who'd raised a lot of great kids. Even her dad thought so. He was thawing on Dante.

"Yeah, Ellen would have our asses if we got into any trouble," Dante added.

"Isn't that the truth?" Jeff nodded. "We have to behave or Momma will kick our butts."

"She isn't our mother," Roman said, his head down, his expression sullen. "She and George are our foster parents."

"Oh, can it, Roman." Dante shoved an elbow into Roman's ribs. "They're the best parents we've ever had in all our shitty lives and you know it. Why don't you give up the poor-lost-boy act?"

"Yeah," Jeff said. "We're together. We don't get in trouble. We eat three squares and they're nice to us. They're good parents."

Roman shrugged. "I guess."

"No 'I guess' about it," Gabe said. "You're just pissed off because you lost the race over here." Gabe nudged him. Roman nudged back, and soon the two of them were tangled in arms and elbows and laughing, which made Anna exhale as the tension receded.

She couldn't imagine what it must be like to grow up without parents, shuffled from foster home to foster home. She'd known them since her freshman year, when she'd met Dante and the rest of the guys. They were like brothers to her. Well, all except Dante. Definitely not a brother to her. "How about some ice cream?"

"That's why we're here, isn't it?" Jeff grinned and leaned over the case, scoping out the flavors.

They told her what they wanted and she served it up. While they ate she finished putting everything away, then bagged up the trash. "I'm going to take this out back while you eat. Then we can go watch movies at my house. My dad rented a couple of horror movies for us."

"I'll take that out back for you." Dante stood and started to come behind the counter.

"Nope." She held out her hand. "It will only take a sec. Finish your ice cream. I want to get out of here."

"You sure?"

"I'm sure. Your job is to watch over the horde. Make sure they don't drip or break anything or I'll have to start cleanup all over again."

"Yes, ma'am," he said with a wink.

Anna laughed, grabbed the trash and headed out the

back door of the shop into the alley. The Dumpster was a short walk over.

The ice-cream shop was set in a series of tall buildings, mainly offices that housed banks and corporations. The shop stayed open late anyway because of the movie theater across the street. Kids always stopped by after the last show. But that meant there were no restaurants or retail and the alley was deserted at night. Creepy as hell for all the kids who worked at the shop, but Anna enjoyed the quiet. Her tennis shoes squicked on the wet ground, the sound echoing off the walls of the buildings.

It was so hot tonight. It had rained earlier and she dodged puddles and discarded soda cans and miscellaneous trash as she made her way down the dark alley. Humidity sucked the breath from her and she was wet with sweat by the time she got to the Dumpster.

She lifted the lid, holding her breath as she hoisted the trash into the container, then hurriedly dropped the lid. Ugh. She hated this part. It smelled so bad in there, like something died. She always imagined something decaying in there, like an animal or even a body. The drawback of having a police-detective father and listening to horror stories at the dinner table about where he'd found the latest victim. Yeah, this alley would be a perfect dumping spot, too. Isolated, no one around at night to witness what went down.

And now she'd creeped herself out. Great.

Shuddering, she turned to head back to the shop, when an arm snaked around her waist and jerked her backward.

Her scream went unheard as his hand clamped tight to her mouth. She squirmed, trying to get away, but his other arm was a band around her, pinning her arms tight to her sides. She kicked out, but he dragged her behind the Dumpster, then fell with her, immediately turning to drop on top of her.

Rocks jabbed into her back as she hit the ground, the breath knocked from her. He was so heavy. His hand was still over her mouth.

No. No!

Her heart pounded so fast she felt the slamming against her chest. She couldn't breathe. Nausea surged in her throat. She was going to throw up. The ground was wet from the rain earlier tonight. It stunk behind the Dumpster. What did he want? He was rolling on top of her, pinning her with his body.

She needed to scream, to let Dante know where she was, but the man's hand still clamped tight over her mouth.

"Don't scream, bitch, or I'll kill you," he whispered against her ear.

She felt something sharp against her throat. A knife.

Oh, God. Oh, God. She froze, tried to still her shaking body, not wanting to do anything that would make him stab her.

Was she going to die?

His breath was bad, just as bad as the garbage in the Dumpster. She felt something hard between her legs as he moved against her.

Please, help me. Somebody help me.

The guys weren't far away. Did she leave the back door to the shop open? She couldn't remember. If only she could scream they might hear her. She was sweating and cold, shivering so hard. Something underneath her was scratching her. She struggled to push him off so she could catch a breath, but he was stronger than she was.

Please get off me. I just want to breathe. I can't breathe!

They'd come help her. They'd get here in time. If only she could scream. She had to get out of this. This couldn't be happening to her.

She squeezed her eyes shut.

Buttons scattered across the alley as he jerked her blouse open, revealing her little pink bra. She'd worn the blouse for Dante, her favorite blouse. Pink and white checks with tiny heart buttons. She'd even chosen white shorts to match. She was lying on the filthy ground now in her white shorts, felt the moisture from the ground seeping through, knew they'd be ruined. *She* was ruined. Tears pricked her eyes, the burn making her blink. She didn't know whether to keep her eyes open, to try to see what he looked like, or keep them shut so she wouldn't recognize him, so he might let her live.

What was it her dad had always tried to teach her? She couldn't remember. She didn't want to be here. She wanted to be inside the shop with the guys. The guys were in there. They'd help her.

He grabbed her breast, squeezed it hard. It hurt. Oh, it hurt. He moved the knife down along her throat to her chest.

"You're mine, bitch. Always mine."

He cut through her bra. She was shaking so hard now that chills racked her body. He bent down and licked her nipple.

Bile rose in her throat and she turned her head away. She wouldn't watch. She couldn't.

But now she remembered what her dad said. *Fight. Don't give in.*

This was different. No way was she going to die. She'd do anything not to die.

Then he cut her. Oh, God, he was cutting her. It burned like her skin was on fire. She felt the warm trickle of blood down her chest. Nothing had ever hurt this bad. She couldn't believe this was happening.

And then she knew. He was going to kill her.

Her dad was right. She had to fight. If she was going to die, she wasn't going to go lying here and letting him do what he wanted to her.

She opened her eyes, stared at him, memorized his face. She wanted him to know she saw him. Then she bit down on his hand and he jerked it away. Taking that brief second, she opened her mouth and screamed. He slapped her so hard she couldn't think through the dizziness.

He clamped his hand over her mouth again, his other hand jerking at her shorts.

Please, please, somebody help me!

"Anna's taking a long time with the trash." Dante got up and went behind the counter toward the back door.

"You know she gets mad when you go back there," Jeff said.

"I don't care. I should have taken the trash out for her. I don't like her out there by herself."

"You just wanna go out there so you can kiss her," Roman said with a roll of his eyes. "I'm ready to go watch movies."

"Yeah, yeah," Dante said as he opened the back door, and heard the scream.

He pushed off the door and ran like hell, not even bothering to see if the others followed. He ran so hard his legs burned, his whole body shaking in fear.

As his eyes adjusted to the darkness, he saw a guy scrambling to his feet near the Dumpster. And he saw feet—tennis shoes. Anna's.

Shit. Shit. He skidded to a stop at the Dumpster.

Anna was on the ground, her clothes undone. It was

pitch-black out there, but he could see her, pale and shivering and bleeding.

Goddammit.

"Grab him!" He motioned to Gabe and the others as they whizzed by him.

Dante had dropped to his knees in front of Anna. She was bleeding at her chest. Her blouse was torn, her face swollen. Tears welled in his eyes and emotion he'd never felt before filled him. He wanted to grab her and cry. He hadn't cried since his parents…

Hold it together for Anna.

"You okay?"

She nodded, jerking the tattered edges of her blouse together.

"How bad are you hurt?"

"I'm fine."

"You're bleeding." He pulled a handkerchief out of his back pocket. "Let me see."

She squeezed her hands tight over her chest.

"Anna, baby, let me see how bad it is."

She lifted tear-filled eyes to his and it shredded a hole in his heart, especially when she dropped her hands and her blouse fell away. The guy had cut her bra in half. Dante swallowed and patted at the spot where the bastard had cut her, just above her left breast. There, he'd carved the shape of a heart.

Goddamn. Son of a bitch. Motherfucker.

Rage blinded him. Dante heard his own breath sawing in and out, felt his blood pounding in his ears. He wanted to tear the guy apart. But right now he had to focus on Anna. He forced himself to smile down at her as he pressed the handkerchief to her chest. He unbuttoned his shirt and shrugged it off his shoulders, leaving him in only his tank top.

"It's okay. It's going to be all right. Put this on." He helped her slide her arms into his shirt, then buttoned every single button. "You stay right here and I'll be back for you, okay?"

She looked up at him, her bottom lip trembling. Then she gave him a brief nod. She was alive. That's all that mattered.

Dante stood and turned to where the guys had cornered the bastard who'd done this. He'd hurt Anna. Dante didn't even want to think about what else he'd done to her.

Anger and rage and guilt boiled inside him. The guy stood there with a smart-ass smirk on his face like he didn't have a care in the world.

"She okay?" Gabe asked as Dante stepped beside him.

Dante swallowed. "He hurt her. He cut her." Dante put his hand on his chest where Anna's wound was.

"Fuck," Gabe whispered.

They all knew, would all feel the same fury that someone would hurt Anna.

Sweet Anna, who didn't have a mean word for anyone, who would never hurt anyone.

The others stepped away as Dante came toward him. The guy jerked back as if he was going to run.

Oh, no, you don't.

Dante tackled the guy before he could get away, flinging his body on top of him. It was insane after that. Instinct kicked in, all those years of street fights with fists and knives. Of survival, of doing whatever it took to stay alive, of defending those who couldn't defend themselves.

Anna hadn't been able to defend herself. This guy was twice her size.

Men didn't hurt women.

The guy rolled and kicked Dante away, then sprang to his feet, pulling a knife. A bloody knife—Anna's blood.

Anger so deep it boiled in his bones raged inside Dante. He saw the blood on the knife and thought of what Anna had gone through. No way was this dude getting out of the alley. The guy waved the knife at Dante, but he was no match for the four of them. They'd gotten into more fights together than Dante could count and they were damn good at working together.

Dante stared him down, holding his attention as Gabe moved behind the man and grabbed his arm, jerking the knife out of his hands.

Fury took hold, then. Dante pulled his arm back and let it swing full force at the guy's face. He staggered as if he was high or something, but Dante didn't care. His fist connected with the bastard's nose and Dante felt the impact, satisfied by the crunching sound. The guy didn't say a word, just pulled to his feet again, ready for more.

Yeah, he had to be tweaking or something to get up after the punch Dante gave him. Dante shoved him back down and the others jumped in, and then it was fists and feet and blood and the guy didn't stand a chance.

He didn't know when the dude had stopped moving, but at some point Dante was out of breath and his fists hurt. He backed off.

"Stop. He's done for." Dante moved away, pulled the others off.

They stood there looking down at the guy who looked nothing like he had when they'd first come on the scene. He was a bloody pulp of a mess. Dante kicked at him, but he didn't move. He was out cold.

He went to Anna, bent over her.

"Anna."

She stared at her attacker, didn't look at Dante.

"Anna." Dante touched her and she flinched. He reached for her shoulders. "It's Dante. Look at me."

She turned to him, then her eyes filled with tears. "Oh, God. Oh, Dante." She fell into his arms and he lifted her, pulled her against him while she sobbed.

He wrapped his arms around her and lifted her. "Come on, let's take you inside."

They took Anna back to the shop and sat her on one of the stools. Dante grabbed some paper towels and wet them so he could wipe her face.

"Is she okay?" Roman asked.

"Don't know." Dante focused on Anna.

She was crying hard now, shook her head, trying to talk even though he knew she had to be hysterical. "He grabbed me from behind, dragged me behind the Dumpster. He ripped my blouse and my bra."

Dante sucked in a breath.

"He cut me, here," she said, unbuttoning his shirt enough to show them all the heart-shaped cut.

"Jesus," Gabe said. "I'm going to kill him."

"Not if I do it first," Roman said.

"You got there before he…" She bent her head down and wept, her fingers clutching Dante's shirt together.

Shit. "Let me help you." Dante rebuttoned the shirt, felt her body shaking, then looked up at Gabe. "Go grab that scum and bring him in here. We need to call the cops."

Gabe nodded and motioned to the others. "Come on."

Gabe and the others left Dante and Anna alone.

"I'm sorry. I shouldn't have let you go out there alone."

"Not your fault."

She could say that, but it didn't matter. "We'll call the cops and your dad. They'll take care of this." Because Dante had failed to.

Chin resting on her chest, she gave a short nod. "Okay."

Gabe burst through the back door, out of breath. "Dante. I think he's dead."

Dante whipped around. "What?"

"He ain't movin'," Gabe said. "I tried to wake him up and he didn't move. We tried to pull him to his feet, but he just went down again like…dead weight. When I went to feel for a pulse I got nothin'."

"It's true," Jeff nodded, his face ghost-white. "He's dead. Oh, man, he's dead, Dante."

Dante turned back to Anna, whose eyes widened. This wasn't good. "I'll go check it out."

She scooted off the bar stool. "I'm going with you."

"No. You stay here."

She shook her head and gripped his hand. "Don't leave me in here by myself. Please."

He blew out a breath, torn between wanting her to stay put, calling the cops and wishing none of this had happened. He should have just taken the goddamn trash out for her. Then it wouldn't have happened at all. "I'll have one of the guys stay with you."

"I'll hang in here with you, Anna," Gabe said, moving next to her.

She shook her head, that stubborn chin of hers lifting as she squeezed Dante's hand. "No. I need to see him."

He sighed. "Okay. Stay right next to me."

They walked outside. He tried to keep her away from the guy, who was still lying there right where they'd left him. Roman and Jeff were standing over him. They stepped aside when he and Gabe got there.

Dante turned to Gabe. "Stay with Anna while I check this out."

Anna resisted, but Dante turned to her. "This is as close as I'm letting you get to him. Understand?"

She nodded, still shaking.

Gabe pulled Anna to his side. Dante went over to the guy and nudged him in the side with his shoe.

"Get up, asshole."

Nothing. He kicked him harder this time.

"Come on, get up."

He kneeled and put his fingers on the man's neck, searching for a pulse. He couldn't find one there, or on his wrist. God, he was a bloody mess and Dante didn't want to do it, but he leaned down and laid his hand over the guy's chest.

The body was warm. He was still warm. But there was no heartbeat, no pulse.

Dante looked up at his brothers. "He's dead."

"Shit. Sonofamotherfuckingbitch." Jeff tore at his hair and started pacing back and forth. "Now what do we do, Dante? We killed him."

Dante stood. "We go back into the shop and we call the cops."

"No."

Dante turned to Anna. "What?"

Anna shook her head, tears streaking down her face. The hysteria had gone, replaced by a calm awareness of exactly what to do. "You have to get out of here. All of you. Now."

Dante went to her, put his hands on her shoulders. "Anna We killed this guy. We were protecting you. Besides, he came at us with a knife. It's kind of self-defense."

"I know that and you know that. But you all have juvie records. You know how it'll look. You still beat him up and now he's dead. You all have to get out of here. I'll call my dad and he'll take care of this."

Dante shook his head. "No. I can't let you do that. I'm not leaving you."

"He's right, Anna," Gabe said. "We can stand up for this."

"No, we can't," Jeff said, his hands balling into fists as he paced. "I don't want to go to Juvie again. We got a nice family and I wanna stay there."

"Me, too," Roman said, sniffing back tears. "Let Anna call her dad and make this go away."

"What are we, a bunch of pussies?" Dante stared them all down. "We did this. We can handle it."

She took them in with her gaze, and knew she'd do anything to make sure they stayed safe.

Anna pulled Dante to face her again. "I couldn't live with myself if something happened to you. To any of you. You saved my life. God only knows what that…guy… would have done to me if you hadn't showed up."

Tears fell down her cheeks. She didn't bother trying to swipe them away.

Dante folded her against him. "Anna, it's okay. You're okay. We've been through worse."

She pushed on his chest and shook her head. "No. I won't let anything bad happen to you because of me. Please, just do this for me. Please."

"Let's go inside." He wrapped his arms around her and led her back inside.

"What do you want to do about him?" Roman asked.

Dante looked over his shoulder at the dead guy. "I guess we leave him there for now."

"What if somebody comes?" Roman asked.

"Not much we can do about it."

Once inside the shop again, Dante checked Anna's

wound. The bleeding had stopped and all she felt was a raw throb she was determined to ignore. She wished she could ignore everything that happened. Concentrating on something other than herself would help. She wiped her face and hands, lifted her chin and stared them all down, determined they were going to see things her way.

"I want you all to go. Now. Hurry, before someone finds the body. I'm going to call my dad and we'll figure out what to do."

"That's not right," Dante said. "You shouldn't have to deal with it."

"I'll have my dad. He'll help. I'm not going to have you be charged when it was you all who saved me. Now go. Please."

"She's right," Roman said. "You know what they'll do to a group of juvies who beat a guy to death, even if he did attack a girl first. We could have just pulled the guy off her, held him and called the cops. We didn't have to beat him up. We didn't have to kill him."

"Come on, Dante," Jeff said. "We can't handle any more on our records. We'll lose the house, our family. I can't do more time."

Dante paced the shop. "It's not right for this to come down on Anna. Hasn't she been through enough?"

She stopped him, cupped his face with her hands. "You saved my life tonight, Dante. All of you. Let me do this for you."

The pain in Dante's eyes, the guilt she saw there, hurt her more than that jerk outside did. "He hurt you. We had to make him pay."

Tears welled in her eyes. "I know. Now let me thank you the only way I can. Go on. I'll handle this."

Dante shook his head. "No, Anna."

Roman gripped Dante's shoulder. "She wants to do it. Let her."

Anna grasped his hand. "I'll call my dad right away. Dante, please."

No way was she going to have him take the fall for this. She'd stand here all night if she had to and argue with him. But finally, he nodded and she exhaled.

"Fine. We're outta here." He pressed his lips to hers, soft and gentle. "Call your dad right now."

"I will."

"We'll head out the back door. We're going to move the…body…behind the Dumpster so no one sees him."

"Okay. And I've got his knife."

The other guys walked out the door. Dante stood there, his fingers wrapped like glue around it as he looked at her. "Lock it behind us."

Anna bolted the back door as soon as the guys left and ran for the phone. Her father picked up on the first ring.

"Daddy?"

"Anna? What's wrong?"

As soon as she heard his voice, she fell apart.

"Daddy, someone hurt me."

One

He shouldn't have come home. He'd promised to stay away, but maybe it was finally time.

Nothing much was different in the old neighborhood. The only thing that had changed in twelve years had been him.

A lot had changed for Dante Renaldi in twelve years. The last time he'd been here had been the night he and the guys had killed someone in an alley. He'd left town right after that with Anna's father's help—more like his insistence—and he hadn't been back since. And in those twelve years he'd mastered the art of killing.

So maybe he hadn't changed much at all.

He vowed he'd stay away. Nothing was going to bring him home again. But one person could bring him home—his foster mother, Ellen Clemons.

Anna's father, Frank Pallino, might have asked him to walk away after that night—and never come back. And he had. But he owed everything he was to George and Ellen Clemons. Those were two people he could never walk away from. He trusted them.

They knew where he'd gone after that night, where he'd been all these years. They didn't know what had happened that night—he owed Anna that much. But he'd stayed in touch with George and Ellen over the years so they'd never think he'd walked away from them after everything they'd done for him.

So when Ellen contacted him and asked him to come home for her and George's twenty-fifth wedding anniversary, there was no way in hell he was going to say no.

Twelve years, thousands upon thousands of miles and a few wars since then, he figured it was time to come home. He'd earned that right, especially after Afghanistan. If Frank Pallino didn't like it, too fucking bad. He'd kept his part of the bargain. He'd left, he hadn't tried to get in touch with Anna in all this time, or with any of the guys. And he had no clue what was going on with Anna.

Coming home could finally give him some answers.

Anna was the big question he was tired of wondering about. He needed to know, had spent too many nights bedding down on foreign soil, staring up at the stars and thinking about her. The only visual he could drum up was her in a shredded pink-and-white blouse, that damn heart-shaped carving on her chest and all that goddamn blood.

Seemed like the only thing in his head these days was blood. He saw plenty of it when his eyes were open, and he saw Anna's when his eyes were closed.

He didn't want that memory anymore. Time for some closure, to remove some of the blood from his mind.

His plan was to get in, get out, make it fast. He'd do his duty to Ellen and George, check on a few things, then leave. He didn't intend to stay. He was used to not staying long in one place, so he planned to treat this like a mission. All he had to do was get the intel he needed, then move on. It wasn't as if he and the guys were friends anymore. Or brothers. There wasn't going to be a reunion.

Once he left he'd find a nice beach for R & R and erase a whole lot of shit from his memory bank.

He'd rented a car at the airport, a nice nondescript midsize piece of junk. It wasn't military issue and there wasn't a chance in hell he'd be driving over a bomb, so this car suited him just fine. He almost felt like a regular guy.

Almost.

Ellen had invited him to stay at the house. He smiled at that. To her he'd always be a kid. One of her kids, one of the many who passed in and out of their lives, but to the Clemonses, they were all "their" kids.

And okay, he wasn't a heartless bastard. He was here, wasn't he? But he wasn't going to sleep in a race-car bed.

He hadn't checked into a hotel yet, just wanted to cruise the old neighborhood to see what was what. Same houses as always, same parks, same sweltering-as-a-motherfucker kind of summer night when the humidity could suck the very life from you, and if it didn't, the mosquitoes would. It was this kind of night he remembered from twelve years ago, a night so hot you couldn't take enough showers to wash the sweat off.

He thought about dropping by George and Ellen's house, but that could wait until tomorrow. It was late and they had kids he didn't want to wake up.

Tonight he wanted to see the old haunts, check into his hotel and get on the right time zone. Tomorrow would be soon enough for whatever reunions had to be done.

He was actually looking forward to seeing George and Ellen, the last foster parents he'd had before Frank Pallino got him emancipated and into the service of the United

States Army. Dante wasn't sure if that was the best thing that had ever happened to him, or the worst. But considering he'd been about to turn eighteen and had no prospects for college or a future, Frank Pallino had probably done him a favor. He had skills now he never would have had if not for the army. Either way, what was done was done, and it was better than jail or God only knows what would have happened to him. He owed the man.

He supposed he owed a lot of people.

The streets were wet tonight. A hard summer thunderstorm had come down just as he'd walked out of the airport. Dante had stood just outside the airport doors and watched the rain. It had reminded him of that night twelve years ago.

Full circle again.

Maybe he shouldn't have come back. As he'd sat at the rental car place watching the rain sheet sideways onto the pavement, the memories pummeled him, those twelve years sliding away. He could still see the alley, could still see Anna the way she looked when he and the guys had walked into the ice-cream shop that night. She'd been decked out in pink and white, her button-down shirt with the little puckers all over it, her dark brown hair in a high ponytail and her caramel-brown eyes mesmerizing him like they always had.

He wished he could remember her eyes and her smile instead of her tears and all that blood. He wished he could remember the happy times instead of the trauma that bastard had inflicted on her that night.

He exited off I-44 at Hampton and headed south, turning down Wilson toward the Hill. The old brick houses all looked the same with their small front porches and well-manicured lawns. Some of the restaurants had changed names, but a lot hadn't, owned by the same Italian families for generations.

Saint Ambrose Church still stood, proud and signaling the old Italian legacy of the Hill. Some things never changed. He toured the old streets where he and his brothers used to hang, wondering which, if any, his real mom had lived in. He had an Italian name, that much he knew. His parents had never married, and he'd never bothered to search his ancestry, figuring there was no point in looking for people who either didn't want to or couldn't keep him. He'd had his foster brothers, and the Clemons family who'd taken him in at fourteen and given him almost four years of the best family life a kid like him could have ever hoped for. That had been good enough.

He left the Hill and made a beeline for Forest Park. The park was deserted, but well lit to keep people like him and his friends from loitering at night. He loved the curving roads that led toward the zoo, the Jewel Box, the art museum, all the places the Clemonses had taken him. They'd made him feel as if he finally belonged to a real family.

His only other family had been his brothers. Now, *those* were some memories, like the nights they'd sit in the park and get drunk or just kick back and talk shit, at least until the cops would chase them out. Those were the good times, when he felt as if he was part of something— part of a unit of people who had your back, who would go to the wall and die for you if it came to that.

He'd found the same thing in the military to some extent, but that was by necessity, not by choice. You had to trust your unit or you'd die out there. He'd made friends, but not brothers. He'd left his real brothers twelve years ago, and he hadn't even told them why, or said goodbye.

Now he just felt alone. Even back home, he was still alone, roaming the deserted streets where once he was in a packed car full of his brothers. Or with Anna.

His cell phone buzzed, so he pulled to the curb and dragged it out.

It was Ellen. "Did I wake you?"

"No. I was out driving around. I was going to come by tomorrow. I got in late, so I didn't want to wake the kids you have staying there."

"Well, there's a problem."

He went on immediate alert. "What's wrong?"

"George isn't here. He went out earlier tonight and isn't back yet."

"Where did he go?"

"I don't know, honey. He didn't tell me. I'm a little worried."

Dante shifted his gaze to the clock on the car dashboard. It was one in the morning.

He knew George Clemons. George was a military man, rigid in his routine. Bedtime was nine for the little kids, ten for the teens, and eleven for the adults. Unless there was an emergency, you didn't deviate from the routine. And he adored his wife. Unless things had changed a lot in the twelve years he'd been gone, something was off.

"You two have a fight?"

Ellen laughed. "We don't fight, Dante. You know that. I love that man the same now as I did the day he asked me to marry him."

And that's what he'd liked about living with them. Stability without tension. The Clemonses were solid. George wouldn't just walk out on Ellen and leave without a word. Which meant something was wrong.

"I'll be right over."

* * *

Dante parked in front of the house just as a hot-looking black Harley pulled into the driveway.

The guy took off his helmet and turned to shoot Dante a glare.

No way. Taller, his arms covered in tattoos and he definitely had a lot more muscle showing under that leather vest than he'd had when they were kids, but Dante would know Gabe anywhere.

Gabe laid the helmet on the back of the bike and headed toward him, a smirk drawing his lips up.

"Finally decided to come back, huh?"

Dante pulled Gabe into a quick hug, then drew back. "It was more like a command that I be here for their anniversary."

Gabe nodded. "Nice of you to show up. And good timing, too."

"Yeah. Ellen call you about George?"

"She's worried, and you know her. Nothing fazes her."

"Let's go inside."

Dante knew Ellen would be happy to see him, but the tight squeeze she gave him spelled a lot more than happiness.

She was past the point of worry and well into terrified.

Now it was up to him and Gabe to settle her down and hopefully figure out where the hell George was while Ellen wrung her hands together and paced the kitchen.

They'd remodeled, torn out the tiny kitchen where he and the guys used to cram their growing, oversize bodies around the tiny table. Now it was bright, with lots of overhead lighting, and a sturdy solid wood table sat in the place of the old metal one. You could seat an army there.

Ellen had coffee ready when they'd walked in. He sat

at the table and downed the brew, stared up at the only woman he'd ever considered a decent mother to him. She looked as worried as she'd sounded over the phone, her short, slightly graying red hair mussed from dragging her hands through it.

"He didn't say anything about where he was going?" Dante asked.

She shook her head and wrapped her fingers around her mug. Her hands trembled. "No. I figured the boys—we have three right now, all in the raging throes of puberty—had just gotten on his nerves tonight and he needed to drive it off."

"You'd think after years as a drill sergeant there wasn't enough attitude in the world that would annoy him," Gabe said. "We never got on his nerves, and if we couldn't rattle him, I don't think anyone could."

The corners of her mouth lifted. "True enough, but he's older now. His patience isn't what it used to be."

"Okay, so maybe that's all it is," Dante suggested. "He went for a drive and he'll be back."

"I thought so at first, but a half hour, hour at most and he'd have been home. He's been gone three hours."

"Flat tire or car trouble?" Dante suggested.

"He has his cell. He'd have called me to let me know. He'd never let me get worried like this."

"I assume you tried to call him?" Gabe asked.

"He didn't answer."

That wasn't good. Dante didn't want to say it, but the one thing George and Ellen had taught him was to be a straight shooter. "Maybe we should call the police, find out if there've been any accidents."

She sank into one of the chairs. "I've been putting that off. I could call Roman."

"Wait," Dante said. "Roman? Why?"

"Roman's a detective," she said.

Dante shifted his gaze to Gabe, who shrugged. "I know. Go figure, right?"

This whole night so far had been mind-boggling. "Okay, call him."

Ellen went to get her phone, a tremor in her hand as she flipped through the numbers. She pressed the button and held the phone to her ear, waiting, her gaze focused on Dante and Gabe.

"Roman? It's Ellen. I'm sorry to call so late, but it's George. He seems to be missing."

She paused a beat. "No, I don't think there's anything to worry about, but Dante thought—" She smiled. "Yes, he's back for the anniversary party. Yes, we've kept in touch over the years. He's fine, honey. But about George…"

Dante listened while Ellen told Roman about George.

Roman a cop. He didn't see that one at all. Then again, he'd never asked Ellen about the guys. His conversations with her had been short over the years, just enough to catch up with her and George, to tell them he was okay. That had been it. Never about his brothers.

He hadn't wanted to know about them, hadn't wanted to think about them, or miss them.

But now, he realized he'd missed a lot. He shifted his gaze to Gabe. Motorcycle and tattoos. What the hell had *he* been up to all these years?

Ellen hung up and laid the phone on the table. "Roman's working a case, but he's going to send some uniforms out around the area to search for him."

Dante could do more. "Is George's phone like yours?"

"Yes."

"What's his cell-phone number?"

She gave it to him. Dante pulled out his phone and entered the number. "I'll be right back."

He went out to his car and grabbed his laptop from his bag, came back inside and set it up.

"That looks like all symbols or a foreign language. Is it?" Ellen asked, looking over his shoulder while he worked.

"Not really."

Gabe leaned over and took a look, then arched a brow. "Dude, where the hell have you been?"

Dante didn't answer. There'd be time for explanations later, after they found George.

"What are you doing?" Ellen asked.

"Triangulating George's position via his cell."

"You can do that?"

"I can do that, provided his cell is turned on or isn't damaged."

It didn't take long. Tracking began to pinpoint the location of the phone on the map, drilling down from the state to the city to the cross streets.

Dante's blood turned cold. He lifted his gaze to Gabe. His gaze narrowed.

"No way," Gabe said.

There? That location?

What the fuck?

"Did you find him?" Ellen asked.

No way was he going to tell Ellen. Not yet. Not until they knew something.

"I don't know, but Gabe and I will go check it out. You stay here in case he comes back." He stood and grabbed his phone. "What's Roman's number?"

She gave it to him and he made the call. Roman was shocked to hear from him, even more surprised about where Dante wanted to meet, but said he was finishing up his case and he'd meet them there.

They walked outside and he turned to Gabe. "You following?"

"Right behind you."

Neither of them stopped to talk it over. There was nothing to say. Not until they got there.

The drive took about ten minutes. Nothing in the city took long to get to. As he drew close to the one place he didn't want to revisit while he was here, his muscles tightened. The last time he'd been here...

He didn't want to remember that night, didn't want to relive it. He'd come back to erase those ghosts of the past, not be reminded of all that blood, of what he and his brothers had done, of what had happened to Anna that night.

But as he pulled down the side street and parked just before the alley, a feeling of dread overcame him.

The one thing he'd learned over the past twelve years was to trust his instincts, his gut. It had never been wrong, and when something felt bad, he was usually right.

This felt bad. Just this once, he wanted to be wrong.

Gabe pulled his bike behind him and the two of them got out.

"I don't like this," Gabe said. "Something's wrong."

"Agreed. This smells like a setup."

"Anyone else know you were coming in besides George and Ellen?"

Dante shook his head.

A black sedan pulled down the street and parked behind Gabe's bike.

Dante smiled as Roman exited the car, dressed in jeans and a polo shirt.

Roman had changed, had filled out. He was muscled, his light blond hair darker now and cropped short.

Dante met him halfway, holding his hand out to shake Roman's. Roman pulled him into a hug.

"I can't believe you're here, man. Where the hell have you been?"

"Here and there."

Roman stepped back. "It's been too long. You just disappeared after…" He shifted his gaze to the alley. "After that night."

"I know. I needed to get away. I'm sorry."

Roman nodded. "I understand. It was rough on everybody."

Dante wanted to ask about Anna, but now wasn't the time. "You ready to check this out?"

"You really think George came here?"

Dante shrugged and shoved his fingers into the pockets of his cargo pants. "That's where I tracked his cell."

"How the hell could you track his cell?"

"I have ways."

Roman slanted a curious look his way. "I want to hear about that."

"Me, too," Gabe said. "But let's get this over with first."

Dante drew in a breath and nodded.

They rounded the corner into the alley, and it was like slamming back in time.

He'd been in the midst of war, been shot at, had ducked for cover as the world exploded around him. He'd been wounded in the line of duty and had spent hours, minutes, seconds wondering if he'd just drawn his last breath.

But he'd never been through anything as awful as that night twelve years ago, when he'd seen Anna lying there covered in blood.

He'd never wanted to come back here again. Ever.

"You okay, Dante?"

He gave Roman a curt nod. "I hate this place."

"Me, too."

"Ditto," Gabe added. "Let's hurry up and get out of here. This place creeps me out."

The Dumpster loomed like a monster in the dark, still positioned in its same spot in the center of the long alley. Now a streetlight shined over it like a monument to that night, forever marking the spot where they killed someone.

"Why here?" Roman asked.

"I don't know. This is where his phone tracked to."

"That makes no sense. George doesn't even know about that night." Gabe paused, looked at Dante. "Does he?"

"I didn't tell him." Dante looked at Roman.

"I didn't, either." They started moving again.

"Jeff wouldn't have said anything, either," Roman added.

"Which means George would have no reason to come here," Dante said. "If anyone had told George, Ellen would find out. Who would want her to know?"

"None of us," Roman said.

The closer they drew to the Dumpster, the tighter Dante's throat became.

When he saw the shoe, he stopped.

No.

"What?" Roman asked, then followed the direction of Dante's gaze. "Oh, shit."

They ran the rest of the way, Dante pushing past the Dumpster to land on his knees on the wet asphalt. His hope that it was an old drunk sleeping it off was obliterated by the sight of the blood, the torn shirt and the heart-shaped carving on George's chest.

Same as Anna's.

Dante felt for a pulse, but George was already cold. There was nothing. He was dead. He lifted his gaze to Gabe and Roman and shook his head.

"Jesus Christ," Gabe whispered as he looked down at George's body.

"I think I might be sick," Roman said, crouching down next to Dante. "This is just like— What the fuck, Dante?"

Dante couldn't speak yet, could only stare at the beaten body of his foster father—his father. The tough but loving man who had been a rock in his life, who had given him a home, had shown him that discipline didn't mean beatings, that love was unconditional, that no matter how many times he'd screwed up, he'd still be loved.

George was dead, killed the same way he and his brothers had killed that guy in the alley that night. And there was a heart carved into George's chest the same as Anna.

What the hell did it mean?

His head swam with questions. He turned to Roman, who had pulled his radio to call it in.

Dante took another look at George, then pushed off his knees and stood, looking around the alley, searching for something…anything that would give him a clue as to why the fuck this had happened.

"Who did this?" Gabe asked, looking as lost as Dante felt.

"I don't know. Ellen said he went out earlier, she thought for a short drive. She tried to call him when he didn't come back, but she didn't get an answer."

Roman had already gone to his car and come back with his evidence kit. He'd gloved up and leaned over

George's body, swallowing hard as he checked George's pockets.

"Yeah, here's his phone." He tucked the phone in an evidence bag and slid his fingers into the other pocket of George's jeans, paused and pulled out a clear plastic bag filled with white powder.

"What the fuck is that?" Dante asked

"My guess is cocaine," Gabe said. "About an ounce."

"And you know this how…?" Dante asked.

"Because he works for Paolo Bertucci," Roman said.

"The mob-guy Bertucci? That family's still around?"

Gabe didn't say anything, just turned his attention to the bag. "What's George doing with coke in his pocket?"

"Good question," Roman said.

The scream of police sirens interrupted any further discussion. Roman bagged the coke as the uniforms arrived. Dante wished they could hide the drugs, but he knew they couldn't.

George, with coke? Had he come here to do a deal? It made no sense.

Black-and-whites blocked off both entrances to the alley. In short order, yellow police tape roped off the alley, and crime scene techs began working the area. The medical examiner had arrived and was looking at the body.

And Dante still hadn't called Ellen. He wouldn't call her. He'd have to do this in person. Did Ellen know about the drugs?

God, right before the couple's anniversary. What was he going to say to her?

Another unmarked car pulled up at one end of the alley in front of the tape. Another detective, he imagined. He'd let Roman handle him.

Dante folded his arms and waited while the car door

opened. The lights were shining on them, so he couldn't see the detective coming at them until he—no, make that she—moved in front of the lights.

He caught the flash of badge clipped to her belt, which was attached to a very nice set of hips, the swing of a dark ponytail and the piece attached to her holster. His gaze lifted to rounded breasts in a polo shirt, and some very wide, very shocked amber eyes.

No fucking way.

Anna.

Two

Anna Pallino's steps faltered when she entered the alley.

First, because she was in this godforsaken alley again, a place she hadn't set foot in since that night twelve years ago. Now she was back again, and someone was dead in the alley. Again.

Second, Dante Renaldi was back.

Those were enough to justify the stutter in her step.

Roman greeted her.

"What the hell is this?" she asked as she caught sight of Gabe standing next to Dante. "Old-home week? Dante comes back and you three decide to have a reunion here?"

"Not exactly."

"Then why am I here?" Something had obviously happened, but why would Roman call her to this crime scene? Because Dante was here?

And why the hell *was* Dante here?

She hated questions with no answers.

"Thought you'd want to know. That's George Clemons back there."

Third reason she almost tripped over her own feet. "George? Oh, my God, Roman. I'm so sorry. What happened?"

He laid his hand on her arm to halt her forward progress. "You need to know, Anna. He's been beaten to death."

She sucked in a breath and grabbed onto Roman, fighting to stay in the here and now. "And? There's more. Tell me."

She saw the reluctance in his eyes. "Tell me."

"Someone carved a heart in his chest. Right where…" He glanced down at her shirt, at her left breast.

Oh, God. No. The heart carving just like hers. Her scar throbbed and she resisted the urge to touch it, to rub the ache away.

George Clemons, beaten just like the guys had beaten Tony Maclin that night.

She took a slow, long breath, then let it out. "I don't understand."

"Anna."

Dante appeared beside her, but she had no time for him. Not now, not when her vision was nothing more than a pinpoint of light.

She had to focus on the scene and only the scene. It was the only thing that was going to get her through this.

She pushed past them both. "I need to see it."

"Don't," Roman started, but she was already on her way to the body. To George Clemons, a nice man who'd raised foster children ever since he'd been discharged from military service.

And his wife, Ellen. Poor Ellen.

She knelt beside the body. Richard Norton was on the scene already, thank God. She was glad to have the chief medical examiner on this case.

"What have you got?" she asked, pulling on her gloves.

"Warm body. Based on liver temp and lividity I'd say he hasn't been dead more than a few hours at most. Won't know cause of death until I do the autopsy. He's a bloody mess."

That he was. Someone beat him badly, worse than the guys had ever pounded on Tony Maclin.

"This is interesting," Richard said, pointing to the heart carved into George's chest.

"Yes, it is."

"Someone loved him to death, I guess."

She grimaced. "So not funny, Richard."

Richard grinned. "Hey, I thought it was one of my better lines."

"George Clemons, our victim here, was Roman's foster father."

His smile died as he looked over his shoulder to where Roman stood with Dante and Gabe. "Oh. That's a pisser."

"Anything else you can tell me?"

"Not until I get him cleaned up and try to figure out what killed him. I don't see any obvious bullet or stab wounds on the body, other than the carving here, but like I said, he's a mess."

"Okay. When will you autopsy?"

"Probably sometime tomorrow or the day after. I'll check my schedule and let you know."

She patted his shoulder. "Thanks."

She stood and walked the scene, looking for evidence, then moved over to talk to the crime scene techs.

"Find anything?"

"No," one of the guys said. "It's like whoever did this vacuumed the place up after he was done. There's nothing. Not even a gum wrapper. The only evidence is the victim himself. But we're picking up whatever we can."

"Okay, thanks."

She turned around and there he was.

Twelve years. Twelve goddamn years and not one word.

"Anna…"

"When did you get back into town?"

So much for the reaction Dante had hoped for. If Anna was surprised or shocked to see him, she was sure masking it well.

"Couple hours ago."

She looked to George, then back at Dante. "Just in time to kill your former foster father?"

Dante scratched his nose. He'd laugh if this whole scene wasn't so sad.

"I think you know better than that."

"You think I… That's so funny, coming from you. I don't *know* anything about you. You've been gone for twelve years, you suddenly show up here and now there's a dead body in the alley. A body you're connected to."

"You're serious?"

"Yes, I'm serious."

"Anna," Roman said, "I don't think Dante—"

"You stay out of this. You're related to the victim. You can't be on this case."

Roman opened his mouth, then closed it. "Fine. You take it."

"I intend to."

"Here's his cell phone and wallet. George left the house about 9:00 p.m. tonight, said he was going for a drive, but didn't come home."

"Is that unusual for him?" she asked.

"His wife said it was," Gabe explained. "He wouldn't be gone that long without calling."

"So how did he end up here, and how did you all end up here?"

"We were with Ellen Clemons," Dante said. "She

called Gabe and me, worried about George, so we went over there to see if we could help."

She finally turned to Dante. "And you just happened to find him here?"

"I found him via his cell phone."

She frowned. "How?"

"I have a program on my laptop. It's not hard if you have the right equipment."

Her gaze drifted south for half a second, and his lips curved. When she lifted her head and met his smiling face, she seemed more irritated than ever.

"What equipment?"

"Laptop. Software."

"I'll need to see it."

"Got a warrant?" If she could be difficult, so could he. She was wasting her time looking at him as a suspect.

"I can get one."

"Then do it. And while you're doing it, why don't you spend some time chasing down who really killed George, because it wasn't me."

"He's right, Anna. This is a waste of time," Roman said.

She inhaled, let it out. "Maybe, maybe not. It's my job to look at everyone."

"You're pissed at me," Dante said. "I get it. I deserve it. But you're not thinking clearly right now and you're mixing personal stuff with business."

Her brows shot up, then knit. She took a step toward him. "Believe me, Renaldi, I know exactly how to do my job. And if you think for one second my feelings are hurt over you, then you're dead wrong. My job is first and foremost on my mind here, so shut up and stay out of my business."

This was a different side to her, something he'd never seen before. She was a completely different Anna.

"Where are you staying?"

He shrugged. "Hotel, probably. I don't know yet. I'll get it figured out."

"Fine." Anna shot a glance at one of the uniforms. "Get his location and phone number for follow-up." She jotted down notes. "What else?"

Roman handed her the evidence bag containing the drugs. "Also found this in his pocket."

Anna's brows lifted. "Looks like coke or heroin."

"It's coke," Gabe said.

She shifted her gaze to Gabe. "You would know, wouldn't you? Bertucci has a lock on distribution and sales in the city. You know anything about this?"

"Not a thing," Gabe said.

What the hell was Gabe into? Dante wondered. Expert on drugs and drug dealing?

"Was he doing a drug deal here?" Anna asked.

"No idea," Roman said. "But George didn't do drugs."

"So you think this was planted on him by the killer?"

"That would be my guess."

"Okay, I'll turn this over to Forensics."

It was fascinating watching Anna, all grown up and in charge now, directing the forensics team, handling evidence, taking photographs and leading everyone in the scene.

She caught him watching her and shot him a look he'd never gotten from her before. A mature kind of cold inspection. He didn't like it at all. The last time he'd seen her they'd been in love. Her looks had been warm.

But Dante had left town. So maybe she was still just a little pissed off at him about that. And maybe he couldn't blame her for giving him an icy, hard stare.

Plus, the circumstances of them meeting each other again weren't exactly ideal.

"That's all for now. I have work to do."

She walked away.

"So Anna's a detective, huh?" Dante looked at Gabe after Roman went to talk to Anna.

"Yeah."

"Kind of a hard-ass, isn't she? That's new."

"You've been gone a long time, Dante."

"I guess I have."

He'd imagined a lot over the past twelve years, but Anna becoming a cop wasn't one of the things he'd thought about. Her married with a couple kids, yeah. Becoming a schoolteacher or a nurse, he could totally picture. He'd even thought the worst, like that traumatic night would turn her to drugs or make her a runaway. A hundred other nightmarish things he'd never wanted to pop into his head had. And he'd taken responsibility for all of them—thoughts that had left him in a cold sweat and guilt that made his stomach feel empty and sick. But a cop? He'd never included that in possible scenarios for Anna.

She looked comfortable in the job, directing the uniforms and whispering with the medical examiner. She knelt next to the body, pointing here and there and actually touching George.

The Anna of twelve years ago would never have done that.

This wasn't the Anna of twelve years ago.

He supposed he had the answer he was looking for. Anna was fine. She'd survived what had happened here in the alley, had moved on with her life and had become a success.

And now there was George's murder in the alley.

What happened here?

Roman walked over to them. "You two are sprung. Dante, let me know where you are once you get settled."

Dante nodded. "Will do." He headed over to Anna, who stood over the crime scene techs as they worked the scene. The coroner's assistants had wrapped the body and were putting it on the gurney.

"I have to tell Ellen." God, he didn't want to do that.

She nodded. "I'm sorry. I'll go with you. I need to ask her some questions."

"This is going to be rough for her."

"I know it will. I still need to ask the questions."

"And I understand that. Which is why I'll be with her."

"Okay. We're wrapped up here. You two going to Ellen's, too?" she asked, looking at Gabe and Roman.

"Yeah," Roman said. "Since we found George, I think it's important we're all there for her."

Gabe nodded. "Someone needs to get in touch with Jeff, let him know what happened. I'll take care of that and then I'll catch up with you at Ellen's."

"All right," Anna said. "I'll meet you all there."

Dante thought about how he was going to tell Ellen on the drive back to the Clemons house. There was no way to prepare her for this. She knew as soon as she opened the door and saw Roman, saw Anna, saw the badge.

"It's bad, isn't it?"

Dante took her hand. "Let's go inside and sit down."

She trembled as he put an arm around her and led her to the sofa. She sat, and Roman slid next to her. Gabe came in right behind them and took up position behind Ellen.

"You remember Anna?" Roman asked.

"Of course. How are you?"

Anna didn't smile. "I'm fine, Mrs. Clemons. I'm sorry to have to tell you this—"

"We found George," Dante said, interrupting Anna.

Ellen shifted on the sofa to face him. "Where?"

"In an alley off Lindell."

Her bottom lip trembled and tears filled her eyes. She squeezed Dante's hand. "Is he dead?"

Dante nodded. "Yes, Ellen. Someone killed him."

She reached up, covered her mouth, then burst into tears. "Oh, God. Oh, no. George."

Dante pulled her into his arms and let her sob. Her loud crying woke the kids staying there. Roman and Anna went to talk to them, assured them Ellen was okay, but that something bad had happened to George. Coming from violent households, this wasn't anything new for these kids. Still, Dante felt bad for them, too. Here they had hopes of a stable life. Now, their lives had been shattered again.

Ellen's life had been shattered, too, in a way she'd likely never recover from. And there was nothing Dante could do to make this better for her.

Dante went into the kitchen to get Ellen some water. Gabe followed. "You get in touch with Jeff?" he asked Gabe.

"Yeah. He's out of town. He's as wrecked about George as the rest of us, and as confused about where it happened. None of this makes sense, man."

Dante nodded. "Tell me about it."

He brought Ellen a glass of water and box of tissues. After a while, she stopped crying and contacted a friend, who came over and collected the kids. Once they were gone, as typical for Ellen, she sat, straightened her shoulders and looked at them.

"Tell me what happened."

Anna looked to Dante. She was giving him the opportunity to take the lead, to decide how much to tell her.

She deserved the truth. All of it.

Dante grasped Ellen's hand. "He was beaten to death. And...someone carved a heart in his chest."

Ellen sucked in a breath and held her hand up to her heart. "Who would do this?"

Dante wished he could tell her about the connection to that night twelve years ago. But he wouldn't. He couldn't. Not without betraying his brothers—and Anna.

"We don't know yet, Mrs. Clemons," Anna said. "But we'll do everything we can to find out."

"Thank you," she said, then turned to Roman. "Will you work the case, too?"

He nodded. "They won't want me to because George was my father, but I'll do everything I can to be involved."

She held out her hand and Roman grasped it.

This was family. Dante had missed it. And he'd come home too late to save it.

"There's more," Anna said. "An ounce of cocaine was found in George's pocket."

Ellen's eyes widened. "Drugs? George doesn't do drugs. Never did."

"Do you have any idea why he would have had drugs in his pocket?" Anna asked. "Maybe one of the foster kids was mixed up in drugs and he was interceding on their behalf?"

Ellen shook her head. "No. None of the boys staying with us have drug-related issues. I can't think of any reason he'd be involved in that. George was strict about no drugs in this house. You took drugs or brought any into this house, you were in deep trouble with him. He'd personally call the police on one of the kids if he found drugs. For him to be found with drugs—" her eyes watered "—it's an insult to his memory."

"We're all pretty sure it was a setup, Ellen," Gabe said, laying his hands on her shoulders. "The police will get it figured out."

She grabbed for a tissue. "But in the meantime, they'll put in the record that he was found with drugs on him. And that doesn't sit well with me. George would be so hurt by that."

She shuddered out a sob, and Dante wanted to make this all go away. He wanted to back up one more day, get here sooner. He wanted to stop all this from happening.

Could he have?

Dante didn't want to leave Ellen, but she said her two younger sisters were coming over. There were funeral plans to be made, and he didn't want to get in the way. They all took their leave with the arrival of her sisters. Dante promised to come back tomorrow. She grabbed him in a fierce hug.

"Don't disappear."

He kissed her cheek. "I'm not going anywhere. I promise. And if you need me—for anything—you call."

She pulled back, her eyes shimmering with tears. "I will."

They all walked outside, and Dante looked up at the clear sky. God, it was still hot out, and he had no idea what time it was.

Late.

Roman and Anna were huddled near his car, whispering. Arguing. Roman finally took off, and so did Gabe, leaving the two of them together.

Anna was about to get into her car, but Dante headed her off.

"Anna."

Her head shot up and she pinned him with a glare, but didn't say anything.

He'd forgotten how beautiful her eyes were. As a teenager, she'd been so pretty with her hair always in a ponytail, her face shaped like a heart, her skin dark in the Italian way, her eyes the color of the finest whiskey. And her mouth—he'd never truly been able to appreciate her mouth, with her full bottom lip that begged for the tugging of a man's teeth.

He hadn't been quite a man yet, hadn't had the time to fully appreciate Anna, never got to see her blossom into a woman.

She was so pretty at sixteen. Now? She could stop traffic.

It had been a rough night. The kind of night when a man thought about grabbing what he wanted before it was too late.

He'd denied himself what he wanted for a long damn time. Things like home. Family.

Anna.

His jeans tightened as she stared at him and he stared back, but he didn't think she was lusting after him the way he lusted after her, since she was probably thinking he was guilty of some kind of crime. Or maybe she thought he was guilty of a lot of sins that had nothing to do with the murder tonight.

He probably was.

"You need something?" she asked.

Loaded question. "Not really."

"Then I need to go. I'm busy."

She was brushing him off.

He wasn't going to let her.

"Anna."

"What?"

"I haven't seen you in twelve years. Have a cup of coffee with me."

Three

Anna's stomach clenched. Just being in the same vicinity as Dante Renaldi again made her dizzy. His presence brought up memories she'd shoved so far into the past she hadn't thought about them in years.

Or tried not to think about them. Tried like hell not to think about them.

Until tonight.

Coming upon that murder scene in the alley tonight and seeing Dante had stolen every breath in her lungs, had made her legs go weak. Her first instinct had been to turn around and walk away—no, run away. She'd almost called another detective in to take the scene, but she refused. This was her job. There'd be no excuse for walking. Plus, Dante, Roman and Gabe had been there and she'd needed to know why.

She didn't like it. It had all been too much like twelve years ago, the night humid and smelling like recent rain, the asphalt streets slick and mirrorlike as she'd driven onto the scene. She'd seen plenty of dead bodies and people standing over dead bodies since she'd been on the force, had worked plenty of crime scenes with Roman. It wasn't until she'd spotted Dante and Gabe that the shock of awareness had hit her. The familiarity had cloaked her in heavy memories she still hadn't been able to break free from, clouding her thoughts and jumbling her normally stellar police process. She was organized and relentless in pursuit of a case. Was this fate getting back at her for her part in what happened twelve years ago?

Fate was awfully fucked up sometimes.

"Well?"

She lifted her head, found Dante staring at her.

Losing herself in thought wasn't like her, either.

"Well, what? I said I was busy."

"I asked you to have a cup of coffee with me."

"I'm on duty, Dante."

"Later."

"I won't be finished for a while."

"I'll meet you in the morning."

She sighed, feeling suddenly tired. "Why?"

"Because I want to talk to you."

"Why?" She knew it was juvenile to repeat the question. She was stalling.

"Have coffee with me in the morning and I'll tell you why."

And so, apparently, was he. She should say no, walk away. Maybe then he'd go and leave her alone, leave the memories alone.

But for some reason, she couldn't let it alone. Curiosity, maybe. And maybe he had some information on George's death. A cup of coffee and some conversation could yield some info.

"Fine. Meet me at Uncle Bill's Pancake House at seven-thirty."

"See you then."

She didn't exhale until he walked away from her and got into his car.

She climbed into hers and drove to the precinct, her body on autopilot while her mind tried to process everything that had happened tonight.

A body in the alley, killed just like the guys had killed Tony Maclin. Beaten to death. And not just any body, but George Clemons, the boys' foster father.

A connection.

Then the heart carving, just like hers.

Shoving the thoughts aside, she drove into the parking lot of the Metro police station, turned the engine off and sat there, needing a minute or two to collect her thoughts and just breathe.

What did it all mean? And why did it happen just as Dante came to town?

Was he the connection?

The station was always quiet at night, she thought as she walked in. She could use a little quiet right now, some time to think about the events of the night. She sat down at her desk and picked up the now-cold coffee, grimacing at the bitterness. She dumped it in the trash and went to the machine for a soda, then stared out the window at the few cars that passed by this time of night, wondering where they were going and what they were doing. Going to work, getting off work, leaving the bars?

Where was Dante right now?

Not that it mattered.

She still couldn't believe he was back after all these years, after all this time and finally having reconciled herself to never seeing him again. She didn't know whether to be angry or curious or how to feel about the ache inside her chest that had settled there ever since she'd seen him tonight.

There'd been too much to process at the crime scene.

Being in the alley again. Seeing the guys there. The body and how George was killed.

Dante.

And she'd still had to do her job.

This was a nightmare.

She took the drink back to her desk and stared at her computer monitor, knowing she had a report to file, and knowing she wouldn't fill in the background information of what she knew had happened twelve years before.

But the past had just collided with the present, hadn't it?

She didn't like mysteries like this. And she definitely didn't like questions without answers.

She rubbed that spot on her chest that always hurt on rainy nights, then opened a new investigation file to make some notes.

She looked at her watch: 3:00 a.m. and damn if she wasn't already anticipating that breakfast.

Four

Anna was an hour and a half late, figured Dante wouldn't hang around and wait for her, or maybe wouldn't show up at all.

She hoped he wouldn't be there. One less thing she'd have to deal with. She was tired and she wanted to go home, take a shower and forget the night had happened.

She walked in and took a look around. He was easy to spot since it was past the breakfast rush hour. There were only two other tables occupied. Dante sat in a booth at the rear of the restaurant, his back to the wall.

Interesting.

She told the hostess she was meeting someone and headed toward where Dante sat nursing a cup of coffee, two menus sitting on the edge of the table.

"You waited." She slid into the booth.

He lifted his head, smiled at her. "Yeah."

"Sorry I'm late. Paperwork had to be done."

He shrugged. "If you didn't show, I'd head out."

"So you ate already?"

"I got hungry after an hour or so, figured you'd chickened out."

She bristled. "I don't chicken out."

He didn't reply, so she poured coffee from the carafe on the table. "You sleep yet?"

"No. I'll sleep later."

"Where are you staying?"

He shrugged. "Don't know yet."

"So maybe you're not staying?"

He lifted the cup to his lips, then smiled. "Trying to run me out of town, Detective?"

He was saved from her biting retort by the waitress, who took her breakfast order—actually her dinner order.

"You look tired. Long night?"

She nodded.

"Why the night shift?"

She took a long swallow of coffee. "More crime happens at night. Less time spent sitting at a desk. We're out on the streets and that's where I like it. Besides, I don't have a shift. People don't die on shifts. I work when I work."

He leaned back in the booth and studied her with his unfathomable gaze. Years ago she couldn't get enough of his eyes, could stare into them for hours, getting lost in the blue depths until she'd lost track of time. She used to think she was the luckiest girl in the world that Dante Renaldi had chosen her as his girlfriend.

They'd sit together in secluded spots like this and make all kinds of plans about their future together.

Until that one night changed everything.

And then Dante had up and left without a word.

So much for their pledge to spend forever together, no matter what.

"You thinking about work, or about me?" he asked, forcing her gaze from her cup of coffee and her thoughts away from the past.

"Work." She wouldn't tell him her thoughts had

been centered on him. He didn't need to know that him showing up had dredged up memories she'd long ago buried.

"Any leads on George?"

"I can't tell you that. It's an ongoing investigation, one in which you might be a suspect."

He laughed, and the sound rippled through her nerve endings.

"You aren't serious about that. It was George who was killed. My foster father."

She shrugged. "So?"

"And I just got here."

"I hear better excuses than that from people who pulled the trigger with witnesses standing right in front of them."

"And probably lousy excuses from those who didn't. Isn't it your job to weed out those who did from those who didn't?"

Wasn't he a smart-ass? "Yes."

"Then I guess it won't take you long to figure out I had nothing to do with George's murder."

She drained the cup and refilled, not taking her eyes off Dante while she poured.

"You're wondering about my motivation for showing up all of a sudden after twelve years, and ending up right in the middle of a murder."

"You have no idea what I'm thinking."

"Some things come back pretty easily." He shrugged. "I used to know a lot about your thoughts."

"I was sixteen at the time, Dante. I didn't have too many thoughts back then that didn't center on you. Pretty easy to figure me out."

He leaned forward, clasped his hands together. "And now you're all complex?"

She frowned. "I didn't say that."

"You didn't have to. It's easy enough to tell." He leaned back. "You'd have to be with the job you do. Solving crime requires a lot of thought."

She cracked a smile. "Any particular reason you're trying to flatter me?"

"Just stating the obvious. No flattery intended. You can't be a fumbling dumbass and make detective."

Settling in and talking to him was easy. She hated that he'd made it so easy.

Her food arrived and just in time, since her stomach grumbled. Vending-machine food for the past ten hours just hadn't cut it. She was starving. She dived in as if she hadn't eaten in… God, she couldn't remember when she'd had her last decent meal. Ignoring Dante, she put all her concentration into shoveling food in her mouth, not coming up for air until she'd scooped the last of her eggs onto her last bite of toast. She avoided licking her fingers because she had company at the table, instead used her napkin to wipe her hands.

When she looked up, Dante was studying her again. "What?"

"You used to pick at your food. I was always afraid you were anorexic."

She snorted. "I wasn't. I was a picky eater. Clearly, I'm not one now."

"Obviously. You crammed every bite of food from that plate into your mouth. I was waiting for you to lick the plate clean."

"I pondered it, then decided against it. You might have been appalled."

He laughed. "Hey, if you're hungry, go for it. Or you could just order another meal."

She drained her orange juice and set the glass and plate to the side. "Not necessary. I'm sufficiently full now."

"It's nice to see you eating."

"I've gained an appetite over the years."

He shifted and looked under the table.

"What are you doing?"

He straightened, his gaze roaming from her face to the rest of her. "Checking to see if you have a hollow leg, because judging from your body there's no way you can eat that much and not gain weight."

She laughed. "I burn it all off working. And it's not like I get three squares a day of food like this. Most of the time I'm lucky to grab a granola bar or crap from the vending machine at the precinct. A full plate like this is a rarity."

"You have someone at home to cook for you?"

Clever. "You mean like a housekeeper?"

"No, like a husband."

"Nice fishing expedition. No husband."

He leaned back. "Just figured by now you'd be married with kids."

"I am married. To my job."

"You're too beautiful to be married to your job."

"That's a sexist remark."

He didn't appear concerned, just took another sip of coffee, then said, "Okay, then. You're too beautiful to be without a man."

"I didn't say I was without a man."

"So you do have someone in your life."

"I didn't say that, either."

His lips curled. "Cagey."

Despite her intent to keep her conversation with him cool, she couldn't help but enjoy this cat-and-mouse game of Twenty Questions. "What about you? You certainly look like too much man to be without a woman."

He leveled one seriously hot look on her that made her toes curl.

"How do you know I'm without a woman?"

She laughed, letting out some of the stress that had been tightening her shoulders. "I think if you had a woman somewhere you wouldn't be sitting here with me."

"You *are* a good detective."

She lifted her cup to her lips and smiled. "That's what my dad says."

"See, this is what surprises me. You never wanted to be a cop like your dad."

Her smile died. "Things changed."

"You mean what happened twelve years ago?"

"I don't want to talk about twelve years ago."

"What if I do?"

"Is that why you're back? To bring up the past?"

"No. I came to see you, to see everyone."

She hated asking it, didn't want him to think she craved the answer. But the question needed to be answered. "Where've you been?"

He shrugged. "Here and there."

"That's a lousy answer to give a cop."

His lips lifted. "Yeah. But, really, not much to tell. I drifted, wandered, picked up work in one spot, then moved to another. I didn't stay in one place too long."

"I could find out where you've been."

His grin widened. "You could try."

"Are you challenging me?" Irritation made her breakfast coil up like an angry snake in her stomach.

He reached across the table and grasped her hand. "No. I didn't come back here to piss you off."

She pulled her hand away. "You're working pretty damn hard on it."

He inhaled, blew it out. "There's nothing to tell you. I saw a lot of the…country. I was restless. And I needed to get out of here."

Escape would have been nice for her, too. But that hadn't been an option. "You picked a hell of a time to just pick up and leave, Dante."

He stared down at his coffee cup, then back up at her. "Yeah, sorry about that."

That was it? She'd been attacked, had gone through the worst trauma of her life, and the one person she thought she could count on had abandoned her when she needed him the most. And all he had for her in the way of explanation was "sorry about that"?

She stared him down, refusing to let him run this time. "You know, that's just not good enough."

To his credit, he didn't flinch, instead held her gaze. "I know it isn't."

"Pretty interesting coincidence that you show up and George is killed."

He drained the last of the coffee in his cup. "Lousy coincidence. I wish I'd been back sooner."

"How much sooner?"

"Soon enough that I could have prevented it."

She leaned back in the booth. "How could you have prevented it?"

"I don't know. Someone lured him to that alley and beat him to death. If I'd been here maybe I could have stopped it."

"Roman was here. Gabe was here. Jeff was here. None of them stopped it."

His gaze shifted to the window where morning traffic crowded the street. "I know. I still think I might have been able to do something." He turned his attention back to her. "Someone else knows about that night—about what happened."

She'd been avoiding thinking that. "Or it could be coincidence."

"Oh, come on, Anna. You're smarter than that. It's no coincidence he was killed in that alley. There's a connection."

"He was found with drugs in his pocket. It could have been a drug deal gone bad."

"Yeah, right. And then they beat him to death and carved a heart on his chest."

She shrugged. "I'm just thinking of all angles."

"There's only one angle. Someone saw what happened twelve years ago."

She looked around the restaurant. No one sat by them, but still she leaned forward. "But why George? He had nothing to do with it."

"I don't know. He had no connection to that night. That's the part that doesn't make sense."

To her, either. She had a lot of thinking to do, and she was too damn tired to do it clearly. She needed to recharge, then tackle it again once she'd had some sleep.

She picked up the bill and slid money to the waitress as she stood. "I need to go."

As she headed out the door, awareness of Dante on her heels pricked at her as she pushed through the front door and toward the parking lot.

"I invited you to breakfast. I would have paid."

She slid on her sunglasses and pulled her keys from her pocket. "I'm capable of paying for my meal. It was nice to catch up with you, but I'm tired and I'm going home."

"I'll follow you."

"I don't think so."

He had the nerve to smile at her. "I'm following you anyway. I want to make sure you get home okay."

"Are you serious? I'm armed. I'm a detective, for the love of God. And it's broad daylight. I've been taking care of myself for a lot of damn years now, Dante. Just because you swept back into town thinking—I don't know what the hell you're thinking—doesn't mean you need to start protecting me. My days of needing you as my bodyguard are over."

She stopped just short of blurting out that he'd failed as a bodyguard the last time she'd seen him, but the words stuck in her throat, refusing to come out.

Even she wasn't that cruel.

He moved in closer. "I'm sure you don't need someone to watch over you. I know you can take care of yourself. But I'm here and this is what I used to do. So I'm following you home."

She hated that he was here, messing up her life, making her want things she'd wanted for a long time, then pushed to the back of her mind, forcing herself to forget.

She inhaled the scent of him. Big mistake, because God help her, she wanted to put her hands on him, and in that moment she realized the feelings she had for him weren't dead.

More likely it was just that she hadn't been laid in a really long time. Dante was still a prime specimen of male beauty. Which was the only reason he had this effect on her. She needed a fast release of tension and he was a man.

But she already knew he wouldn't be a quick fuck and out the door. They had too much history.

And dammit, they'd never had sex.

That night twelve years ago had gotten in the way.

It still would.

She tilted her head back and offered up an uncaring shrug. "Do what you want. I'm going home."

She got into her car and pulled out of the parking lot, refusing to check and see if he followed.

She already knew he would.

What would happen when they got to her house?

She'd turn him away. Or maybe he'd just drive right past when he saw she was fine, which of course she would be.

Just fucking fine.

Yeah, she was fine, all right. So fine she buried herself in her work to avoid alone time. Because alone time meant thinking about her life.

Or lack of one.

Wasn't that why she worked her ass off, agreeing to pull extra shifts all the time? So many of the guys had families and commitments. She didn't, so why not work?

Things might have been different for her if Dante hadn't left.

Then again, maybe they wouldn't have been different at all. Maybe their teen romance would have run its course and she would be right where she was now.

But she couldn't change the attack, couldn't change what had happened to her that night. And hadn't she always wondered what it might have been like if Dante had stayed? If she'd had him to hold on to, would she still feel so lost, so empty inside?

Ugh. Could she be more dramatic?

Lost and empty. Please. Her life was just fine.

And there was that *fine* word again, that word that seemed so…inadequate and unfulfilling.

She pulled into the driveway and opened her car door,

so deep in thought she startled when Dante appeared right next to her.

"Jesus. How did you sneak up on me?"

He smiled. "I guess you *are* tired." He took the keys from her hand and headed toward her front door, making her run to catch up to him.

"Hey, I can do that," she said, fighting him for the keys.

"I'm sure you can."

He stepped up to the front door, twirling her keys.

And stopped so fast she tumbled into his back.

"Dammit. Why don't you look where you're— What are those?"

"I don't know. Got a boyfriend?"

"I already told you I didn't." She crouched down to pick up the flowers that had been left lying in front of the door.

"Don't touch them."

"What?" She tilted her head back to stare up at him. "What are you talking about? They're just roses."

Dante bent down to examine them. "There's a card. You see what it says?"

She hadn't noticed the card tucked in with the flowers. It was typed, not handwritten.

Did you like the gift I left you in the alley?

Her skin broke out in goose bumps, nausea bubbling up inside. She leaped up and backed away from the porch.

"Oh, shit. Goddamnsonofabitch. Who did this?" She whirled around, her hand on the butt of her pistol.

"Whoever it is might still be here, hiding, watching to see your reaction." She saw Dante reach behind him, lift his shirt, saw him pull out a Glock. A few minutes ago she'd have asked him if he had a permit, would have used it as an excuse to find out more about him.

Right now she was glad for the backup.

"Call it in," he said. "And don't go inside. I'll look around."

"Don't get in the grass. There might be footprints."

He turned to her. "I'm not an idiot."

She cocked her head to the side as she lifted her phone. "I don't know who the hell you are, Dante."

"Yeah, well, we'll talk about that later."

Yes, they would.

She made the call, then started walking around the porch, looking for any evidence like footprints or discarded cigarette butts—any lucky clue.

Usually there weren't such things, but sometimes one got lucky.

"I don't see anyone lurking around the bushes or around your neighbors' houses. I checked your backyard and the alley. There's no one."

Anna looked down the street, then up. This wasn't going to happen to her again. She'd suffered the most incredible fear she'd ever known. Nothing would ever scare her like that again.

"I don't know what kind of game he's playing, but I'm not joining in."

Crime scene techs showed up. Anna directed them to the flowers and card. They photographed and bagged the evidence. Anna had them wait outside and directed them to check for footprints and fingerprints while she unlocked her front door.

Dante put on a pair of gloves and nestled in right by her side.

"You aren't coming in with me."

"You'll have to arrest me to stop me, because for all we know he could be inside waiting for you, and you've got nobody backing you up."

"And you aren't a cop."

His deep blue gaze bored into hers as he lifted the Glock and pointed it inside the house. "Trust me when I tell you I know how to use this gun. Either call for backup or let me go in with you."

Her teeth hurt from grinding them. She nodded. "Fine. Stay behind me and do exactly what I say."

She caught the slight lift of his lips. "Yes, Detective."

She waited for the techs to dust and lift prints from the doorknob, then turned the knob and nudged the door open with her foot. Light streamed in from the gauzy curtains in her dining room, making it easy to see inside the living room.

"Nothing looks out of place," she whispered to Dante. "I'm moving inside."

She felt Dante on her left flank as she stepped in, her gun pointed slightly down, her finger poised on the trigger. She made a sweep left, then right, seeing nothing out of the ordinary. While she moved to the right, Dante swept to the left, opening the closet door while Anna headed into the kitchen.

Once they cleared those areas they went together down the hall and checked the two bedrooms and bathrooms.

Everything was clear.

"Nothing's been touched. Nothing even looks like it's been moved even an inch. He wasn't inside."

"Or he's good at putting things back in place."

She sighed. "I'll let the techs in and have them dust for prints, but I don't think he was in here. I'd know."

"Yeah? How would you know?"

"Instinct."

He nodded. "That I understand."

"I'm going to have to give my captain an update on all this. This sucks."

"First you need to get some sleep. There are dark circles under your eyes."

He reached out, swept his thumb across her cheekbone.

His touch sent shock waves through her body. Unprepared, she took a hasty step back and stumbled. Dante caught her with his arm wrapped around her, tugging her against him, which only made things worse. He was warm—solid, and not at all what she wanted.

This was all too much.

"You okay?"

"Yeah. Fine." She jerked away from him and turned around, headed outside to the techs and led them into the house.

While they worked making a dust bowl out of her entire house, she contacted her captain and left him a message, letting him know about the flowers and card, then told him she'd give him a full report when she came on duty again.

Dante kept his distance, but she felt his gaze on her, as warm as his touch.

She didn't like the familiarity, the sense of closeness he wanted when she knew so little about him.

She had too many questions. Like why he had a gun and he'd swept through her house like a cop who knew what he was doing. Those were answers she was going to get from him.

He moved in next to her. "I know you're tired. And the tech guys are done now, so you can get some sleep."

She looked up and realized the CSU team had packed up and were leaving, shutting the door behind them. She hadn't even noticed.

"Okay, good."

She walked to the door and waited. He came toward her and stopped in front of her.

"If you'd like, I can stay."

"Stay and do what?"

His lips curled, and warning bells rang. She'd walked right into that one. She really was tired. "I don't need you to stay."

"He could come back."

"If he does, I can handle it."

Dante surveyed the double dead-bolt lock on her door. "I guess you're secure."

Anna felt anything but secure at the moment, especially since she was leaning against the door and Dante was about a quarter of an inch away from her, all that testosterone sending her libido firing in a way it hadn't since...

Since the last time they'd been alone together. She'd been full of raging teen hormones back then, which she sure wasn't now.

Now she was a competent adult capable of taking care of herself, yet here he was, trying to act as if she was in need of saving.

She hadn't needed saving in a long time. These days she saved herself.

"You need to go."

He laid his palm against the door above her head, his body hot and enticing as he stared down at her with sea-blue eyes that made her want to dig her teeth into his shirt and rip it off, then bury her face in his neck and lick the bead of sweat that had formed there.

"Is that what you really want?" he asked.

His breath blew against her hair, and she was ten seconds from either self-combusting or grabbing him by the shirt, planting her mouth on his and taking him up on what he was so obviously offering.

"Yes, it's what I really want."

He paused, his lips curling in a smile that told her he knew it wasn't at all what she really wanted.

He slid his hand behind her, his touch making her tremble as his fingers swept across her back.

But then she heard the click of the doorknob. She moved to the side as the door opened.

"Okay, then. See you later."

Her heart rate skipped double time, her palms were wet and her body tingled with the awareness that she was so affected by Dante she was shaking all over. And just as fast as he had her primed and ready to throw him to the floor and have her way with him, he was gone.

She wasn't over him at all. Not at all.

She hit the dead bolts, rubbed that spot on her chest with her knuckles and headed toward the bedroom, but she was damn sure not going to sleep now.

Bastard.

Five

Dante stood at the end of Anna's driveway and leaned against his car. He needed a few minutes to cool his body down, and the summer heat wasn't helping any.

So, okay, he figured following Anna home would piss her off. Maybe that's what he'd wanted to do, just to get a reaction out of her, to fire up that cool control that she wore like body armor.

He was glad he'd followed her, that he'd been here to see those flowers and that card.

What he hadn't counted on was the heat that had flared up between them.

Twelve years ago they'd had passion, but it had been young—intense yearning with nothing to show for it.

What passed between them inside just now had been very adult, very hot, and nothing like what they'd had when they were younger.

But that wasn't what he'd come home for.

In fact, it had been a stupid move to go inside her house, to allow himself to even think he could get close to her again. He'd crossed the line and pushed the limits and become that almost-eighteen-year-old boy again, totally crazy over the sweet innocent girl he loved but knew he shouldn't have.

Now he was thirty years old and he still couldn't have her.

The rumble of a motorcycle turning down the street caught his attention. He walked toward the driver's side of his car as Gabe pulled to a stop and cut the engine on his Harley.

"Reminiscing about the good old days?" Gabe asked.

"More or less. What are you doing here?"

"Taking a ride. Thought I might find you here." Gabe looked up at the house, then slanted a glance back at Dante. "Though I kind of figured you'd be smooth enough to get inside."

"I was inside."

Gabe arched a brow. "Done already?"

Dante laughed. "Asshole. Listen, someone left roses and a note on the front porch for her."

Gabe grinned. "Secret admirer?"

"No. The note said, 'Did you like the gift I left you in the alley?'"

Gabe's demeanor changed in an instant, harsh anger slashing across his face. "Son of a bitch. The killer is stalking her?"

"I don't know. Her CSU team took the flowers and note in for Forensics to go over, and they dusted the place for prints."

"Any sign of forced entry? Was he in her house?"

Dante shook his head. "Doesn't look like it."

"Shit. What the fuck is going on, man?"

"I don't know. We need to get everyone together to talk about it, though, figure this whole thing out."

They both went silent then. Dante thought about George, about why he'd gotten mixed up in all this.

"You find a place to stay yet?" Gabe finally asked.

"No."

"How long you plan on hanging out here?"

Dante cocked his head to the side. "I wasn't going to stay long, but now that this thing happened with George I might have to change my mind about that. Why?"

"Because if you're staying a few days or a week you can put up with a hotel. If it's going to be a long visit, I could maybe help you out. If you're looking to stay permanently—"

"I'm not staying permanently."

"So which of the other two is it?"

"I hate hotels." Which wasn't an answer to Gabe's question, but Dante didn't have an answer. He didn't know how long he was going to be here. It had been an impulse to come in the first place. He wouldn't have, if not for Ellen asking him. And then George was killed. And now he'd seen Anna…

Gabe nodded. "Yeah, I hate hotels, too. Follow me. I have some friends that just built some condos. Some aren't sold yet and I can hook you up."

"That'd be great, thanks."

Dante climbed into his car and followed Gabe. The one thing he'd always loved about St. Louis was that it didn't matter what your destination was. Nothing was very far away. You could get from the city to the country in a matter of fifteen minutes, minus rush-hour traffic.

The condos were nice. Things sure had changed around here. Progress. Old shit got torn up, and new stuff got built. That's the way it had always been, and so Dante expected it always would be. Just because he had a vision in his head of what his hometown had looked like when he'd left didn't mean time would stand still.

Buildings changed. People changed. Everything and everyone grew.

He followed Gabe to the parking lot of the main office. Gabe got off his bike and Dante got out of his car. "Just wait here. I'll go talk to management and see what's available."

"Sure."

These were pretty high-class condos. Gabe, in his worn jeans and sleeveless shirt and with his neck and arms covered with tattoos, didn't seem the type to even know the management. But Dante knew all about labeling people. And assumptions.

Never assume anything.

Gabe was out a few minutes later with a grin on his face. "Building D. We'll head west down the main road and turn right."

Dante followed him to the building and pulled up in front of one of many cookie-cutter-type condos.

"Grab your stuff. I've got the key."

Dante pulled his bag from the trunk of his rental car and followed Gabe to the door on the main level, just off the entrance. Gabe slipped the key in the lock and blissful air-conditioning greeted them.

"It's furnished," Dante said as he walked in. "Someone live here?"

"No. They keep it available for visiting corporate clients."

"Uh-huh." Dante laid his bag on the floor and checked out the spacious kitchen, oversize living room and two bedrooms. Everything he might need was here, from pots and pans to flat-screen TV and even a game console. The beds were freshly made and the place had a new smell.

He walked back out to the living area. Gabe was on

the couch, the television was on and he was playing a game.

"Make yourself at home."

Gabe grinned. "I am."

"So where do you live?"

"Right across the walk from here."

"Convenient."

He took a seat next to Gabe and picked up the other remote, started punching buttons. It was a war game. Piece of cake.

"What exactly do you do now, Gabe?"

He lifted a shoulder. "This and that."

Which was the same answer Dante had given Anna—totally vague. "Which means what, exactly? That you're a fry cook at the local burger joint, or that you're an ax murderer?"

Gabe leaned to his left, punched a few buttons and knocked out Dante's player on the game. "No, I prefer guns. You don't have to get as close to the victim that way."

Dante laughed. "Funny. But these condos are upscale, so you must be doing something."

"Yeah, I'm doing something. Mostly freelance."

Gabe killed Dante's last player. Dante cursed. "Freelance sounds like illegal. What are you into?"

"You sound like Anna, always asking questions."

"I'm not a cop, though. And you're working for the Bertuccis now?"

Gabe started the next game. "Yeah. Paolo Bertucci. He runs the mob here in the city."

"Your boss?"

"Yeah."

Not the line of work Dante expected Gabe to get into. "For how long?"

"About two years."

"Good work I guess."

"It pays the bills."

Working with the mob could be lucrative business. It could also get someone killed. "What do you do for Paolo Bertucci?"

Gabe was focused on the game, his fingers flying on the controller. Dante was trying to keep up, but Gabe was kicking his ass.

"Jack-of-all-trades. Anything from running errands to enforcer duty."

"You like the job?"

"Like I said…it pays the bills."

Working for the mob also meant you kept your mouth shut, and Gabe wasn't stupid. Still…

"You think Bertucci's connections in drugs had anything to do with George's death?"

Gabe paused the game, shifted his gaze to Dante. "I don't know. He moves drugs in this city. Doesn't mean he's directly involved. He leaves that to the peons."

"Like you?"

Gabe laughed. "I'm not a drug dealer, man."

Which meant Gabe was higher up on the Bertucci food chain than just a peon.

They used to be as tight as brothers. Real brothers, not the foster brothers they had been. There had been no secrets between them. They'd known everything about each other, had spent many nights up in their room in the Clemons house where they'd been fostered sharing all the shit they'd been through as kids. It had bonded them because their hells of abuse and shitty childhoods had been so similar.

And now they were strangers circling each other, neither of them willing to divulge their secrets.

Dante leaned back on the sofa and dragged his fingers through his hair. "Not much like the old days, is it?"

"Guess not."

"You into something big?" Dante knew he had no right to ask, especially since he hadn't told Gabe shit about himself.

"Just stuff I don't want to talk about. With you, particularly, since I don't know where the hell you've been the past twelve years."

"You've been here the whole time?"

"No. Left right after…right after the thing went down with Anna. I had to get the hell out. That whole scene freaked me out."

Damn. Gabe had skipped town the same time he had. "I didn't know you'd left, too."

Gabe slanted him a look. "I didn't know about you, either, until after I came back. Where'd you go?"

"Dallas first. Big city, easy to get lost in. Figured I should get out of here, give Anna some space. I thought if I wasn't around that whole mess would just disappear. Guess you must have had the same thought. How long did you stay gone?"

"I've been back here two years. I guess we all need to come home eventually, huh?"

Dante smiled at that. "Ellen asked me to come back for her and George's anniversary."

"Man, that shit sucks for her."

"It does." He didn't even want to think about it. "Anyway, I agreed to come back because I figured it was time anyway."

Gabe nodded. "So we both left right after the attack."

"Looks like it. Roman and Jeff never left, though?"

"No, they both stayed."

"Nothing is like I expected it to be," he said.

"Why? Because you didn't get a big welcome-home party?"

He shot Gabe a look. "No. I don't know what I expected. Sure as hell didn't expect to find out Anna was a detective. And, Roman, too. That's a shocker. And you—look at you. All tatted up and gone biker. A real badass now."

Gabe laughed and stretched his legs out in front of him, then popped his black shit-kicker boots up on the table. "The one thing I found out when I came back? The world around here didn't stop turning just because I left."

It sure as hell didn't. Didn't make Dante feel any better, but he'd done what he'd been asked to do, and he'd done it for Anna's sake. At the time it seemed like the right thing to do.

It *had* been the right thing to do.

But at the time he'd thought Gabe would be around to watch over her. The others had been younger, not as well equipped to be her protectors.

"I didn't know you were leaving," Dante said. "I might have stuck around otherwise."

"I didn't know you had left, either. Sorry, man."

Dante shrugged. "Not your responsibility. Anna managed okay, though. She had her dad to take care of her. How's she seemed the past couple years since you've been back?"

Gabe grinned. "Feisty. Driven. She's out to get the bad guys in a big way."

In the short time he'd seen her at the crime scene, he could see that about her.

"Which means what, exactly? That the two of you meet up more often than not?"

"You might say that." Gabe chuckled.

Curious, Dante leaned forward. "Something else going on with you and Anna I should know about?"

"Like what?"

He didn't want to ask. But he needed to know. "You have something going on with her?"

Gabe frowned. "Why would you think that?"

"You showed up at her house this morning."

Gabe let out a soft laugh and shook his head. "You dumbass. It's not like that. I look out for her."

"Maybe you're not the right person to be doing that, considering what kind of business you're in."

"Yeah, and you think you're better equipped to do it, mystery man?"

"Hell, I don't know." Dante stood and walked to the window, raked his fingers through his hair. "I'm talking out my ass, Gabe. I'm tired. I've been up all night." He turned to face his onetime best friend and brother. "It's good to see you. I'm glad you're here. And thanks for giving me this place to stay."

Gabe stood. "Get some sleep. I'll check in with you later."

He held out his hand. Dante clasped his arm and pulled him in for a tight hug.

He never got close to people, hadn't since he'd left here. Gabe and the others had been the only people he'd truly counted on. They were the only ones he'd ever told his secrets to. He trusted them with everything without question.

Or he had at one time.

Like Gabe had said—everything had changed in twelve years.

"It's good to have you home again," Gabe said.

"It's good to be home."

He was surprised to discover he actually meant it.

* * *

Anna was armpit deep in the thing she hated most—paperwork—when Dante strolled into the squad room and made a beeline for her desk.

She frowned. "Who let you in?"

"Some guy named McClaren."

"Remind me to withhold his donuts."

"Funny."

He made himself at home by sliding into the chair next to her desk, extending his long, lean legs out in front of him. He wore a dark gray T-shirt that stretched tight across a very well-developed chest, his muscled biceps peeking out from the hem of the short sleeves.

And just like before, the stupid sex chemicals in her body roared to life. God, now that he'd grown up he was devastating, which she would have already been well aware of if he hadn't left her twelve years ago.

She refused to be attracted to him. She intended to stay angry. His reappearance had brought unpleasant things, just like the last time she'd seen him.

He might even be considered a suspect. She wasn't about to be attracted to a suspect.

She turned her attention on him, determined to remain cool and aloof.

"Something you want?"

He gave her a half-lidded look that made her squirm in her chair, so she chose to ignore him and concentrated on her paperwork instead.

"I take it you're busy?"

"Master of the obvious, aren't you?" she replied while not really studying the file in front of her.

"Want me to help?"

She lifted her gaze to his. "You a cop?"

He smiled at her. She'd always loved his smile. He'd

made promises to her with that smile. Promises he hadn't kept.

"Not a cop, no."

"Then you should leave and let me be one."

"I thought I'd hang out with you awhile and we could catch up. Maybe we could go grab something to eat."

"I'm on duty, Dante."

"You're doing paperwork, Anna. Unless your captain thinks it's a bad idea for me to be here and throws me out."

She wished. As far as her captain knew she could be interviewing a witness or an informant at her desk. And he wasn't even at the precinct at the moment, so the likelihood of him throwing Dante out were as remote as James Patterson strolling into the squad room to interview her for his next book.

She should be so lucky.

"Catch any bad guys tonight?"

"I think they stayed inside out of the heat."

"Smart of them."

"What about you?"

"Did I catch any, or was I one of them?"

He was a mind reader. Her lips curved while she made some notes in the file and closed it. "You said it, I didn't."

"I'm not a bad guy, Anna."

"So you say."

"Anything on George yet?"

"I'm not discussing a case with you, especially one you're directly involved in."

"Indirectly."

"Whatever." And no, she hadn't found a thing, something she noted in the file she opened next. Unfortunately, she had no suspects. There were no prints at the scene and no witnesses. The only reason George

Clemons was dead was a direct link to that night twelve years ago. And because of all of them.

Because of her.

Then there was Dante conveniently showing up at the same time a murder was committed. A murder of someone he was tied to.

And she knew nothing about Dante or where he'd been. No record, no priors, he showed up in no criminal databases, which she supposed should have relieved her, but the odd thing was he showed up nowhere. At all. It was as if he didn't exist after he left here. Which made her more suspicious, not less.

She knew a lot of guys worked odd jobs for cash, so they never reported income, but for twelve years? Come on.

It made her wonder even more what the hell he'd been doing for the past twelve years. And why he was suddenly back. He said he was back for George and Ellen's anniversary party. But then George turned up dead. She didn't like it. Not at all.

As much as she wanted to keep the past where it belonged, as much as she didn't want to encourage Dante, especially after last night, maybe it wouldn't be a bad idea to get close to him, to find out where he'd been and what he'd been doing while he was gone. Because if he was connected in any way to George's murder...

"Anything on the flowers and note?"

She shook her head. "Forensics got no prints, which doesn't surprise me. The scene around my house came up clear, too. It's just like the alley."

"What about the alley?"

Dammit. "Nothing. Never mind."

"Talk to me, Anna."

"No. I'm not discussing this investigation with you."

She laid her head in her hands.

"Tired?"

"Like you wouldn't believe."

"Did you sleep?"

"I got a little." Mainly what she got was a whole load of frustration, staring at the ceiling and fantasizing about Dante.

Hot, steamy fantasies. Naked ones.

Ugh.

As if late June wasn't already hot enough...

Cool fingers swept across her neck, pressing in and massaging the tight muscles there. For a split second she forgot she was at work, that there were other cops there.

Then she jerked her head up and shrugged his hand off. "Stop that."

His lips curled. "You don't want me to stop."

"You said that yesterday."

"You didn't want me to stop then, either."

She looked around, expecting to find the entire squad room of cops staring at her.

No one was even in the room.

Shit.

"You can't do that here."

"Where would you like to do it?"

She sighed. "You've been back in town for a little more than one day. We hardly know each other anymore. Why the hard press to get in my pants?"

He took a seat in the chair. "Is that what I'm doing? I was just asking you out for a meal."

She slanted him a look. "You're asking for a lot more than a meal."

"What if I want to get to know you again, figure out what you've been up to all this time."

"We aren't going to find out any more about each other over a meal today than we did yesterday."

He laughed. "One short conversation? You think that's all we have left?"

"I don't have time for relationships in my life, Dante. I'm busy."

"I didn't ask you for a relationship, Anna. There are things we need to talk about, and you know it. We all need to talk, not just you and me."

He wanted more from her than talking. She knew it and he knew it. She hadn't been a cop for seven years—a damn good cop—by ignoring signals and body language. Dante's body language told her a lot about his intentions.

Intentions she had no desire to act on.

Okay, maybe she had desires, but she knew nothing about him.

"You want to talk, how about you start by telling me the truth about you?"

He leaned back, a look of wariness on his face. "What truth?"

"About where you've been for the past twelve years." And why he left in the first place.

That shut him up.

"And why you show up here and suddenly someone close to you is dead."

Now he looked pissed. A sure sign of something to hide. "Circumstance. I had nothing to do with George's death."

"So you say. But it sure is a coincidence that George is murdered—" she looked around to make sure no one had wandered into the squad room "—in a place very familiar to you, that no one knows about, on the same night you come back after being gone for twelve years. I'd like an explanation for that one, Dante."

"So would I. I'd also like an explanation why after the murder someone left you a love note and flowers showing off about the murder. And it couldn't have been me since I was with you on the scene."

She opened her mouth to argue the point, but instead clamped it shut.

"We do have a lot to talk about, Anna. You, me, Gabe, Roman and Jeff. Our past has suddenly been dumped right into our laps again. And like it or not, we have to deal with it."

She didn't like it.

"I'll think about it."

"You do that."

Great. A get-together with the same people she'd been with twelve years ago.

A reunion she didn't want to have.

Dante sat in his car and stared at the nondescript brick building that housed the metropolitan police station. Cops wandered in and out as he pondered what his next step would be.

Why hadn't he just told Anna where he'd been and what he'd been doing for the past twelve years?

Because his life was a big giant secret and he never knew from one minute to the next where it would take him or what his identity would be when he got there. And he knew better than to just start spilling his guts.

He didn't exist, not officially, and the fewer people who knew that the better.

If he was lucky he could get in and out of town without anyone knowing who he was and what he did.

His superiors would like that a lot.

He'd done the right thing by not saying anything,

even if the end result had been the mistrustful look in Anna's eyes.

He'd been the one who put that look there in the first place, so he was going to have to own it.

Which didn't mean he'd have to like it.

He started up the car and drove away.

Six

Sleep had been an illusion, a fantasy. Anna had come home after getting off duty, stripped off her clothes and climbed into a hot shower to scrub the remnants of the day from her body, her mind filled with the possibilities of this case.

By the time she'd crawled into bed, the thick shades pulled down to block out the morning sunlight, she was exhausted. But sleep had been in fits, and dreams had been filled of that night twelve years ago, of being pinned down and helpless, the burn and screaming pain of a sharp knife carving into her chest. And suddenly it wasn't her anymore, but George, a shadowy figure standing over him as he cried out for help, the tip of a knife glinting silver and menacing in the moonlight.

She woke with a gasp, her hand immediately going to her chest to rub the ache that never seemed to go away. Dragging her hand through her hair, she got up, dressed and made coffee.

Cup full of life-infusing brew, she stepped out onto the back patio.

It was brutally hot outside already, the humidity rising like the steam coming off her coffee. She took a seat on a cushioned chair, glad she had a shaded patio to cool her bare feet. If it was this hot in June, what was August going to be like?

Unbearable. And this kind of heat bred crime.

But she wasn't on duty right now and she'd barely brushed the cobwebs out of her mind. It wasn't time to think of work yet.

She sipped her coffee and watched the birds peck at the feeder in the corner of the yard. She'd impulsively bought it this spring, thinking her backyard needed some life and color—much like her life—but hey, she had to start somewhere, and the yard was easier. She'd added flowers and bushes, and had spent a couple weekends digging into the dirt with her shovel, sweating her ass off and loving every minute of it.

She didn't need a social life if she had a backyard project, did she? Try telling that to her father.

Now she had to remember to water everything and put seeds in the bird feeder, but at least she had something out here to look at besides a couple trees and some grass.

She sipped her coffee and smiled at the birds fighting over the seeds.

The only thing missing from her life now was a rocking chair and a cat.

She laughed, thinking her dad would not be amused by that thought. He was already bitching about her getting close to thirty and not giving him grandchildren.

As if that was a priority.

As if any man would want to deal with all the baggage she'd bring to a relationship, the scars from the past, both physical and emotional. She could hardly stand getting naked in front of a man. Nudity required explanation of her scar, and since she'd never told the truth about that night, she had to lie about how she'd gotten it. Sex was much better in the dark, wearing some clothes. Not that she had a problem with sex. She liked it just fine, but the whole relationship and marriage thing? No thanks.

As if she was even interested in getting married and having children, anyway.

Her work hours were shit, she had frequent nightmares, the past still had a stranglehold on her and she liked her independence. She dated rarely, slept with men even more infrequently and took her sexual frustration out on her job.

Yeah, she was one hell of a catch.

Her cup empty, she went inside to refill and saw her phone vibrating across the kitchen counter.

It was a text message from Dante asking her to call him when she woke up.

She pressed the call button and he answered on the first ring.

"I didn't expect you to answer me right away," he said. "Figured you'd still be asleep."

"I don't need a lot of sleep."

"So you've said. You ready to meet with all of us tonight?"

No. She didn't want to meet with any of the guys, but figured Dante would keep insisting. And if he didn't, Roman would. Roman worried like an old woman. "I guess so. How about pizza at my place at six?"

"Okay. I'll round everyone up. I'll bring the beer."

"Won't this be fun." The best kind, too—they'd be talking about a murder, and she'd have to once again relive that night.

She clicked the phone off and leaned against the counter, ignoring the throb of the scar on her chest.

There had to be an explanation for George being killed in the alley, for the uncanny resemblance of his murder to the death of Tony Maclin. And for the carving of the heart on the victim's chest.

But there was also the matter of the flowers and the card. No explaining that away as coincidence. Someone had wanted her to know about the murder. The flowers had been a gift. A sick gift, and there was no way to neatly tie this up as a coincidence, no matter how much she wanted to.

She had time, so she headed to the medical examiner's office. Richard Norton hadn't autopsied the body yet and she wanted to take another look.

She walked into the nondescript one-story brick building, which was always cold as a tomb even outside the examination rooms. She figured they deliberately kept it that way to discourage visitors, but on a day as hot as this she welcomed the arctic temperature indoors, passed her way through security and signed in to view the body being held in storage downstairs. The attendant outside the room went in with her.

She pulled the sheet back. George hadn't been cleaned up yet—they'd do that when they autopsied him, but the carving on his chest resembled hers. Same location, left side of the chest, crude, as if it had been done in a hurry just to make a point. His wound looked deeper than hers, though, as if someone had dug down hard with the knifepoint. She wondered if George had still been alive when the killer had taken the knife to his chest.

Tony Maclin had been toying with her when he'd carved the heart into her skin. She still remembered the burning pain, how much it had hurt.

Had George felt the pain? Or had he already been beaten so badly he couldn't feel anything at all by that point, not even the knife cutting into his skin?

Her scar tingled. She wanted to rub it, to remember, but the tech's presence prevented her from doing so.

We're connected now, George. You're not alone.

"See something on him?" the tech asked.

"No. Just wanted to take another look, see if there was something I missed."

She covered him with the sheet and the tech closed the drawer.

It had been a waste of time to come here. She didn't know what had drawn her.

She stared at the silver drawer where George Clemons lay and thought how easily that could have been her twelve years ago. If the guys hadn't been there, if they hadn't rushed to her rescue, she could have ended up on a slab in this ice-cold room, dead at sixteen.

Everything she was now, everything she'd worked so hard to become, would have been obliterated that night in the alley. She'd have been buried underground, locked in a box, surrounded by dirt.

The room got hot. Her vision began to swim and her throat tightened, cutting off her breath.

No. Not now. This couldn't be happening.

She had to get out of here.

"I'm done," she said, forcing her breaths to slow down even as dizziness took over.

This was such a shitty time for a panic attack.

She pivoted and pushed through the double doors, already feeling the cold clamminess, the numbness in her fingers and face.

Get out. Get out now.

"M.E.'s behind schedule but has him on tap for tomorrow," the tech remarked casually as they walked into the elevator. "You coming back to watch?"

Anna nodded, barely focusing on his words as he

pushed the button and the elevator pitched and rolled. Nausea rose in her stomach and she leaned back against the wall for support. She needed to lie down, to feel something cool against her face.

She'd never fallen apart in front of anyone. If someone found out, they might tell her she couldn't do her job.

Could the tech see her sweat? Did he notice how pale she was? She tried to stay calm, to keep from breathing too fast.

When the doors opened, she walked slow and easy past the desk, but as it was, she could barely walk at all. She could no longer feel her legs past the pins and needles stabbing them.

"See you tomorrow," the tech said, waving her off.

"Yeah, tomorrow."

Her car seemed a thousand miles away as she shoved the door open, the blast of summer heat only making the queasiness worse. She was going to collapse right here on the front steps. She needed to lie down, to curl up in the fetal position so she could breathe.

But it was so hot out here. A few more feet, then she'd be in the car. She could turn on the air-conditioning and lie down.

She breathed in and out as fast as she walked, which only made it worse, she knew, but once the panic hit the only thing that mattered was getting to safety, being able to shut the doors and lock everyone out.

She weaved through the lot and knew she looked like a drunk. She could only hope no one saw her.

A few more feet. Just a few more feet. She fumbled in her pants pocket for her keys. Where were her keys, dammit? Finally she grasped them, dug them out and hit the remote, the sweet sound of the car unlocking her salvation. Sweat poured down her face and back as she

grabbed the door handle and slid inside, punched the lock
and started the engine.

She cranked the A/C down to the sixties, punched up
the fan, the sick feeling overwhelming her as she breathed
in short pants, trying to remember to take in slow breaths
and exhale easily.

She pushed the seat back as far as it would go and
leaned over, shoving her head between her knees.

This was going to pass. She was going to survive it.

She was drenched in sweat, but the cold air-
conditioning was a lifeline. Every minute that passed had
her chest loosening up so she could draw a breath. Within
fifteen minutes she could lift her head without wanting to
pass out or throw up. She swiped her wet hair away from
her face and looked around, thankful no one had come
by the car to see her embarrassing show of weakness.

When she was no longer shaking like a leaf, she put
the car in gear and headed home.

Dante made sure to arrive at Anna's house earlier than
everyone else. He wanted a chance to talk to her first.

When she opened the door, she looked gorgeous. Her
shorts and tank top showed off incredibly toned legs and
arms.

But she also looked pale and tired, with those dark
circles still under her eyes. And that worried him.

"You don't look like you slept at all."

She pulled the door open. "If I want that kind of
browbeating I'll go see my dad."

"How is he, by the way?"

"Doing okay, other than being grouchy as hell. He had
to retire a few years ago because of a knee injury."

"Job related?"

"Yeah. Went running after a suspect and blew out

his ACL when he tripped in the dark. After a couple surgeries, it was obvious he wasn't going to be able to work as a detective again, so he took early retirement."

Dante followed her into the living room. "Bet that pissed him off."

"Like you wouldn't believe."

He held up the case of beer he'd brought. "Where do you want this?"

"Fridge is fine."

He put the case in her refrigerator and pulled two out, handed one off to her after popping the top off.

She pulled her legs up and crossed them, took a long swallow and sighed.

"Long day?" he asked.

"Day off. But yeah, still a long day."

"Maybe you should have caught up on some sleep."

She lifted her head and looked at him. "I get the idea this whole sleep thing weighs on you."

He laughed. "It does when it looks like you haven't had much of it lately. Working too many hours, or is it nightmares that keep you awake?"

He'd cut a little close to the truth, so she decided to change the subject. "Do you think everyone will be here by six?"

"I know evasive tactics when I see them, Detective. But in answer to your question, yes, they'll be on time."

"Did you get hold of everyone?"

"I got hold of Roman and Gabe, and Roman said he'd call Jeff."

"Okay."

"So on your day off did you do any detecting on the case?"

She wasn't about to tell him about her ridiculous trip to the morgue to stare at George's body. "No."

"You working this case by yourself?"

"Well, Roman can't since George was indirectly a relative."

"But no other partner?"

"No."

"I thought you cops always worked with partners."

"Not always. And we're short-staffed, so we work cases alone or with uniforms. Roman and I aren't partnered, though we have bumped into each other on cases now and then."

"Funny that you both ended up in law enforcement. He's the last person I would have expected to become a cop."

She took another drink of her beer and wrapped her hands around the bottle, making sure to keep her focus on Dante, on the present, and not on the past. "I would think you would have been more surprised that *I* ended up in law enforcement."

His lips curled. "That, too, but Roman was always a little wild and undisciplined. You at least had the familial background for it."

"People grow up and change. Maybe the incident twelve years ago altered Roman's perspective enough to make him want to pursue law enforcement."

"I guess it did change some of us. Or maybe it affected all of us in some way, affected the choices we made in our lives after that night."

Cryptic words.

She wanted to ask him if that night had changed him at all, and if it had, how. He was catching up on all of them. But his secretiveness was beginning to piss her off.

The doorbell rang and she rose to answer it.

Gabe was at the door, with Jeff.

"I hope someone ordered pizza," Jeff said as he strolled in with his usual abundance of showmanship. "I'm starving."

Dante had never thought he'd be back here, let alone reunited with the old gang in one place. With Jeff and Gabe showing up, and Roman walking in a few minutes later, it was as if he hadn't been gone.

They were all older now, but the smiles and laughs were the same. They were different, and yet the same.

Jeff had come in wearing a suit—a suit, of all things. No way would Dante have predicted that.

"A suit, Jeff?"

Jeff waggled his brows. "Gotta maintain my slick image with the ladies, ya know?" He flicked the lapels of his jacket. "They like me suave and sophisticated."

Anna rolled her eyes and slapped a beer into Jeff's hand. "He's in insurance sales. Hence, the suit."

Dante laughed. "Is that right? And how are insurance sales?"

Jeff popped the top off his beer. "People keep drivin' cars, buyin' houses and they keep dyin'. Business is good."

"And ninety-five percent of his customers are women. Go figure," Roman said, taking the other beer Anna offered.

"Can I help it if the ladies like me?" Jeff asked, throwing his arm around Roman.

Dante always thought Jeff and Roman looked the most like brothers. Both about the same height and with light hair, Roman's was more surfer-boy blond, whereas Jeff's was sandy, but Dante and Gabe used to tease them about being the golden boys.

"So any wives or kids?" Dante asked as he sat on the sofa next to Jeff.

"Oh, God, no. I'm still playing the field, hoping like hell never to get caught."

Dante laughed.

"How about you?" Jeff asked.

"No. Not married yet."

"I'm so glad you're back, man. I missed you. It was rough when you and Gabe left."

"Yeah. I'm sorry. I didn't know he left the same time I did."

"Where've you been?"

He was going to have to answer that question soon. Probably sooner rather than later, judging from the way Anna hovered on the edge of their conversation. "Around. Here and there."

Jeff laughed. "That sounds like you don't want to answer. Like you've been in jail or somethin'."

"No. Not jail."

"On the beach in Bali with the perfect woman?"

Dante laughed. "Uh, no."

"Hey, man, I can dream, can't I? I always pictured you running some con with a sexy brunette, then taking the money and leaving the country, living out your days in luxury."

Jeff always had a vivid imagination. It's how he'd survived a hellish childhood filled with abuse.

"I like the way you think, Jeff, but no. That sounds more like your fantasy."

Jeff took a long gulp of beer and nodded. "Yeah, that's me. Always on the lookout for the perfect woman."

"Who's running away from you," Gabe replied, sliding into an unoccupied chair. "Which is why Jeff is still single."

Dante shook his head. "The more things change…"

"The more they stay the same," Roman said, taking a spot on the sofa on the other side of Dante.

"What about you, Roman?" Dante asked.

He shrugged. "Haven't settled down yet."

"But rumor has it Tess might be the one," Jeff said with a teasing glint in his eyes.

"Oh, yeah?" Dante asked. "Who's Tess?"

Roman's cheeks turned pink. "A woman I've been seeing for a while now."

Roman had always been shy around girls. Even now, Dante could tell he was uncomfortable talking about Tess. But he wanted to hear more. He wanted to know more about all of them. He'd missed so much.

"Dante, you're the elusive playboy, just like me," Jeff said. "You and I can hook up and it'll be like old times all over again."

Dante laughed. "You know, Jeff, I always thought you just used me to get women to buzz around you."

Jeff leaned forward. "You'd think that, ya know? But for some reason I haven't been all that lonely since you've been gone. Maybe you weren't the babe magnet we all thought you were. Maybe it was me all along."

Gabe snorted.

"Hey, I'm not exactly lonely," Jeff said, shooting Gabe a glare.

"No, but you are full of shit."

Jeff raised his arms and laid them over the back of the sofa. "See, Dante, this is what you've missed out on. You planning on stayin' now that you're back?"

His gaze hit Anna just as Jeff asked the question. "Don't know yet. I'll be here for a little while."

"No, he's not staying," Anna said right over the top of him.

"Not staying? Come on, Dante, we just got the old gang back," Jeff said.

But the pizza arrived, so that shut down most of the conversation as they all gathered in the kitchen to fill their plates and refill their beers.

When they gathered in the living room, Dante figured this was as good a time as any to bring up the murder.

"So you're probably wondering why you're all here."

"Because you're back in town, we figured," Jeff said. "And to pay tribute to George, the best father any of us ever had." Jeff raised his beer. "To George."

They all drank.

Dante glanced to Anna, who was leaned back on the sofa engrossed in the conversation. She didn't seem to be in any hurry to fill them in on why they were really here. He nudged her foot with his. "Do you want to do this, or should I?"

She narrowed her gaze at him and actually looked irritated. "Now?"

"If not now, when?"

"Fine." She turned her attention to the rest of the guys. "This is actually not a welcome-home-Dante party."

"It's not? Does this mean I have to chip in for the pizza and beer?" Jeff asked.

"Cheapskate," Roman said.

"Hey, I need to save all my money for the ladies. They like to be shown a good time."

"Which means what, exactly? Bowling? Dollar-movie night?"

"Fuck you, Gabe. My women are always satisfied."

"That's not what I've heard," Roman said.

Gabe snorted. Jeff flipped him off. Dante laughed. This was just like old times.

"Guys," Anna said, wrangling them in. "Can we get back to why we're here?"

"Oh. Sure, honey," Jeff said, shooting all the guys a glare. "Why are we here?"

"We need to talk about George's murder."

That got their attention. Jeff frowned. "I know. It sucks. Funeral is Thursday."

"I'm not looking forward to it," Roman said. "Poor Ellen. I went by to see her this morning. She's trying her best to be cheerful, but you can tell she's crushed."

Jeff nodded. "She's going to be lost without George. The two of them—they went together, ya know? One just doesn't belong without the other."

Dante could tell Jeff was getting choked up. He stood. "That's right. This murder has ruined Ellen's life. George was everything to her. We have to figure out why it happened. Someone beat him to death in the same alley where Anna was attacked that night. And carved a heart on his chest—same as what happened to Anna."

Anna moved around in front of the sofa to face them. "Also, after the murder, someone left flowers on my front porch with a note that asked me if I liked the gift they left in the alley."

"And before any of you ask," Roman said, "we don't have any clues. No evidence left behind at the scene. No fingerprints, nothing."

"What the fuck. So what does that mean?" Jeff looked at Roman, at Gabe, then at Dante.

"We don't know," Roman said. "Tony Maclin died in the alley twelve years ago. He's the guy who carved the heart in Anna's chest. We were the only ones in the alley that night."

"Tony Maclin? That was his name?" Dante asked.

"You didn't know, did you?" Anna asked.

Dante shook his head. He'd always just been that guy in the alley, the one who'd hurt Anna. "This is the first time I've ever heard his name."

Not that it made a difference, he supposed.

"His name was Tony Maclin. He was a high school senior, about to graduate and go to college. He lived in South County."

Dante frowned. "He lived in the county? What the hell was he doing in the city that night?"

Anna shrugged. "Don't know. When I became a cop I looked at his file. It never really shed any light on why he was there."

That just left more questions in Dante's mind, and dredged up more memories about that night.

"Back to George though," Anna said, nudging Dante out of the past and into the present, reminding him of what they all had to talk about.

"Right. It's no coincidence George was killed in the same place, that someone cut a heart in his chest, that he was beaten to death," Dante said, folding his arms and looking at all of them.

"Dante," Anna warned.

"What are you saying?" Roman asked.

The one thing he didn't want to say. The one thing none of them wanted to say out loud. But it had to be said. "The obvious. Someone else was in the alley that night when Anna was attacked, and when we beat Tony Maclin to death, whoever was there saw what we did."

No one said anything, so he continued.

"Someone sent us a message."

Seven

Anna stood to move next to Dante. "It wasn't a message. It could still be a coincidence."

Dante's brows lifted. "You don't really believe that, do you?"

"It's my job to look at all the angles. I can't use tunnel vision on this and tie it into what happened twelve years ago as the only option, when it could be something else entirely." She turned to all of them. "There could still be the drug angle."

"Wait," Jeff said. "What drug angle?"

"George was found with coke on him," Gabe said.

Jeff snorted. "George? Do drugs? He'd slit his own wrists before he'd let drugs anywhere near him."

"Agreed," Dante said. "But this is still connected to that night twelve years ago. The drugs were planted."

"You don't know that," Anna said. "The drug angle is a viable option."

"Anna," Dante said, laying his hand on her shoulder. "Same location, same cause of death? The heart cut into his chest? Come on. It's the same damn thing that happened that night. You can't ignore it."

"He's right," Gabe said. "Plus, they killed George, and that ties it to us. Someone else was there that night."

"Dante is right about this," Roman said, grimacing. "Someone saw what we did and is punishing us for it."

Anna agreed, but the cop in her wanted to deny. "Who would have been there? Why wait twelve years to send a message? And what kind of message is killing George? He had nothing to do with it."

"No, but he's connected to all of us," Dante said.

Roman grabbed her hand, forcing her attention on him. "And you know as well as I do that murder only makes sense to the killer. Look at what Tony Maclin tried to do to you that night, Anna. Did that make sense?"

Tony Maclin. The mention of his name always brought that night, still so clear in her mind, rushing back. The smells, the sounds, her walk to the Dumpster to empty the trash. She hadn't seen anyone that night, not even her attacker. And after she'd been attacked, there'd been panic, and pain, and the guys rushing to jump on Tony Maclin.

She hadn't known his name until the next day, when his body had been found and the media had reported on it.

They'd put Maclin's picture on the news. Just a kid, like the rest of them. Clean-cut, looked like a nice guy.

He hadn't been a nice guy in the alley when he'd grabbed her and dragged her behind the Dumpster and held a knife to her throat.

And a part of Tony Maclin would always remain with her.

The scar throbbed, reminding her of him, of what he'd done to her.

Now the past had caught up with the present.

Could someone else have been there that night? She

racked her brain to recall if she'd seen anyone else around, someone who could have seen what had happened. But her mind wrapped around the events that stuck out in her mind—the attack on her, and the guys beating Tony Maclin.

If someone else had been there, why hadn't they stopped what happened to her? Why hadn't they stopped the guys from killing Tony?

She could still see them pummeling him, hear their fists connecting with his flesh.

She tried to muster up sympathy for the way they'd pounded on him, the blood flying from his face, the way he looked when they'd finished with him, but all she'd felt was satisfaction that he hadn't gotten away, that he'd felt some of the misery he'd inflicted on her.

She'd waited years to feel guilty about him dying in the alley that night, and she never had.

Justice had been served that night. It might have been vigilante justice, and it might have been cruel, but she lived with the scars of that night, and she knew she'd never have survived the attack if Dante, Gabe and the others hadn't been there for her. Instinctively, she knew Tony Maclin would not have let her live. He hadn't just been out to rape her. He intended to kill her. Maybe it was the drugs he was hopped up on that had left him without coherent thought, but she knew she wasn't going to come out of that alley alive.

No, she felt no guilt over him dying instead of her.

She owed the guys everything. Including keeping her mind open about the attack on George and the connection to twelve years ago. She had to protect her guys.

"So somebody knows. Now what do we do?" Jeff paced back and forth, downed the last of his beer and crushed the can. He raked his fingers through his hair. "This is fucked up. I need a cigarette."

He pushed open the slider and stepped through into the backyard. Anna watched his hands shake as he lit a cigarette, the smoke billowing out through his mouth and nostrils.

"I'll go see if I can calm him down," Roman said.

Gabe leaned back against the sofa. "What do you think, Anna?"

"I don't know. If I were being honest I'd say I'd like to live in complete denial about the whole thing."

"Can't say I blame you for that," Gabe said. "You don't want to relive it or have it come back again."

She didn't, but it wasn't going to be avoidable. "Do you guys remember seeing anyone in the alley that night?"

Dante shook his head. "No, but we were all focused on what had happened to you. Once we saw Maclin and grabbed him, that was it."

"Dante's right," Gabe said, throwing an arm over the top of the sofa. "There was tunnel vision. We only saw him, and then there was you."

"I do remember sweeping the alley," Dante said, taking a seat in one of the chairs across from the sofa. "We wanted to make sure Maclin didn't bring anyone with him."

Gabe leaned forward. "You're right. I remember that, too. After we left you, before we got out of there. We panicked, wanted to make sure no one saw what we'd done."

"And?" Anna asked.

"There was no one," Dante said. "We checked one end of the alley to the other. There wasn't a sign of anyone."

"But that doesn't mean someone hadn't been there

before," Gabe said. "Someone could have been there watching the whole time."

Dante nodded. "And then taken off when we brought Anna inside the shop."

"Shit," Gabe said.

"But why wait? If someone saw you guys beat up Maclin, why not report it right then?" Anna asked.

"Scared?" Gabe offered. "Maybe whoever was in the alley with Maclin was high, too, not even sure of what he was seeing. Plus, no way would he call the cops."

"Okay, that makes sense. Self-preservation and all that. But what did that have to do with killing George? What's the connection?" Dante asked.

Anna blew out a breath. "That's my job to figure out."

Jeff and Roman came back in.

"In the meantime, all of you need to be on guard and be careful," Anna said. "We don't yet know what the connection is between George's murder and what happened twelve years ago."

"And whoever did this has some connection to you, Anna," Jeff said. "You don't worry about us. You gotta watch your own back."

She smiled and nodded. "I always do, Jeff."

They chatted for a while, the guys catching up with Dante, who, Anna noted, still wasn't all that forthcoming about where he'd been for the past twelve years, giving them excuses about traveling and doing manual labor here and there and how much he'd enjoyed seeing the world.

He looked so at ease as he bullshitted with the guys, not at all tense about all this like Jeff was. Roman was used to threats, because like her, it was the nature of their jobs. Gabe was laid-back because he lived his life with the criminal element. He was always looking over his shoulder.

Was Dante a criminal, too?

She needed to find out.

Jeff and Roman headed out. Since Gabe kept checking his phone, not a half hour later he said he had a "meeting." She didn't want to know what kind of meeting he had, nor was she going to ask.

Gabe stood at her door and laid his hands on her shoulders. "You keep eyes in the back of your head. I don't like what's going on."

"You do the same."

His quick grin didn't comfort her, because she knew he took chances he shouldn't. "I always watch my own back, honey."

He kissed her cheek and walked out the door. She closed it, locked it and turned to find Dante standing right behind her.

She skirted around him and went into the living room, picking up empty beer cans. After she dumped them in the trash, she pivoted and he was right there behind her again with a stack of cans in his hand.

"Goddammit, Dante."

"What?"

"Quit sneaking up on me."

"You're a cop. I wouldn't think anyone could get a stealth drop on you."

Unnerved, she shoved him aside and went back into the living room. "Normally no one does. You've got ninja skills."

He laughed and slid onto the sofa next to her, stretching his long, lean legs out in front of him.

"Don't get comfortable."

"You don't have to work, do you?"

"No."

"It's still early." He stretched his arms over the back of the sofa.

She refused to notice the lean muscle of his forearms, or the dark hairs. Or his tan skin that made her want to ask where he'd been outside lately.

"I'm tired."

His grin irritated her. "I make you nervous."

"No, you don't." She leaned forward to pick up the pizza boxes.

"Anna."

He laid his hand on her arm and pulled her back. "Talk to me."

His touch had an effect on her. No man's touch did that. She hated that Dante's did. He was a closed-up mystery, a few pieces of a giant puzzle. She wouldn't ask him again where he'd been.

"We have nothing to say to each other anymore."

He swept her hair away from her face. She knocked his hand away.

Instead of being offended, he smiled. "I like that you're tough. It makes me worry a little less about you."

"You have no right to worry about me at all." She pushed off the couch and grabbed the empty pizza boxes, shoved them in the trash can in the kitchen. This time she knew Dante was behind her, her senses tuning to him. She put the lid on the trash and turned around.

He was so big. Big guys tended to freak her out, at least when they invaded her personal space. Caged between him and her kitchen counter, she expected the normal panic to set in. She took things with men slow and easy. Too much too fast and things took a nosedive.

But everything about Dante was familiar to her, from his scent to the color of his eyes to the way his skin felt under her hand. She balled her fingers into her fists to keep from reaching out to touch him, to find out if he still felt the same to her. She took a deep breath, inhaling the crisp scent of him. Her heart banged a hard rhythm against her chest, but this time it wasn't the familiar choking panic—it was something else entirely.

"I do make you nervous. I never used to do that."

"I'm not nervous. You're crowding me and it's pissing me off."

He took a few steps back, his brow furrowing. "You still freaked out about that night?"

"No."

"Anna."

"No." She walked past him, but he reached out and gently grasped her arm, pulled her against him.

Though she would have clocked other men for grabbing her, she melted against him. Dante's body was familiar to her. She couldn't help herself, she had to touch, to test her reaction. She slid her palms along his biceps. Hard muscle and soft skin eased across her hands, making her tingle in places that just flat out never tingled.

And he let her, this time not pushing to be the aggressor. He let her explore without moving in to take.

Men and her and relationships—yeah, that didn't go well. Maybe she didn't try hard enough. She put all her energy into her work and there was nothing left over for guys. Sex wasn't worth all the hype anyway. Quick release and out the door—that was her motto. It had worked well over the years for both her and the guys she chose.

When she was a hormone-filled teenager—before that night—and she and Dante had been filled with heat and desire for each other, then yeah, there'd been the promise of something incredible.

But all that had changed.

Now she was chest to chest, hip to hip, thigh to thigh against one solid wall of muscle, and she felt stirrings of something she hadn't felt in a very long time. Something hot and delicious, like her blood had just slowed down in her veins and begun a slow heat.

Her skin prickled with goose bumps, her breasts felt full and her nipples tightened. She jerked her head up and read flat-out desire all over Dante's face. He hadn't budged, wasn't moving his hands, but, oh, man, were there clear signals in his eyes.

She'd never been so tempted to take what was so obviously being offered, to lift her fingers and touch his mouth, to taste him, to forget everything and fall back twelve years and take up where they left off.

And she still had no idea who he was, where he'd been, or what his involvement was in the murder the other night.

She took a step back and he let go, cocked his head to the side and gave her a lopsided smile.

Was he playing her?

Damn.

"Get out."

His smile died. "I don't get you."

"No, you don't 'get me' at all, and you're not going to."

She walked to the door and opened it.

He stood in front of it. "I'm worried about you, Anna. About what happened."

"Then or now?"

"Both"

"Don't be."

"I don't like what's going on. And I can't believe you're not taking it seriously."

Her palm began to sweat as she held the doorknob. "I'm taking it plenty seriously. That's what this meeting was about."

"But I don't think you see yourself in the mix."

"How could I not see myself in it? I was there. And I'm the one who got the flowers and the note. Believe me, I'm in it and I know it. But I also know I'm not the one who killed Tony Maclin." That's what worried her. The guys did. She understood there was a connection between what they did and George being killed in the alley. She knew there was a reason someone had left her the flowers and the note. She just didn't know what the connection was.

He stepped outside the door. "Keep your eyes open and watch your back."

"I always do. I'm a cop, remember? I can take care of myself. You do the same."

He nodded and walked away. She shut the door, locked it and couldn't help but watch him as he made his way to his car, got in and drove away.

She turned and went to the kitchen counter, grabbed the glass Dante had drunk from earlier and bagged it.

If he didn't want to share what he'd been up to the past twelve years, she'd find out for herself.

She might be emotional about him, but she wasn't stupid.

Pent up, his head filled with thoughts of friendship and murder and Anna, Dante drove around, needing to think, to process everything from tonight.

It had been great to reconnect with all the guys. He'd sat back and listened to them talk, watched the way they interacted with each other. They'd all grown up and changed, just like he had. But in so many ways they were exactly the same as they'd always been. Jeff still thought he was slick, Roman was still the glue that held them all together as brothers and Gabe still hung back and observed, a lot like Dante did.

And then there was Anna, the Snow White to all of them, though they'd never been dwarves, but they sure as hell had rallied around her from the beginning when they first met her. They'd probably all fallen madly in love with her from the first day she'd showed her sunny smile and disposition and refused to let the school bullies push around the new kids. With her dad as a cop, the other kids had left them all alone, and Anna had become their champion.

No one had stuck up for them before. They'd never been worth anyone's time.

Anna had stood in front of all of them as if she could single-handedly take on the school bullies. Not that they'd needed her help, of course. Dante had gotten used to being the new kid in school and had to fight his way out of plenty of scraps. So had the other guys, but a couple of the group of foster kids were younger than Gabe and him, and he and Gabe protected the younger boys.

And then Anna had told the bullies where they could shove it.

Fourteen-year-old Anna, skinny as heck with braces on her teeth, looking tough as steel as she squared her shoulders and warned the boys they'd better back off.

Dante and Gabe, bigger than the boys threatening them, had taken a couple steps forward. Dante supposed they'd looked menacing enough to get the bullies to back the hell off. Anna, looking pretty smug and satisfied, had turned to them and grinned and told them all to stick with her because her daddy was a cop and she'd make sure no harm would ever come to them.

Oh, yeah. They'd all fallen in love with her that day. And were loyal to her after that.

Except when Dante had run out on her right after the worst night of her life.

That hadn't been the most loyal thing he could have done.

Then again, he'd done what her father asked him to do, what he thought was best.

Or maybe he'd just been scared as hell and wanted to get out of town. Who had he been protecting then—Anna or himself?

He found himself at the alley, pulled over and got out. The tape had been removed, so he walked down toward the Dumpster. It was late, dark and so humid he was drenched in sweat in a matter of minutes, no different than a lot of hellholes he'd been in over the past twelve years. Only this time he wasn't hiding from the enemy and swiping sweat from his eyes to clear his field of vision.

This time he was alone—just him and his memories.

A rumble of thunder rolled in the distance. Rain was coming, just like that night twelve years ago. The ground had been wet and Anna had been wearing those cute white shorts that had ended up muddy and bloodstained. He walked behind the Dumpster, still able to clearly see her pushed against the brick wall of the building, holding the tattered edges of her blouse together, her eyes wide with shock, blood streaming down her chest.

His hands balled into fists. If he could, he'd beat the hell out of Tony Maclin again. Dying once wasn't enough punishment for what the bastard had done to her. He needed to suffer over and over again.

Just like Anna continued to suffer.

She hid behind the bravado of her detective's badge,

but Dante saw the haunted look in her eyes, especially when they'd stood in this alley where George was killed.

She still wore that look today, hidden behind her tough look and the badge she wore. He saw the fear in her eyes when he came close, felt the tension in her body when he touched her. She hadn't forgotten one minute of what had happened to her twelve years ago.

So who the hell had dragged it all up again by repeating the crime?

Who wanted them to remember?

Eight

"Somehow I thought I'd find you here."

Anna looked up and cast a smile at Roman as he entered the squad room.

"I couldn't sleep anyway, figured I'd go over some of my cases. What are you doing here?"

He took a seat at the desk across from hers and opened his laptop. "Same thing. How's George's case going?"

"You know I'm not supposed to talk about it with you. You're not on this case."

He gave her a look. "Come on, Anna. You know how it works. Officially, yeah, I'm off the case. Unofficially…"

His sentence trailed off. And yeah, she did know how it worked. His name wouldn't appear on any official records or notes on the case, but he'd work the case with her. That's just how it was done. She'd do the same thing if it was someone close to her who'd been killed.

"You talk to the captain about it?"

"Yeah. He told me I was off the case. I argued with him. He told me I was off the case."

She leaned back in her chair. "Then he told you that you could work it unofficially, right?"

"Well, yeah."

She shook her head. That's the way it worked. Even the captain knew the drill. With uniforms? No. With the detectives? There was more leeway. You didn't push out a decent detective just because of involvement.

"Just watch your step on this one and don't screw it up," Anna said.

"I'm as good a detective as you. Your dad made sure of it."

She grinned. "Yeah, he sure did, didn't he? He'd accept no less than perfect from either of us."

"I owe him everything, so let's make him proud by bringing in the bastard who killed George."

She pushed a few buttons while Roman opened his system.

"How are things with Tess?" she asked while she let Roman take a look at the case file on George.

"Great. She's working a heavy-duty tax case for a national company, so we haven't seen much of each other lately. She's doing a lot of traveling."

She peered around her monitor. "That must suck."

"It does. I thought things were getting serious, but she's a career woman. Hard to pin her down. I think she's married to her job."

Anna scooted her chair so she could see Roman. "And does that mean you want her married to you instead?"

He laughed. "Ever the matchmaker, aren't you?"

Was she? She'd never thought about it that way, but she'd like to see her guys settled. None of them were yet, and it was time. Maybe if Roman got married, that would get Jeff to think about grabbing a woman and settling down. And who knows—maybe even Gabe would turn his life around.

She could wish, anyway. "You know I want you to be

happy. Tess is a sweetheart. What's wrong with tying the knot?"

"Not sure if I'm ready for that step yet, but maybe down the road things could be headed that way."

She was glad to hear it. She loved him like she loved all the guys. He, like Gabe and Jeff, were the brothers she'd never had.

Dante, on the other hand, was something entirely different.

"So, got any new leads?" he asked.

"Nothing. There was no trash service that morning, no witnesses located. Forensics report on the bag of drugs came back as suspected—an ounce of coke. Pretty good stuff, too. Street value is about eight hundred dollars."

Roman whistled. "Any prints on the bag?"

"Yeah. George's. No one else's."

Roman grimaced. "That's convenient."

"Isn't it? Anyway, autopsy is scheduled for this morning, so I'll head over and watch that. You're welcome to come with me if you'd like."

He shook his head. "There's no way I could watch George's autopsy. I can work the case with you, but that? I just couldn't."

"I understand. I'll go and find out all I can about George's murder."

"What's there to find out? Somebody beat him to death and cut him."

"Maybe that's all there is to it, and maybe there's more. Hoping the M.E. can tell me more. Maybe the CSU will find hair or fibers or something the killer left behind."

"Yeah, you know as well as I do that shit only happens on television. The amazing find under the microscope that solves the case in the last five minutes."

"True," she said with a laugh. "We should get so lucky. It would up our solve rate, wouldn't it?"

"Yeah, and we'd all get commendations. But that doesn't happen. Most of our cases are solved with good old-fashioned legwork and dumbass luck."

"I'll take dumbass luck right now. I want to get this guy."

"Me, too, honey."

Anna was right on time for the autopsy, gloved and masked and in the room. Dr. Norton had George on the table, ready to cut when she walked in. She stayed quiet and out of the way while the doctor did his inspection of the body and dictated his report, though half the time she wondered if he was talking in his official report or if he was talking to her.

"Somebody really did a number on this guy. Bruising on the torso, especially the ribs. Looks like he was kicked several times."

"Any shoe impressions on the skin?" Anna asked.

"None apparent. Looks like whoever kicked him did it with the toe of their shoe or boot. We found no fingerprints on the body itself, no hair or fibers that didn't appear to belong to the victim or the victim's clothing. You'd think a crime like this someone would leave something, especially if it was an argument that escalated into the beating this man took."

Damn. Someone had been thorough in making sure they didn't leave any evidence, which meant it wasn't a spur-of-the-moment crime of passion or anger. This was a deliberate attack and whoever had done it had been meticulous.

"What about the knife wound on his chest?"

The doctor leaned over and examined with his fingers,

then put the magnifying mirror over the heart-shaped wound and motioned her over.

"It's crude, as you can see. Maybe the carving of the heart was done in a hurry, as an afterthought. The cut isn't too deep." He measured. "About two centimeters in."

"Any estimate on the type of knife?"

The doctor looked up. "Yeah, sharp and pointy."

"Ha-ha."

"The cut isn't jagged, so the knife wasn't serrated. Small blade. Some kind of pocketknife, probably."

"We found a bag of coke on him."

Richard nodded. "We're running a tox screen. I'll let you know what we find."

The rest of the autopsy was unremarkable, and Anna left disappointed. She'd expected something that would give her some clues to chase.

Right now she had nothing more to go on than she had when they'd started the investigation.

No witnesses, no fingerprints, no DNA evidence, nothing.

And that just plain sucked.

With nothing to go on and frustration eating away at her, she went to Forensics.

"You get anything on that glass?" she asked Patty, one of the techs.

"I ran that earlier. Hang on." Patty went to a stack of reports and grabbed a file, flipped it open and strolled back toward her. "Whoever's prints those are is clean. Not in the system at all. Any system. AFIS, Interpol, nothing. They're clean."

Interesting. "Okay. Thanks, Patty."

She supposed that was a good thing he didn't come

up anywhere, but she'd run a background check on him and it was as if he didn't exist.

No one didn't exist. There were records of everyone. Everyone except Dante, and that wasn't normal.

She decided to pay Paolo Bertucci a visit.

Bertucci lived in a sprawling, private, gated area with plenty of acreage that gave him space away from neighbors, unsurprisingly. His house was a remodeled two-story brick mansion set back in a thick wooded area. Perfect to give him enough privacy, especially with the gate and the security system he'd put in making the place look like a celebrity lived there.

Anna was certain Bertucci thought himself a celebrity of sorts. He frequented the clubs, always had two or three women on his arm. He dressed in designer clothes, wore expensive jewelry and drove flashy sports cars and high-dollar SUVs. He always had an entourage of bodyguards trailing him.

Unfortunately his celebrity status had more to do with his mob connections than Hollywood. And they hadn't been able to officially tie him into anything hard to make an arrest. All they could do was watch, make notes and work with the feds on gathering evidence, hope their informants continued to bring them information and maybe someday take the bastard down, because Anna knew he was dirty.

She pulled to the front gate, rolled her window down and flashed her badge at the camera. After a minute or so the gate started its slow roll open and she drove down the long concrete driveway toward the house. A tall dude in a tight black T-shirt meant to show off his sizable muscles met her out front. She'd just bet he had a piece tucked into the back of his pants.

He leaned against her window. "Can I help you?"

"Detective Anna Pallino from St. Louis Metro. I'm here to see Paolo Bertucci."

"You have a warrant?"

"He commit a crime that I need a warrant for? I just want to have a conversation with him."

"About what?"

"About none of your fucking business."

He glared at Anna, a look meant to intimidate. She stared back, not even bothering to remove her sunglasses.

He finally pushed away from her car. "Just a minute."

The guy went inside. Anna got out and leaned against her car, surveying the impeccable landscaping filled with colorful flowers, the trellis with climbing roses and the copious wide windows on all levels that offered a clear view of approaching vehicles. The windows were probably bulletproof, too. You didn't get to the top of the mob food chain like Bertucci did without making enemies.

The double front doors were thick as hell, which meant no one could kick them in.

The place was a fortress.

Muscle man returned within a few minutes and motioned her inside. She stepped in, impressed with the Italian-marble flooring, the wide-open floor plan that led to an expansive living area on the right and a dining area on the left.

The furnishings, the artwork on the walls and tables— everything screamed high dollar.

"This way. Mr. Bertucci is out back in the pool area."

Must be nice. She was taken down a long hallway, past the kitchen where a cook was busily chopping vegetables and didn't even bother looking up at her. She'd just bet the staff here saw a lot, and were paid very well not to notice a damn thing. Or ever say a word about anything they "didn't" see.

The kitchen was huge, with stainless-steel appliances, a giant center island and an eating area that would serve all her friends and possibly the entire precinct. Since she loved to cook, Anna would kill for a kitchen like that. She could spend hours, days and possibly the rest of her natural life enjoying that kitchen.

Muscle guy opened the back door and led her outside to what had to be the Garden of Eden. A sheltered arbor covered with greenery provided cool shade where a table sat filled with drinks. Beyond that was a sizable pool where Paolo Bertucci lay floating on a raft in his board shorts, his buffed hairless body well tanned, his bald head reflecting the sun with the same intensity as the giant diamond earring in his left ear. He was surrounded by a bevy of beauties sporting very tiny bikinis.

Anna was most definitely overdressed.

"Ah, Detective Pallino, welcome to my home."

"Thank you."

"Can I offer you something to drink? Sangria, perhaps?"

"No, thanks, I'm on duty."

"Then how about some lemonade or iced tea."

Both sounded great. It was hot and the back of her shirt stuck to her. But she stepped out into the bright sunlight and walked to the edge of the pool. "No, thank you. I'd like to ask you a few questions."

"You can ask. Depending on the questions, I may or may not answer."

"There was a murder in an alley off Lindell two days ago. A man named George Clemons."

Paolo stared at her, then shrugged. "Name doesn't mean anything to me."

"I'm sure it doesn't, but he was found with an ounce of cocaine on him."

"Mmm, bad boy. Someone kill him over the drugs then?"

"If they did, I'm sure they would have taken the drugs with them, don't you think?"

Paolo raised his hands, the two diamond rings on his fingers glinting in the harsh sunlight. "I wouldn't know anything about that."

She crossed her arms. "I would think you'd know a lot about the drug trade in my city, Mr. Bertucci, since known dealers are seen coming and going from your house all the time."

Bertucci flattened his lips. "You watchin' my house, Detective?"

"Me personally? No. But I believe you're well aware that you're under surveillance, so I think we can cut through the crap and get down to an honest discussion."

He sat up on his raft. "I don't know what you're talking about. I have a lot of friends who come and go. Sometimes there are parties. That's probably what your surveillance people see."

"Uh-huh. Look, I'm not here to bust you for drugs. I want to know if you have any dealers working the area around the alley where the murder occurred."

He laughed. "Like I'd tell you if I did. Maybe it was your friend Gabe."

He'd throw Gabe under the bus just to piss her off? "Gabe's not a suspect."

"So you want me to give you a name?"

"That'd be helpful."

He took the cocktail offered by one of the bikini-clad women and grinned up at Anna. "Now, that would be me doing your job for you, wouldn't it?"

"I would appreciate the help," she said, gritting her teeth the entire time. "We just want to question anyone who might have been around the alley at the time of the murder."

If there was recognition on Bertucci's face, he didn't show it. Instead, he shrugged again. "I'll have to put some feelers out and see if anyone knows anything."

Right. In other words, she wasn't going to get shit from him. "If you hear of anything, or your memory has an epiphany and you think of anyone who might have been in the alley that night, do let me know. I'll leave my card with one of your associates."

"You do that. Always nice to see you."

"Likewise."

"You're a beautiful woman, Detective Pallino. And it's a very hot day. Care to take a dip in the pool?"

She gave him a lift of her lips. "Gee, Mr. Bertucci. I'm kind of overdressed for a swim."

"My ladies here have many extra bikinis. Or you could go without."

She eyed the women, who looked as though they couldn't care less if Paolo added one more to the harem. They must be well compensated. Ugh.

"Thanks for the offer, but I have to get back to work."

"Some other time, perhaps."

Yeah, around the time pigs sprouted wings. "Have an enjoyable day."

Bertucci was cool and not very forthcoming with information, but it was always a brain game to spar with him, and she had to admit she enjoyed it. And he knew something. She was sure of it. She just didn't know what he knew, or how he was connected to George's murder.

The bad thing was, if Bertucci was connected, then Gabe was connected.

Did Gabe know anything? Was he withholding information from her?

Now, that really would piss her off. Would he place his position with the Bertuccis over the death of his foster father?

Sometimes she wasn't exactly sure where Gabe's loyalties lay.

Maybe she needed to find out.

Once summoned, you didn't ignore Paolo Bertucci. Gabe had been in the area anyway when he'd gotten the text from Bertucci's right-hand monkey, so he'd ridden over.

Bertucci was on the patio in the backyard, his typical group of bikini babes serving lunch.

"You're just in time for some salsiccia-and-polenta sandwiches. You hungry?"

"Sure, boss, thanks." Gabe grabbed a bottle of beer from the center of the table and popped it open, leaned back and waited. Darla brought him a sandwich. He thanked her and ate, watching the girls frolic in the pool. Paolo talked on the phone while he ate and barked instructions to one of the black-clad morons standing guard over him.

Finally, he wiped his mouth with his napkin, sat back and lit a Cuban. "Detective Pallino dropped by today."

"Yeah? What did she want?"

"To grill me about some dead guy in an alley. They found drugs on him and she thinks I'm connected."

Gabe finished the last bite of his sandwich and pushed his plate to the side, then grabbed another beer. "She's got nothin'."

"That's what I figured, too. She wouldn't have come fishing at my house if she did."

"So no problem then."

"She's your friend."

"Yes, she is. And you've known that since the beginning. I've never hidden that from you."

Paolo nodded and smiled. "I know. Your honesty has always been refreshing, Gabriel. That's one of the reasons you've risen so fast in my organization. I trust you."

"And I appreciate it, Paolo. Anna might be my friend, but you know where my loyalty lies."

"I also know having a 'friend' like Anna can be useful."

Gabe leaned back in the chair and offered up a sly smile. "It serves its purposes. She cuts me slack and feeds me information even when she doesn't know she's doing it."

"Because you know all the right questions to ask, and because she trusts you."

"She thinks I'm not going to cause problems for her, and so far I haven't—that she's aware of."

"Cultivate that relationship."

Gabe crossed his fingers. "We're like this."

"Good. But keep in mind the time may come when you may need to sever that tie."

Gabe shrugged. "Whatever needs to be done for the greater good. Like I said, I know where my loyalties lie."

"Good boy. Everything set up for tonight?"

"Yeah. MacKenzie and Smith are meeting me at eleven. Shipment comes in at midnight."

"Excellent. Let me know how it goes."

That was his signal he was no longer needed. He stood. "Will do. Thanks for lunch."

"Care to stick around and play with the ladies?"

He took a quick glance at the mounds of available breasts floating in the pool. He leered at the ladies, then turned to Bertucci. "Tempting as hell, but some other time, Paolo. I want to scout the warehouse in advance, make sure nothing's going to pop up that might surprise us."

Gabe left the house, climbed on his bike and headed out toward the location of the drop tonight.

Bertucci was a lot of things, but stupid wasn't one of them. That's why it had taken Gabe two years of working for him to get where he was now.

People like Paolo Bertucci ran these cities, smuggling in drugs right under the noses of the cops, lining the veins of the rich, the middle class and the poor. And the ones Paolo got to push it? They were the real victims.

Gabe had no idea what George had been doing with drugs in his pocket, but those drugs were linked to Bertucci. Someone had planted them there. Someone connected to Paolo's hierarchy.

And there wasn't a damn thing Gabe could do about it. He could find out with a little legwork and clear George, but it would blow his cover. And he'd spent two years getting himself dug into the Bertucci organization. No way was he going to screw this up. He'd get his ass fired for one thing. Or dead if Paolo found out who he was really working for.

So he'd have to keep his mouth shut and hope Anna could figure it all out, while he sat on the sidelines and played dumb.

Sometimes he really hated his job.

Nine

Anna was frustrated. She updated her reports and got into her car, not wanting to spend the better part of her shift stuck in the precinct.

She drove past the alley, though she wasn't sure what she expected to find there. Nothing, which was exactly what she saw. It was empty.

She pulled over and got something to eat, then grabbed her phone, impulse punching Dante's number.

"Anna?"

"Yeah."

"What's up?"

"Did I wake you?" She cringed, realizing not everyone kept night hours like she did.

"No. I'm up."

Now what? Idiot. Why did he still twist her up inside and make her feel like a tongue-tied sixteen-year-old? "I…I want to talk to you. You busy? You're probably going to bed soon aren't you?"

She heard the soft chuckle. "No. I'm up. Come over."

"Okay." She hung up, feeling stupid and hot and sweaty. Damn him for getting to her that way.

She drove over and knocked on the door of the condo.

He answered, looking delectable in a pair of jeans and a well-worn gray T-shirt that snugged tight against his body. His hair looked mussed, like he'd run his fingers through it several times.

"Are you sure you weren't sleeping?"

"I'm sure I wasn't sleeping. Come in."

He closed the door after she walked in. The television was on, though turned down low. He had a laptop open on the dining room table.

"Working?"

"Not really," he said, pushing it closed as he headed to the kitchen. "Online games. It's an addiction."

She laughed. "I guess it's good to have something to do to pass the time."

"You want something to drink?"

"Water, if you have it."

He pulled out a bottle of water for her and a soda for himself.

She felt ridiculously out of sorts standing in the middle of his living room, though this really wasn't his place, so she didn't understand her discomfort.

"Decent place."

"Gabe scored it for me, and yeah, it beats the hell out of a hotel."

She took a seat on the sofa, unable to take her eyes off him as he slid next to her. What was it about him that, even after twelve years and total abandonment, he could still capture her interest in a way that made her palms sweat and her heart beat faster?

It had to be the shadowy element. She'd been drawn to him when he was the bad boy, the kid with the rocky, brutal past. And now he'd swooped back into her life as mysterious as ever, possibly even mixed up in a murder investigation. She should be steering clear of him and focusing on him as a suspect. Instead, she was breathing in his musky male scent and wishing she had the guts to put down her water and climb onto his lap and do what she'd fantasized about doing for the past twelve years.

She breathed in and out, her focus on the sun-bleached hairs on his arm and the broad muscle of his biceps. She hadn't even realized she was staring until her gaze reached his face and he was smiling down at her.

"Lost in thought?"

She leaned back and took a long swallow of water. "Yeah."

"About the case."

"Of course."

From the smirk on his face, she could tell he knew damn well what she'd been thinking about.

Bastard.

"You going to tell me why you came over?"

She'd love to. If she actually knew what had compelled her to drive over here.

"I'm stuck."

"On?"

"This case. But Roman's the one I should brainstorm with."

"He around tonight?"

"I'm sure he is. I could call him."

"But you didn't. You called me. So talk to me."

He made it sound so simple when everything was actually convoluted. Like being here in the first place.

"Anna, it's me. You can talk to me."

She shifted to face him. "You want me to erase twelve years of 'I don't know where the hell you've been or who you are' as if they don't mean anything, Dante. I can't do that, especially when you won't tell me anything."

"I was in the army."

Her brows shot up. "The army?"

"Yeah. When I left here I joined the army. I needed to get away, start over, start a different life, but I was unskilled, so I knew I needed training. The army gave me that."

"How long were you in the army?"

"Still am."

"You… Really?"

"Yes."

"So you're on leave?"

His lips curled. "You could say that."

She frowned. If he was military, his fingerprints would have showed up in the database. "Are you Special Forces or something?"

He leaned back. "Why do you ask?"

"I ran your prints. You don't show up."

"You ran… When?"

"I used a glass you drank water out of and ran fingerprints on you."

His brows rose. "Why?"

"Duh. Because you wouldn't tell me a goddamn thing about yourself or where you'd been for the past twelve years. I don't like mysteries, so I wanted some answers."

His smile was infuriating. "Get any?"

"No. You don't show up on any databases. No license, nothing. Why is that? I can't imagine you'd be any good to Special Forces not knowing how to drive a car."

"I do special projects undercover. They don't want me showing up on any databases. Let's just leave it at that for now."

She opened her mouth to argue, but Dante placed two fingers at her lips. "Please, Anna."

She was supposed to believe him, take his word.

They'd been everything to each other at one time.

But right now, he could be a killer.

People changed. She knew it, saw it.

But how much did they change? All those years ago she knew exactly who he was and what he was capable of.

He'd saved her life that night. But he'd also taken a life.

She'd never been so confused about anything—or anyone—before.

"So tell me why you're here."

She should leave, keep her distance, listen to that inner voice that kept telling her to be wary of Dante.

Instead, she decided to see where this led.

"Autopsy showed nothing out of the ordinary other than George had been beaten and cut with a nondescript sharp knife, probably some random switchblade. No stray hairs or fibers, no fingerprints from the scene. The bag of drugs was clean, but it had George's fingerprints on it. The scene and the body itself were almost too clean. It was as if whoever had done this had been meticulous about prepping the scene or making sure he'd leave nothing behind."

"A lot of crafty killers watch television and read books these days. Many are well versed in crime scene technology."

"True, but people think they know what to watch out for, and they still leave something at the scene we can pick up on. This guy left nothing. Not even a shoe print."

Dante leaned forward, resting his forearms on his knees. "Which means what, exactly?"

"I don't know, other than he knows what to do to not leave any evidence behind."

"Maybe he's done this before."

"I did a search on similar crimes and found nothing."

"Which doesn't mean your suspect hasn't killed before. He just hasn't killed in this way, right?"

She leaned back. "True. But how could we not know this guy was in the alley that night twelve years ago? Wouldn't we have seen him?"

"Lots of hiding places in that alley, Anna. You were in shock, and the guys and I were focused on two things— you and Maclin. There could have been an elephant in the alley and we wouldn't have noticed."

"You're probably right. Shit." She took a drink and set the bottle down on the table in front of her. "But why kill George?"

"I told you. It's a message. He's here and he knows what happened. Now he wants us to know. And he wants to hurt us—us being me and the other guys. George was our father—the closest thing to a father we had. Killing him hurt us."

Anna nodded, acknowledging the pain they must all be going through. The funeral had been brutal for all of them. She'd stayed in the back and watched them as they'd surrounded Ellen, watched their faces as the coffin was lowered into the ground. She'd felt the gut-wrenching sorrow emanating from all of them, especially from Ellen as she'd let tears fall from her cheeks and stood stoically at the grave site. It had been a horrible experience.

She shook off the memory and lifted her gaze to Dante. "But why wait twelve years to send his message? Why didn't he do it earlier?"

He shifted, drawing his knee onto the sofa. "I've been thinking about that. Maybe he was waiting for me to come back so we'd all be here."

And maybe Dante was the one who had set it all in motion. Maybe he was the killer.

She hated thinking it, but there it was.

No. He wouldn't do that to George. He'd loved him. She remembered him telling her that George was his father. He'd admired and respected him and he and the other guys had finally found a home—a family—with the Clemonses.

So she pondered his suggestion, the fact that all of them who had been in the alley that night were now back in town. "That's the only thing that does make sense. If he wants to show off—to show us that he knows—he had to do it in front of all of us and you weren't here. For a while Gabe wasn't here, either. It wasn't the right time."

"Yes."

"Which means it's someone local, someone who's been tracking our movements all these years. How would he even know who we are?"

"You know as well as I do, if you want to find out who people are, you can figure it out. You worked in the shop right there. Easy to backtrack from there."

This was all so surreal. "You're right. So now he's done it. What's going to be his next move?"

Dante dragged his hands through his hair. "Hell if I know. Maybe it's a cat-and-mouse game and he wants you to find him."

"Ugh. This *is* as bad as television."

"Ready for a beer now?"

"I'm on duty."

"I won't tell anyone."

She smiled. "No, thanks. I'm so tense I probably wouldn't stop at one, and it would be my luck I'd get called in by my captain, he'd smell alcohol on my breath and then there'd be hell to pay."

"I'm sure you wouldn't be the first detective to drink on the job."

"No, I wouldn't. But that's not who I am."

He leaned back and studied her. "Still a good girl, aren't you?"

She stood, her irritation spiking hot. "You don't know anything about me, Dante."

Dante loved seeing the flash of heat in Anna's cheeks. Even if he'd pissed her off, which he seemed to be able to do easily.

"I guess I don't. You never used to spark up as quick as you do now."

"You never used to irritate me as much as you do now."

He laughed. "Then sit down and tell me about yourself." He patted the sofa. "Sit."

Her jaw clenched. "I'm not a dog."

"Please."

She slid onto the sofa and grabbed the bottle of water, eyeing him warily. She had reason not to trust him. The circumstances of their first meeting after he'd gotten back hadn't been ideal. And she'd gone on a fishing expedition to find out more about him. Hadn't found anything, either.

She still didn't know it all.

"Tell me what happened after that night," he said.

"You mean after you left?"

"Yeah. I'm sorry I left you."

He wanted to say it over and over until she believed him, until she forgave him.

She shrugged. "No big deal. I handled it."

He could continue to apologize for that, but what would be the point? What was done was done and he couldn't change the past.

"Yeah, you did handle it. Look at you now."

Ignoring him, she said, "After that night I went on living just like normal. I went back to school and tried to pretend nothing had happened."

"That must have been hard."

"It was. The guys—Roman and Jeff—stuck by me, but I was so freaked out about someone connecting us to the murder in the alley that I distanced myself from them."

"But no one knew you were there."

"I was working that night, remember? The police questioned me. I told them I had closed up and hadn't heard anything out back."

Guilt hammered at him. It had been a mistake leaving. He could have waited awhile, could have argued harder with her father about leaving right away.

Yet he couldn't go back and change the past. His guilt would always be there, so he'd just have to live with it.

She had paused, so he nodded. "Go on."

"Anyway, after that I motored through classes, had no social life and went on to college where I majored in criminal justice. Then I became a cop."

"So you could take down bad guys like Tony Maclin."

"Something like that."

"Only I don't think it was that simple, was it?" He swept a stray hair away from her face. She stilled, her eyes so expressive, so wary. He wondered how badly that night had scarred her. "Did you get counseling after the attack?"

"Yes. I had no one to talk to and my dad felt inept about it, so he found someone for me to talk to. With those records being confidential I was protected and so were the rest of you. Plus I didn't elaborate much to the therapist, just said I had been jumped."

He hated that she couldn't even be honest in therapy. "I'm sorry."

She shrugged. "Don't be. It wasn't your fault. You didn't attack me in the alley that night."

"But if I hadn't left, and if we had called the police, you wouldn't have had to bottle this up inside all these years. And now we have this…"

"I can deal with it, Dante."

"Can you?"

She laughed. "I'm stronger than you think, a lot stronger than I was that night. Being a cop requires you to toughen up. I've been shot at, kicked, slapped, punched and swiped at with a knife. Being a cop isn't easy."

"No, I don't imagine it is. But it still doesn't mean you should have had to endure the aftermath of that night alone."

"I wasn't alone. You all saved my life."

Then he ran. So did Gabe. And left Anna alone to pick up the pieces and hide their crime. Yeah, he was some savior.

"You don't always have to be tough." He leaned in and palmed the nape of her neck, massaging the tension he felt.

Her eyes widened, but it wasn't fear he saw there. "Yes, I do."

He decided to push his luck and drew her toward him. "It's okay to lean on someone else."

She reached out, touching his chest. She wasn't shoving him away, just resting her fingers there.

He should leave her alone. If he was a good guy, he'd do that.

He wasn't a good guy.

"I don't lean on anyone, Dante."

He gave her a devastating smile, then bent his lips to hers. "Try."

Ten

Anna gasped as Dante's mouth met hers. Her mind fired off a million reasons why this was wrong. She was on duty. Dante could be a killer. She was angry with him for leaving her.

His lips were soft as they slid across hers, making her forget all her objections. She encountered a solid wall of muscle as she braced her hands against his chest. It would be easy to push away, to break the kiss.

But how long had it been since she'd allowed a man to get this close?

Dante wasn't just any man, and it had been years since the last time she'd touched his lips, since the last time she'd felt his body against hers. Then they'd been kids. Now they were adults with adult passions and needs.

The last of her resistance melted away as she sagged against him. He wrapped his arms around her and dragged her onto his lap where she felt just how much of a man he really was now, and how far out of her element she was. Yet she didn't want to stop, instead let her fingers dive into his hair as he eased back against the sofa and deepened the kiss, his tongue sliding between her lips and teeth.

She shivered at the intimacy of the contact, no longer needing to worry about pulling back because she was too young and they had to take precautions about going too far. She could go as far as she wanted to.

She always pushed men away. The act of sex, while not unpleasant, wasn't something she lingered on.

With Dante, she'd want to linger, to explore. She lifted her fingers to where their lips were connected, skimming them over his jaw, his neck, down to where the corded muscles of his shoulders exposed his sheer power.

Powerful men in intimate settings scared her.

He didn't.

She adjusted, sweeping one leg over his hip to straddle him, her mouth still latched onto his as passion exploded inside her. Dante gripped her hips and rocked her against his erection. She whimpered against his mouth and drove herself against the rock-hard evidence that his need was as great as hers.

The first thing that would have to go was her gun, followed shortly by her clothes. Too many clothes.

Her phone vibrated. Dante's fingers traveled up her rib cage, creating an even sweeter vibration along her nerve endings.

The pulse of her phone was incessant, dragging her away from the drugging euphoria of Dante's kiss. She pulled back and grabbed her phone out of her pocket, looked at the display.

"Damn." She pushed the button. "Detective Pallino."

She listened, clarity slicing through the sexual haze. "When?"

She looked over at Dante, whose lazy smile died as he read her expression. She slid off his lap, regret hollowing her belly as she caught the disheveled look of his hair and the ridge pressing incessantly against the zipper of his jeans.

"I'll be there in fifteen minutes." Still trying to gather her wits and catch her breath, she put the phone in her pocket as she looked at Dante. "Another murder in the alley."

He was off the sofa in an instant, dragging his fingers through his hair. "Killed the same way as George?"

She nodded, tucking her shirt back into her pants.

"I'm coming with you." He grabbed his shoes.

She should say no, but he was a part of this, too, and she felt a bit raw at the news there'd been another murder. She wanted him there with her. "Okay."

They were on scene within fifteen minutes, the familiarity of the roped-off alley making her stomach roll. She had to hold it together. This was her case. She'd called Roman on the way over and he said he'd meet them there.

Gloved and their shoes covered, they moved toward the crime scene. The body was positioned on his back in the same location near the Dumpster. The victim looked like a businessman, had on a suit and nice shoes. His tie had been thrust to the side, his white shirt torn open and bloodied. From a distance she could already see his chest, see the carving of the heart. Her stomach rolled. He was beaten so badly his face was unrecognizable.

Blood was everywhere.

"This is worse than last time," she said.

Anna squatted and surveyed the wreckage that was once a human being. The M.E. was already on the scene.

"Same as the last one," Dr. Norton said. "Time of death was earlier tonight. Based on temperature and lividity I'd say maybe three or four hours ago."

She looked at her watch. It was three in the morning. So anywhere from 11:00 p.m. to midnight.

Anna reached into the victim's pocket and pulled out his wallet.

The familiar name and picture on the driver's license stopped her breath. Her heart pounded so hard she heard the mad rush of her blood in her ears.

"No. This can't be right." She looked at the face, unrecognizable because of the blood and swelling. His hair was so matted with blood she hadn't noticed the sandy coloring.

Dante dropped to his knees next to her. "What is it?"

She turned to him. "It's Jeff."

Dante frowned. "What? No, it's not."

Hands shaking, she handed him the driver's license.

Dante looked at the license, then the body. "That's Jeff?"

Anna bowed her head. "God, Dante." She didn't know what to do, what to say.

"It can't be."

"It is." The face was distorted and swollen, but it was Jeff's hair, his body.

"You know this vic?" Richard asked.

She nodded. "From high school."

Richard laid his hand on her arm. "I'm sorry, Anna."

This changed everything. It was what she was afraid would happen when George had been found in the alley.

The murderer had started killing her guys.

She squeezed Jeff's arm. "I'm so sorry."

She hadn't jumped on this fast enough and now everyone was in danger. Her gaze lifted to Dante, his face filled with hard anger as he stared down at Jeff's body.

Her misery turned to fury. This had to stop. She had

to hold it together. It was her job to be objective. She continued searching the body, so glad it wasn't Jeff's sweet face staring back at her. At least he didn't look like himself as she reached into his inner jacket pocket. When she pulled out the white bag, she cursed.

"Drugs," she said to Dante, who grimaced.

"Come on." Dante cast her a disbelieving look.

She bagged it and handed it over to the CSU team.

There was blood spatter around the body, this time the crime scene not so neat. Blood pooled under Jeff's head.

"His skull is likely fractured," Richard said. "I don't know if he was hit with something or if your killer pounded his head into the pavement. I'll be able to tell more once I autopsy him. Again, no gunshot wounds or other obvious signs of stabbings other than the carving here."

Pain racked her body. All she wanted to do was curl up and cry. Instead, she sucked it all inside, rose and finished working the scene. Because maybe this time there'd be some goddamn evidence they could use.

When Roman showed, Dante touched her arm. "I'll tell him."

She gave him a curt nod and went back to walking every square inch around the body with the forensics team. There had to be something here. No one was that good at hiding the evidence of his presence.

She lifted her head only when Roman cursed so loud several uniforms stopped and stared. He made eye contact with Anna, his face drawn with shock and sadness. She shook her head.

Not now. They could all fall apart later.

Roman came over to her, his face drawn, his skin pale. "What do we know?"

"Nothing. Same as last time. A lot of blood spatter, though. This time he was meaner."

Roman squatted and lifted the cover over Jeff's face.

Anna didn't want to look again. It wasn't Jeff anymore anyway.

"Jesus," Roman muttered. "We need to find out who did this."

"Do a canvas around this area," she directed the uniforms, motioning to the people milling around the taped barrier at both ends of the alley. "They might be nothing more than gawkers, but they could be potential witnesses, too. And I want Forensics taking pictures of all those people. Our suspect could be lurking, getting off on revisiting the scene to watch the action."

They began to wrap Jeff for transport. She had just seen him. He had been laughing and joking with all of them at her house. Anna's heart clenched, the pain in her chest tightening to a near-unbearable level. Her scar throbbed and she rubbed at it with the heel of her hand.

You and me are one now, Jeff, in a way I never wanted.

Now there were two other people with matching scars like hers. And she was the only survivor.

She and one of the uniforms hit the other end of the alley to talk to the people there. No one saw anything, just happened to be leaving one of the bars when it closed and saw the police cars so came over to see what was going on. But they still took names and numbers to interview these people later. They might have been standing outside the club and seen whoever was in the alley. Often people saw something and didn't even realize what they'd seen was important.

Anna walked outside the alley and down the street, turning the corner to get a view of the buildings that fronted the alley. It was all corporate and banking on both sides, so unlikely anyone would be inside, but she wanted to know.

She motioned Roman over. "Let's find out what offices flank the alley. I want to know if anyone was pulling an all-nighter. Maybe looked down out their windows into the alley the nights of the murders. Maybe some corporate junkie on deadline."

"You got it." He laid his hands on her shoulders. "You gonna be okay?"

She lifted her gaze to his. "I'm so pissed right now I want to tear someone apart. But I'll be fine as long as I'm working. We just need to find out who's doing this."

He nodded, his expression grave. "We will, honey."

"We have to tell Ellen."

He closed his eyes, opened them again. "I hadn't thought about that. Want me to go with you?"

"No. Grab some uniforms, get into those office buildings and get that started. If we can pull a witness out of anyone in there, it could make this case. I'll go talk to Mrs. Clemons."

Dante came up behind Anna. "I'll go with her. I was just over there to visit Ellen."

Roman looked pained. "This is going to destroy her after just losing George."

Dante put his arm around Anna's shoulder. She felt the sting of tears and blinked them back.

This wasn't about her grief. This was about finding a killer. Her pain could wait. "We'll go do that before I head back to do my report."

"I'll get started on the list," Roman said.

She nodded. "I'll meet you back at the station."

She turned and they all watched as Jeff's body was loaded into the transport van.

Anna pulled Roman into a hug, squeezing him tight.

She pulled back and searched his face. "You be careful. You know what's going on here."

He gave her a sober nod, then his gaze shifted to Dante. "You look out for her."

"Not going anywhere."

Telling Ellen was about as horrible as Dante predicted it would be, and had to have torn Anna up inside. He felt Anna tense up next to him when Ellen sobbed and turned her face into Dante's shirt.

Anna remained stoic, did her job, gave her sympathies and let Dante handle most of it. Dante had put his arm around Ellen and held her when she would have crumpled to the floor. He knew how she felt, knew every kid who'd stayed with her was like one she'd given birth to.

"I'll be in touch after the autopsy is completed and he's released to the funeral home," Anna had told her. The raw agony in Ellen's eyes was enough to make Dante tear up. And nothing brought him to tears.

They'd tried Gabe's phone a few times, but it had gone straight to voice mail. Dante wanted to deliver the news in person so he hadn't even left a message. He'd catch up with Gabe as soon as he could.

They left Ellen's and climbed back into Anna's car. She sighed and leaned her head against the headrest.

"What now?" he asked.

"Now I need to drop you off. Then I want to go to Jeff's place."

"Why?"

"I don't know where he was tonight, or where he was when he was taken to that alley. Maybe his house will give us some clues."

She picked up her phone and called for the evidence team, then called Roman and asked him to meet her there.

"I can drop you off on the way."

He slanted a look at her. "I'm not going home. And if you drop me off I'll just follow you."

The ride was silent, and he wasn't surprised when she pulled up in front of his condo.

"Thought you were going to Jeff's place."

She put the car in Park and turned to face him. "This has to be dealt with first. I want you to pack up and go back to wherever it is you came from."

He figured this was coming, knew she'd want to protect him.

"I'm not leaving, Anna."

"You have to."

He saw the fear in her eyes, the desperation, and knew he'd have to tell her everything in order to convince her he wasn't going to die.

"Let's go inside and talk about this."

"Fine. I'll help you pack and I'll escort you to the airport." She followed him inside.

Dante noticed her hand on the butt of her gun as he opened the door and flipped the lights on. He moved in front of her. "It's okay. There's no one here."

"You sure about that?" she asked.

After tonight he wasn't sure of anything anymore.

She shoved ahead of him. "I'm going to check your bedrooms if you don't mind."

He didn't mind, but he wasn't going to let her check them alone. He moved with her, his hand within reach of his own weapon. Once they cleared the house, she stood in the middle of the living room, her arms crossed.

"You have to leave, Dante."

"I'm not going."

"Are you insane? You realize there's a killer out there who wants all of you dead."

"Yes."

"So you're going to stay and do what? Paint a target on your back?"

"You want me to leave and let the other guys become targets? I can't let that happen. Not when I could stay and possibly do something to stop it."

She lifted her chin. "That's my job."

"Yeah, it is. And I can help."

"Really, how? You're not a cop. You don't have the resources available to you that I do. You might be able to ride along with me now and then, but frankly you hinder my investigation and it would be easier for me to do my job if you'd just get the hell out of my way. It would be one more person I—one more potential victim I don't have to worry about."

One more person—what? He'd like to know what she was going to say before she stopped herself.

"You can't anticipate what the killer will do, Anna. You don't know who he's going to target next."

"No, I can't. But I can sure as hell make sure it isn't you."

He wanted to explore how she felt about him. What had been about to happen before she'd gotten that phone call could have brought them closer together, at least physically.

He wanted to clear the cobwebs of the past. That's why he'd come back. He wanted to be sure Anna was okay, that they were okay.

Now no one was okay.

"I can take care of myself. And I'm not leaving."

He felt the boil of tension inside her as she stepped up to him and gave him a shove that was more frustration than anger. "Why are you being so goddamn stubborn about this?"

He slid his hands up her arms to wrap around her wrists, pulling her fully against him until her head rested on his chest. Holding her was killing him, making him want her. He wanted to wrap himself around her, inside her, until they both stopped hurting.

"My brother was murdered tonight. My foster father was killed a few days ago. There's a potential serial killer on the loose targeting the people I care the most about, including you. Do you really think I'm going to walk away from that?"

She lifted her head to look at him. "You walked away before."

The stab to his gut hurt like a cold, sharp knife. She'd said it to hurt him, to make him leave. And she was right. She didn't trust him to stay when she needed him. "I deserved that."

He saw the pain in her eyes and would have done anything to take it away. "Then leave now."

"No. Not this time. Not again."

"This is my job to do."

"This is more than your job now. And I'm not leaving you alone to fight this bastard."

She sighed. "He's going to try to kill you."

He nodded. "And probably you, too."

"You're not equipped to deal with someone like this. I can't let you risk it."

Dante's lips curled. Maybe it was time to let her know who and what he really was. "Honey, I've killed more people than this guy ever will. Trust me, I can handle this crazy fucker."

Eleven

Anna stared up at Dante in dumbfounded shock.

"What the hell are you talking about?" She pulled away.

"Let me start at the beginning. I told you I joined the army when I left. But I need to explain why I left."

She folded her arms. "That would be a good place to start."

"Twelve years ago when I walked out on you, it was because I figured I needed to get out of town fast. I wanted to separate us, Anna."

"Why?"

"I was afraid of the fallout from the murder, of anything tying you to me. I figured distance would help."

"That doesn't even make sense."

"Now, maybe. Back then it made a whole lot of sense to me. Anyway, during my time away, let's say I learned how to handle myself. And I can watch over you."

"That's what you mean when you said you killed a lot of people. You were black ops."

He didn't answer, but his eyes gave him away.

She backed away, irritation grating on every nerve ending. More lies. More cover-ups. More about him she didn't know. What else was there? "I don't need you to watch over me. I'm a trained detective. What's it going to take for you to realize I can take care of myself?"

"A little backup couldn't hurt. Not with some insane killer out there. Look at what happened to George, one of the smartest men I ever knew. He would have never let himself get blindsided like that. And Jeff wasn't exactly a moron. He knew to watch his back. We came from the streets. It was tough out there. Instincts like that are never lost. We had just told him last night to watch out for himself and now he's dead. So whoever's doing the killing was smart enough to get the drop on him. They could do the same to you, so no matter how tough and capable you think you are, you can still be hurt."

Anna flinched. Dante knew he'd insulted her, but he needed her to see reason. This wasn't a game, and it wasn't a back-and-forth about which of them was better prepared to take care of themselves. It was life and death and they had to start watching out for each other.

"I'm moving into your place."

She looked horrified. "What? No."

"Until this guy is caught, I'm not taking any chances with your life."

"And I said no."

"You want to make sure I stay safe, don't you?"

"You would if you got the hell out of town."

"You need me."

She sighed. "Because you're some supersecret agent?"

"Not exactly, but that could work to our advantage, and it's the reason I didn't just spill to everyone about who I was. It's not something people are supposed to know."

"How can you help?"

"I can get information you can't. I have carte blanche in this country. Hell, anywhere, for that matter."

"Again, how?"

He hooked his thumbs in his jeans and gave her a smug smile. "Basically, I don't exist."

"So what you're saying is that you're above the law?"

"Pretty much, yeah. So let me help, Anna. You need all you can get on this, and I'm damn good at taking care of myself."

"You might be good at what you do, Dante, but just like you said to me, it still doesn't mean you can't be killed. Sticking around here thinking you're immortal cock of the block is the surest way to end up dead."

"I'm better than most at watching my own back. And people who do what I do know how easy it is to slip up and end up dead, so believe me, I know how to be careful. I haven't stayed alive this long by being stupid."

She wanted to believe him. But she wanted him to stay alive, too. And maybe she could use his help down the road, because bureaucratic red tape was the worst, especially once you got into the nitty-gritty of working a case. Brick walls were frustrating. If she hit one and Dante could help her bust through it, then he could be useful.

"Fine. You can stay in town."

He smirked. "I was staying anyway."

"Smart-ass. But you aren't bunking at my house."

"I'll just sleep in your driveway if you don't let me in."

"I'll have you arrested for trespassing."

"Won't stick."

She wanted to kick him. "Goddammit."

"Quit arguing with me. I'll pack a bag and then we can head over to Jeff's house."

"You can't just investigate this case with me. You're a civilian."

"I know. I need FBI credentials."

Her eyes widened. "What? You can do that?"

"Yeah. I can pull some strings and make it happen."

"Just like that."

"Not exactly. I've been working on it for a couple days now, figuring I might need them. It'll take some maneuvering and a few phone calls, but yeah, I can get FBI ID."

Who the hell was he that he could grab fake credentials? "You'll never get that bullshit past my captain. He'll want to verify you with the actual FBI."

"And he'll be able to—with the actual FBI. I work for people who'll clear it."

"Jesus, Dante. Really?"

"Really. Give me a few minutes to make a phone call and see if I can push things along. Then I'll pack a few things."

Anna was rarely impressed, but she was impressed. If he could pull off what he said he could.

After he packed, they went outside.

"I'll meet you at Jeff's condo. I have to go somewhere."

She arched a brow. "Supersecret black ops stuff?"

"Something like that."

She shrugged, figuring he could do what he wanted. She had a murder investigation. "I'll see you there. Or not."

He walked over to her car and pulled her against him. "You can pretend you don't care, Anna, but I know you do. If you didn't, you wouldn't have tried to boot my ass out of town."

She lifted her gaze to him, half angry and half scared to death. "I don't want anyone else to die before I get this case figured out. You don't mean any more or any less to me than the other guys."

His lips curled in a smile that told her he knew she was lying. "Bullshit." He pulled her against him and kissed her soundly. The emotion of the night got the best of her and she grabbed a handful of his shirt, held on and kissed him back, terrified she'd never see him again.

When she pushed away, his eyes had gone as dark as the storm churning within her.

"Do you always take without asking?"

He swept his thumb over her bottom lip. "No." He leaned in and brushed his lips over hers again. "No," he whispered against her mouth. "Want me to apologize?"

She shuddered against him, then pushed him away, not sure if she was more irritated at him or at herself.

"I'll see you at Jeff's. Be careful."

She nodded, and climbed into her car, her lips still tingling from his kiss.

Oh, sure. Become an FBI agent.

Great idea, Dante. It was a good thing he'd already set things in motion a couple days ago, because he needed it to happen now and it wasn't like he could pull this whole FBI thing out of his ass in an instant.

And speaking of his ass, his superiors were going to have his over this. The one thing he'd never done was abuse the power they gave him.

Until now, anyway. He was on vacation, and now he wanted FBI credentials. Sure, he could do almost anything, but he had some tap dancing to do to explain this.

First thing was to meet with a local contact, and since security was paramount he couldn't do it with Anna around.

A half hour after he left Anna, he arrived at a house in South County.

Nice neighborhood. Well established, with thick, full trees and well-maintained lawns.

And one expensive, big fucking house. Colonial-style, two-story, with those columns and big windows and a lawn that looked as if whoever lived here hired people to take care of it.

Dante went to the address he'd been provided and through the gate toward the side door to the garage. The garage door was open, so he walked in.

"Good thing my wife is in Tahiti with the kids," the guy said who greeted him.

He was in his fifties, slightly graying hair short in a military kind of cut.

"Sorry to bother you. This is kind of urgent."

The guy had a glass half filled with amber liquid and a couple ice cubes. "Whatever. Come on into my office."

Dante followed him through the garage and into the house.

He led Dante into a downstairs study, motioned for him to take a seat on the other side of his cherrywood desk.

"Someone will be here shortly with your paperwork."

"Thanks."

Dante looked around the room while his host worked on the computer. Military medals were framed on one wall, law certificates on another, political awards and the like.

He'd been out of the country for a while, but not too long to finally recognize who his contact was—he was influential and a big player.

This was going to cost Dante next time he got an assignment, which would probably end up being in some shithole he might have been able to turn down otherwise.

The man finished typing in his computer. "Background complete, without question."

"Thank you."

Someone entered the office and handed an envelope to the man, then left.

He removed the contents, reviewed them, then handed them over to Dante.

"These should be sufficient for your needs."

They were. "Thanks. Sorry to bother you."

"The request came from high enough up that I figured it was important for national security."

Oh, Christ. "It is. Thank you. I'll get out of your way now."

The man nodded, led him back out the way he came.

"Stay safe, Dante."

"I will."

Dante got the hell out of there as fast as he could, grimacing at the cost of what he'd just done.

He tucked the badge into his pocket and backed out of the man's driveway.

Fuck it. He never called in favors or abused power like some of the other guys did.

This one was necessary, and worth it.

Now maybe he could do some good.

He entered the address to Jeff's house into the GPS unit in his car. Anna was waiting outside when he got there.

"Roman here yet?"

"He just called. He'll be here in five. And I assume you're now an FBI agent?"

He moved beside her. "I'm trusting you with some pretty sensitive information, Anna. Don't blow my cover when I could help you with this case."

She shrugged. "Why would I when it'll be so much fun watching you play secret agent?"

"Not a secret agent."

"Whatever."

"You can't tell anyone about me, not even the other guys. Not even Roman. As far as anyone knows, I really am an FBI agent. I was on vacation and when the murders started happening I decided to get involved."

"Uh-huh. And why the mystery beforehand? Why wouldn't you have just told them what you did for a living when you first got here?"

"I'll figure out some explanation for that. Hell, I'll lie."

"You *are* lying."

"I know."

She rolled her eyes. "However you want to play this, but you know what they say about lies."

"My life is a lie, Anna. I don't sweat it much."

And her life was all about the truth. He could see the mistrust on her face. They'd just taken two steps backward, but there wasn't much he could do about it. This was his life, what he did.

They lived in two different worlds.

Roman showed up along with two uniformed police officers. Dante took a step back to observe how this went down, mainly because he didn't want to get in the way, but also because he liked watching Anna work.

Flashlights in hand, Anna, Roman and the uniforms surveyed the perimeter of the house looking for signs of forced entry and for footprints.

"There's a window here over the kitchen," she said. "It's closed, but not locked."

"That could be an entry point," Roman said.

Anna nodded. "We'll have to dust it for prints and

check for footprints." She shined the light on the ground. "Lots of bushes here under the window. I don't see any broken branches, but since this window is over the back porch he could have climbed onto the porch railing and lifted the window that way without rustling the bushes or leaving prints on the ground."

They headed around the front once they determined there were no other points of entry. Once inside, Anna was methodical. She was a born leader, giving the uniforms—and Roman—directions on how to proceed. She didn't rush in, was in no hurry to scour Jeff's house for clues or to see if his place was in shambles. She took each room step by step in order to preserve any evidence they might find, and she kept control over everyone under her.

She operated a lot like he did, with a cool head under pressure. It would be easy to want to know right away what had happened in Jeff's house, to need to know now if the killer had taken Jeff from there, if there had been a struggle.

The living room was clean, and so was the kitchen.

"Nothing in the sink or on the counters looks disturbed. Sink is clean. Wow, the counters are clean, too. This place is immaculate."

"Man, Jeff was a neat freak. I didn't know that about him," Dante said.

"Don't you remember how he'd put a napkin in his lap whenever you all would come to the shop for ice cream? You'd make fun of him."

Dante squinted as he tried to remember, then his lips lifted. "You're right. And he'd clean the counter after we all ate. How could I forget that?"

Anna smiled at the memory, then ached at the loss.

"So if our suspect got in through this window it doesn't

show," Anna said. "You'd think there would have been some cast-off dirt from his shoes."

"He could have cleaned up," Roman said.

She nodded.

It was a one-story house, so they moved into the first bedroom.

Nothing there.

"I have blood here," Anna said, motioning with her flashlight in the hallway.

"Possible drag marks with more blood," Roman noted.

They followed the trail toward the door to the master bedroom. The door to the bedroom was open and Anna flipped on the light.

"Here," she said.

Dante peered over her shoulder. The room was a mess and it was obvious there'd been a struggle. The bed had shifted, marks on the hardwood floor showing where it had been pushed away from its normal spot. The bedside-table lamp was broken and there was blood on the floor next to the bed.

Anna moved into the bathroom and switched on the light, careful of every step she took to avoid any contamination. The uniforms waited outside the bedroom. Roman did, too, on the phone requesting the ETA on the crime scene unit.

Dante stayed in step with her, matching her every movement so they wouldn't contaminate the area.

"Looks like it started in here."

Dante nodded. "Mirror is broken. There's blood on the mirror and on the broken glass on the floor. Looks like the suspect was hiding in the shower. When Jeff walked in, the suspect came up behind him and shoved his head in the mirror."

Anna grimaced. "Probably. Enough to disorient him but not knock him out."

She followed the drops of blood back into the bedroom. "It continued in here. Jeff stumbled out of the bathroom—or maybe the suspect dragged him in here. There was a struggle and Jeff turned to face his attacker, who jumped him and they landed against the foot of the bed. That would explain the marks on the floor from the bed being pushed."

"Jeff wasn't a small guy, so his attacker had to have some power to bring him down." Dante bent down and pointed to a spot at the foot of the bed. "More blood here."

"Probably from his head injury. My guess is whoever did this was bigger than Jeff. He'd have to be to subdue him and carry him out of here."

Dante stood. "Unless he used some kind of drug."

Anna shifted her gaze from her notepad to Dante. "He could have started the beating here, knocked him unconscious."

Dante shook his head. "I don't think so. Jeff might have been a smooth talker, but he was a tough son of a bitch, always had been. When we were kids and got into fights, he'd never give up and he was as tough as they came. We had to pull him off the other guy more than once."

"That hadn't changed," Roman said, coming into the room. "He could still hold his own."

Dante nodded. "Which means the killer would have to beat him pretty hard to knock him out. And then there's no guarantee your suspect would be able to keep him that way until he got him in the alley to finish the job. I don't think he'd want to risk Jeff waking up on the way to the alley. My money's on drugging him."

She surveyed the bedroom. "You may have something.

There's not enough blood here for the kind of a beating he sustained."

"Which means he finished him off in the alley."

"Right. Tox report will let us know if he was drugged and with what."

She walked outside the bedroom, followed the drag mark trail. "It just stops abruptly."

"He carried him," Dante said. "That's why the drag marks end here in the hall."

She nodded. "Which means maybe our killer left some evidence on Jeff's body."

"We can hope. It also means our killer isn't a small man, because Jeff was sturdy."

They had something to go on now, a lead of some kind, which was more than they had before. Even a small step was progress. Dante wanted this guy bad. Two people he thought of as family were dead. It needed to end here.

Crime scene technicians arrived and Anna and Dante moved out of the way to let them process the scene.

"If we're lucky," she said to Dante and Roman as they stood outside, "some of that blood will be the suspect's."

"We're never that lucky," Roman said.

"You're right, but I can wish for it."

Anna went to talk to the crime scene techs, leaving Dante outside with Roman.

"You seem pretty interested in the case for a civilian," Roman said to him. "I mean, I know you and Jeff were brothers, just like we all were, but, man, you being here just muddies up the crime scene."

"I'm not a civilian, Roman," Dante said, pulling out his FBI badge.

Roman's eyes widened. "No shit?"

"No shit. Sorry I didn't tell you before. I needed to

keep it on the down low because of potential undercover situations."

Roman nodded. "Understood. So you're on this case now?"

He gave Roman a straightforward look. "How could I not be? First George, and now Jeff? I worked a little magic and asked to be assigned to the case."

"Huh. How'd you do that?"

"I have contacts in the state offices who requested FBI involvement."

"Good to have friends in high places, I guess. You in the FBI. Christ, Dante. I never would have figured you for a government job."

That was an understatement. "Me neither."

"I'm glad you found something legit. I was worried about you, wondering what you'd really been doing all this time."

Dante laid a hand on Roman's shoulder. "Now you can stop worrying. I'm doing just fine, and you have an extra hand to help work this case."

"What does Anna think about you being in the FBI, and getting involved in the investigation?"

Dante shrugged. "About what you'd expect she'd think about it."

Roman laughed. "That's what I figured. She likes to work alone, thinks she can do it all herself. She's like a superhero, single-handedly saving the world one bad guy at a time. But on this one? She needs someone to watch over her. She needs us all to watch over her. I don't like this."

"I don't, either."

Hours later, Roman headed out along with the CSU team. Everything was wrapped up, yellow tape and a sign across Jeff's house marking it as a crime scene.

Anna stayed behind to take a few more photographs, then packed up her kit in the trunk.

"Where to now?" he asked Anna.

She blew out a breath. "Home, I guess. I'll file a report when we head into the office tomorrow. Or later today. I'm beat and need a few hours' sleep."

They headed back to Anna's house. Dante frowned when Anna pulled into her driveway.

"You should leave your porch light on. Especially since you come home in the dark so often."

"Yes, Dad," she said as she unbuckled her seat belt and opened the door.

"I'm not kidding," Dante said, moving in front of her as he stepped onto the porch. "You leave yourself vulnerable. Especially now. Remember what happened last time."

"I see really well in the dark and I'd know if something was out of place," she said.

"Still, it pays to be careful." Dante checked the front door.

Nothing this time.

"No flowers or love notes?"

"None that I can see."

She seemed disappointed, searched the porch. "Huh. That's interesting."

She slid her key in the lock and opened the door, flipped on the lights and walked in, releasing the strap over her holster to lay her hand on the butt of her gun as she scouted the room. Dante searched the bedrooms, gun in hand while Anna took the kitchen. They had the house entirely searched, including the closets and crawl space in a matter of minutes.

Dante slid his gun into his pants when they met in the living room. "Clear," he said.

"Here, too," Anna said. "I'm also not stupid. I know there's a killer targeting all of us. I won't take any chances."

He came up to her and brushed his knuckles over the soft skin of her cheek. "You look worn-out. You need a glass of wine, a hot shower and a good meal, not necessarily in that order."

"I need to lie facedown on my bed and pass out."

"You won't sleep well. I'll bet all those gears in your head are still spinning."

She hated that he presumed to know her thoughts, her feelings. How could he when he'd been gone so long? She'd changed, dammit. "Maybe."

"Go take a shower. I'll be right back. Lock the door behind me."

"Then how will you get in?"

He leveled a devastatingly sexy smile on her that made her feel anything but tired. "Give me your keys."

"Where are you going?"

"To get food."

Her stomach growled, betraying the statement she was about to utter about not being hungry. "Fine."

"Go shower." He grabbed her keys and she locked the door behind him, headed into the bathroom and turned on the hot, steamy water. Only then did she let the reality of the night intrude on the walls she'd so carefully constructed around her world.

Jeff was dead. Same as George. Both killed in the same manner as Tony Maclin all those years ago. Both of them carved with a heart just like hers.

Now she had two bodies in the same location. And that night twelve years ago still remained a secret. She couldn't use it as background because she'd never reported it. If she reported it now, it would ruin Dante's,

Gabe's, Roman's and even Jeff's lives, not to mention her father's.

Shit.

She stepped under the water and let it pour over her head, wishing she could just disappear, forget all this was happening. She wanted it to go away, didn't want to deal with it.

And Jeff was dead. Dammit, Jeff was dead.

The full force of that reality finally slammed into her.

The sob tore from her throat and she couldn't do anything to hold it back. She shoved the heels of her hands against her eyes to try to stop it, but she couldn't. Instead, she slid down the shower wall and sat on her heels, crying buckets for Jeff, releasing the pain she'd been holding back since she'd discovered the bloody, beaten body in the alley was her friend.

"I'm sorry. I'm sorry."

When she'd let out all she had in her, she was drained, exhausted. She opened her eyes and climbed to a standing position, her legs shaking. She laid her hands against the wall and just breathed for a minute, then grabbed the shower gel and poured some in her hands, soaped her body and rinsed.

Dante would be back soon. She needed to finish up and the water was getting cold. She rinsed her hair and wrung it out, then turned the shower off.

That's when she glanced down at her scar and saw blood.

Her heart began to hammer against her ribs.

You're imagining it. It's not there.

She knew that. She looked down again, certain it would be gone, a figment of her overtired, overstressed imagination. But a thin river of blood traced around the scar, started to run down her breast, then her belly and legs.

No. It's wasn't there. She rubbed at it, but blood kept coming.

Her breathing quickened and the familiar clawing sensation choked off her throat.

No. Oh, God, no. Not now.

She pushed open the shower door and fought to focus.

The towel. She had to find the towel.

And breathe. *Breathe, Anna, breathe.*

She did. Faster and faster. She was bleeding, she had to get help, now.

Someone help me, please. He's going to hurt me.

She stumbled out of the shower, tripping over the bottom edge and falling to the tile floor.

And that's when she saw it, all over the floor. More blood, rivers of it, all around her, pouring from the cut on her chest. She pressed the towel there.

"Stop bleeding. Son of a bitch, stop bleeding."

And through it all, her throat closed as if someone had put his hands around her neck and had begun to squeeze. She fought for every breath, sucking in air as if each inhale was the last one. Panting, she tried to get up, but she was nauseous, dizzy, soaked with sweat. And the tile was cool. She was so hot.

"Help…me."

She couldn't breathe. She was bleeding. He was going to kill her.

The blood continued to surround her. She was going to drown in it.

Dante put the takeout on the kitchen counter, surprised Anna wasn't out of the shower yet.

Then again, she deserved a long, hot shower after

tonight. She looked a wreck and he knew damn well how much Jeff's death affected her, despite her attempts at maintaining a cool, professional resolve.

He went to the bathroom door and listened. No shower running, so he knocked.

"Anna? I'm back with food."

And that's when he heard the shuffling and a faint whisper.

"Help me."

He turned the knob. Door wasn't locked. He pushed it open. She was lying on the floor naked, curled up in a ball, the towel clenched in a death grip around her, her breath sawing in and out.

She was drenched and shaking.

He bent over her and touched her skin. It was cold. "Anna."

She flinched when he touched her. Fuck, she was so pale.

She lifted trembling hands to his. "Blood."

Aw, shit. He'd seen enough post-traumatic stress disorder in the field to know a panic attack, and she was in the throes of a big one. "Honey, there's no blood on you."

He picked her up, despite her attempts to fight him off. He put the lid of the toilet down and sat her on it, then shoved her head between her knees. "Breathe, Anna. Slow and easy."

She ignored him at first, her arms flailing as her instinct to fight was strong. But he kept her head shoved down between her knees and kept his voice calm. "You know what to do. Breathe slow. You're hyperventilating."

In the meantime he grabbed a washcloth and ran it under cold water in the sink, didn't bother to wring it out, just slapped it on the back of her neck. After a few minutes she stopped shaking. A few minutes more and her breathing began to slow down. He swept the washcloth down her back, then over her face.

Finally, she seemed calm enough, so he let go of her neck. She raised her head a fraction, but braced her hands on her knees.

"Better?"

She was shivering. "Cold now."

He grabbed her robe from the hook on the back of the door and laid it over her. She slid her arms through it and wrapped it around herself.

"Need a drink of water."

"Okay." He found disposable cups by the sink, so he filled one and handed it to her. No way was he leaving her alone.

"Sip," he instructed.

"I know."

Her voice was clipped. Angry. She was embarrassed. He understood that, but she'd have to deal with it.

She took several sips, breathed a little, then a few more sips until the cup was empty.

She shoved her hair away from her face and blew out a hard breath. She still looked pale, but not as bad as she had when he'd walked in.

"Think you can stand now?"

"Yeah." She reached for the sink, but instead he helped pull her up, then slid his arm around her waist.

"I want to get dressed, comb my hair. I'm okay."

He could let her go now. "Holler if you need me. I'll be in the kitchen."

"I'll be out in a minute."

He shut the door, then leaned against the wall, listening to the sounds she made. Normal sounds.

Only then did he exhale and calm his own breathing.

Jesus. She'd scared the shit out of him.

Yeah, she'd hidden it well, but the trauma Anna suffered twelve years ago had stayed with her.

And the guilt churned within him.

He pushed off the wall and headed into the kitchen, warmed the Chinese food in the microwave and spread it out on plates. Anna finally surfaced. She'd put on shorts and a tank top and had combed her wet hair. Her face had lost that deathly pallor and she seemed steady enough now.

She hadn't been the only one shaking in there.

"Take a seat."

"Making yourself at home in my kitchen?" she asked as she slid into one of the chairs at the table.

"As a matter of fact, I am." He put a plate and a soda from the fridge in front of her.

"How long have you had panic attacks?"

She lifted her gaze to his, a hot bite of anger in her eyes.

He held her gaze. He wasn't going to let this go, and she knew it.

"Twelve years."

That didn't surprise him. "You take medication?"

She shook her head and pushed her plate to the side. "No. No drugs. Therapist tried to shove those on me. I tried them but they made me fuzzy. I hated not being clearheaded."

"So how do you deal with the attacks?"

She laughed and took a long swallow of soda, then dabbed at her lips with the napkin. "Obviously, not well."

"They often come with hallucinations?"

She inhaled slowly, then dragged it out. "Rarely. At first, yeah, but hardly at all anymore. Tonight was a bad one. Sorry."

They ate for a while in silence. He was hungry, so he devoured most of his, while she picked at hers and slid the food around with her fork. But at least she ate some.

"You don't have to apologize to me, Anna. You went through hell twelve years ago. Everyone deals with trauma in different ways."

"Obviously I haven't dealt with it."

"This case dredged it all up again, didn't it?"

She stared down at her plate, nudged the rice with her fork and nodded. She didn't want to admit to anything. Dante knew that to her this was admitting weakness. He knew what that felt like.

"Your panic attacks have increased?"

She lifted her gaze to his. "Since the night we found George."

"You still seeing a therapist?"

"Not for years."

"Maybe you should consider seeing one."

"What for? It's always going to be with me, Dante. It's never going away."

He wasn't going to let her get off that easily. "Then maybe you should consider stepping away from this case and letting some other detective handle it."

She laughed. "Are you serious? No one knows as much about this case as I do."

"Then let some other detective and Roman handle it. Roman knows as much about it as you do."

A fast and sharp no was her reply.

"Why not?"

She shrugged and fiddled with the soda can. "Because he wants me involved."

"Who wants you involved?"

She didn't meet his gaze this time. "The killer."

"Yeah? And you know this how?"

"He didn't leave Roman a gift at his front door, did he?"

"Maybe that's exactly why you should give this case up."

"Bullshit. I'm a cop and I've got cop instincts. I'm not handing off this case just because I freak out and hyperventilate every now and then. I've had these attacks for years. They come and go. I can handle them."

He laughed. "Yeah, you were handling it like a champ in there a few minutes ago."

If looks could kill, the glare she pinned him with would have dropped him dead on her kitchen floor. She stood, anger darkening her cheeks.

"Fuck you, Dante. Get out of my house."

He only smiled at her. "I'm not leaving. Especially not now."

Her hands clenched into fists. He liked her with a little fight in her. It gave her strength and it made him feel better. It hurt him seeing her crumpled and weak on the floor.

"You think I can't throw you out of my house?"

"I'd like to see you try. I'm staying put. You need someone to watch over you."

She laughed at that. "I haven't needed anyone to watch over me since you left me twelve years ago. I can take care of myself."

He shrugged and stood, heading into the living room. "So you keep telling me, but from where I'm standing you're doing a piss-poor job of it. The boogeyman could come in here and scare you right into a panic attack. You'd drop like a candy ass."

When she launched herself at him, he was ready for her, just as he was always prepared for an attack. Only this was Anna, and he'd never serve a lethal blow to someone he cared about.

What he hadn't been prepared for was her fury and the way she leaped on top of the chair and the kitchen table, flying over it to land on him.

He might be holding back. She wasn't. She'd shoved her knee into him. He grabbed her arms and tossed her over his head, sending her flying onto the carpet.

Like a cat, she landed on her feet and without hesitating even a second came at him again. And even though he was more than twice her size, she wasn't deterred. Whoever had taught her these maneuvers had done a damn good job. She knew her moves.

But he was better. He could have put her in a hold she couldn't get out of, could immobilize her. Hell, he knew how to kill in just one move. But that wasn't the idea here. He wanted to see what she had. And what she had was good. Good kicks, great maneuvers, she countered whatever he came up with, and she wasn't afraid to go after him.

Plus, it helped that she was pissed at him. Healthy anger made for a stronger opponent. All that peace-loving martial-arts stuff was a load of crap.

Go for the jugular. Go for the kill. That's what Anna was doing. She was mad enough to kill him right now, and if he'd been a weaker man he'd be under her and she'd be ready to deliver a death blow.

Not that she would, but she'd be capable of it with a lesser opponent.

She leveled a kick that could have broken his nose if he hadn't feinted back.

Yeah, his girl was ready to inflict some pain.

Good for her. He took her leg and lifted it, tossing her onto her back. Then he leaped on top of her.

Time to end the game. He pinned her underneath him

and splayed his arms and legs over her, waiting to see if this position would trigger another panic attack.

She was breathing in and out heavily now, but all he saw in her eyes was spitting-mad fury.

"You're good," he said.

She fought for breath, her breasts rising and falling with the effort. "So are you. Otherwise you'd be dead by now."

He laughed. "I don't think it was your intent to kill me."

"Don't flatter yourself. If I wanted you dead, you would be."

"You don't have it in you to kill someone you care about, Anna."

She arched a brow. "And you do?"

"You have no idea what I'm capable of."

"You know what? You're right. I don't have any idea what you're capable of because I don't know who the hell you are anymore. Now get off me."

He jumped up and held out his hand for her. Instead, she rolled over on her belly and rose on her knees. He shrugged, but when she turned around there was a Glock in her hands, and she was pointing it at him.

"Now who wins, Dante?"

Twelve

Dante stared at the gun in her hands, then lifted his gaze to hers, no fear in his eyes. "You gonna shoot me?"

She lowered the gun, shoved it back in the pocket of the chair where she always kept one of the spares. "Just trying to prove to you that I do have a few tricks up my sleeve."

"Noted. Feel better now?"

Despite her utter fury, her lips lifted. As a matter of fact, she did feel better. And maybe Dante had something to do with that. He'd deliberately baited her, no doubt to shock her out of her feel-sorry-for-herself mood. There was nothing she hated more than having a panic attack. Having one and Dante finding her in the midst of one, with the bonus of delusions? The worst thing that could ever happen to her.

Instead of coddling her, though, he'd pissed her off, which had made her so angry she'd come after him like a bull.

Which had been exactly what she needed. Now she felt stronger. More capable.

So, yes, she did feel better. And damn him, he knew she would.

"Thanks."

He smiled. "You're welcome."

He held his hand out for her and this time she took it, letting him haul her up to stand. "How did you know what to do?"

"I've done my share of time in Iraq and Afghanistan and other unmentionable places. I spent some up-close-and-personal time with people who have PTSD, and know how to deal with it. It has a lot of different faces. Some people you have to hug. Some you have to slap around a little."

She went into the kitchen and grabbed fresh sodas, handed one to him. "Yeah. Coddling me wouldn't have made me feel better."

"I know that much about you, Anna."

She pulled her legs up on the sofa and wrapped her arms around them. "And yet I don't know a damn thing about you, Dante. So tell me."

"What do you want to know?"

"Why the army?"

He took a gulp of soda, then set it on the table next to him. "I wanted to be all I could be."

She snorted. "No, seriously. Why the military?"

"I was a month away from turning eighteen. I knew college wasn't in the cards for me. I just wasn't ready for it back then. But I knew I needed order and discipline in my life, so the military seemed right for me. I had all this pent-up energy and aggression and I needed an outlet, some training. I talked it over with George and he told me to choose whatever I wanted. I chose army."

She studied him and Dante knew he'd have to choose each lie carefully. The military part was easy, because that was the truth. But how he got there—that was all lies. It wasn't George who'd gotten him there—it had been her father, and it hadn't been his choice to leave.

That he wouldn't tell her. She didn't have to know why her dad had wanted him out of town after that night.

More lies.

"And I guess you must have liked military life if you're still in it."

He slanted a smile her way. "It's a lifestyle. I got used to it."

"So you don't like it?"

"I didn't say that."

"You're not saying much of anything. You didn't say you like it or don't like it. You're very noncommittal."

"And you're a very good detective."

She laughed. "It's my job to probe, to get beyond the surface to the truth."

He'd have to be careful what he said around her. "I do like it. At first it was regimented. I had no freedom. It was a lot like being a foster kid, always having someone tell you what to do. It sucked. But after a few years, I had more and more responsibility, and more and more authority. The further up the food chain you go, the more you get."

"What do you do for them?"

"Black ops are special assignments. I sometimes work with a team, sometimes alone. It depends on what they need me to do."

"Do you like the work?"

Did he? He never thought about it. It was just what he did. "It pays the bills."

"Dante, seriously."

"I don't know, Anna. It's just what I do. I'm used to it. It's part of me."

"And what is it that you do?"

"I can't tell you specifically about the operations I've done. They're classified."

She wrinkled her nose and studied him. "So you go in and do the dirty work, the hard missions that no one else can do."

"Something like that."

"Does it involve a lot of killing?"

"Sometimes." No point in lying anymore.

"Hence the rewards."

"Yeah."

"So now that you're off the grid, I imagine you can do almost whatever you want."

His eyes took on a devilish sparkle. "It has its perks."

He knew she didn't trust him. He didn't blame her.

"Like assuming false identities, Mr. FBI Agent?"

"That'll help with the case. I'll be able to pull strings you can't. Get faster results on DNA."

She leaned back against the sofa and twirled the soda can around between her hands. "What DNA? So far we haven't found a single piece of useful trace."

"Jeff's bedroom was a mess. Surely your techs will be able to scrape up something from there."

"True. It sure as hell was messier than the alley, which looked as if it had been scoured by a cleaning service. Whoever grabbed Jeff didn't take the time to clean up his place before dragging him out of there. There was a definite struggle in there. I'm hopeful we can pull some DNA, prints, blood or fibers—something out of there that'll give us a lead, because so far we've found nothing in the alley from either murder."

"Something will come up."

She yawned. "It has to."

Her eyes drifted closed and he let the silence stretch between them, hoping she'd fall asleep.

It didn't take long. Five minutes, maybe, and she was out, the rhythmic rise and fall of her chest telling him she was asleep.

He scooped her up and she woke, her eyes wide and alert.

"I'm taking you to bed."

She arched a brow. "I don't recall inviting you."

He laughed. "I'm dumping you in your bed. Then I'm going to my own bed to sleep."

She laid her head on his shoulder. "Now I'm insulted."

He rolled his eyes. "There's just no pleasing you, is there?"

"Yeah, I'm tough like that."

After he deposited her on her bed, she grabbed the blanket and pulled it over herself.

"Thank you, Dante," she murmured.

"You're welcome." He closed the door to her room and headed toward his own, leaving it open so he could hear anything that might not sound right. As he sat on the edge of the bed he took a deep breath and released it, hoping it would relieve the tightness in his chest.

Maybe he'd bought into Anna's tough act, because seeing her down on the floor of her bathroom tonight had just about knocked him out.

She wasn't a superhero. She was vulnerable, and she had a lot more demons to fight than just the bad guys out there.

His short vacation was about to get longer.

Anna heard the buzzing, knew it was her phone, but wanted more than anything to ignore it.

Phone meant work or bad news. She'd had all the bad news she could handle. She was full up.

And she'd had nightmare-free sleep. Couldn't she just continue with that?

The buzzing intensified.

"Well, hell." She reached out from under the covers and grabbed her phone, read the display and punched the button. "Yeah."

It was Roman. "You sound like you're asleep."

"I was. What's up?"

"I did some research into the companies in the buildings backing the alley. The north-side building has a key-card entry system that logs who goes in and out and when. There were three people there last night during the time period of the murder."

She sat up in bed, swept her hair out of her face and blinked several times to force her eyes open. "And the south-side building?"

"Security guard signs people in and out. He said no one was in the building last night, so it's just those three on the north side."

"Okay. Got names?"

"Yup. Figured you'd want to do interviews."

"You figured right. What time?"

"About eleven?"

The clock said she had an hour. "I'll meet you there."

She threw on clothes and decided against making coffee, figuring she'd hit a drive-through on her way to meet Roman. That way she wouldn't wake Dante.

She crept down the hall, saw him sleeping facedown on the bed, his gun peeking out from under his pillow.

She closed his door. As she tiptoed out of the house, she felt a twinge of guilt for not waking him.

He didn't have to do everything with her, and he needed the sleep as much as she did, especially after dealing with her meltdown last night.

At least that's what she told herself. The reality of it was, he was already too close to her and she needed the break.

She'd fill him in on the interviews later.

She climbed into her car and headed into town, zooming into a drive-through for some much-needed caffeine. Roman was waiting for her in the lobby of the bank building.

"Where's Dante?" he asked.

She shrugged. "Not joining us on this one. I'll catch him up to speed later on."

"Okay. So there's a law firm that takes up the entire third floor. Two associates were working last night 'til about two in the morning."

She walked alongside Roman toward the elevator. "Third floor would give them a good view. Who else?"

"Some corporate jock, head of a marketing firm on the fifth floor. He was here until past midnight. His offices only front the north side of the building, though."

She nodded. "Okay. We'll talk to the corporate jock just in case, but I doubt he'll be of any use. I'm primarily interested in the attorneys. Are they clocked in now?"

"Yeah. I checked at the front desk when I got here."

She lifted her phone. It was almost eleven-thirty. Damn, she really had gotten some sleep.

Dante had also called her. Twice. She hadn't answered, instead sent him a text that she was running down some leads and she'd get back with him later.

Roth, Llewelyn and Macy was a typical law firm. All expensive wood paneling and quirky architecture as the elevator doors opened. Fresh flowers flanked the reception desk, along with the attractive young blonde sitting behind it.

"May I help you?" she asked.

Anna flashed her badge. "I need to see Margaret Atkinson and Larry Stevens."

She lifted her nose a couple inches in the air. "Do you have an appointment?"

"No," she said.

"Then may I ask what this is regarding?"

"No, you may not. But you can pick up your phone and tell them this is police business and they can hustle their asses out here, or we can do this down at the station."

The girl's eyes widened. "One moment, please."

It didn't take long to get a response. But instead of the two associates she got an older guy with slightly graying hair and a very expensive suit.

"I'm Roger Macy, one of the senior partners of this firm. Can I help you?"

"Detective Anna Pallino of the St. Louis Police Department. We're investigating a murder that occurred in the alley last night. We understand two of your associates were working late last night and would like to speak to them to ascertain if they saw anything."

"Ah, yes. We heard about the murder in the alley behind this building. Two of them so far, right?"

"That's correct."

"Was it someone who worked in this building?"

"No, sir. The victims are unrelated to the tenants here."

"All right. Let me gather my associates in the conference room. Do you mind if I'm present for the questioning?"

"Not at all."

Lawyers. Anna looked to Roman, who shrugged.

They were led to the conference room and instructed to wait. The room was stark white, no pictures on the walls. It had a long, smooth cherry table and a ton of comfortable chairs, a credenza on either side and a stellar view of the alley through the wide windows.

"Good view of the Dumpster," Anna said.

"Not sure what you could see in the dark." Roman pressed his nose to the glass.

Anna looked over his shoulder. "Doubtful someone would be looking out that way. But maybe they heard something and looked down. Plus, there's a light over the Dumpster area. We'll see."

They turned when the door opened. Macy came in with a man and a woman, both in their late twenties, good-looking. Both looked nervous, though the guy pressed his hand to the small of the woman's back as if to comfort her.

Hmm.

She was pretty, with long, dark blond hair pulled up in a sleek ponytail. She wore a pencil skirt and a nondescript white silk blouse. He was in a gray suit, impeccably tailored.

Macy introduced them both.

"Have a seat. This isn't an interrogation," Anna said. "We know you were both working late last night, and a murder occurred outside in the alley behind this building."

Margaret Atkinson nodded. "We heard the sirens while we were working, then saw it on the news this morning."

"Yes. We were wondering which offices you were working in."

"Here in the conference room," Larry said. "We're working on the same case. Trial's coming up, so we're reviewing depositions and witness lists and preparing pretrial motions."

"Did you at any time have cause to look out the window here?"

Margaret looked at Larry, then shook her head. "No, we pretty much stayed at the table the entire time."

"We have a deadline," Larry added after watching Margaret while she spoke. "We didn't leave the conference room."

"It was a late night and we had a lot of paperwork to do," Margaret said.

"You didn't hear anything unusual outside?" Anna asked.

"No. We were wrapped up in…the case," Margaret said, her nervous gaze darting to Larry. "We didn't hear a thing. Until the sirens, of course."

Larry offered a serious look. "We're very focused. A bomb could go off and we wouldn't have heard it. We didn't leave our chairs, until as Margaret said, we heard the police arrive."

"We went downstairs then to see what was going on," Margaret said, "but they wouldn't let us pass because they already had the police tape up."

"At that point we figured we should get out of everyone's way, plus we had to be here early this morning, so we wrapped things up and headed out," Larry added.

"What time was that?" Anna asked.

"Around two," Larry said.

Anna remained silent, wondering if either would add anything.

Larry looked from Margaret to their boss. "We have the paperwork prepared if you'd like to check it all over."

Macy waved his hand. "Unnecessary."

"How long were you in this room?" Anna asked.

"Hours."

"Most of the night," Margaret said, her gaze once

again flitting to Larry before coming back to Anna and Roman. "From the time the office closed until we left. We ordered takeout to be delivered. I think…Larry, you have the receipts for that?"

"I do."

"Motions had to be filed this morning," Margaret said. "So we stayed and worked through the night until we were finished."

"Uh-huh."

"Detectives," Mr. Macy said, "I'm sure you can tell my associates didn't see or hear anything."

They were getting nowhere. Anna pulled her card. "Please do your best to try to remember everything from last night. Even the smallest detail could be of use. An unusual sound, anything that seemed out of the ordinary or may have caught your attention, even if it was for only a few seconds. If you got up to glance out the window and you saw anything that springs to mind, give me a call."

"They certainly will, Detective," Macy said, sliding her card across the table and slipping it into his coat pocket.

She thanked them and they left the office.

As soon as they hit the elevator and the door closed, Anna turned to Roman.

"Working on briefs, my ass. Maybe she was in *his* briefs."

"Agreed," Roman said. "The only thing they saw in that conference room was each other. The killer could have hung a body outside the window and they wouldn't have noticed."

Anna wrinkled her nose. Crude, but accurate as far as the witnesses. "Yeah, pretty useless. The two of them were skirting glances back and forth like crazy. I think they were more afraid of the boss finding out they'd been boinking all night instead of working."

The corporate dude on the other floor was a bust, too. His office fronted the street instead of the alley. He'd only worked until about eleven, had parked on the street side and he hadn't seen or heard a thing.

Useless. They were due for a break, and soon.

Thirteen

Dante was parked in front when Anna drove past the precinct, so she parked on the street and walked up toward him.

He leaned against his car, arms crossed, his expression unfathomable behind his mirrored shades. Did he have to look so impossibly sexy in his worn jeans and tight T-shirt?

Women passing by on the street paused, looked over their shoulders and ogled. And why wouldn't they? He was gorgeous. Well worth a second look. Even a third.

She wanted to kick them for ogling, which was ludicrous. He wasn't hers. She had no claim on him. She didn't know what pissed her off more—the women staring or her irritation over it.

He seemed to be oblivious to the stares he got, his attention fully on her.

"What are you doing here?" she asked, deciding to ignore his rock-god status from the sidewalk groupies mentally dragging their tongues over him.

"Figured you'd show up here eventually." He pushed off the car and came toward her.

"I'm surprised you didn't use your supercomputer to figure out my whereabouts."

"I could have, but no point. You were with Roman."

"How did you know that?"

"I called him when I woke up and saw you weren't there. He told me you were meeting him."

"Smart-ass," she said, starting up the steps. "You talk to my captain yet?"

"As a matter of fact, we had donuts and coffee together this morning."

She stopped, pivoted on the steps to face him. "You did not."

The corners of his mouth lifted. "Did, too. He likes me. Actually, he really likes me since I brought him donuts."

Captain Pohanski was a dick. He didn't like anyone. He didn't appreciate his precinct messed with. And he especially didn't like the FBI, who he often referred to as a bunch of inept, interfering ass wipes.

"I can guarantee Pohanski doesn't like you."

"If you say so." He waited for her to turn and go inside.

"You're bullshitting me."

He dragged his sunglasses down the bridge of his nose and gave her a look with those baby blues of his that melted her to the steps.

"You going in or not?" he asked.

She turned and went inside, grateful the air-conditioning was in prime working order today. Between the heat, the way he looked and those steamy looks he was giving her, she was hot. Plenty hot.

"Pallino."

She cringed at the sound of Captain Pohanski's bellow. "Yes, sir."

"Get in here."

She lifted her gaze to Dante's, who took a seat at the chair next to her desk and stretched out his legs. "I'll just wait here."

"You do that."

She took a slow walk toward the captain's office.

Pohanski was a short round Pillsbury Doughboy of a man, with a ruddy complexion and jowls. His shifty, narrow eyes made him look more like a criminal than a cop. He was also a damn fine police officer who knew his shit. He had thirty years of perfect service under his belt and ran his precinct loosely, preferring to let his cops do their jobs rather than keeping his thumb on top of them. But you never, ever wanted to be called into his office, because if you got caught on his radar, you got an ass chewing you never forgot.

What the hell had Dante gone and done?

"Shut the door."

Oh, hell.

She did, and moved in front of his desk, which looked as if it had been burglarized. There were crumpled notes, Post-its everywhere—Pohanski didn't believe in technology—pencils, two empty coffee cups, a mountain of files, one dusty desktop computer that wasn't turned on and about fifteen note pads.

"This murder investigation you're working? The two dead in the alley?"

"Yes, sir."

"A real clusterfuck."

"Yes, sir."

"Could be a serial."

"It's looking that way."

"Any particular reason you haven't filled me in about it lately?"

"I was on my way to do that when you called me in, sir."

"Uh-huh." He tapped the pencil on the quarter of an inch of desktop that was visible. "So this Dante Renaldi, the FBI agent that's insinuated himself into the case."

"Yes, sir. About that…"

"Sharp sonofabitch. I'm a little pissed off about the government bureaucracy and the fact that he's pushed himself onto this case, but he explained about George Clemons and Jeff Barrone and his relationship to them. In his shoes, I'd do the same thing. I hate the FBI and all their bullshit, but I like him."

Anna's fumbling excuses for Dante got caught at the back of her throat. "Sir?"

"Keep him close to you."

Pohanski looked down and started scribbling notes onto one of his pads.

That was it?

"Uh, I'll do that. Thanks."

She turned to make a hasty exit.

"Pallino?"

She pivoted to face him. "Sir?"

"What's with the roses and note to you?"

"Killer's trying to piss me off."

"Is it working?"

"It is."

"Keep me informed. The media's going to get their teeth into this case. I'm going to have the higher-ups crawling so far up my ass I'll have my teeth cleaned. Get it solved and soon."

"Yes, sir."

Before he found something else to grill her about, she turned and got the hell out of there, shutting the door behind her. She headed back to her desk where Dante was still sitting, a smug smile on his face. She slid into her chair and gave him an evil glare.

"What did you do to my captain? Drug him with the donuts?"

"I have a way with people."

She rolled her eyes at him. "No one has a way with Pohanski."

Dante arched a brow. "A smooth talker like you can't wrap him around your pretty little finger? Come on."

"Screw you." She booted up her desktop and started entering information on the case.

"So what did he say?"

Like she'd tell him. "He just wanted an update on the case."

"Uh-huh. He likes me, doesn't he?"

"He thinks you're going to be a hindrance to this case and I should keep you as far away from it as possible."

Dante laughed. "Liar."

She shifted her gaze to him. "Okay, fine. He did like you. He wants me to stick to you like glue. What the hell did you tell him?"

"Bullshit, mostly. But all the right kinds of bullshit. In my line of work I've had to schmooze every type. I know how to work people to get what I want."

She leaned back in her chair. "Is that what you've been doing to me? Working me?"

"You know better than that. You know *me* better than that, and don't give me that crap about you not knowing me. You of all people know me better than anyone."

She wanted to say she didn't know him at all. There were parts of his past she didn't know, but she was learning more every day. And she wanted to find out more—about where he'd been, what he'd been doing, what he'd been through all these years, and how all that had shaped him into who he was now.

Mostly she wanted not to care about him at all.

The problem was, she did care, and that pissed her off more than anything. She'd spent years building this great wall of I-don't-give-a-shit-about-anybody. She kept watch over her guys because she owed them, but she didn't love anyone. When you loved someone, they could hurt you. They could leave you.

She'd been really successful at keeping her heart under wraps all these years. Her job had helped with that, keeping her busy enough that she didn't notice the loneliness. The panic attacks and memories of that night kept her from getting close to anyone. She guarded herself well.

Until Dante came back. Until this case reminded her she hadn't been alone all these years. That she did have people she loved.

People she loved that she could lose.

And now it was like twelve years ago—her and all the guys again.

Only now they were one guy short. Jeff was dead. Someone hunted them all. Someone wanted them all dead.

"Hey, Anna?"

She lifted her head to see Roman coming into the squad room. "Yeah?"

"You need to come outside and see this."

Puzzled, she and Dante headed out the front door, the same way they'd come in.

Roman inclined his head down the street where her car was parked.

Her heart stumbled when she saw the single rose and the card attached to the windshield wiper of her car.

"Goddammit." Dante pushed past her toward her car with his long, lean strides. She and Roman hustled to keep up with him.

"I saw it when I was driving up," Roman said. "I pulled in behind your car and already called for a forensics team."

She nodded, but her focus was on Dante. He was pissed. She'd never seen him so angry—not since that night twelve years ago.

He pivoted in a three hundred sixty degree circle, hand on the butt of his gun as if he could spot the killer on this busy street.

"He's not here, Dante."

He shot her a glare. "You sure about that? It's downtown, cars buzzing by, sidewalks crowded with people. He could be right goddamn here right now watching you. You need to go inside."

Her dander up, she went toe-to-toe with him. "Don't tell me how to do my job."

He got closer to her. "And don't be so hardheaded about this that you end up dead."

Equally as furious with Dante and the killer, she pivoted, leaned over her car and examined the bloodred rose and white card tied to it with a red ribbon.

"Ballsy fucker, isn't he?" Roman said.

"He's pissing me the hell off." Anna wanted to tear him apart. And she wanted to read that goddamn card. "Where's CSU?"

"It's going to take them a few minutes, honey. Let me get my kit." Roman went to his trunk and popped it open, grabbed a few pairs of gloves and tweezers from his kit.

"We need photographs first," Anna said, gloving up and grabbing Roman's camera. She took a step back and shot some photos from a distance, then took a photo of

YOUR PARTICIPATION IS REQUESTED!

Dear Reader,

Since you are a lover of suspense fiction – we would like to get to know you!

Inside you will find a short Reader's Survey. Sharing your answers with us will help our editorial staff understand who you are and what activities you enjoy.

To thank you for your participation, we would like to send you 2 books and 2 gifts – **ABSOLUTELY FREE!**

Enjoy your gifts with our appreciation,

Pam Powers

SEE INSIDE FOR READER'S SURVEY

YOUR READER'S SURVEY
"THANK YOU" FREE GIFTS INCLUDE:

▶ 2 Suspense books
▶ 2 lovely surprise gifts

PLEASE FILL IN THE CIRCLES COMPLETELY TO RESPOND

1) What type of fiction books do you enjoy reading? (Check all that apply)
○ Suspense/Thrillers   ○ Action/Adventure   ○ Modern-day Romances
○ Historical Romance   ○ Humour   ○ Paranormal Romance

2) What attracted you most to the last fiction book you purchased on impulse?
○ The Title   ○ The Cover   ○ The Author   ○ The Story

3) What is usually the greatest influencer when you <u>plan</u> to buy a book?
○ Advertising   ○ Referral   ○ Book Review

4) How often do you access the internet?
○ Daily   ○ Weekly   ○ Monthly   ○ Rarely or never.

5) How many NEW paperback fiction novels have you purchased in the past 3 months?
○ 0 - 2   ○ 3 - 6   ○ 7 or more

YES! I have completed the Reader's Survey. Please send me the 2 FREE books and 2 FREE gifts (gifts are worth about $10) for which I qualify. I understand that I am under no obligation to purchase any books, as explained on the back of this card.

191/391 MDL FH7Q

FIRST NAME   LAST NAME

ADDRESS

APT.#   CITY

STATE/PROV.   ZIP/POSTAL CODE

The Reader Service — Here's How It Works:

Accepting your 2 free books and 2 free gifts (gifts valued at approximately $10.00) places you under no obligation to buy anything. You may keep the books and gifts and return the shipping statement marked "cancel." If you do not cancel, about a month later we'll send you 4 additional books and bill you just $5.99 each in the U.S. or $6.49 each in Canada. That is a savings of at least 25% off the cover price. It's quite a bargain! Shipping and handling is just 50¢ per book in the U.S. and 75¢ per book in Canada.* You may cancel at any time, but if you choose to continue, every month we'll send you 4 more books, which you may either purchase at the discount price or return to us and cancel your subscription.

*Terms and prices subject to change without notice. Prices do not include applicable taxes. Sales tax applicable in N.Y. Canadian residents will be charged applicable taxes. Offer not valid in Quebec. Books received may not be as shown. All orders subject to credit approval. Credit or debit balances in a customer's account(s) may be offset by any other outstanding balance owed by or to the customer. Please allow 4 to 6 weeks for delivery. Offer available while quantities last.

If offer card is missing write to: The Reader Service, P.O. Box 1867, Buffalo, NY 14240-1867 or visit: www.ReaderService.com

BUSINESS REPLY MAIL
FIRST-CLASS MAIL   PERMIT NO. 717   BUFFALO, NY

POSTAGE WILL BE PAID BY ADDRESSEE

THE READER SERVICE
PO BOX 1341
BUFFALO NY 14240-8571

NO POSTAGE
NECESSARY
IF MAILED
IN THE
UNITED STATES

her car in relation to the police station. Once she got the pictures, she nodded to Roman who had the tweezers in his hand.

"Envelope isn't sealed." He deftly pulled the card out of the envelope enough for them to read it.

Number two, Anna. Did I kill him good enough for you?

She jumped back as if she'd been burned. Angry tears pricked her eyes. She blinked them back, refusing to let him get to her. "Not for me, you son of a bitch. Never for me."

"He's playing you," Dante said. "He's trying to upset you."

"You know what? It's working. I am upset. He's playing this game and killing people I care about. People you care about. And he's doing it for me? I don't fucking think so. He's doing it for himself. For whatever his agenda is. And he's trying to lay it on me. That's bullshit."

"Pohanski is coming out," Roman said.

Anna whirled, then groaned. "Great. Just fucking great."

Her captain came over just as the CSU team arrived. "What the hell is this?" he asked as he leaned over her car. "More love notes?"

"It would seem so."

"Fucking hell." Pohanski smoothed his hand over his bald head. "You light a fire under CSU and get this wrapped up in a hurry."

"I'll do that, sir."

Pohanski stormed off. She instructed the CSU team to pull the flower and card, dust her car for prints and get the hell out of there. She put a couple uniforms on crowd control, and she, Dante and Roman headed back inside.

"I can't even believe he put that on my car outside the police station."

Dante slid into the chair next to Anna's desk. "When you think about it, it's a great idea."

Anna's brows shot up. "Yeah? Explain it to me."

"Cops going in and out. Busy street with heavy traffic downtown, people not paying attention. Easy to get lost in a crowd and no one expects anyone to do anything out of the ordinary right outside a precinct station."

"He has a point," Roman said. "Hiding in plain sight. We've seen that plenty of times on cases."

Anna laid her head in her hands. This case had just gone from bad to worse.

Roman stood. "I'm going to head over to the lab and light a fire under Forensics' ass. We need tox results on Jeff, the results of those drugs both Jeff and George were found with. And now we have this."

Anna nodded. "Thanks, Roman."

Her phone buzzed. She pulled it and looked at the display.

"Oh, no."

"What?" Dante asked.

"It's Gabe. We never got around to telling Gabe." She watched the phone buzz until the call went to voice mail. If she had to tell one more person about Jeff she wasn't going to make it.

"I'll take care of it."

She met his gaze. "I can do it."

"You go check out the autopsy. See if they find anything."

She nodded. Neither task was going to be a pleasant one. She stood and so did Dante. "I'll do that, thanks."

He moved to leave.

"Dante?"

"Yeah."

"About outside?"

He looked around the squad room, then smiled and brushed his knuckles across her cheek. "Just tension, Anna. Don't worry about it."

She relaxed. "Thanks."

She knew she couldn't face the autopsy. There was no way she could stand over Jeff's body and watch them take him apart piece by piece as if Jeff hadn't been a live person a day ago. She might be a coward, but she'd rather hear about what they found rather than see it for herself.

She dragged her heels heading over to the M.E.'s office, then finally went inside. They told her the autopsy was in progress, so she stalled for time, called Roman who was cooling his heels at the lab with nothing to report. She headed out to her car to finish up some paperwork. By the time she came back inside, it was over.

"You missed it," Richard Norton said as he dried off his hands.

Perfect timing. Jeff's body had already been returned to the refrigerated compartment, so she wouldn't have to look at him, wouldn't have to face him—or her own failure at catching whoever was doing this.

"I got tied up. What did you find?"

She followed Richard to his office. "Whoever did this had a much better time wailing on this guy than he did the one before. He was beaten more severely, especially around his face. Relatives wouldn't have been able to recognize him if they'd been looking at him."

She knew. She hadn't known it was him at first. But the image of Jeff's bloody, beaten face would remain with her forever.

More nightmares to look forward to.

"Cause of death was skull fracture and corresponding

brain bleed. If you'd been to the autopsy, I could have showed you."

She was glad she'd missed it.

"Plus his airway was swollen from being choked, his nose broken, ten ribs fractured, his lungs bruised…"

Anna had to buck up and listen to Richard go over the autopsy results as if Jeff were just another victim, instead of someone she'd known almost half her life. If she let it get too personal, Pohanski would pull her from the case. She could only hope that Jeff had been unconscious for most of it, that he'd fallen blissfully under and had died without knowing a lot of the pain.

That's how she was going to think of it, anyway.

"Did you pull anything off the body? Prints, fibers, anything of note?"

"Prints, no. Pulled a few fibers from his skin and clothing. Those could have likely come from his house, or they could have come from the killer. Sent those off to the lab to be tested. He had marks all over him, obviously, from being beaten, but your suspect must be using thick gloves when he beats them and only the tip of a shoe for the kicking. We have no shoe imprints on the body, no fingerprints. He's as clean as the first guy. Once we washed all the blood off, we found bruises, scrapes and cuts. He had a deep gash on his head. Your killer took the victim's head and pounded it on the floor of the alley. Brain swelled up like a watermelon and filled with blood. Your vic didn't have a chance. Like I said earlier, this kill was much more vicious than the last one."

Anna grimaced.

"And then of course we have the same crude heart carving over his chest as the previous victim."

"I need tox-screen results as soon as you can get them to me."

Richard nodded. "Yeah, he was injected. There's an injection spot on his right bicep. I saw in the file his bedroom had been wrecked and it looked like he'd been taken from there to the dump site. I can tell you for certain he died in the alley, so he was alive when he was taken from his house. By the time he was found in the alley he'd only been dead a few hours. I'll tell the lab to rush the tox results for you."

"Okay. Thanks, Richard."

"You have any leads on the killer yet?"

She shook her head. "Nothing yet. This suspect is so clean he's squeaking right through."

He patted her shoulder. "You're tough and tenacious, Anna. No killer is that thorough. You'll catch him."

"I appreciate the confidence. And yes, I will."

She had to. She would. No one else was going to die.

Dante met Gabe at his condo and filled him in on everything that had happened last night. And today.

Gabe leaned over, his forearms on the knees of his jeans.

"Damn." He shook his head. "I can't believe Jeff's dead." He lifted his head and shot an angry glare at Dante. "The bastard took him from his house?"

"Yeah. Blood in the bathroom and the bedroom was a mess. Looked like a mean fight."

"That should yield some evidence. Anna will be happy."

Dante shrugged. "Maybe. First time he was Mr. Clean. This time, not so much."

"Good. You don't make a mess like that without leaving something of yourself behind."

"Spoken by someone who knows something of crime scenes?"

Gabe lifted his lips and stared down at Dante's badge. "Not saying a thing to the FBI."

"Sorry about that."

"Yeah. What the hell, man? Couldn't you have said something?"

"Not really. Maybe. Fuck, I guess I should have. I'm so used to being undercover I just don't tell people. And I'm never around people I know, so…"

This lying thing sucked. He was usually really good at it. This time, he was weaving so many lies even he didn't know what he was saying. He should have just told the truth from the beginning.

Anna was right.

But then he wouldn't have been able to become FBI guy, and that was going to help the case, so he'd live with it.

Gabe regarded Dante with something that looked a lot like mistrust. Dante wondered if Gabe was thinking he was the one being investigated. He hoped not. There was already time and distance between them, and he needed to keep Gabe close, for Anna's sake.

"So you're undercover right now?"

Dante smiled. "No. I got myself assigned to the local P.D. so I could help investigate George's and Jeff's murder."

"But you're on the government's payroll."

That part, at least, wasn't a lie. "Yeah."

"Huh. Can't see you as a fed."

"No? What did you see me as?"

"I dunno. Nothing on the legal side, that's for sure."

Dante laughed. "Thanks, Gabe."

"Hey, just call 'em like I see 'em. There's a reason you and me hightailed it out of here as fast as we could after the shit went down all those years ago. And it wasn't because we were saints."

"You're right about that."

"So for you to turn out to be FBI after all we've been through—man, you got lucky."

"I know, right? I cleaned up my act, decided to stay out of trouble for a change. I developed goals and ambitions."

"I had goals and ambitions, too. Only mine were a little different than yours."

"Like what?"

Gabe gave him a knowing look. "Do I look stupid?"

"I think you can trust me, Gabe. Me of all people."

Gabe laughed. "You say that like we're supposed to know each other. We don't know shit about each other anymore. I don't trust you any more than you trust me."

Dante leaned back, realizing Gabe was right. They knew nothing about each other anymore. His perceptions of the guys, and of Anna, were stuck in time—twelve years ago. They were all different people now.

He couldn't help but be hurt that his onetime best friend and closest brother didn't trust him at all. And that was on him. He'd have to live with that.

"You're probably right. But you know what? I don't give a damn if you trust me or not. The only thing I care about is keeping you, Roman and Anna safe."

Gabe nodded. "I think that should top all our lists, especially Anna. Knowing her, she's worried about all of us and not herself."

"Likely."

"Then we need to make sure that we all keep watch over her. We have the skills to keep her safe."

"I'll talk to Roman about it."

"Okay."

"In the meantime, I guess I don't have to tell you to watch your back."

"We said the same thing to Jeff last night. Didn't help him much, did it?"

Dante frowned. He was beginning to wonder if any of them were safe. And who the killer's ultimate target really was.

Anna dreaded her next stop, but she knew it had to be done. She didn't bother to knock. Plus, she still had a key in case the door was locked.

She turned the knob and rolled her eyes. Of course it wasn't locked. Her father still thought that just because he had a house full of weaponry, he was invincible.

"Dad? You here?"

"Out back."

The slider was open to just the screen. She looked around the living room. Needed a good dusting, but he was keeping the clutter under control. Then again, Frank Pallino had always liked order in his environment, whether at work or at home. Minimal knickknacks and still the same furniture that had been here when Mom had been alive, which was why Anna's tension level settled to a reasonably calm state whenever she came home.

As she walked through the kitchen, she smiled at the gold-and-white curtains over the kitchen sink, and the brick-yellow Formica tabletop with its shiny metal legs that had stood the test of time and who knows how many years. It even still had the matching chairs she remembered sitting at for years. That thing had to be an antique.

Her dad was out back with Rusty, his golden retriever. Anna had gotten Rusty from a shelter a few years ago after Dad had retired from the force, figuring he'd needed a playmate, someone to keep him active. They'd always had dogs when she was growing up. After the family dog,

King, died when Anna was around twenty, Dad hadn't gotten another. He'd insisted he did just fine without having to deal with an animal underfoot all the time. Anna moved out when she joined the force and she knew her father was lonely.

Plus, he'd put on some weight around his middle, no doubt from spending too many days watching TV and drinking beer. No amount of nagging on her and on her father's physical therapist's part had gotten him out of that damn chair.

She knew he'd been depressed. His life had been as a cop, and he hadn't known what to do with it after he couldn't be a cop anymore. Having to retire at fifty years old sucked. Her dad still had a lot of life in him, a lot of energy.

And then she'd gotten Rusty, only a year old and one rambunctious dog.

Oh, man, had her dad been pissed at her, had yelled at her and told her to take the damn dog away. But she'd refused. She'd moved into the house with her dad and the dog and told her father that the shelter had a strict no-return policy, and furthermore, she was going to give up her job and become his physical therapist if he didn't start cooperating.

That had gotten his attention. And the dog wriggled his way into her dad's heart fairly quickly. How could he not? Rusty was affectionate and sweet and learned fast once he found a family to love him.

Since her father wasn't going to allow her to quit her job on the force, he reluctantly straightened up his act, started back on his therapy and welcomed Rusty into his house. Though Anna was certain he secretly fell madly in love with the dog at first sight. They'd been inseparable ever since and she credited Rusty with her father's amazing recovery.

Now he took Rusty to the senior center a couple times a week. The older folks loved Rusty. And together Dad and Rusty did safety talks at the local schools.

Her dad had found things to do to stay busy. He felt useful now, and she was so grateful for that.

She stood at the door and watched Rusty go after the ball her father tossed. Rusty bounded back, ball in his mouth, making a game of keep away, but his dad grabbed the ball, dog spit and all, and tossed it again.

She laughed and stepped outside. "He can do that all day long, can't he?"

Her dad turned to her. "As long as I'm willing to throw it."

"I see you're bending pretty good."

"Yeah, the water therapy is helping."

He came inside and Rusty followed, eager to see Anna, as always. She bent and petted the dog, who then bounded off to his water bowl while she and her dad sat at the kitchen table.

"What's going on?" he asked, his keen eyes boring into her.

"How do you know something's wrong?"

"Because I know you. There are worry lines across your forehead, plus you look like you haven't slept in a week."

"Good thing I don't come to you seeking compliments about how great I look."

He laughed and cupped her cheek with the palm of his hand. "You have boyfriends for that."

"Sure, Dad."

"So what's going on? Problem case?"

She hesitated, knowing this was going to be tough. "There's a lot I have to talk to you about."

He leaned back in the chair. "Start at the beginning. I'll listen."

"Dante's back in town."

He frowned. "Since when?"

"A few days ago. George Clemons was beaten to death in the alley the other night. It was the same spot where I was attacked. A heart was carved on his chest. Here." She placed her fingers where her scar was.

Her dad pushed his chair back. "Jesus."

"It gets worse. While we were following up on that murder, Jeff Barrone was beaten to death last night. Same alley. Heart carved on his chest."

Her dad's eyes filled with tears. He stood. "Oh, shit, baby. Come here."

She could be the strong, invulnerable detective all she wanted with everyone else, but that never held water with her dad. To him, she would always be his baby girl, and she knew it had destroyed him that night she'd called him from the ice-cream shop. He'd rushed over there and she'd known from the moment he got there that he was more devastated by what had happened than she had been.

Since her mom had died when she was six years old, she knew he'd felt as if it had been his duty to protect her, and he had failed that night. Not to her. There was no way he could be with her all the time, and no one could have foreseen what could happen. But she had seen the guilt on his face, and she'd have done anything to wipe that away.

He patted her back and stroked her hair, and somehow, she did feel better.

He stepped away and they sat again, but he held tight

to her hand. She looked down where their fingers were joined.

Her lifeline. What would she do without him?

"I've been busy the past few days. Had some school functions with Rusty and some doctor appointments and therapy sessions. Haven't even caught up on the news or read my paper. I didn't know. Why didn't you tell me?"

"I've been kind of busy myself, but knew you'd want to hear it from me."

"Are you all right?" He swept his knuckles across her cheek, the concern on his face so deep it made her heart ache.

"Yes."

"No one knows about the connection?"

"Of course not."

"Maybe you should tell them."

She cocked her head to the side. "Not gonna happen, and you know why."

He sighed. "You shouldn't have protected Dante that night."

"And we've been over this a hundred times. Let it go, Dad."

He shrugged. "Fine. So it's obvious someone else was there that night. Someone saw the whole thing and identified all of you, and now he's playing this sick game of cat and mouse and murder."

She nodded. She wasn't going to tell him about the note and flowers. Knowing her dad, he'd camp out at her house with his gun, putting himself at risk.

"Got any thoughts on who it might be?"

"I have no idea. Someone who was with Maclin, or maybe somebody he was meeting. Maybe it was even a person walking through the alley that wasn't connected to him at all. Though they wouldn't have known who we were."

"Easy enough to find out if you try hard enough."

"I suppose." She'd pondered all the angles until her head throbbed.

"Why wait twelve years, though? Why file it away all this time?"

"That's what's bugging me, too. The only thing I can come up with is Dante. Gabe was gone for a while, and he came back. Now Dante's back, which means we're all here now."

His father nodded and dragged his fingers through his hair. "That's the only goddamn thing that makes sense. Jesus, Mary and Joseph, this is a mess. And you can't tell anyone at the precinct about it."

"I know."

He lifted his gaze to hers. "Though you can if you need to."

"No, Dad. I can't and I won't. Too many people could be hurt if I did. The guys…you. I'll never tell what happened twelve years ago."

He shook his head. "We should have never played it that way. I shouldn't have let you talk me into keeping that secret."

"We had to protect them. They saved my life."

"And now someone's trying to take theirs. We have to figure out why."

"No. *I* have to figure out why."

He took her hand. "You're not in this alone, girlie. I might be retired but my cop brain isn't. Go back to the beginning."

"The Maclin case?"

"Yeah."

"Dad, I've been over the case time and time again. Mainly because I wanted to know what had been done as far as investigating it. They'd developed no leads and after a while it went cold. And we know why."

"So reopen it. Do some investigation into similar crimes, and lo and behold the Maclin case is gonna come up. He was beaten to death in the same alley, so you'll have a legit reason for being in his file."

She pondered his line of reasoning. "I was also working in one of the buildings then, so I was interviewed as a potential witness for his case."

Her dad crossed his arms. "Convenient, huh? That's why you'll suddenly remember Maclin's case from twelve years ago."

She laid her head in her hands. "Lying sucks."

"Yes, it does. But use it to your advantage now and bring in the Maclin kid's file into your current investigation."

She sighed. "I guess so. But there were no witnesses. I remember that much. And I lied and said I closed up shop and was out of there before he died."

"It never hurts to look again, see if there's anything you missed."

"Okay. I need to get back to work."

He stood and hugged her again, then held her out at arm's length. "You get to the point you need to spill your guts about that night, you do it. You don't worry about me or the guys, you just do it, okay?"

"I'm not going to tell anyone about that night. You'd lose everything. They'd be arrested."

"They were juveniles then, honey. That was a long time ago and I doubt anything would stick now. They were defending you. And now they're being targeted by a murderer. As for me… You don't worry about me."

She kissed his cheek. "You're my father. I love you. I'm always going to worry about you."

Fourteen

"What's all this stuff?" Dante asked.

Anna looked up at him. He'd just taken a shower, his hair still damp as he pulled up a seat at her kitchen table.

He smelled like soap—something with a fresh pine smell. Whatever it was, it slid into her senses and made her want to lean over and shove her nose in his neck. Between his scent and the sleeveless shirt that showed off all his tanned muscle, it brought back last night, before she'd gotten the call about Jeff.

They'd started something hot together and hadn't finished it.

Probably for the best anyway.

Yeah, right. She needed to keep reminding herself of that, because her libido was pinging so loud she was surprised Dante couldn't hear it.

He swept some of her loose hairs behind one ear, then gave her a dark, dangerous look. The kind of look that made her swallow, hard. She couldn't help but stare at him. His face had the kind of physical beauty that made her just want to sit and stare at him, just like it had been with those women on the street. It had been like that when they were younger, too. Girls were jealous she'd landed him as a boyfriend. She'd been damn smug about it. She knew how lucky she had been to have Dante. Tall, dark and handsome fit him to a tee then—even more so now, only one could add dangerous and devastating to the mix.

And a mysterious element that seemed to cling to him no matter how much he told her of his past.

"You keep staring at me like that and I'm going to get you naked and spread you on top of all these files on the kitchen table."

Now, *there* was a fantasy she could spend hours imagining.

Forcing herself to blink, she said, "You don't want to do that."

His lips curled. "Yeah, I do."

"I have work."

He seemed to ponder whether he was going to let her do her work, or pick her up and toss her on the kitchen table. If he chose the latter, she wasn't certain she'd have the will to put up much of an objection.

"Okay, tell me what all these files are."

Admittedly, she regretted his choice, but she turned to the folders. "They're the files from the Tony Maclin case."

He arched a brow. "How did you get those?"

"Remember I told you they interviewed me on his murder case because I worked at one of the businesses that fronted the alley that night?"

"Yeah."

"I pulled his file and brought it into this case, claiming his murder was exactly the same type, in the same location."

"Do you think it's a good idea to bring that connection into play?"

"If I didn't, someone else would. And then I'd be asked

why I didn't bring it up since I had been questioned about his murder."

"You could always say you were sixteen at the time and you forgot."

She shot him a look. "That's right. I forgot the time I was questioned about a murder. Come on, Dante. I'm a detective. It's my job to make that connection. Especially having been a part of the file."

He sighed. "I guess you're right. I don't like it, though. It drags the past into the now."

She shrugged. "Unavoidable. It's already here."

He laid his arm over her chair, the heat from his body making her all too aware of him.

"That must have been hard on you, having to answer questions, pretending you had no idea what had happened that night."

She shrugged. "I got through it."

"I'm sorry—again—for you having to do it alone."

"I wasn't alone. My dad helped me through it."

"I'm glad he was there for you."

Because I wasn't were the words he hadn't said. But they'd already been said before. No reason to keep repeating them.

She went back to trying to focus.

"Anything in particular you're looking for?"

"Not really. I talked to my dad today. He said to pull the files and look again."

Dante leaned back in the chair. "What else did your dad have to say?"

She lifted her gaze to Dante's. "About the murders, or about you coming back?"

"Both, I guess."

"He was surprised to find out you were here, agreed the timing of the murders might have something to do with your return. The killer might have wanted us all here at the same time, and that's why he waited for you to come back."

Dante nodded.

"He also thinks maybe I missed something the first time I looked at Tony Maclin's file, so I should look again."

"I can't imagine you overlooking anything."

She shrugged. "It's possible. I wasn't investigating a case the first time I took a look at it. Or the second, or the third. I kept going back to it, but it's not like I went over it with a fine-tooth comb. It was more of a cursory overview. Morbid curiosity, you know?"

And she'd never really given Maclin's file the detailed look she needed to give it, because every time she opened it up it reminded her of that night.

"Yeah." He shifted his focus to the file folders spread out on the table. "Okay, so what should we be on the lookout for?"

"I don't know. Anything that might give us a clue or help us with the current case. Something the original investigators might have missed. Interviews, photos, evidence, something I might have missed when I looked at it."

He pulled a folder and opened it up. "Let's start digging."

They both went silent and perused the files. She opened the envelope containing the crime scene photographs and wrinkled her nose.

Looking at Maclin's bloody, beaten body again conjured up memories she'd tried so hard to eradicate. It was like being back there again. She could still smell the humid night, the blood, could still feel his hands on her, touching her, ripping at her clothes.

Try as she might, she couldn't suppress the shudder.

Dante glanced over. "Hard to look at?"

"Not really."

"Liar."

She shot him a glare. "Hard for you to look at?"

"No. He deserved what happened to him. I don't feel remorse. But I wasn't a victim that night. You were. It's easy for me to look back at that night and feel nothing but hatred for him, and sadness for what you had to go through."

She studied him, his relaxed posture, the lack of tension on his face and in his body. He wasn't lying. Then again, in his line of work he was probably good at masking his true feelings. "He wasn't the last person you killed."

He didn't flinch. "No. And you've seen a lot of dead bodies since Tony Maclin," he reminded her.

"Yes."

"So just look at those photos like any other crime scene. Let it go, Anna."

He was right. She had to take the emotion out of it— had to take herself out of it and look on Tony Maclin as just another victim.

Even though she'd been *his* victim, even though he'd tried to rape her, would have likely killed her. She stared down at the photos of his body and felt the familiar stirrings of tension swirling around her.

She closed the file. Just as she had every other time she'd gone through it, looking at it without really seeing what was in there because it reminded her too much of that night.

"Useless," she whispered.

"Maybe you should let me look through these instead," Dante said.

She shook her head. "I should be able to do this."

She hated feeling weak. Twelve years later and Tony Maclin still held her prisoner. Even in death he still terrorized her.

"You can't help but feel close to his case. He traumatized you. Are you supposed to forget it ever happened?"

"I want to. I want to be over it. I want it to not bother me anymore." She tilted her head toward him. "For God's sake, Dante, it's been twelve years."

"And you still carry a scar—not just psychological, but an actual, physical scar—from what he did to you. I don't think there are timelines for just getting over that."

She turned away from him. "There should be. Many women get over attacks like that and go on to be—"

"What? Normal? You think you're not normal?"

She snorted. "Those panic attacks I have are totally normal."

"Face it, babe. You didn't exactly choose the best career to distance yourself from the dregs of humanity. You remind yourself every day of the evil out there. Facing down rapists, drug dealers and killers isn't exactly the best way to get over trauma, ya know?"

She allowed a smile. "You may have a point."

"And you work yourself almost nonstop, so it's not a surprise you're always so tense. You don't give yourself time to relax."

She shrugged. "I figured if I worked all the time, I wouldn't have to think about it."

"Sometimes you have to face it. It's the only way to let go of it."

"I like my method better."

She lifted her shoulders, then dropped them again, the tension mounting.

"Yeah, your way is working great. I'll bet you're just a bundle of knots back here."

He slid his fingers into her hair. Her ponytail holder had started to bother her, so she'd taken it out and slid it on her wrist, leaving her hair loose. His fingers running rampant along the back of her neck and along the tenderness of her scalp was not good for her concentration. Not that she was really focusing on the Maclin files anymore anyway.

He rubbed the base of her neck, the area that was always so sore.

Oh, yeah. Right there. She dropped her chin to her chest and gave up. He swept her hair over one shoulder and stood, moving behind her to use both hands now, digging into those tight spots with his thumbs.

"Am I hurting you?"

"No. Harder."

"Your muscles are like bricks here."

"Tell me about it."

He alternated between hard and soft, and she yielded to the mastery of his hands. She was such a sucker for a good neck massage. Dante had strong, firm hands, and he didn't seem to be in any hurry to stop.

Most men couldn't handle her tough muscles, stopping after only a few minutes and flexing their fingers as if her muscles had caused them pain.

Wimps.

Dante kept going, digging at the tight spots until they melted under his sweetly brutal assault. He knew exactly how far to push, how much pain she could take, when to back off and move somewhere else. He never stopped. She almost felt guilty.

Almost.

"You a licensed massage therapist or something? You're really good at that."

He laughed, the deep sound vibrating through his fingertips and skittering through her nerve endings to all her sensitive feminine parts.

"No. You have a high pain tolerance."

"Mmm. Lucky me."

She wondered how long she was going to let this go on before she put a stop to it. The Maclin files lay scattered across her kitchen table, forgotten. She really should get back to—

But then he hit a tight knot and dug at it, and she melted.

"Oh, that's really good, Dante. God, your hands are like magic. Right there."

She heard his harsh intake of breath and stilled. "What?"

"You do realize that's sex talk."

She laughed. "Sorry."

He moved his hands across her muscles again. "I don't think you're sorry at all. I think you're trying to torture me."

"You keep rubbing my shoulders like that and I'm likely to start moaning."

"You start moaning and I won't just be rubbing your shoulders."

She enjoyed this easy banter, especially the sexual undertones. And what was wrong with that? They knew each other. She probably knew Dante better than any other man she'd actually had sex with.

Maybe it was time to find out what she'd been missing all these years.

His touch glided across her neck and down to her shoulders, his fingertips light now instead of firm. Admittedly, she liked the butterflies dancing around in her stomach.

If their relationship came with a past, so what? He had to know they had no future. She knew it. He belonged… somewhere else, was just hanging around because of the case. When it was over and they caught the killer, he'd be on his way, and she'd go back to her life the way it was.

But the thought of exploring with him was tempting. It was a new feeling, one rich with promise.

She liked his hands on her, and wanted more than just a back rub.

She tilted her head back to peer up at him, not at all shocked to see the dark desire in his eyes as he stared down at her.

Nor was she surprised when he cradled her head in the palm of his hand and bent to take her lips in a soft, searing kiss. She melted into the kiss, losing herself as his lips swept across hers, his tongue sliding inside to claim hers.

He moved to the front of her chair, lifting her to draw her against him. Plastered against his hard, hot body, she could only moan and clutch his shirt while his hands roamed over her back, his fingers tangling in her hair to angle her head for a deeper kiss.

His passion ignited hers and she wanted to get closer to him. Standing wasn't going to cut it. She broke the kiss, shocked at the raw hunger she saw in his eyes, at the same time needing to see it there, desperate to know what she felt wasn't one-sided.

"Come on," she said, sliding her hand in his so she could take him to her bedroom.

He tugged on her hand to pull her back. "No. Right here. I've been thinking a lot about right here."

He would, wouldn't he? The thought of it shot her desire up to the ceiling.

He lifted her and placed her on the kitchen counter,

jerking her tank top out of the waistband of her shorts. She lifted her arms and he drew the shirt over her head, his mouth coming down on hers at the same time his hands pressed against the bare flesh of her belly. Her abdomen quivered at his touch, the idea of surrendering totally to him both thrilling and utterly terrifying.

Oh, no. That wasn't going to work. She had to touch him, had to feel his skin, too, had to take control. She pulled at his shirt and he lifted it out of his pants.

She took a moment to appreciate his broad shoulders, lean waist and tanned skin, then reached out to let her fingertips wander over his chest where a fine sprinkling of dark hair was scattered, then disappeared, only to reappear lower by his belt buckle.

She lifted her gaze to his. He wasn't smiling, his eyes a half-lidded dark, stormy blue, his jaw clenched. She knew he was at the boiling point, which made her want to push his buttons. She reached for his belt buckle and pulled the flap out.

"Later," he growled and pulled her to edge of the counter before cupping the back of her neck and putting his mouth on hers again.

She gasped at the contact of her skin to his that was both joy and shock. She hadn't been close to a man in so long, and never one who exuded as much passion as Dante. She purposely chose men she could dominate so she could set the pace, so she could be in control. With Dante, she knew that wouldn't be the case.

She'd have to surrender, and she'd never done that before.

Could she do it?

Dante released Anna from the kiss.

God, she had a stranglehold on his body, and damn if

it took every ounce of restraint to hold back, when what he really wanted was to strip her naked and be inside her right now.

But while he saw passion flare hot in the honey-brown depths of her eyes, he also saw a flicker of fear, and that meant he was going to have to slow things down. Because she could put on whatever show of bravado or tough act she wanted to, but he knew better. He felt the tension when he kissed her. He'd been with enough women in his lifetime to read the easy yield versus the hesitant one.

Anna was hesitant, and that meant things weren't a go.

She might think she was ready, and maybe her body was willing, but her mind hadn't yet come along for the ride.

He laid his hands on the counter on either side of her thighs and took a deep, cleansing breath, then raised his gaze to hers and offered up a smile, one that let her know how much he wanted her. Because he really did want her. His cock was hard and his whole body ached for her. But this wasn't about what he wanted.

She arched a brow. "You're kidding, right? I'm half-naked here, Dante."

He took a long, slow look at her, from her messed-up hair that made her look sexy as hell, to her lips, swollen from his kisses, to her bra that barely covered her spectacular breasts, to her flat belly and those barely there shorts and her oh-so-hot long legs.

"You're still dressed. All the important parts of you, anyway. I think we need to talk about this before we jump into having sex."

"Are you fucking kidding me? Isn't that usually the woman's line?" She grabbed her tank top and pushed him away, leaping off the counter at the same time.

He turned. "Anna."

"Don't. Just don't." She pulled her shirt back on, then grabbed his and shoved it in his chest.

"You're angry."

She whirled around to face him. "You think? I've just been rejected."

"I didn't reject you. I just want to talk."

"Manspeak for I-don't-think-you're-hot-enough-to-fuck." She stormed off into the living room.

He laughed and followed. "That's not what I said. You are definitely hot enough to fuck."

She stopped in the middle of the room and narrowed her gaze at him.

Okay, maybe laughing had been the wrong move. Good thing her gun was in the other room. Then again, she did have that hidden Glock in here somewhere.

"Don't you dare laugh about this. You don't get a woman all hot and bothered, then say you want to talk. Are you some kind of moron?"

"I guess I am. Look, you seemed tense."

She threw her hands in the air. "Of course I was tense. You were kissing and touching me and I was turned on like crazy. Also, I haven't had a decent orgasm in like six freaking months. Are you reading my lips here? Six. Months. You'd be tense, too, wouldn't you?"

Dante gaped at her. Anna threw him a murderous glare.

"Are all men this dense or just you? Jesus, Dante, do I have to draw you a road map to my vagina, or are you grabbing a clue?"

He finally lost the smile. "I'm beginning to."

"Good. So can we get down to the sex so we can get back to work, or do we just want to scrap the whole idea?"

She wanted to get it over with? Really? Was sex a

chore for her, a task to get through so she could get back to the exciting part of her life—her job?

Who the hell had she been having sex with, anyway? Was it the men she'd been with, or was it the past that had gotten her all screwed up?

This was going to take some finessing, and a hell of a lot of patience.

"Anna."

She narrowed her gaze at him as he approached.

"What?"

"You see sex as a battle to be won."

She backed away. "That's ridiculous."

"Is it?" He caught up to her, took her hand and pulled her toward the sofa, dragging her on top of him. She went willingly, but damn she was stiff as a board.

"It's not ridiculous. You're tense. All my hard work massaging those tight muscles just went down the drain."

She sat astride him, pressing her hands on his chest—keeping distance. "That's because you pissed me off. We were doing fine in the kitchen—until you stopped."

"Because I could tell you weren't ready."

She cocked a brow. "Really. And how could you tell?"

"It was in your eyes. Your body was saying yes, but the rest of you wasn't on board."

She fisted his shirt in her hands. He wasn't sure if she was frustrated, turned on or preparing to take a swing at him.

"Psychoanalyzing me, Renaldi?"

"No, just reading some clear signals that told me to back off. When we have sex it's going to be because you're ready for it. Totally ready for it."

She surged against him and his cock roared to life. He gritted his teeth, refusing to let her control the game. "Seems to me *you're* totally ready."

"We aren't talking about me. We're talking about you."

She leaned forward, her hair loose and draped around her beautiful face. "I am ready." She rocked against him again and he thought for a few seconds about giving up and throwing her to the sofa and taking what she was offering. Why bother worrying about whether or not she was psychologically ready? Physically she was totally in the game, right? She was offering, and it had been a long time since he'd been inside a hot woman. It would be easy, they could both get off and ease some of the tension. Then they could concentrate on finding a killer.

But this was Anna, and something was off with her. He didn't just want to fuck her, he wanted to make love to her, wanted her to be with him—really with him. Not just two bodies grinding together, but engaged in a way that went beyond just the physical.

And he didn't think he'd get that if all they did was rip each other's clothes off and go at it.

Not right now, anyway.

She needed a slow, seductive dance. He intended to break down her barriers no matter how long it took, no matter how painful it was going to be—for both of them.

And the one thing he knew about her was that she liked to be in control. He'd bet that extended to the bedroom, too, where maybe the average guy wouldn't notice that she wanted to be in charge so she could playact the game of sex.

Like now, when she slid her hand between them to rub his erection, hoping to distract him.

"I'm ready, Dante. Let's get to it."

That was part of her problem. Her body was all over

his, hot and sexy and doing all the right things. God, was she doing all the right things. In fact, if she continued to do that he was either going to explode or throw her on the floor and shove inside her so he could come. And he'd make her come. And she'd be happy about that, too. They'd both be happy.

But there was a disconnect in her eyes. Her body might want the sex and the release that went with it, but the rest of her hadn't shown up to the party.

And he really wanted her focused on what they did together—what he did to her—not just her body, but her mind, her heart and her soul.

Maybe it was too much to ask of her, given what she'd been through, but he was willing to give it a try.

He wrapped his arm around her and flipped her over onto her back, looming over her, keeping watch as her eyes widened.

"You're ready, huh?"

She smiled. "Totally."

"For anything?"

He saw the glint of wariness, but she masked it by lifting her chin. "I can take whatever you've got. Bring it on."

And then he knew for sure she looked on sex as a challenge to be won, not something to be shared.

He was going to change that.

When she reached between them to touch him again, he grabbed her wrist and held it pinned to her side. "No."

She frowned. "Why not?"

Instead of answering her, he kissed her, a deliberately gentle kiss with just his lips, meant to slow down the tempo. He knew she wanted him hot and bothered and eager for penetration. Which he was. He really—oh, hell, yes—was. But he was also a man used to denying himself what he wanted.

He could wait.

Anna had no idea what kind of game Dante was playing, but the rules had changed and she didn't have the upper hand anymore, which she didn't like one bit.

But he was kissing her in this slow and deliberate way that made her head fuzzy, and all her limbs went lax until all she could think about were the delicious things he was doing with his mouth.

So when he rolled to his side and slid his hand under her shirt to snake his fingers along her stomach, her guard was down and her concentration was focused on his hands and how very much she craved his touch. And when he cupped a breast, his thumb drawing lazy circles across her bra-covered nipple, she whimpered in protest, wishing she was already naked so she could feel the touch directly.

She was a languid pool of nerve endings, a sensual puppet, and Dante pulled all her strings. Somewhere in her sex-fogged brain was the thought that this wasn't how it usually played out. She always had control. She was the one who set the pace, the scenario, and she never, ever handed the reins to a man.

But when Dante hooked his leg over hers, his denim-clad thigh rubbing against her center, and he took her mouth at the same time he pulled the cup of her bra down and found her nipple, a million stars exploded behind her eyes. All coherent thought fled as he plucked the bud between his fingers and drove his thigh against her sex, his mouth devouring hers, his tongue exploring in a sensual dance she had no hope to resist. All she could do was clutch his shirt in a death grip and hope she could continue to draw breath through his assault.

His fingers were on a march, sweeping over her breasts, her abdomen and lower, her breath catching as he slid his hand into her shorts.

He pulled his lips from her mouth. She opened her eyes and found him watching her, something far too intimate to bear, especially considering where his hand was. She scrunched her eyes closed and buried her face in his neck.

"Anna."

His fingers danced along the top of her sex, dipping into her panties. She arched against him as wild sensation burst and she lost all hope of controlling this game.

"Anna, look at me."

He asked too much of her. She bit down on her lip when his fingers slid lower, but couldn't resist the moan of sheer pleasure as he found the tight bud and began to play with it.

"Anna."

She tilted her head back and opened her eyes, meeting his gaze at the same time he tucked two fingers inside her. Her lips parted and she gasped, lifting to take more, feeling every sensation as his thumb swirled around the tight knot until she thought she might explode.

"Don't hold back," he whispered, pinning her with his gaze. "Release for me."

She'd never known a man like this, who could take her from anger and frustration to sweet pleasure in mere minutes. But as she rode the crest of his finessing fingers, she knew without a doubt she couldn't hold back.

It had been too long and, damn him, he was just too good.

And as the pulses began deep inside her, she knew that

he felt them, too, saw the smile of triumph on his face as she rocked against his hand and let go.

She gripped his arm, lifted her hips, and his name spilled from her lips.

"Dante."

He took her mouth in a deep, searing kiss as she climaxed, absorbing her cries as waves of pleasure crashed over her, leaving her shaken and trembling against him.

And still, he held on to her, his fingers continuing to coax every quake within her until he finally withdrew.

She expected him to strip her and take her then, but he only held her, kissed her, took her down gently from the rollicking roller coaster of sensations and emotions of her orgasm until she couldn't help but ask him.

"Dante."

He looked down at her. "Yeah?"

"We're not finished yet."

He grinned. "No, Anna. We're not. Not by a long shot."

"Shouldn't we…"

"Get back to work? Yeah, we probably should."

He shifted her upright.

Was he serious?

"But—"

He cupped her chin with his fingers. "I think you need to trust me before we go any further. Let's take this slow."

She glanced down at the ridge against his jeans that showed the pleasure had been all one-sided, and wondered how he could deny himself like that.

"I'll survive. Let's get back to work. We have a killer to catch."

She inhaled, let it out and watched him head into the other room.

Trust him? She didn't know what to make of him.

She stood and headed into the kitchen.

Fifteen

"**Y**ou've got one hell of a smile on your face."

Anna lifted her head, lost the smile and narrowed her gaze at Roman, who leaned a hip against her desk. "I do not."

He frowned and crossed his arms. "What's going on?"

"Nothing's going on. I'm working here."

"You're working with a smile. That's not like you."

Geez. She came into the office in a halfway decent mood and she got an interrogation. "Why are you being so nosy?"

He slid into the chair next to her desk. "Why are you being so evasive?"

Damn Dante, anyway. This was why she preferred being tense. Her being relaxed made people suspicious. "I'm not being evasive. I got a good night's sleep, that's all."

Roman laughed. "Yeah, that is unusual for you. And strange considering everything going on. What brought on the sleep?"

She adjusted the files on her desk. "I kind of had a bodyguard. Dante's staying with me."

Roman arched a brow. "Is that right?"

"He insisted."

"And you're no pushover. So what gives?"

She shoved the files away and gave Roman a pointed look. "You suddenly have a problem with Dante?"

"I just wonder if he's really who he says he is."

She looked around, though Dante wasn't there anyway. He'd gone with Ellen Clemons to help her make Jeff's funeral arrangements, something she admired him for doing and knew wasn't going to be easy for him.

He told her he'd catch up with her later. After he'd followed her to the precinct, of course. And that had been after much arguing on her part that she could drive herself to work without an escort. But he'd insisted. She'd told him he could shadow her if he wanted, but it was a waste of time.

He had, and had pulled off when she'd entered the lot.

Anna was grateful for the reprieve after last night's intimacy. She needed time to regroup and figure out just what they meant to each other.

But now she had Roman in her face questioning Dante's motives, and she didn't need that today.

"I don't understand, Roman. He's FBI. He has the credentials." Which he wasn't, but at least Anna knew who he was.

"Is he? It just seems strange that all this shit starts going down the minute he steps into town."

She nodded. "We've discussed that, figured our suspect started this chain of events as soon as Dante came back. You know, all of us who were there that night are now in the same place?"

"Or it could be something else."

"Like what?" He stared at her until she caught on to his thought process. "You think Dante is the killer? Why? That would make no sense, and he was with me…"

But he hadn't been with her specifically at the times the murders had been committed, had he? She thought back to the two murders. After, when she got the calls, yes. But she couldn't pinpoint time of death to Dante being with her the whole time, could she?

"Dante would have no reason to kill George or Jeff," she argued.

"Not that you know of, but what do any of us really know about him anymore? He's been gone for twelve years, Anna. Do we really know where he's been and what he's been doing all that time?"

"Why would you accuse him of this? Is there something you know about him that you're not telling me?"

Roman shook his head. "I'm not accusing him of anything. Jesus, Anna, I'd hate if he was the one. And no, I don't know anything concrete. But I don't like how close he's gotten to you so fast after he came back, and how you've let him. Two people get killed in the same manner as Tony Maclin, in the same alley. They get hearts carved on their chests, and suddenly Dante's moving in with you. That's just a little convenient.

"It's you I'm worried about. I don't want the way things were between the two of you in the past to cloud your judgment now."

She lifted her chin. "My eyes are wide open."

"Are they? I just want you to be careful."

"I am careful. I know who he is." At least she thought she did.

"You know, who we all were back then isn't who we are now. You can't accept him based on who he was twelve years ago. We're all different now."

"I know that, Roman. That's part of why I'm trying to keep Dante close. I'm trying to find out who he is now. I'm doing my job."

He looked at her as if he didn't really believe her, but finally he nodded. "As long as you do it with your eyes wide open."

She wondered if she did know. Dammit, she hated that Roman had thought the same thing she'd thought. Only she'd discarded the idea, hadn't followed through.

Was Roman the one thinking clearly and she was seeing only what she wanted to see?

Was Dante sliding past her defenses, purposely ingratiating himself into her life, into her heart, so that she wouldn't see what was going on right under her nose?

Roman was only looking out for her, making her see logic. Her judgment wasn't exactly clear where Dante was concerned. And Roman was always logical when working cases, never let his emotion cloud his judgment. That's what made him a good cop.

Was she letting emotion get in the way of seeing what was right in front of her?

She'd accepted everything Dante said at face value without any proof. How did she know for a fact he was who he said he was? He'd given her the perfect excuse not to be able to verify his background. Black ops, in the wind, unable to be tracked.

Shit. She pushed back from her desk and stood, heading into the break room for a coffee.

After pouring a coffee she moved over to the snack machine, searching for something to munch on, loading her quarters in and deciding on a package of nuts.

Could Dante get legitimate FBI credentials if he did anything other than work for the government? Her captain had certainly bought his ID, and Pohanski was no dumbass. Surely he'd have had Dante checked out, verified by the FBI, but no way could she go to her captain and ask him if he'd verified Dante. That would only cast suspicion on Dante, and that's the last thing she would do.

She leaned her forehead against the metal side of the snack machine, wishing every damn thing didn't have to be so complicated.

"You taking a nap?"

She jerked upright and turned around to find Dante leaning against the doorway of the break room. "How did you get in here?"

He held up his badge. "Hall pass."

She blew out a breath. "Right. Of course."

He frowned and came into the room, stopping in front of her to run his hand down her arm. "You upset about something?"

She took a step away. "No, just busy."

"Bullshit. What's wrong?"

"Nothing. Just have a lot on my mind."

"The Maclin file?"

"Yeah."

"Find anything?"

"No. I want to interview his family."

Dante shifted his gaze to the doorway, then back to her. "That's risky, don't you think?"

"Why?"

A couple uniforms came into the break room, so Anna led Dante out the side exit. The brutal heat slammed into her and made her breath catch. At least they were alone out here.

"Isn't it obvious?" he asked when they moved along the far wall on the side of the building, a place set up for smokers. None were outside right now, so they had privacy.

"Isn't what obvious?"

"Maclin's family. What are you hoping to find out?"

"I don't know. Maybe I can get some information out of them. I want to meet them, talk to them, see what they have to say about their son and that night. The case is twelve years cold now."

"Not to them it isn't. You know what he was to you. To them, he was their son, and he was murdered."

She lifted her chin. "I know what he was to them. Still, it's a lead we need to follow."

He leaned against the brick wall and shrugged. "Up to you."

"Yes, it is. You want to come along?"

"You know I do."

"And it won't bother you."

"To meet Maclin's family? No. Why should it?"

He seemed so cold at that moment, she wished he hadn't shifted his sunglasses over his eyes so she could see them. She could read a lot in a person's eyes.

Like whether or not they were lying to her.

Dammit. Why had Roman planted the seed of doubt in her mind? Was Dante a killer? Could he be sweet and gentle and touch her body the way he had, and be a cold and ruthless killer, too?

She knew he could. Lots of killers were like that, completely fooling the people closest to them into believing they were warm and loving, when in fact they were utter psychopaths.

She didn't want to think about this. Not now.

She went inside, grabbed her file and notepad and met Dante in the parking lot.

"I'll drive," he said. "You give directions."

She could argue the point that he had no legal right to commandeer a detective's vehicle, but decided to pick her battles with him. She slid into the passenger side and told him where to go.

The Maclins still lived in the same house in Kirkwood where Tony had grown up. Anna directed Dante up Lindbergh, then off a side street.

"Nice," he said. "Our lives would all have been a lot different if we could have lived in houses like these."

There were large lots with some smaller homes, and then some bigger, all with perfectly manicured lawns, mature trees and beautiful landscaping.

The Maclin home was one of the bigger ones, a two-story white frame house with dark green painted trim. Triangular gables spread across the top of the home, and a wide porch was set off at the side of the house. A couple expensive cars were parked in the driveway in front of the three-car garage. Anna wondered what sat inside the garage.

"Rich kid," Dante said, wrinkling his nose as he pulled up the circular driveway and parked. "What the hell was he doing in an alley in South City that night?"

Anna met him around the front of her car. "That's something his parents could never tell us, according to his file."

"Maybe they know something more now."

"Doubt it," she said, ringing the bell, "or they would have let us know by now. They want their son's killer found."

Dante didn't say anything, just kept a straight face as they waited for the door to be answered.

"Bet they have a butler," Dante said, whispering in her ear.

She nudged him with her elbow.

The door was answered after Anna rang it a second time. A tall, slender woman with short blond hair answered. She was well dressed—country-club type, Anna would guess, based on the crisp capri pants and button-down silk short-sleeved shirt. Expensive sandals, too.

"Susan Maclin?" Anna asked, revealing her badge.

"Yes? Is something wrong?"

Anna introduced herself and Dante. "We're here about your son's case."

Susan's hand went to her throat, her eyes widening. "Is there new evidence? Did you find his killer?"

Anna almost felt guilty getting the woman's hopes up. "No, ma'am, we're just looking into a few cold cases. Mind if we come in and ask you some questions?"

She opened the glass and screen door. "Of course not."

Susan Maclin led them inside, where it was icy cool, thankfully. The place was open and spacious as they followed her from the front to the back of the house.

"I hope you don't mind the sunroom. It's where I spend a lot of time. It's air-conditioned, of course."

Anna looked at Dante, who shrugged. "It's fine, ma'am," he said.

"I'll bring us some iced tea."

"Not necessary," Anna said. "We'll try not to take up too much of your time."

"Oh, it's no bother at all. I'm so grateful you're re-opening the case. I'll be back in a moment."

She glided out of the room, her blouse seeming to flow like water. The woman was so elegant and graceful. Anna slunk into the chair, feeling the weight of guilt settle on top of her.

Susan Maclin looked frail and vulnerable.

And hopeful, her brown eyes widening with that look a parent got whenever a cop opened up an old, unsolved case. She'd seen that look before on the faces of loved ones whose child or parent or spouse had been a victim. All they craved was closure. Anna's and Dante's presence here represented the hope that it could come sometime in the near future.

Only, Susan Maclin would never have closure for her son Tony's murder.

Shit.

"Stop it," Dante whispered, taking a seat in one of the oversize chairs next to her.

Anna shifted her gaze from all the beautiful knick-knacks over to Dante. "Stop what?"

"Looking so guilty."

"She's making us tea."

"I'm sure it's already made."

"Don't you feel guilty?"

"No. And you shouldn't, either."

"Here we are."

Anna sat up straight and managed to put on her nonsmiling detective's face for Tony Maclin's mother as the woman handed her a glass of iced tea.

"Thank you."

Susan took a seat across from Anna and Dante, held herself in rigidly perfect posture as she faced them. "You're welcome. So tell me what news you have about my son's case."

"Is your husband around?"

Her hopeful look faltered a bit. "I'm afraid Bob doesn't live here anymore. We're divorced."

"I'm sorry," Anna said. "If you don't mind my asking, for how long?"

"Is that relevant?"

"Everything is relevant in a murder investigation, Mrs. Maclin."

"We divorced five years after Tony was killed. His death put a strain on our marriage, as you can probably imagine." Susan swept her perfectly coiffed hair away from her face.

"I can imagine. So you stayed here in the house?"

"Yes. Bob's family is in Chicago. The memories here…they were hard for him. He relocated. Which made it difficult for Sam."

"Sam?" Dante asked.

"Tony's younger brother."

"Oh, that's right," Anna said. She remembered the younger brother being mentioned in Maclin's file. But Dante wouldn't have known about him. She shot him a look and he covered nicely, turning to Susan.

"Does Sam live here with you?" Dante asked.

"Off and on. He's a sculptor, an artist like me, though I paint." Her eyes filled with tears. "Like Tony was going to be, before he died. He was so very talented…"

Anna waited while Susan composed herself, trying to feel sympathy for this woman who'd lost her son. But her son had taken something from Anna that night twelve years ago, and Anna's life had never been the same.

And while she didn't mourn Tony Maclin's death, she felt bad for what Susan Maclin lost because of that night. A son. A marriage.

If they hadn't killed Tony…

"Even after all these years, it's still so difficult," Susan said.

Anna lifted her chin. "Yes, it is."

Susan frowned. "Excuse me?"

"We're sure it is difficult for you," Dante said, taking over for Anna when she couldn't. "I'm sorry we have to put you through this, but we just have a few questions. We're hoping to update the file. You never know when a new lead could help us find the person who killed your son."

Susan pulled a tissue from the box on the glass table in front of them, dabbed her eyes and nodded. "Of course. I'll tell you anything you want to know."

"Tell us about Tony," Anna said. "There's not much in his file. I'm curious, since you live out here, if you have any idea what he was doing in an alley in South City that night. Did he have friends who lived over there?"

"Not that I know of. Tony had a tight circle of friends, all local to the area. He was involved with the art club and with sports. His father insisted he do something other than sit inside and paint, so he played soccer."

"Varsity?" Dante asked.

Susan met his gaze and smiled. "Yes. Bob got him involved with sports when he was a kid. The usual stuff—baseball, soccer, basketball. He wasn't big enough for football when he got older, but he had agility, so he gravitated toward soccer, and was good enough to make the varsity team in high school."

"Did he enjoy sports?"

She nodded at Dante. "Well enough, I suppose, and it was an outlet for his frustrations."

"What kind of frustrations?" Anna asked.

Susan's lips lifted. "It's an artist thing. When you work on a piece, and it's not going the way you want it to, it can be so incredibly frustrating, because it's here in your soul—" she fisted both hands against her chest "—but you can't bring it out on the canvas. He got to let out that anguish on the soccer field. I think it helped clear his head so he was better able to work on his craft."

"He painted. Like you?"

"Yes," Susan said.

Anna looked at the artwork on the walls in the sunroom. Beautiful paintings of women dressed in flowing dresses standing at the edge of a beach, ocean water lapping near their feet while the women searched the water as if they were looking for something. There were birds or sea creatures in the distance, sometimes lighthouses. In some there were children—sometimes one boy, sometimes two, building sand castles or frolicking in the water.

"You paint with an impressionistic feel," Anna said. "They're lovely."

Susan beamed. "Thank you. My work has been on display in galleries all over the country."

"Was Tony as good as you?" Anna asked.

"Better, I think. His talent was raw, but so good. He was set to attend college in New York that fall."

Guilt hammered at her. "I'm sorry."

As if she hadn't heard Anna's apology, Susan went on. "He was so nervous about moving away, about moving to New York and attending college. He seemed so distracted that summer."

"Distracted how?" Dante asked.

"*Jittery* is the only word I can come up with. In and out of the house a lot. Wasn't concentrating on his painting much, which was unusual for him."

"What about his friends?" Dante asked. "Anything change with his friends?"

She sighed, clasped her hands together in her lap. "Everything changed with him before he died. His personality, the way he acted with his friends. I don't know what was going on with him."

"Did you know he was on drugs?" Dante asked.

Anna shifted her gaze to Dante, not sure whether this was the right time to ask that question. But she'd brought him along and hadn't coached him on the questioning, so she had to accept his involvement in the interrogation of Maclin's mother.

"I didn't. I suppose in retrospect it makes sense considering his behavior, but Tony was always such a good kid. And he played sports. I'd like to think the drugs they found in his system was an anomaly, something he'd just done once."

Ha. Fat chance. Anna knew better. If he was out of his normal area and high, chances were he was either looking to buy or trying to sell. "It's possible. What about his friends?"

"Nice kids. We'd known them all from the time Tony was little."

"No troublemakers, no one who stood out to you as someone you didn't want your son to be around?"

"Not at all."

"What about newcomers into his circle?" Dante asked. "Anyone come over or infiltrate his group that you didn't recognize?"

"Not that I can recall, but it's not like we stood guard over his social group. We trusted him. He had a lot of freedoms because he was a good boy."

At their exchanged looks, Susan added, "Sam might know, though. He was only a few years younger and went to the same high school, sometimes hung out with Tony and his friends."

"Is he around?"

"Probably working in his studio. Let me see if he'll come talk to you."

After she left, Anna turned to Dante. "What do you think?"

"I think, like a lot of parents of teenagers, she was blind to whatever it was her son was up to."

"And we still don't know what that was."

"No, but maybe his brother does."

Susan returned with a guy dressed in spattered khaki

overalls and a tattered T-shirt. He had long, shaggy dark hair and was wiping his hands with a rag.

"This is my son, Sam. Sam, this is Detective Pallino and Special Agent Renaldi. They're working your brother's case."

Sam kept his head ducked down and hair fell over his eyes, so Anna couldn't get a read on his expression.

He looked shy, didn't make eye contact.

Or maybe antisocial. Anna couldn't tell which just yet.

"Hi."

"Hi, Sam. I'm Anna Pallino, and this is Dante Renaldi."

"Hey, Sam," Dante said, taking Anna's cue that they needed to be friendly.

"Sam," his mother said, "they thought maybe you could tell them about Tony's friends."

He looked irritated to have been disturbed. "What about them?"

"We need to know who his friends were, who he hung out with prior to his death," Anna said.

Sam shrugged and leaned against the wall, wiping his hands with the rag. "The usual people."

Susan smiled apologetically at them, then laid her hand on Sam's shoulder. "They need to know names, Sam."

"Tim Long. Travis Aducci. Heather Sanderson. Uhh, Mark Charich, Evan Amarola, Jill Serlins…"

Anna wrote the names down as Sam went through the list. He seemed to have a decent memory, since they ended up with about twelve names.

"Thanks, Sam," she said. "I'm sorry about your brother."

"Uh-huh." He turned to his mother. "I was in the middle of my project. I need to get back to it."

Susan shifted her gaze back to Anna.

"Just a couple more questions, if you don't mind,"

Anna said. "Sam, where were you the night your brother was killed?"

He didn't lift his head, continued to wipe his hands on the rag. "I was here."

"With your parents?"

"We were out that night at a party for some friends," Susan answered. "I thought Tony and Sam were both home, but I guess Tony went out and left Sam by himself."

"Did Tony tell you he was going out?" Anna asked.

Sam shrugged. "I was in the studio working on a project. I didn't know he left until my parents came home and asked where he was."

"And what time was that?"

"All this information is in the police file, Detective," Susan said.

"Yes, it is, but we do like to go over the information again, if you don't mind. It helps to freshen the case."

"Of course. Answer the question, Sam."

"What was the question?"

"What time did your parents come home?"

He shrugged again. "I don't remember. Why are you here now after all these years? You didn't find his killer then. Do you have a lead or something now?"

"No, we don't. We're just checking out some cold cases to see if something new will come up."

Sam lifted his head and Anna saw a spark of anger there. "All you're doing is upsetting my mother. You don't have anything new, so why don't you leave?"

"Sam, that's rude."

"So? They're rude for coming here after all this time, bringing up Tony's death again." He looked over at Anna and she saw the anger directed at her, his words sharp and focused. "He's dead. Someone killed him and you don't know who did it. Leave it alone."

Sam turned and left the room.

"I'm sorry," Susan said. "Tony's death really upset him all those years ago. It upset all of us, as you can imagine. It's taken a lot of years to put the pieces back together."

"I'm sorry if our coming here has reopened old wounds, Mrs. Maclin," Anna said. "I think we have enough now."

She headed toward the door, hoping Susan would lead them out. She could already feel the sensation of the walls closing in on her. She needed to get out of here.

"It's no problem," Susan said. "Sam's not always so antisocial. He really is a nice young man. It's just about this…about Tony…that gets him upset."

"We understand," Dante said.

"If we can help at all," Susan said, "if it gets you closer to finding Tony's killer, please come see us at any time."

Anna stiffened and Dante laid his hand at the small of her back, leading her toward the door.

"Thank you, Mrs. Maclin," Dante said. "You've been very helpful. We'll be in touch."

As soon as they were out the door, Dante all but shoved her toward the car, opened the door and pushed her inside. Once he started up the car, he cranked the A/C to arctic level.

"Relax. Breathe. And not too fast. I need your head clear so we can debrief that meeting. No panic attacks right now."

She concentrated on her breathing, on the cold air-conditioning flying at her face. Pulling away from Tony Maclin's house helped. As soon as they were on the highway again, the tension in her body lessened. He pulled into a fast-food drive-through and got them both something to eat and drink, then parked in the restaurant's lot, where they ate silently.

Anna knew Dante was watching her.

"I'm fine now."

"You're not fine. You feel guilty because Susan Maclin is grieving over the loss of her son."

She shrugged and shoved a couple French fries in her mouth.

"Remind yourself what her poor, sweet, athletic, artistic son did to you that night twelve years ago. How he jumped you in the alley, dragged you behind the Dumpster, held a knife to your throat, cut off your clothes and carved a heart across your breast. How he laid on top of you and pulled your shorts off. What he would have done to you—"

She held her hand up. "Enough."

"Don't feel guilty because he's dead. He got what he deserved."

She shifted in her seat to face him. "Did he? We could have handled it differently, could have held him, called my dad or the cops."

"And then what? You saw where they live. That place screams money. His dad's a lawyer, Anna. Did you know that?"

"Yes."

"He would have gotten a slap on the wrist. Probation. And you would have been called to court to testify against him. Would you have been able to do that, or do you think they would have plea-bargained him out of it? The case might have never gone to trial. Rich boy would have been back out on the streets, sniffing coke and doing the same damn thing to another girl."

She lifted her chin, refusing to let Dante get to her. "Stop it."

"Stop what? Stop trying to make you see that just because a rich, entitled drug-dealing prick like Tony

Maclin didn't get the chance to keep doing what he did to you that night you shouldn't feel guilty about it? You expect me to feel bad because we beat the shit out of him and he happened to die because of it? Hell, Anna, I've killed people who did a lot less than he did."

Shocked at his revelation, she frowned. "What does that mean?"

He turned away from her. "Nothing."

"Dante."

"We're not talking about me. I don't feel any guilt over that night. I'm not sorry for what happened. I'm glad we beat the hell out of him. I'm glad he's dead. No regrets. You shouldn't have any, either."

Dante was right. She shouldn't have any. That night twelve years ago had been the worst night of her life.

Tony Maclin had terrorized her.

He might have been the sweetest, brightest star in Susan Maclin's life. But to Anna, he'd been a monster. And that one single act continued to haunt her.

She hadn't done anything wrong that night so long ago. Nothing except try to protect the guys who had saved her life.

Yet somehow she was continuing to allow herself to be victimized by the crime that had been committed on her.

She lifted her gaze to Dante, the one person who had gotten to her first, who had scared Tony Maclin enough to pull away from her before he had done even more damage to her.

She owed Dante her life.

But Roman's words stayed in her mind, coupled with Dante's statement of a few moments ago.

He seemed so nonchalant about death.

Had he killed innocent people? And if so, who?

   Could she trust him? God, she really needed to. They
were growing closer, and she needed to be able to lean
on him, both professionally and personally.

   She had to know. But how?

   How was she going to find out whether she could trust
him or not?

   The only way she knew how to get at the truth, of
course.

   Point-blank.

Sixteen

Anna kept thinking all through dinner, not sure how to approach what she wanted to talk about with Dante.

They grilled burgers outside and she fixed salad. They ate, had some beers and mostly talked about nothing. Dante didn't press her, either, which she appreciated, but she caught the sidelong glances he gave her.

He knew there was something on her mind.

After the dishes, he opened a bottle of wine and handed a glass to her and took one for himself. They sat on the sofa in the living room.

"You want to talk to me about what's on your mind?"

It was now or never and she wasn't one to hold back. She half turned to face him. "Roman thinks I shouldn't trust you."

He didn't seem shocked or angry. "Yeah? What did he say?"

"That we don't really know all that much about you since you were gone, and that despite your FBI credentials, all the killings began when you showed up. And we need to look at all the angles, which include you being a suspect."

He seemed to consider it for a moment, then nodded. "He makes a good point."

That was it? Roman made a good point? She'd expected him to disagree, to yell, anything but quiet agreement. "But my captain verified your credentials."

"Do you know that for a fact? Did you ask him?"

"No. But I also know Pohanski wouldn't accept you on face value, so that FBI badge has to be legitimate."

"Okay."

"That's all you have to say? I've basically accused you of being a murder suspect and you find that acceptable?"

Dante shrugged. "Roman's right to be cautious about me, or anyone who tries to insinuate themselves into your life. I'm glad Roman's got your back and is protecting you. It means he cares about you and he'll be extra sharp looking out for you."

"Goddammit, Dante, you're not taking this seriously. I practically pointed the finger at you as the killer."

He leaned back, relaxed and offered up a half smile. "Is that what *you* really think?"

She gaped at him, then stood, threw her hands in the air and began to pace. "I don't know what to think anymore. You make me crazy."

He climbed to his feet to block her. "Yes you do. You have great instincts, Anna. Use them."

She pinned him with a look. "Is that how I'm supposed to trust you? With my instincts?"

"You want more tangible proof?"

"Yes, dammit, yes, I do. Shouldn't I?"

"Is that what it's going to take for you to trust me?"

She didn't know how to answer him. It was her job to look for evidence, for tangible proof of innocence. Not just someone's word. It didn't matter if it was Dante.

"I have a safe-deposit box. I've had all my military

records put in there by my attorney. Your name is on it as well as mine. I'll give you the key and you can go look at everything."

"My name? What is my name doing on there?"

"You're the only person in my life that I trusted, Anna. If something happened to me when I was…out there, I needed to have someone listed to have access to the documents that proved I existed. If I die, there are instructions that the key to the safe-deposit box go to you. My attorney has your information and knows to contact you in the event of my death. My birth certificate is in there, my military documents, everything I've done— at least the stuff I can talk about. And money. A lot of money."

She collapsed onto the sofa, stunned by this revelation. "Why me?"

"Because you're all I ever thought about during all those years. Every night I was doing shit duty with nothing but a rifle, the sand and the stars, and all I could think about was you. Every assignment I got sent on when I thought I might not come back, you were the last thought in my head. I knew if something happened to me, I wanted word to get to you that I hadn't just disappeared and made nothing of my life. I wanted someone to know—I wanted *you* to know that maybe I had done something that mattered."

She saw the pain in his eyes, the tight set to his jaw, knew what it cost this proud man to admit that he needed someone to care about him.

She stood and went to him, pressed her body against his. "Thank you."

He didn't respond, didn't wrap his arms around her. Usually she was the one taut with tension. This time it was he who stood rigid and unmoving.

"Thank you," she said again.

He didn't budge. "For what?"

"For believing in me. For caring about me all these years."

"I've cared about you my whole life, Anna. I did a shitty job of showing it, I ran when I shouldn't have, but I never once stopped thinking about you or caring about what happened to you."

Tears filled her eyes and she almost broke, not sure she deserved a man who gave more than she could possibly give back. But she knew she had to try to show him the kind of love he needed.

She rose on her toes, cupped his face in her hands and pressed her lips to his, feeling shaken to the core.

She heard the growl low in his throat. His arm snaked around her and he jerked her fully against him. His lips met hers as his hand wound into her hair, holding her head in place as he devastated her with his kiss. His hand roamed down her back to grab her ass and he squeezed possessively, whether to warn her off or bring her closer, she didn't know.

Probably to warn her he wasn't going to accept her backing away, that she'd better be in it until the end, or walk away now.

She didn't want to walk away. She'd made her decision and she wanted Dante.

She knew what being intimate with Dante was going to cost her, what he was going to ask of her. It would be nothing like what she was used to. He'd bare her to the core, strip down her emotions and make her reveal her feelings, everything she tried hard to keep bottled up inside.

The thought of it made her feel naked.

With Dante, she couldn't keep anything locked up.

Not when he slid his hands up her body, cupped her face between them and brushed his lips across hers, his tongue flicking out to tease and entice. She shuddered in a breath, her nipples tight, aching points against the silk of her bra.

She burned for him, needed him more tonight than she ever had before. His confession had scraped raw her need for him. She'd always thought herself damaged, but hadn't realized how damaged he'd been by his past, how much he needed to be healed.

They were a matched set. Two screwed-up souls who gravitated toward each other like magnets.

"You need me," she whispered when he trailed his lips down her jaw to her neck.

He raised his head, his half-lidded gaze so intense it made her shiver with delight that it was directed at her. So much power in that look. A lesser woman might be afraid of all that desire.

A few days ago, she might have been afraid. Not anymore. Now she craved it.

"I do need you. And you need me, too." He reached for the hem of her tank top and lifted the shirt over her head, tossing it to the ground. She followed suit, sliding her hands under his shirt, feeling the searing heat of his skin as her hands traveled upward toward his chest. He grabbed his shirt and pulled it over his head, throwing it on the floor near her tank top. He skimmed his fingers up her arms, then across her chest, circling the heart-shaped scar.

She held her breath when he bent and traced the scar with his tongue.

She'd always hated that scar, hated that she couldn't get rid of it, that it would always remind her of that horrible event in the alley twelve years ago.

Dante lifted his head and traced the scar again with his thumb. Now, the scar throbbed, but in a different way as her nipples tightened with need and an ache for Dante that grew more powerful every time they were together.

"This scar doesn't define you. It's part of you. Part of the beauty of who you are."

She released the breath she'd held. She'd always thought it ugly. Only Dante could make her hideous scar turn to something beautiful as he bent and licked it again, then the seam of her bra, pulling the cups down to capture a nipple in his mouth to suck. Bursts of pleasure made her back bow as she pushed her breast farther into his mouth until she thought she'd die from the exquisite sensation.

When he pulled away she was out of breath.

He found the front clasp of her bra and unhooked it, pulling the straps down her arms and adding that garment to the fast-growing pile of clothes on the floor.

His gaze roamed over her, her nipples pebbling under his inspection. His erection made her throat go dry, made her feel like a teenager again—uncertain and shy.

"We've never been naked together," she said, then cleared her throat because she could barely get the words out.

"That's going to change tonight."

He undid the button on his jeans, then the zipper, and dropped his pants. He'd gone commando. Somehow that didn't surprise her at all. It also made her want to unleash a little feminine growl, because he was magnificent. Everything she'd imagined about him hadn't been adequate. He was built and muscled and thick and pulsing and while her throat was dry, other parts of her definitely were not. Just looking at him dampened her, made her swell and throb and want. He made her body come alive in a sexual way like no man who'd come before him. The way he looked at her had a lot to do with that—like a predatory beast whose patience had run out, who needed to mate and mate now. What woman wouldn't be primed and ready when a man like Dante looked at her that way?

She licked her lips, realizing it was all for her.

He dropped to his knees and drew her cotton shorts and panties over her hips and down her legs, tossing them to the side, then lightly grasped her ankles, slowly lifting his hands upward, over her calves, her knees, then her thighs, spreading them apart.

When he raised his head to look into her eyes, her legs began to shake.

"You are so beautiful, Anna." He pressed a kiss to each of her thighs. "And you smell wild and sweet. Right here."

He pressed a kiss to her sex, his tongue darting out to circle her clit. She placed her hand on his head, grabbed a handful of his hair and gasped as he took a long, slow lick. She lost her balance and all sense of awareness as he pleasured her with his mouth.

"Dante." His name fell from her lips as the only coherent thought in her head.

He moved his hands behind her to cup her buttocks, to hold her solidly, to bring her toward his mouth. She held on tight, afraid she was pulling on his hair because it was just so damn good, but she couldn't stop. She was lost in the sensations, lost in this unbearable intimacy as he took her right to the edge and made her hover there.

"You're teasing me," she whispered, watching him. She couldn't not watch him. It was the only control she had left.

He lifted his gaze to hers and she swore his eyes were smiling at her.

A devilish, wicked smile.

He swept his tongue across her, dipped inside her, and she was lost. Her climax hit with a resounding force, and she tilted her head back and simply let go. Dante held tight to her while she rocked against him, so incredibly, wildly free, so uncharacteristic of her that she shocked even herself.

And when he pulled her down to the carpet and climbed up her body, pressing soft kisses to her hip bone, her belly and her breasts, she was able to catch her breath and wonder how she had lost herself so completely.

But she could do this. She could give herself to him and still retain herself, could show him he was worthy of being loved, and still hold a part of herself intact.

Dante knew the second Anna tensed up again, could feel it in the way her body locked up.

She was a master at control.

Fortunately, he was good at breaking down walls. And he was determined she wasn't going to lock him out, no matter how afraid she was to let him in.

And when she fought to roll over on top of him, he understood.

It was what he'd told her about the safe-deposit box. It had gotten to her.

He stopped her, pushed her onto her side.

"I don't need a pity fuck, Anna."

Her eyes widened for a fraction of a second, then narrowed. "I don't know what you're talking about."

"Don't you?"

She started to get up, but he held her there, draped his leg over hers.

"I can get plenty of pussy, honey. That's not what I'm after with you."

Her chin jutted up and he knew he'd pissed her off, which was exactly what he'd been going for.

"This isn't sweeping me off my feet, Dante."

"No, I'm sure it isn't." He grazed his fingers up her arm, felt the tension coming off her. "But I also know you're trying to control this. You lost control a few minutes ago, and it scared you."

"Don't psychoanalyze me, Renaldi. It pisses me off."

Ignoring her, he said, "I liked you out of control, Anna, your body shaking against my mouth when you came. You threw your head back and all you thought about was your own pleasure."

She shot him a mutinous glare. "Stop it."

He traced the veins on her skin, from her collarbone to the well between her breasts. Her nipples puckered and hardened. "You need to stop listening to your mind and start listening to what your body wants."

He bent and took a long, slow lick of one nipple, rolled his tongue around it, then captured it between his teeth, flicking it with his tongue until she hissed.

He almost laughed. She was the only woman he knew who could be pissed off about being turned on.

When he pulled her nipple into his mouth and sucked, she grabbed the back of his head and drew his mouth to her breast, holding him there while he fed on her nipple. After he worked it for a while, he pushed her onto her back and moved to the other nipple, watching her reaction.

Her eyes had closed, her hands clasped into fists and her body arched as he played with her breasts.

That's what he wanted. Anna engaged, listening to the needs of her body instead of walking through the motions of sex as if it was a road map. She had a lush, beautiful body that was made to be loved, and he knew she'd either had lousy lovers in the past or she just hadn't allowed any man to take his time and give her the attention she deserved.

He was going to give that attention to her, by sweeping his hand over her rib cage, her belly, watching her stomach ripple as he dipped a finger into her belly button, then palming the spot just above her sex, letting his fingers dangle right there, but going no lower.

Her eyes shot open and she watched him warily as he danced around the spot he knew would give her pleasure.

"Dammit."

He was propped up on his elbow, his fingers dancing around her sex, and she was giving him death glares. He had her right where he wanted her, not at all trying to control him, instead focused on his next move.

So instead, he leaned over and gave her a deep, soul-penetrating kiss at the same time he laid the palm of his hand over her sex, then dipped his fingers inside her.

Her body clenched around his fingers as her tongue wound around his. His dick pounded, demanding release.

He could wait. This was all about Anna, about her release, her satisfaction. He wanted her limp and relaxed, all the tension squeezed out of her before he slid inside her.

"You bastard," she whispered as she broke the kiss, reaching for his wrist to guide his movements, to show him what she wanted.

"Yeah," he answered her. "Show me what you want."

She lifted against his hand, searching for more. He gave her more as he pleasured her with his fingers at the same time. Her mouth fell open on a soft cry as she released, the spasms of her body tight around his fingers, her nails digging into his arm.

But it was the way her body bowed that he found so

damn hot, the way she put everything into her orgasm that made sweat break out on his brow as he held on to her, his fingers inside her while she rocked through it for what seemed like a full minute until her body relaxed against the carpet.

Yeah. When she let go, she really let go. He wanted to be inside her when that happened, wanted to feel her sweet release surrounding him. He was damn near shaking with the anticipation of it.

So much for retaining his own cool.

He dragged her off the floor and pulled her onto his lap, leaned against the sofa, and swept her hair away from her face, pulling her down for a kiss.

Her mouth tempted him, always had. Besides the sassy things that came out of it when she spoke, she had full, sweet lips and she knew how to kiss. She wasn't tentative about it and she'd always thrown herself fully into a kiss. He loved a woman who did that. Back when they were together before, it had taken every bit of restraint he had to keep from getting her naked and taking her. For some reason, he'd had scruples then.

Now he didn't, and she wasn't sixteen anymore. He could have her, and he intended to.

Right now.

Anna had barely caught her breath, certain Dante was trying to kill her.

Could a woman die from too many orgasms?

She might like to try to find out.

She was at war with herself, still making an attempt to keep that part of herself locked tight despite Dante's assault on every square inch of her body and soul.

But the way his mouth took possession of hers, the deep relentless kisses that made every part of her throb with need, it was as if he knew her game and he was making sure she fully understood he wasn't going to allow her to hold back.

And how could she when his lips brushed hers like that, when the velvety softness of his tongue rasped against hers, demanding she give him everything?

How could she hold anything back when he used his mouth and hands on her in ways that made her cry out in wild abandon, and yet her body still throbbed in anticipation, wanting even more of him?

And now she sat on his lap, the tender, throbbing part of her rubbing against the thick, hard part of him, and he wasn't even attempting to push her into moving to the next step. Instead, he was kissing her again, as if they had all night to do this, which wasn't at all the usual way she approached sex. By now it would have been over with and the guy would have been long gone.

And she would have been frustrated, wholly unsatisfied or busy satisfying herself.

She sure as hell wouldn't need to be satisfying herself tonight. Clearly Dante wasn't the kind of man to leave a woman to see to her own needs. Since she'd been with him she'd had multiple orgasms. He'd had none.

He finally pulled his lips from hers and as she stared down at his incredible blue eyes, her heart lurched. She traced his lips, her fingers wandering over the stubble of beard across his jaw, remembering what that felt like rubbing against her inner thighs. She shivered.

"Cold?" he asked while at the same time sweeping his thumbs over her nipples.

"No. Hot. You make me hot." Hot and slick and wet and so ready for him.

His lips lifted, which only made him look more dangerous.

"Good. I like you hot. Now climb on and ride me."

Dangerous and wickedly bad. "I'm not sure I like you ordering me around."

He gripped her hips and lifted her. "You can order me around later."

She slid down on him and grasped his shoulders, biting her lip at the feel of him as he entered her.

It was heaven and hell as he filled her, stretched her, and she wasn't sure she'd ever felt anything that made her body tingle with so much awareness. She kept her gaze glued to Dante, and this reminded her why she'd always kept herself disconnected during sex. This intimacy, the way Dante moved inside her and looked at her, forced her to connect with him.

There was no way she could rock against him, filled with him, and not be affected. This wasn't a quick coupling in the dark—it was no-holds-barred, lights-on, open-eyed lovemaking with a man who wouldn't accept anything less than her total surrender.

He drew her forward and grasped her hips, dragging the most sensitive part of her against him.

"You're torturing me," she whispered as she braced her hands on his shoulders.

"Then torture me back." He lifted, burying his cock to the hilt inside her.

She let out a gasp, then curled her fingertips into the crisp hairs of his chest, determined not to let go, not to shatter completely.

"Everything I am is here for you to see, to touch, to taste," he said, rising up to meet her again as he took her hands in his. "I won't hold anything back from you."

Damn him for his honesty, for letting her see the naked truth in his eyes. His fingers dug into her hips and he dragged her against him again, taking her so close she had to bite down on her lip to keep from catapulting over the edge.

"It's only fair to give me the same, Anna. Let go."

Sweat slickened their bodies as they glided over each other. Anna lay on top of him and he grasped hold of her hair in one hand, tugging until it hurt. She liked his possession of her, thrilled to it in a way she couldn't explain.

"Let me have you." He flipped her over onto her back and plunged deep inside her, his mouth grinding against hers the same way his body did, taking full control now.

She lifted her gaze to his, her hands sliding over his skin. "Give me all of it, Dante."

There was such power, such passion in his eyes, but this time, she refused to look away, refused to do anything but meet that power head-on as he lifted up and slammed against her. She reveled in it as the force of his thrusts sent her over the edge. She climaxed with a wild cry, and he went with her, groaning and taking her lips in a hot kiss that shot her orgasm even higher. She'd never felt sensations like this, borne of passion that met emotion.

Breathless, she could only hold on as the waves continued to pound at her from every part of her body until she had nothing left, until she fell, lax and boneless. Dante lifted off and lay next to her, panting as hard as she was.

He grasped her hand and laced his fingers with hers. The contact was so sweet she didn't know what to do with it, so she lay there, staring up at the ceiling, unused to this brightly lit aftermath. Usually it was dark and whatever guy she was with would be in as big a hurry to dress and get away from her as she was to get away from him. There would be no words, no cuddling, just mumbled pleasantries and a quick escape.

Instead, Dante shifted and pulled her leg on top of his body, then laid his palm on her stomach, tracing invisible patterns over her skin. He didn't seem in any hurry to escape.

"You're thinking again."

She turned her head to look at him. "Yeah."

"Can't you just take a minute to enjoy the moment without analyzing what it means?"

"It would be a first for me if I did."

He drew circles around her navel. "Try."

"Everything's changed now."

"Between us, you mean."

"Yes."

"It's supposed to. When this happens between a couple, things change. You can't avoid it."

She turned on her side to face him. "I wasn't ready for it."

His lips quirked. "You can't plan for everything, Anna. Sometimes things happen."

"I know that. In my line of work, I react to the unexpected."

"But this isn't work. This is your life. And you like your life to be orderly and planned out because it's the one aspect you can control."

She frowned. "I hate when you do that."

"What?"

"Seem to know so much about me when you've been gone so long. Am I that easy to figure out?"

"No, but you aren't so different from before. You think you are, but you aren't. You always liked your life orderly, and you liked controlling the situation. That much about you hasn't changed. Everything about who you were didn't change that night twelve years ago, Anna."

Huh. Interesting.

She thought it had. She thought everything about her had been altered by that one act. She'd always felt her entire personality had undergone a radical transformation, that she'd become someone completely different. "Really?"

"Really. You're still the same Anna now as you were back then. Yeah, you grew up. We all did. And parts of you changed. You have to because of what happened. But who you are in here—" He laid his hand on her chest, over her scar. "The soul of you. That's still Anna, the same Anna I've always known."

Somehow, that gave her a great deal of peace.

Seventeen

Anna and Dante worked diligently the next day on the list of Tony Maclin's friends. Several were clean-cut, average students who were so far away from the drug element that after running a diligent background check they were easy to eliminate from the suspect list. A few had moved out of state, one lived out of the country, and two had died together in a car accident during college.

That left four who were questionable and who lived locally. Anna brought Roman in on the list of names.

After the three of them ate lunch in one of the interrogation rooms, they divvied up the four names and decided to head out separately to do interviews.

"I don't think Anna should go alone," Roman said. "Whoever is doing these killings might be tailing her."

She bristled. "I refuse to have a watchdog or bodyguard. You two should be more concerned about yourselves."

"And you need a partner," Roman argued. "Neither of us had someone leaving us love notes and flowers."

They walked out to the parking lot and Anna turned to stop them. "The notes and flowers were left when I wasn't around. Whoever it is doesn't want to face me."

"Right now he doesn't," Dante said. "But that could change anytime."

"We'll get through this list faster if we split up. And I don't want to change routine."

She knew Dante warred with his protective, Neanderthal instincts, but she lifted her chin and refused to back down.

"Fine, but you stay in touch at all times."

She hadn't realized how tense she was until he gave in.

"And I'll take two of the names on the list," Roman said, snatching two files.

"Fine. We'll meet back here afterward."

"At least check in with me when you're on the road?" Dante asked.

She nodded, surprised when he came over to her and yanked her against him to press his lips to hers. "Talk to you soon."

She blew out a breath and laid her hand on his chest. "Was that absolutely necessary to do in public?"

His lips curled. "Yeah, I think it was."

She watched him walk away, enjoying the fine view of his ass before turning to see Roman's quirked brow.

When Dante drove away, Roman turned to her.

"A change in your relationship?"

"I don't want to talk about it." She walked toward her car, but Roman followed, so she stopped, turned to face him.

"I trust Dante," she said before he asked the question.

"Why?"

"We talked, got some truths out."

"Yeah? What did he tell you?"

Things she couldn't tell him. "I just do. You know me, Roman. I don't lay my trust on someone easily."

He shrugged. "I guess you know best. I still want you to be careful."

She laid her hand on his arm. "I know you do, and I appreciate you looking out for me."

"I always will, Anna, no matter who it is. But just because you trust him doesn't mean I will."

"Fair enough."

"You be careful out there."

"I will."

Evan Amarola, the guy on her list to check out, apparently had moved out of his family's home in the Kirkwood area and now lived with three of his buddies in a four-family flat off Grand, which was a far cry from the suburbs.

These were older homes, some in disrepair, and not a lot of trust in the faces of people as she drove by and parked.

The grandmother of one of Evan's buddies owned the fourplex. She was a suspicious old woman with pink curlers in her hair, a faded flowered cotton housecoat and a cigarette hanging out of her mouth. She left the screen door locked when she answered the door.

"What do you want?"

"Is Evan here?" Anna asked, flashing her badge.

The woman, Mrs. Baker, squinted as she read the badge. She wrinkled up her leathered face even more. "What'd he do now?"

"Nothing, as far as I know. I'd like to ask him some questions about a friend of his."

"One of these other losers who lives with my grandson?"

"No, ma'am. Someone he went to high school with."

"Eh. I guess you can come in. He's still in bed. Let me go kick him."

Anna opened the screen door and stepped in.

The house smelled like cat pee, cigarettes and not-recently bathed old woman. Anna was grateful for her strong stomach, because the three together were a lethal combination.

Three cats wound their way around her legs, and she saw evidence of a few more skirting in and around the furniture.

"You can sit down if you want," Mrs. Baker said, the cigarette still clenched between her teeth.

Given the stench in the room, there was no way in hell Anna was going to sit on the furniture. "I don't intend to stay long, but thank you."

"Want some coffee?"

Anna's stomach lurched. "I'm good, thanks."

Mrs. Baker shrugged. "Suit yourself. I'm going in the kitchen to work my puzzles. The kid'll be out in a minute."

Anna stood in the center of stink central and waited, trying to hold her breath.

Fortunately it wasn't too long before a barefoot guy in jeans and no shirt yawned and headed down the hall. His short hair stuck up in all directions and he looked like hell.

"You wanted to see me?"

"You Evan Amarola?"

"Yeah."

"I need to ask you some questions about Tony Maclin."

Evan cocked his head and frowned. "Tony? That was like, ten years ago or somethin'."

"Twelve," Anna corrected.

"I didn't have nothin' to do with that."

"Didn't say you did. What I'm interested in is who he was hanging out with at the time of his death."

"Oh. Well, shit, I don't remember. Tony had lotsa friends."

"Any sell him drugs or get him involved in drug dealing?"

"Drugs? Probably. Tony was pretty stressed about college and it started to freak him out. He was different senior year."

"How different?"

"Nervous. On the go all the time. Started missing school. He was always really good with his classes, but they didn't seem to matter to him anymore."

"You ever see him do drugs?"

Evan looked hesitant.

"Whatever you have to say isn't going to hurt the guy now," she reminded him. "He's dead."

"Yeah, I saw him do some coke and E at some parties. And before school he smoked a little pot to relax."

"Would you say he was doing drugs every day?" Anna asked.

"Maybe."

"Who was his dealer?"

"I don't know."

Anna wondered what Evan did know. According to the information she'd been able to dig up, he and Tony were close. Closer than Evan was letting on based on his answers. "Did he seem to have drugs on him pretty regularly?"

"Yeah."

"Did someone at school deal?"

"I don't know. I didn't do drugs."

Anna gave Evan a sidelong look. "You know, considering you've been in and out of jail for the past twelve years, and all of them on drug and theft charges, I'm going to have a hard time believing that answer, Evan. Want to try again?"

"Okay, maybe I did party a little. But I wasn't dealing."

"I'm not accusing you of being his dealer. I'm also not trying to pin anything on you. What I need is to figure out who Tony's source was back then."

"Why?"

"You don't need to know the answer to that," she said. "But I'd sure appreciate the help."

She could see the wheels turning in Evan's mind.

"Yeah? What could I get for this information?"

"Nothing. Other than me not coming back here every day to hassle you."

His face fell. "Oh."

"You either know the answer to the question or you don't. If you do, I'll keep coming back here, or bring you down to the station, until I get the answer I'm looking for. It'd be a lot easier to get it now. Then I leave and you don't see me anymore. Trust me, you don't want me getting familiar with you and what you do in your leisure time."

"I don't remember his name," Evan said in a hurry. "He was a college student though, some guy who graduated from our high school a few years ahead of us. All the kids used him."

"Do you know what college he went to?"

"Wash U. He was a med school student there." Evan grinned. "I think he was paying his way through medical school by dealing at some of the high schools."

It shouldn't take much investigating to figure out who the guy was.

"Thanks, Evan."

For the first time since this whole nightmare began,

Anna had a speck of hope. She climbed into her car and headed out.

When she pulled onto the street, she noticed another car pulling out from the curb, going in the same direction as her. Normally she wouldn't think that strange— probably someone who lived in the area, except when she turned north, so did the car. When she changed lanes, so did the car behind her.

To test her theory, she made a right turn at the next stoplight.

As did the car behind her.

She kept her movements normal, didn't speed up or slow down or appear to be looking in her rearview mirror. She wanted to make sure she wasn't simply being paranoid.

Damn Roman and Dante for putting those kinds of thoughts in her head, but it wouldn't hurt to be careful.

It was a greenish-colored Jeep, older model, kind of beat up. She wasn't going to call it in until she knew for sure, because if she did and it turned out to be nothing she'd be ribbed for being paranoid.

Then again, there was a killer on the loose, and she was a possible target. She probably wasn't being paranoid enough.

She made another turn, this time right again, doubling back to where she'd started out.

The car, which had managed to stay within a few cars of her, made the right turn again.

She turned left next time onto Arsenal and headed west.

He followed.

At the first street she could she turned into Tower Grove Park, figuring if this was coincidence he'd go straight.

The two cars between them passed, and he turned into the park.

She pulled over. So did he.

Heart pumping, she called it in, including his tag number, then got out of her car, her hand on her gun.

He was already getting out of his car. When she recognized him, her heart rate sped up.

"Stay in your vehicle."

"I need to talk to you."

"Get back in your car, goddammit."

He kept coming toward her. Why the hell was Sam Maclin following her?

"Sam, get in your car or I'm arresting you."

He stopped, held his hands up. "For what? For wanting to talk to you? For asking you why you came to my house to harass my mother?"

"Turn around and put your hands on the hood of your car."

"Jesus Christ."

He laid his hands on the hood of the car. She came up behind him and kicked his legs apart, grabbed a wrist and slapped handcuffs on it, then the other. Then she turned him around to face her.

He was just as angry now as he had been when she and Dante had come to see him and his mother.

"Why are you following me?"

"To tell you to back the hell off my mother."

"You could have handled that with a phone call."

He smirked at her. The bastard. "It's more effective in person."

"Is that a threat?"

"I'm not threatening anyone. You upset my mother by dredging up Tony's murder. She's not sleeping again, taken to wandering the house at night. Leave it alone."

She studied him. "Any particular reason you want me to leave it alone?"

Could he be the one leaving notes on her car? Could he be the killer?

"Yeah. I just told you. It upsets my mother. When she's upset she can't paint."

She stepped closer. "How long have you been following me?"

"I came to the station to talk to you, saw you leave, decided to follow."

"Uh-huh. Like I said, a phone call would have been easier."

"And like I said, it's not as effective. Figured I could talk you out of reopening my brother's case if I talked to you in person. A phone call just wouldn't do it."

He had attitude coming out his ears, and a demeanor she just didn't like. "You're a real smart-ass, Maclin."

A black-and-white screamed into the park and slid to a stop in front of them.

Sam caught sight of the squad car and shot a glare at her. "Great. So now you're going to arrest me for what? For wanting to talk to you about my mom and my brother?"

"There are friendlier ways to have done it, Sam. And you were the one harassing me. You don't follow a police officer."

"You want us to take care of this creep?" one of the uniforms asked.

She studied Sam. He had no fear in his eyes as he glowered at her, ignoring the uniforms. If he'd exhibited even one ounce of fear, she'd have let him go with a warning. But without that, he freaked her out.

Killers showed no fear.

"Take him in," she said, grabbing his arm and handing him over to Lincoln.

"You'll be sorry," Sam said as the officer took him away.

She ignored him and slid back in her car, then headed toward the precinct.

Dante was already back at the station when she arrived. She grabbed a cup of coffee and sat at her desk.

"My guy didn't pan out," Dante said. "He was like a saint, so squeaky-clean I felt dirty interviewing him."

Anna nodded. "Well, I guess that's too bad."

"What did you find?"

"Cat pee, stale cigarettes and unbathed old lady."

Dante made a sour face. "Fun. Did you get anything out of it other than that?"

"I did," she said, and gave him a rundown of what Amarola had told her.

Dante nodded. "That's a solid lead. Now we need to find Dr. Drug Dealer."

"Yeah. Also, I was followed on the way back."

"What?" Dante sat up in the chair. "By who?"

"Sam Maclin."

Dante's eyes narrowed. "Son of a bitch. You grab him?"

She took a sip of her coffee and nodded. "He's in holding."

Dante stood. "I want to talk to him."

She grabbed his arm. "Not right now. I want him to cool his heels for a while. He's got an attitude."

She knew that wasn't Dante's first choice, and from the look on his face it was probably a good idea not to let him anywhere near Sam at all.

"What did he say to you?"

"To back off his mother and the reopening of the investigation."

"Huh. He couldn't have called you?"

Funny that they were on the same wavelength. "That's the same question I asked him."

Dante stared at the back of the precinct toward the holding cells. "Is he worried about his mother or himself?"

"That's what I'm wondering. You think he was in the alley that night?"

"It's possible. He was fifteen at the time. File says he was at home. And he sometimes ran with the same crowd as Tony."

"Guess we should check that out."

"Check what out?" Roman asked as he came in. "Did you get a lead?"

"Yes, and that isn't what we're talking about." Anna filled him in on what she found out from Evan Amarola, and what happened with Sam.

"He tailed you? That's suspicious as hell, especially after the roses and cards. We need to figure out where he was the nights of the murders."

"I'm going to go talk to him," she said, grabbing her notebook and a pen.

"I'll do some backtracking on his whereabouts the nights of the murders," Roman said.

"His mother isn't going to like that."

"And?" Dante asked. "You're not trying to be her friend. You're trying to solve a case."

She stopped, realized what she'd been doing. Her first thought was how this would affect Susan Maclin because she'd already lost one son. What was she thinking?

She had no objectivity here. She lifted her gaze to Dante. "You're right."

Roman laid a hand on her arm. "You interview Sam first, see what you can get from him about the nights of the murders. We'll go from there. I'll do the background on him."

"Okay."

They called for Sam to be brought into an interrogation room. He didn't look any less subdued after spending some time in holding. In fact, he looked more pissed off than ever, and focused his glare on Anna.

"He's got a bug up his ass about you," Dante whispered as they entered the room.

"So I noticed." She and Dante took a seat across from Sam.

"You've been read your rights and you understand those rights?" Anna asked.

"Yeah."

"I understand you waived your right to have an attorney present for questioning?"

He shrugged. "I didn't do anything wrong. What do I need a lawyer for?"

"We need to know your whereabouts on the nights of June twenty-third and June twenty-seventh."

"Why?"

"Do you know where you were those nights?"

He shrugged. "Probably in my studio working on some art."

"Do you know that for a fact?"

"No, but that's usually where I am. I'm working on a project, so I've been spending a lot of time in there. Why?"

"Two people were killed in the same alley your brother was killed in."

"Huh. So?"

Wasn't he a real bleeding heart. "They were beaten to death, just like Tony."

He leaned back in his chair. "Again. So? What does this have to do with my brother?"

"That's what we'd like to know," Dante said.

He shrugged again, refusing to look at Dante and keeping his gaze focused only on Anna. "People get killed all the time, especially in the city."

"That's hardly a high-crime area," Anna said. "And to be beaten severely in the same manner as your brother, in the same location, isn't a coincidence."

A flicker of interest lit in his eyes. He sat straighter in the chair. "So you're saying whoever did these murders is the same person who killed Tony?"

"I'm not saying that."

"So what am I doing here, and why are you talking to me about it?"

She let the question linger in the air, until recognition dawned in his eyes.

"Are you fucking kidding me? I had nothing to do with those murders. I was working at the time."

"Can anyone verify that?" she asked.

"Yeah. My mother."

"Someone other than a family member?" Dante added.

He rolled his eyes. "The studio is at the house. So no, no one else but her."

"That's too bad," Anna said, feeling a small twinge of guilt for going after yet another member of the Maclin family. Then again, he'd come after her today, and in doing so put himself on her radar. He had no one to blame but himself.

"You've put yourself in a bad position, Maclin," Dante said. He stood and walked around the table to Sam's side, then stared down at him. "You harassed and threatened the detective here, and you have a connection to a prior crime in the alley with a similar method of death."

"What connection? Because he was my brother?"

"Because you can't verify your whereabouts on the night your brother was murdered, and now these murders. Doesn't look good for you."

Now the venom in his eyes was directed at Dante. "This is bullshit. You're trying to railroad me because you don't have any other suspects."

"And you're trying to deflect because you killed the two men. Maybe you even had something to do with your own brother's death that night twelve years ago."

Sam shot out of the chair and lunged at Dante. "You're full of shit!"

Two uniformed officers hustled into the room to subdue Sam, cuffing him and slamming him into the chair.

Dante hadn't even flinched, hadn't moved from his spot against the desk. He just smiled at Sam as he was restrained.

Sam glared at Dante, then at Anna. "I want a lawyer."

And just like that, the interview was over.

"Sure," she said.

She and Dante left the interview room and met up with Roman in the hall.

"That was interesting," Roman said, coming in from the viewing area. "He's hiding something."

Dante shrugged. "Maybe not. I was baiting him. It could be he was pissed off at the implication that he had something to do with his brother's death, which we all know he didn't."

Anna nodded as they headed down the hall back to the main squad room. "But he might have had something to do with the current murders."

She stopped. They were alone in the hall, so she lifted her gaze to Dante and Roman. "If he did, he's cagey. Doesn't appear to act as if he recognizes us."

"A good killer wouldn't," Roman said. "He's not going to play his hand."

She let out a sigh. "We'll see how this plays out."

"Let the guilt go," Dante said as they moved back to the desk. "You want this case over with. If Sam's your guy, it's over."

"And Susan Maclin would lose another son."

"Neither of which would be your fault."

She threw the notepad on her desk, irritated at herself for the knot in her stomach.

Dante was right. This wasn't her fault.

"You need to focus on something else," he said. "Let's find that medical student and work the drug-dealer angle."

"You're right. What we need to do is figure out who was connected to Tony's high school who was also in medical school back then."

Dante sat, crossed his legs at the ankles. "Shouldn't be too hard to narrow it down. Not a ton of people go to medical school."

"That's what I figured, too." She turned to the desktop and started her search.

Dante stood and leaned over her shoulder. "Is that the Wash U website?"

"Yeah." She wrinkled her nose. "I was hoping it was going to be easy, but hell, it's hard to even get a list of staff and medical students. You have to know exactly who you're looking for."

She searched a while longer, then shoved away from the desk and stood.

"This is bullshit. We're getting nowhere."

"And you're tense and not thinking clearly."

She shot him a glare. "Don't tell me how I'm thinking. I'm as clear as I can be."

"With the death of a friend on your mind and Sam Maclin added to the list. We'll call the school and get them to release the names of all graduates of Tony's high school within a specific date range who went to Washington University and attended medical school. Then we'll go from there."

She nodded and made the call. When she hung up, she said, "They'll have it for us tomorrow."

Maybe something would pop soon. It was about damn time.

That evening she went home and changed into a dress to go to the funeral home for Jeff's visitation, something she dreaded but had to do.

They all had to do it, and she took comfort in having Dante by her side.

They met Roman and Gabe outside, both of them wearing suits just like Dante.

Gabe came up to her and kissed her cheek. "You look beautiful."

She'd worn a simple black sheath with short sleeves, nothing special, but still she smiled up at Gabe. "Thanks. And you all look classy in your suits. Jeff would have loved to see you dressed up like this, especially you, Gabe." Anna smoothed the lapels of his dark suit and fought back tears.

"Aw, shit, Anna. Don't cry."

She lifted her gaze to Gabe. "I don't know if I can do this."

Roman smoothed his hand down her back. "They said the casket will be closed because… Well, you know."

Anna turned to Roman and shook her head. "It doesn't matter. He's still in there and we all know it."

Roman nodded. "But we're all together, and we'll handle it."

Dante swept his hand behind her neck. Even without words she felt comforted by his presence next to her as they all walked inside together.

What was she going to do when this case was over and Dante left?

She'd deal, just as she always did. She'd go back to the way her life was before he swept into town and turned her life upside down.

No problem, right?

Ellen Clemons was there, holding vigil in front of Jeff's casket. Her eyes were swollen from crying. Anna's heart went out to her.

Anna hated funerals, hated that they represented loss. She'd hated them ever since her mother died of cancer when she was six years old. She hadn't understood then that her mother was gone and would never come back, but slowly it had sunk in that it was just her and her dad left. She'd never feel her mother's arms around her hugging her, never smell her mother's perfume, never see her mother's smile again.

Death sucked. It ripped the people you loved away from you, sometimes well before you were ready for it to happen.

Often way before you were ready for it.

Sometimes brutally. She'd seen it plenty of times when she had to notify next of kin in a murder case she investigated, had seen families crumple when they were given the news about their son or husband or brother or sister. It was devastating.

Losing Jeff to a sick killer? There was no reason for

that, no way to explain it. No wonder those families fell apart when their loved ones were inexplicably taken away from them.

As she tensed, Dante stood behind her and rubbed her shoulders and whispered in her ear.

"Breathe. You can get through this."

His touch, the sound of his voice, reminded her to stay in the here and now.

"I'm fine."

"Yes, you are. Did I mention you look incredibly sexy in black?"

She turned to face him. "That's a totally inappropriate statement for this venue."

A smile tugged at his lips. "It's never inappropriate to tell you you're beautiful. Now relax."

She shook her head, but the rising panic had disappeared.

Probably part of his plan. She'd have to thank him later.

While she visited with those she knew and hung close to the guys, she also surveyed those who wandered in, wondering if Jeff's killer was here. Or maybe he'd be at the graveside service tomorrow. She planned to attend, not only to pay her respects, but to see who showed up.

"See anyone who looks out of place?" Roman asked.

She shook her head. "I don't know Jeff's friends, but we should make sure to have the funeral director make us a copy of the guest sign-in list."

Roman nodded. "I'll go take care of that now."

"How are you holding up?"

She lifted her head and smiled as Gabe moved in next to her and slid his hand in hers. "I'm doing okay. Did I mention that you clean up nice?"

Gabe looked so different, and yet not at all out of place

in a dark suit, his hair combed back away from his face. She was so used to seeing him in a do-rag and tank top, with worn jeans and boots, his tattoos showing, that she almost couldn't accept him looking like a businessman.

"What? I can do suits."

She arched a brow. "Yes, you certainly can. You look very handsome."

He leaned in and whispered in her ear. "Makes you want to leave Dante and run off with me on my bike, doesn't it?"

His comment caught her by surprise, and she laughed, nearly out loud. "Stop it, damn you. I'm supposed to be solemn."

"Bullshit," Gabe said as Dante and Roman surrounded her. "Jeff wouldn't have wanted our tears. He'd have wanted us to laugh and celebrate his life."

"I agree with that," Dante said. "And then he'd want us to kick the shit out of the son of a bitch who killed him."

Roman nodded. "And that's our job, to make sure we catch the bastard who did this."

They were right. Jeff wouldn't have wanted them to be down and depressed. "We'll catch him. In the meantime, we'll head out tonight and have a drink in Jeff's honor," she said.

"And a roll of the dice at his favorite casino," Gabe said.

Anna's lips curved. "Jeff would have liked that. I'm game."

Despite the night starting out so badly, they'd had a great time at the casino, doing shots and shooting craps. By 2:00 a.m., though, Anna was yawning and barely able to keep her eyes open, so she and Dante left. Roman and Gabe decided to play on.

Normally alert on caffeine and adrenaline, Anna was

appalled to realize she'd fallen asleep on the way home. Having Dante in her life was making her lazy.

But it was also nice, she realized as she laid her head on his shoulder when they walked to the front door, to have someone to lean on at the end of a really hard day. He opened the front door, flipped on the lights and did the customary search of her house.

She yawned, though she woke herself enough to be alert for anything out of the ordinary. Everything in her house was secure, so she kicked off her shoes and fell onto her back on the center of the bed, letting her eyes drift shut.

"I'm too tired to even get undressed."

"So you're going to sleep like that? In the middle of the bed on top of the covers?"

"Thinking about it."

"I don't think so."

"I'm immobile. You'll have to sleep on the couch."

"Wanna bet?"

"Yeah. How much you got?"

He grabbed her feet and started rubbing them, and she moaned.

"That's not going to get me off this bed. If anything it'll ensure I'll fall asleep faster."

Except he moved from her feet to her calves. She felt the press of his body on the bed as he straddled her, his hands sliding under her dress to caress her thighs.

She shivered.

"Oh, that's nice. But I'm still not moving."

He slid his hands higher, found her panties and drew them down her legs. All thoughts of sleep fled as her body came to life in a roar of desire, especially when he pressed a soft kiss to her inner thigh.

"I'm pretty sure," he murmured against her skin, "that I can get you to move."

She shuddered out a sigh. "Give it your best shot."

When he put his mouth on her, her hips shot up and she clenched the blanket, lifting against the heat and wet of his mouth. She could only think of the pleasure he gave her. He was the center of her universe right then.

Yeah, he made her move, all right, made her rock against him until she shattered so fast her head spun.

Then he was above her, his face so damn beautiful she had to reach up and touch him, to assure herself he was real, that she hadn't fallen asleep and dreamed all this.

But when he kissed her, when his lips swept across her mouth and the velvet softness of his tongue rasped against hers, she knew it was real, that he was solid and hard and hot against her.

This was life and she intended to celebrate it tonight. After all the death surrounding her for the past weeks, she wanted nothing more than to feel utterly, completely alive.

Dante lifted her dress over her hips and slid inside her in one smooth movement that made her gasp, made her draw her knees up and plant her feet on the bed so she could rise to meet his thrusts.

They were silent, but they didn't need to speak. Their bodies did all the talking as they moved in unison, both of them knowing exactly what to do, what to say to each other. It was as if they'd been doing this forever, not as if this was only the second time they'd made love.

And when he gripped her hips and drove deep, she felt the hot stirrings of orgasm once again and raked her nails down his arms, demanding he give her that release.

He stilled, smiled down at her and then lowered his body on hers, kissing her with an intensity that brought the climax she sought. She wrapped her arms and legs around him and rolled through the orgasm, felt his body tighten and held him as he came, this time not afraid of the intimacy. Instead, she needed it, needed to feel close to him, to feel him shuddering against her as she did against him.

He stayed on top of her, his face buried in her neck as they breathed together. It was almost as if there was something he wanted to say, but hesitated.

She wondered what it was, because he rolled to his side and pulled her with him. She listened to the sound of his heartbeat, content to just be with him.

"I like being with you, Anna."

Somehow she didn't think that's what he'd wanted to say.

She wondered what he really had on his mind.

Dante had lived a solitary existence for so many years that getting close to Anna had come as a shock.

Oh, sure, they'd been in love before, but that had been teenage love. And hell, what had he known about it back then? He'd had no example to learn from. He sure hadn't had much love and affection as a kid, no great parental guide of a loving couple to emulate. His time with George and Ellen had been short. He'd grasped the concept of a loving family, but they hadn't been his from the start. He hadn't trusted in the permanence of it. And then he'd had to leave.

Life in the army and in Special Ops was all about working on his own. He hadn't put down roots, hadn't had time or opportunity to fall in love. His thoughts over the years had always come back to Anna, had always centered on her. He figured it had to do with the trauma she'd gone through and how guilty he felt over leaving her after that night. He never thought it had to do with love. He didn't know love.

Now he wasn't so sure. Yeah, he felt protective, especially with a killer out there targeting all of them. She was vulnerable and he needed to make sure nothing happened to her.

But what would happen after the killer was caught? And what about now?

Making love to her was different than being with other women. He couldn't explain why. It was just…different.

God knows she wasn't easy. She was one of the hardest women he knew. She had issues. Lots of them.

So why, lying next to her like this, did it feel so damn right?

And what the hell was he going to do about it?

Eighteen

"Aha," Anna said a couple days later as she reviewed the tox-screen reports on George and Jeff. "First, the packets found on George and Jeff were cocaine, which wasn't found in either of their systems."

"No surprise there," Dante said.

"Agreed," she said. "But the bastard did drug Jeff. Tox screen verified he had a high enough dose of morphine to knock him out fast."

She handed a copy of the report to Dante, who nodded. "He'd have been unconscious in under a minute."

"Yeah," Roman said. "A lower dose and you party. A high one like the amount found in Jeff and you pass out fast."

Anna studied the report. "Easy enough to get if you know a dealer, or you can get some from a friend. But getting some from a friend usually means pills. This was injectible, not party. The M.E. found a puncture wound on Jeff's upper arm. Someone would have to know just how much to give him to render him unconscious so he could transport him to the alley and finish the job."

Dante grimaced. "So he finished him off while he was out cold? Pansy-assed fucker."

"It looks that way," Roman said. "I'd like to get my

hands on the son of a bitch, give him a taste of his own medicine."

Anna nodded. "Me, too. Who would do this? And what reward is he getting out of beating an unconscious man to death? There's no fight in him. It doesn't make sense. I don't understand his motivation."

"I don't think the killer has a motivation, or gets any pleasure from killing," Dante said. "He just wanted Jeff dead."

Anna closed her eyes for a brief second, mourning Jeff all over again.

"At least now we have something. He used morphine in injectible form. We have a way of tracking him."

Roman stood. "I'll do the legwork on that. Maybe my informants can tell me who's out there selling it. I'll see if I can pull in some favors from some dealers and identify the guy who bought the shit."

Anna nodded. "My guess is it's not someone buying in volume for resale. Probably a quantity larger than individual use, but smaller than a dealer would want. He doesn't need a lot of it. We also need to check local hospitals and see if there've been any thefts of injectible morphine. It might not be a street thing."

"I'm on it," Roman said. "Also, our guy Sam isn't squeaky-clean. He's been arrested a couple times. Once for petty theft when he was eighteen. Another time a couple years ago for possession of marijuana."

"Interesting."

"Probation both times. He's never done any time."

"See, this is what happens when you're rich," Dante said, focusing on Anna. "Remember what I told you at the Maclin house?"

Anna nodded.

"What?" Roman asked.

Dante looked around. The precinct was busy today, but the other detectives were on the phone or buzzing around the squad room. "Trying to get her to give up the guilt about Tony Maclin. I told her if he'd have lived he might have walked."

Roman nodded. "Likely. Money buys good lawyers and a lot of freedom, unfortunately. That's why our boy Sam was sprung right after he called his lawyer."

She shrugged. "We didn't have anything to hold him anyway."

"We need to keep our eye on him. And on the alley," Dante said. "Two dead is enough."

"The alley is under surveillance," Anna said. "We've installed surveillance equipment, plus have extra security driving through there on the hour, twenty-four hours a day. Our killer is going to have a hard time bringing anyone else there."

At least they had that much. Now they had to zero in on him and find him.

She took the report they got from Washington University and studied it. There were eight names on there that had gone to Tony's school within the appropriate time frame.

Dante looked over her shoulder. "Now we need to narrow down that list and figure out which one of them could have been dealing drugs back then."

"I don't think we're going to get Sam's cooperation."

Dante snorted. "Not likely. But I know someone who can help."

She tilted her head back to look at him. "Who?"

"Gabe."

"I don't see how Gabe can help."

Anna stood in the kitchen that night making a salad.

Dante made up hamburger patties while they waited for Gabe to show up.

"Gabe has connections we don't," he said.

She laid the knife down on the cutting board and leaned her hip against the counter. "I thought you had all the connections I didn't have."

"Gabe has all the illegal ones."

"Ah. And you think he might be able to figure out what names on that list of medical students were involved with drug dealing?"

Dante shrugged. "It's worth a try."

"You also realize if Gabe's deeply tied to the mob it's likely he won't tell you."

"Maybe he won't. But when it comes to protecting the people he considers his family, he might throw us a bone."

She took the knife up again and started cutting. "And he might decide saving his own skin is worth more than family. Paolo Bertucci isn't someone you mess with. He has powerful connections."

"Then we'll see how deep the brotherly bonds really go."

"I guess."

Dante knew Anna didn't understand the kind of ties he'd forged with his brothers all those years ago in the foster home. But it had gone deep, at least for Gabe and him, and he'd like to think for the other guys, too. He wished he'd stayed in touch with all of them, but especially Gabe.

He wondered if it would've made a difference in the life Gabe had chosen for himself.

He didn't fool himself into thinking he had that kind of influence on the choices people made or the roads they traveled. Gabe was who he was because he'd chosen it and was content. Nothing Dante did, whether he'd stayed in town or left, would have made any difference in Gabe's life.

The doorbell rang. "I'll get it," Dante said, ever mindful of the killer on the loose. One hand on the gun tucked into his pants, he looked out the peephole and saw Gabe. He opened the door and Gabe grinned back at him.

"Checking me out?" Gabe asked.

"You know it."

"Then you should know I'm heavily armed," Gabe said, sauntering in wearing loose-fitting dark cargos and a black sleeveless top, his hair covered up by an old, worn-backward St. Louis Cardinals ball cap. Even Dante had to admit the guy put out the vibes of a total badass. He was well muscled and looked like someone you didn't want to fuck with.

"You look like a thug," Anna said, moving past Dante to hug Gabe and plant a kiss on his cheek.

Gabe wrapped an arm around Anna's waist to hug her back. "I'd like to think you care, but I'm sure you were frisking me."

She laughed. "Off duty. Promise. I'm even having a beer to prove it."

Gabe shifted his gaze to Dante. "If she's drinking, I'm following."

"Beer's in the fridge. Help yourself."

"What, I don't get served around here?"

"A subpoena maybe, depending on what you spill," Anna said, lifting the knife she'd been slicing with to point it at Gabe. "And depending on how much of my beer you drink."

Gabe grabbed a beer from the refrigerator and popped the top, then made himself at home by sliding onto a bar stool at the counter. "Thought you said you were off duty."

"Never agreed what you said would be off the record."

"Ouch."

Dante laughed. "Better make that clear before you start spilling your secrets."

"Off the record for the night then, Detective?"

Anna made an affected sigh. "If you insist." She lifted her beer and took a long swallow, then resumed slicing tomatoes.

"Roman coming tonight?" Gabe asked.

"No. He's bound and determined to run vigilante over the alley to make sure the killer doesn't show up there. Plus, since he found out there's been no missing morphine from any of the hospitals around here, he's running down the morphine angle with some informants. So it's just us."

"A threesome, huh?" Gabe waggled his brows.

"In your dreams, perv," Anna said, dumping the tomatoes in with the bowl of lettuce. She handed Dante the plate with the burgers on it. "You two go out and start the grill. You're in my way."

Dante grabbed his beer and the plate and waited while Gabe opened the sliding-glass door to the backyard.

Dante flipped the switch on the gas grill and set the temperature, then lifted his beer, taking a drink.

"She's in rare form tonight," Gabe said. "It's unusual for her to be in a good mood. Is that you?"

Dante shrugged. "I have no idea. Her moods are up and down."

Gabe's lips lifted. "She's a woman. That's to be expected."

"You an expert?"

Gabe smiled as he took a sip of his beer. "I've had my share."

"But not one to settle down with."

Gabe stared out over the backyard, took a couple swallows before answering. "What do you think, man? Look at my lifestyle. Not really conducive to having a woman in it."

"You could change your life."

Gabe didn't meet Dante's gaze. "No, I couldn't."

"You stuck in something you can't get out of?"

Now he did turn to Dante. "Is that why I'm here? You and Anna planning an intervention? Because if so, forget it. I'm exactly where I need to be."

Gabe didn't say it was where he wanted to be. Where he *needed* to be.

A big difference in Dante's mind.

"No, it's not why you're here tonight. I know better than to get involved in your business."

"Good."

Dante threw the burgers on the grill, and they drank in silence for a few minutes, until Anna came and joined them.

"So, did Dante tell you about Sam Maclin?"

Gabe shifted his gaze to Dante. "No, he didn't. What's up?"

Anna filled him in on their initial visit, and Sam's following her.

"There's a hornet's nest you shouldn't have poked. Why the hell would you want to go there?"

"To see if we could ferret out some additional information on the case," Anna said.

"Did you?"

"Obviously, since Sam came after me and told me to stop digging."

Nothing seemed to shock Gabe. He sat there calmly and took it all in. "He's a suspect in the murders?"

"We don't know yet," Anna said. "But we're keeping an eye on him."

"Interesting. So what do you need me for?"

"We have a list of the people who went to medical school at Washington University within a few years' time frame of Tony's senior year," Anna explained. "According to one of Tony's friends, a Wash U med student was Tony's dealer. We need to find out who that was."

"You have...connections, I assume," Dante said. "You know people."

Gabe arched a brow. "And?"

"We're hoping you could find out if any of those people are or were involved in drug dealing, distribution... Maybe also find out if this list of friends of his are involved, too."

Gabe nodded at Anna's point-blank suggestion. "You think one of his buddies might have been there that night and might have a reason for wanting us dead? Or even this med student?"

"I really have no idea," Anna said. "But we're chasing every angle we can."

"Isn't this your job?"

"It is. I've narrowed down the names from Washington U, and got Tony Maclin's friends' names from Sam. But you know as well as I do that sometimes people who show up clean might not really be."

He nodded. "Give me the names. I'll see what I can find out."

"Thanks. And maybe you could also give us a lead on the drug distribution in the city and county. If we could talk to some of these people, track any of them back to Maclin or any of his friends..."

Gabe frowned. "You're asking a lot of me, Anna."

She nodded. "I know. I don't want you to put yourself at risk, but if there's any way you can tiptoe around this and still get us some information, I'd appreciate it. It's for all of us, Gabe. We already lost George and Jeff. I don't want any more of you to die."

Gabe looked away for a few minutes, as if he struggled with what was the right thing to do. Then he looked back at Anna and said, "I'll try my best. But they watch my every move. They know my connection with you. So if I find anything, you have to be careful how you use it. Understand?"

Anna nodded. "I understand. Thanks, Gabe."

Dante watched the interplay between Gabe and Anna, like an intricate dance. She knew what to ask, and Gabe knew just how to answer. Obviously they'd played this game before, the mobster and the detective.

Dante was aware of who Gabe worked for. Anna had told him, but until now he hadn't wanted to believe how deeply he was embroiled with the mob.

Though he supposed he shouldn't be surprised. It wasn't like working for Paolo Bertucci meant you were his waiter or a day trader. At least, it wasn't the stock market you were trading in.

When the burgers were done, they ate at the table outside. Anna had made salad and fried potatoes.

"You're awfully good at this domestic shit," Gabe remarked as they ate. "Some guy is going to snap you up someday, fill your belly with babies and lock up your guns."

Anna snorted and waved her fork at Gabe. "I'd like to see the man who can lock up my guns."

"So you're okay with the belly filled with babies?" Dante asked.

She narrowed her gaze at him. "Is that a proposal?"

"I'd be afraid to propose to you when you have a pointy object in your hand."

She laughed. "Good answer, Renaldi."

"You two are so romantic, it's sickening," Gabe said. "Should I leave?"

"No, smart-ass," Anna said. "You're on dishes."

Gabe recoiled. "You trust me with your dishes? There's a reason I eat off paper plates."

Dante rolled his eyes. "I'll do dishes. You two talk strategy."

Anna watched Dante carry the plates inside, a mix of feelings settling over her. She was relaxed, an unusual sensation for her. Maybe it was Dante and Gabe. These were the two guys she'd always trusted the most, and were probably the two men she should trust the least.

Incongruous. And damned disconcerting. She had no idea what to do about either of them.

"What's wrong?"

She shifted her gaze to Gabe. "Nothing's wrong."

He leaned forward, lowering his voice, though Dante was running water in the kitchen and Anna doubted they'd be overheard.

"Bullshit. You watch Dante like you want to lick him all over—and by the way, that makes me kind of want to toss my dinner all over your patio, so knock it off when you're around me—but at the same time you look at him like he's a suspect. What's up with that?"

She narrowed her gaze at him. "Are you sure you're not a cop? You're awfully good at reading people."

He laughed and leaned back. "Yeah, I think you know better."

"I do. I'd be a lot happier if you were a cop."

"You'll get more of the information you're looking for since I'm not. Now, what's going on with you and Dante?"

She couldn't help but let her gaze drift back to the kitchen, where Dante stood, his hands in the sink as he rinsed her dishes and loaded them into the dishwasher. Such a powerful man doing such a domestic chore without complaint.

She didn't understand him. At all.

She turned back to Gabe. "Do you trust Dante?"

"What do you mean?"

"It's a simple question. He's been gone twelve years, then suddenly shows up and people start dying in the alley where I was attacked."

"You think he's connected? Do you really suspect him?"

"That wasn't my question. Do *you* trust him?"

"You mean do I think he could have killed George and Jeff? Hell, no."

"Just like that. You don't even know where he's been all these years."

"I don't have to know. I know him, know who he is and what he's capable of. Out of all the guys, I know him best. He's not capable of it no matter where he's been for the past twelve years. When we were kids, he took care of all the younger guys and wouldn't let anyone hurt them. He stood by me when it mattered most, and I got into some deep shit when I was younger. He could have turned his back and not gotten involved, but he stood toe-to-toe with me and took heat on his own just to keep me safe. That's not someone who's going to start picking them off one by one.

"Whoever's doing the killing is someone who doesn't care about people. Dante cares."

She nodded, watching Dante in the kitchen.

"You're mad at him because he left twelve years ago. Don't judge him because of that. Who made you doubt him?"

"Roman."

Gabe nodded. "Roman's careful of you, like we all are, but he probably sees you getting closer to Dante and he's afraid for you. You know how Roman is. He's always been the worrier. He'd throw any of us under the bus to protect you. You were there for him when he was younger, so he'll want to keep you safe. And he was hurt when Dante left. He's got some issues about that, too."

"That's true."

"And because he was older than Jeff he took it on himself to be the one to watch out for you after Dante and I left, didn't he?"

"Yes."

"Besides, that night in the alley twelve years ago bonded all of us to you. We're all going to look out for you for the rest of our lives. And even if one of our brothers gets a little too close we're going to be wary on your behalf."

"Like Roman did."

"Yeah. The only thing you have to answer is—do *you* trust Dante?"

She inhaled and let it out. "I honestly don't know yet. I want to."

"There's your answer. And you should probably figure it out before you two get any closer."

She smiled at him. "You're a good friend."

He smiled back. "I'll always be here for you, Anna. No matter what you need."

She swept her hand across his cheek. "Thank you, Gabe. I love you."

"Whoa. You trying to steal my girl?"

Gabe leaned back in the chair and propped his feet on the table as Dante walked out. "You know it, bro."

"Well, knock it off. I saw her first."

"No you didn't. Jeff did. Or maybe it was Roman."

Anna rolled her eyes. "You're both full of shit. I saw all of you first, when you were being bullied by those assholes on the football team. And I saved you."

Dante and Gabe looked at each other and nodded.

"You sure did," Gabe said, his lips twitching.

"We'd have been toast if you hadn't threatened them with having your daddy the cop kick their asses."

Anna leveled a mutinous glare at Dante, then at Gabe. "Fuck you. Both of you." She stood and went inside, but a smile lit up her face at the memory of the first day they'd met. She really did love these guys.

Which made her miss Jeff even more. And made her realize that this thing with Dante was getting out of control.

She was growing more and more comfortable with him and it was beginning to make her more and more uncomfortable.

Nineteen

Anna had sent Dante with Roman to work the drug-dealer angle, needing them both out of her hair long enough so that she could go see her dad. She found him walking up the street with Rusty as she pulled to the curb.

"Working up a sweat?" she asked as she walked up the steps to the front porch.

Her father let Rusty off his leash and into the house so he could get a drink. "The knee feels strong lately."

"You look pretty good now that you took off some of that beer weight."

"Hey, I still have my beers. Rusty just works them off me."

She laughed. "High five for Rusty, then."

"How's the case coming along?"

"We have some leads. Nothing major breaking yet."

She went inside and got them both something to drink, then came back, bringing Rusty with her. The dog curled up at her dad's feet and went to sleep.

"So why are you really here?"

Her gaze shot to his. "Can't a daughter visit her father?"

"Anytime. But why are you really here?"

She narrowed her gaze at him. "You're very cynical."

"And still a good cop."

She laughed. "Yeah, you are."

"So?"

She leaned back in the rocker and stared at the street, at the normalcy of the neighborhood she knew all too well, wishing life were as simple as it had been when she was a kid. "I don't know. It's a lot of things."

"So, it's Dante."

"He's part of it. The case is part of it. I just feel out of sorts."

"You're frustrated because this case isn't easy to solve and it involves people you care about. And Dante isn't making your life easier because you can't fit him into one of your neat little organizational slots."

She turned her head. "What does that mean?"

"You like order, and he's chaos. He's turned your world upside down and made you feel things, and you don't like to feel things."

She looked out at the street again. "Hmmph."

"So I'm right?"

"I don't know. Maybe. You make me sound like a robot."

"Not a robot. Just afraid to put yourself out there and risk being hurt. It's not like you've paraded a bunch of boyfriends in front of me over the years, Anna. You've never brought a guy over to meet me."

He was right. She hadn't. Mainly because she'd never had a serious relationship with anyone. "No one was worthy."

"You haven't brought Dante by since he came back, either."

She shrugged. "He won't be staying long."

"Did he tell you that?"

"Not exactly. I just know."

"So you're already ending things between the two of you before you know how he feels about it."

She shifted in the chair to face him. "I just know, Dad. We're not going to end up together. He has his life and it's somewhere else. I have mine and it—"

She didn't even know how to finish that thought. She couldn't see that far into the future, but she did know her life wouldn't include Dante. Why get her father's hopes up by dragging Dante into his life?

"It what?"

"I don't know. We just won't end up together."

"Or maybe you're afraid you won't end up together. That he'll leave you like last time."

She frowned. Her dad was just as bad as Dante at reading her thoughts and emotions. Damn men. "When did you get so good at this relationship stuff?"

He laughed. "Honey, I'm the last person you should be talking to about love. I wish to God your mother was still alive. She'd have been great to talk to about this. But she isn't, and all you got is me."

Her lips lifted. "I'm okay with having you. You've done a great job giving me advice, Dad."

He reached out to grasp her hand. "Thank you, baby girl. But I know you. I know your heart. I know you loved Dante once, and I have a feeling you still do."

She inhaled, let it out and kicked the rocker back with her foot. The rocking relaxed her.

"I sent him away, Anna."

She sat up. "What? Sent who away?"

"Dante. After that night. It was me who sent him away."

She pulled her hand away from her father. "I don't

understand. Dante said he wanted to get away, that he got George to sign the emancipation papers for him."

Her father shook his head. "He said that to protect you, because I asked him not to tell you it was me. I went to Dante, told him it would be best if he left town and put some distance between you and him."

"No. He said it was his idea to go."

He gave her a small smile. "Again, he told you that to protect me. He never wanted to go."

Her stomach hurt. "Why would you do that?"

"Because I was afraid after what happened to you. I was afraid for you. And God, I was so grateful to him for saving your life, but I was afraid for him, too."

"So you sent him away, in what? In gratitude? To protect him? From what? That doesn't make sense."

He rubbed his right brow, something he always did when he was troubled. "I'm not explaining this right."

"No shit, Dad. I don't understand this. Why did you send him away?"

And why did he go? Did her father threaten Dante in some way? Dante had seemed like a grown man to her. But he hadn't been quite yet eighteen. Close, but not quite. And her father had been a cop. He could have leveled all manner of threats against Dante to get him to leave town.

"I told him it was in his best interest to lie low for a while, just in case Tony Maclin's murder was somehow tracked back to him. I was trying to protect him, Anna. You gotta believe that."

She stayed silent, but a part of her was furious at her father for orchestrating all this, for separating her and Dante all those years ago.

"I wanted you to be safe, and figured if I could get Dante out of here, and get you through this mess with

Maclin—keep you and Dante apart, there'd be no way to tie you two to the crime."

"That doesn't even make sense. What about all the other guys?"

Her father didn't answer. Of course. She hadn't been dating them, hadn't been as close to them as she'd been to Dante. This had been his way to separate her and Dante. She'd have naturally stayed away from Gabe and Roman and Jeff at the slightest urging, because as fond as she'd been of them, she hadn't loved them like she loved Dante.

"You did it to break us up."

He had the decency to look away. "Not entirely."

"How could you do that to me? To Dante?"

"I was panicked, not thinking straight. When I saw you that night, covered in blood and in shock, and you told me what happened, all I could think about was you. I didn't care about anyone else but you, Anna. I made the best decision I could for both you and Dante at the time. I separated the two of you to protect you both. You can hate me for that if you want, but don't blame him for leaving. He honored my wishes, believed me when I told him it was to protect you.

"He'd have done anything to protect you—even if that meant leaving you without saying a word."

All these years she thought Dante's leaving had been his idea, only to find out it had all been orchestrated by her father.

Good intentions or not, it hurt.

She stood and went to the railing, and leaned against it, facing the street. "Things might have been different if he hadn't left."

"Yeah, they might have. And they might have been worse. I'm sorry I lied to you, Anna. But I still believe I made the right choice."

She turned around and faced her father. "I can't deny this hurts me, Dad. All these years I assumed it had been Dante's choice to leave."

To leave me. She couldn't bring herself to admit that, not even to her father.

Her dad looked down at his feet. "I'm sorry."

"You saying you're sorry doesn't make up for you tearing us apart."

He lifted his head. "I won't apologize for doing what I thought was right at the time. You were sixteen and you'd just been through a horrible trauma. You didn't need Dante in your life right then."

The sting of tears burned her eyes, and suddenly she was sixteen again. And Dante was the one person she *had* needed, more than anyone.

"You had no right to make that decision for me."

"I had every right to make that decision for you. I'm your father."

"Goddammit." She swiped the tears from her cheeks. She wrapped her arms around her middle, hoping it would help the ache go away.

"I hope someday you'll be able to forgive me," he said. "I did what I thought was right."

She didn't say anything, couldn't, afraid if she tried, she'd fall apart right there on her father's front porch.

"Please don't hate me, Anna."

She pushed back the misery and fought back the tears. "You're my dad. I can't hate you. But dammit, I'm mad at you right now."

"You have a right to be."

She grabbed her phone to check the time. "I need to go."

He stood. "Okay."

He looked so damn miserable she couldn't help herself.

She threw her arms around him and hugged him. He squeezed her tight and she wanted to hang on to him like this forever.

But she wasn't his little girl anymore, and hadn't been for a long time. She let go and took a step back, saw the tears in his eyes and hated that they'd had this fight.

"I love you, Anna."

She kissed his cheek. "I love you, too, Dad."

"Bring Dante over soon, okay? I'd like to see how he turned out."

She nodded. "I will."

As she climbed into her car and headed back to the station, she realized this changed everything.

Dante hadn't left her. He'd been forced to leave.

How was she going to maintain her distance knowing that?

This was why she didn't have relationships. She flat out didn't have time to sort through the emotional aspect of it all.

Especially not now when a killer was on their heels.

Dante would understand that. His primary motivation was finding the killer, too. They'd concentrate on that and push their relationship to the background.

It was the best thing to do for everyone involved.

Coward.

She ignored that inner voice and headed back to the station. Dante and Roman were back.

"There are several dealers working morphine in the area," Roman said. "But only a handful have the mix in injectible form."

"You get names?" she asked.

He nodded. "Dante and I followed up and went to talk to a couple of them. Obviously no one wanted to talk, so we didn't get much. I'll keep trying."

Anna nodded. "I got a call from Gabe. He's got some information for us on the drug-dealing angle, so we're going to meet with him."

"When?"

"About ten."

"I'll catch up with you," Roman said. "There are a few of these dealers I can catch at night, so I want to see if I can talk to them. We need a damn break in this case and if we can get one of these dealers to ID whoever bought the morphine we're looking for, we'll have a solid lead."

"Okay," Anna said.

"I'm hungry," Dante said after Roman left. "Let's grab a bite to eat before we head to the house."

"Sure."

Dante grabbed his keys.

"Dante?"

He turned and smiled at her, and everything about him seemed different.

Was it because of what her father had told her about him?

"What is it?" he asked.

"Um, how about pizza?"

"You read my mind."

They ate dinner, talked, even had a beer, and all the while Anna couldn't help but see Dante differently.

She'd been so angry with him for so long, had thought he'd abandoned her and had only his own interests in mind when he'd left all those years ago.

Now she knew the truth, and it had changed everything.

Or almost everything. The past, at least.

But the present was the same, and the future…

That, she didn't know. And she wasn't about to guess.

She and Dante were going to meet Gabe at her place. When she opened the door, her eyes widened.

"You have a hot date later?"

Gabe frowned. "No. Why?"

"Because you look amazing."

Gabe wore a tight, black short-sleeved shirt, his dark hair free of his customary do-rag tonight. And with his full, muscular physique packed into his jeans, he was simply gorgeous.

And blushing under her scrutiny, which was adorable.

"Stop it," he said and moved inside.

Dante was in the kitchen drinking a beer. He already had one out for Gabe.

"Aren't you looking pretty," Dante said. "Got a date?"

"What the fuck is it with you two? You trying to set me up?" Gabe asked as he pulled out a chair and flopped into it, then popped the top on the can.

"He's embarrassed because I gushed over how hot he looked."

Dante arched a brow. "I'm going to keep a close eye on both of you."

"You want the info I brought with me or not?" Gabe said, clearly irritated, which Anna found oh so amusing.

"We're all ears," she said. "And eyes, handsome."

Gabe swore. "Once more, Pallino, and I'm out of here."

"Sorry. I'll be good." She held up her hand. "Promise."

"I did a little scouting on our friend Tony Maclin's past and who the dealers were in his area at the time. I found three heavy ones who fit the profile—Don Osher, Crey Robinson and Adam Marcovelli."

Anna wrote down the names, opened her laptop and started typing.

"Osher is currently doing twenty-five to life for murder, so he's out." She typed in the other two names.

"The other two are clean. Both have local driver's licenses, so they're a possibility."

"Let me have your laptop," Dante said, then opened up a database that looked like nothing Anna had ever seen.

"What is that?"

"Can't tell you. It's classified."

"Dante."

He gave her a quick look. "Not kidding."

Gabe stood and came over, glanced down at the laptop. "Huh."

"What does that mean?" she asked.

"Nothing. You're like a superhero of information technology, aren't you?"

"I can get around a few roadblocks."

"More than someone in the FBI, I think," Gabe said, grabbing his beer and sliding into his chair. "That's no database I've ever seen."

"Me neither," Anna said.

Her gaze burned into Dante's back, but he didn't look up, just continued to jump from screen to screen so fast she got dizzy. Finally, she gave up and took her chair.

"You sure he's FBI?" Gabe asked.

Anna just shrugged. "That's what his credentials say." She wouldn't blow Dante's cover. Not even to Gabe. If Dante wanted Gabe to know who he really was, he could tell him himself.

"Crey Robinson," Dante finally said, pushing back from the chair.

"He's the one?" Anna asked. She looked at the laptop screen. There was the entire history of one Creighton Robinson and a picture of him in a white coat, looking arrogant like a lot of doctors did.

"He was doing his undergrad work for medical school

while Tony Maclin was in high school. He's finishing up his surgical residency at Washington University now."

Finally. Finally, they had a lead.

Dante called the hospital. "He's on duty tonight. Night shift."

"We need to go talk to Dr. Robinson." She went to Gabe, bent down and kissed him on the cheek. "You are awesome."

Gabe grinned. "I know."

"You also need to be doubly careful."

He wrapped his fingers around her wrists. "So do you. We don't know what his target is other than tracking us down and killing us."

She nodded. "I know. But we'll get him, Gabe. I won't let anyone else die. I'll catch him."

He stood and pulled Anna into his arms for a hug. "I know you will."

After Gabe left, Dante grabbed the car keys. "We can head over to the hospital now."

Anna laid her hand on his arm. "Wait. I need to tell you something."

He paused. "Okay."

"I talked to my dad. He told me he was the one who made you leave twelve years ago."

Dante laid his keys on the counter, then leaned against it. "He didn't make me leave. Nothing would have made me leave if I hadn't wanted to."

He was being noble, giving her dad an out. "You were a kid, underage. He was a cop. I know how it works. You didn't have a choice."

He brushed his knuckles across her cheek. "I always had a choice. I made the decision to leave. I'm no hero, Anna."

Yes, he was. "You left to protect me."

"I left to protect myself."

She laughed. "Why are you making this so difficult?"

"Because I don't want you blaming your father for this. We both decided me leaving was the best thing to do. For you. For me. For the situation. He isn't the bad guy here."

"I didn't say he was."

"But you're mad at him, aren't you?"

There he went again, reading her body language or moods or whatever the hell he did that he was so adept at. She shrugged. "A little. He kept that information from me. He kept you from me. He took the choice away from both of us."

Dante smiled. "That's the teenage Anna digging in her heels. What does the adult Anna think about it?"

Oh, sure, he had to get all logical about it. Damn him. "The teenage Anna refuses to allow adult Anna out of the closet long enough to render an opinion. Teen Anna is still pouting about it."

He laughed, pulled her into his arms and kissed her, long and hard until she melted against him. Her head spun and her body came alive. When he pulled away, he said. "That was definitely adult Anna kissing back."

He kissed her again. "Forgive your dad. It's in the past and that's one thing that should stay there. The army made me stronger and gave me skills and opportunities I might never have had. I have no regrets. Your father's a fine man and I'm grateful to him for what he did for me."

"He said I needed to bring you over. He's mad you've been back in town and haven't stopped by to say hello."

"Let's do that before we head over to the hospital. We have some time."

"Okay."

Maybe that would help. She still felt bad about her dad, about how they left things, even though they'd hugged and said their I-love-yous. Getting him and Dante together again would be a step in the right direction. She was proud of everything Dante had accomplished in his life. She wanted her father to be proud of him, too.

The house was dark when they pulled up in front. It was still early, at least for her dad, who never went to bed before midnight.

Anna frowned.

"Your dad have plans for tonight?"

"Not that I'm aware of. He's always home in the evenings. Maybe he's out walking Rusty."

Dante pulled out his phone. "It's eleven-thirty."

"He's a night owl. Habit from years of working night shift. He wouldn't go to bed before one or two."

She went to the door, rang the bell, didn't hear Rusty's bark. She turned to Dante. "That must be it, since I don't hear Rusty barking. They must be out for a walk."

"How far do they go?"

"Just around the block usually. He wouldn't go as far as the park. Not this late at night."

"Maybe he went to bed early."

She laughed. "My dad hasn't gone to bed early one night in his entire life."

"Okay. So let's check the block."

She started to walk down the path, then stopped. "He would have left the porch light on. And the house lights."

She turned and headed to the front door, turned the knob. The door opened. The hairs on the back of her neck rose. She lifted her gaze to Dante and lowered her voice. "Something's wrong. If he went to the bar or out somewhere he'd have left lights on, and Rusty would be here. He'd bark. And Dad only leaves the door unlocked when he's home."

Dante pulled his gun and stepped in front of Anna. She pulled her gun, too, moving next to Dante. "I know the layout of the house better, and Rusty knows me. If he's in here and he comes running, I can calm him down."

He nodded. "Stay close to me."

She pushed the door open, leaving the lights off. If someone was inside, she didn't want him to know they were there. Familiar with the layout of the house, she moved inside, stepping light and easy through the living room. As her eyes adjusted to the darkness, she noted nothing seemed out of place. That was good. Dante pressed his shoulder against hers. She nodded and they moved into the kitchen.

That's when she saw it, highlighted by the moonlight shining in through the back door onto the floor.

Blood.

Her heart slammed into double time and she broke into a sweat.

Dante saw it too and turned to the side, his gun pointed up as they followed the blood trail from the dining area to the back door. She reached out for the handle and Dante grabbed her wrist. She jerked her gaze to his.

"Prints," he whispered.

Shit. She didn't want to think like a detective right now. Her dad might be out there. Dante grabbed a towel from the counter and handed it to her. She nudged the partially open slider and walked outside.

More blood on the patio. Panic rose and she swallowed past the dryness in her throat.

Not now. She refused to let it consume her. She forced her breathing, in and out, with normal breaths. Shaky breaths.

"Anna," Dante whispered. "Hold it together."

She waved him off and stepped off the patio and into the yard.

That's when she heard the whimper and hurried to follow the sound.

It was Rusty lying next to her father. He hadn't barked, hadn't moved, because he was protecting her dad.

No.

Her dad was at the back of the yard near the bushes. She dropped to her knees, saw the blood everywhere.

Tears pricked her eyes. "Dad."

He was unconscious, blood all over his face and body. His shirt had been ripped open and half a heart had been carved into his chest. The killer hadn't been able to finish. Something had stopped him. She laid two fingers on the side of her father's neck, fervently praying.

She couldn't find it, searched again. There! Faint, but it was a pulse.

"Dad. Daddy, it's me, Anna. Can you hear me?"

He didn't respond.

She heard Dante on the phone. She assumed he was calling for an ambulance and for police units, but it was all white noise to her.

"Anna, I'm going to check the area."

She nodded and leaned over her father again.

He didn't respond and she wanted to curl up next to him right there on the ground and offer him comfort. She swept her hand over his hair. "Stay with me, Daddy. Help is on the way."

She picked up her father's hand and held it—along with her breath—until she heard the wail of the ambulance and saw the lights out front. Dante came back, too.

"Front door wasn't messed with, but back slider was. Uniforms are here, too, doing a canvass of the area. More black-and-whites are on the way, and I've called Roman."

Anna wasn't really listening, at this point didn't give a shit about the suspect. All she cared about was her father making it out of this alive, and surviving the attack.

Dante dropped to the ground and checked her dad's vitals, then shifted his gaze to hers. "He's still here, Anna."

"I know. He's going to make it. He has to."

The EMTs arrived a few minutes later and started working on her dad, and Anna got out of their way. She'd been to enough crime scenes during her tenure with the force to decipher their language. It wasn't good. His blood pressure was dangerously low, he was in shock and he'd lost a lot of blood. They put him in the ambulance and headed off.

"Go," Dante said. "I'll wait for Roman to show up. You keep watch over your dad."

She nodded.

"Anna."

She stopped.

"I know he's your father and you have every kind of emotion tied up in this. But keep your eyes open at the hospital. If your dad saw this guy, the killer knows it and he may be on the lookout to finish the job he started. I'll make sure they send a uniform to watch over him, too."

She nodded and hurried off to her car so she could follow the ambulance to the hospital.

She wasn't leaving her father's side. Not until he woke up.

And he would wake up.

He had to.

Dante paced the back porch, Rusty at his side. He curled his fingers in the dog's fur. A perfect witness. He was sure the dog had seen everything.

"Wish you could tell us who did this, Rusty." Because

so far no one else could. Anna's father had been found in the backyard, but the yard was surrounded by a fence and tall trees, obscuring the vision of his neighbors on either side. Dante had gone to talk to both. One had been inside watching television and hadn't heard or seen anything. The ones on the other side weren't home, and there was a park behind his house. Uniforms were canvassing the rest of the neighborhood, but so far had come up with nothing.

How had this night gotten so fucked up? He dragged his fingers through his hair and wished he could be at the hospital right now with Anna. No matter how many times he lifted his phone out of his pocket, the display was empty of messages from her. Nevertheless, he pulled it out again.

And again, nothing. Did that mean she had nothing to tell him, or was she in a corner somewhere having a panic attack?

He had to get to her.

But he also wanted this crime scene to yield something. Not only had Roman showed up, so had Pohanski, once he'd heard it was Anna's father who'd been the victim of the latest attack.

Pohanski supervised the crime scene himself, breathing down everyone's neck to make sure not a single thing was missed. Then he pulled Dante and Roman aside as the CSU team made their sweep.

"What the living fuck is going on here?" he asked.

Dante filled him in on what they'd found at Frank Pallino's house.

"So someone broke into his house, beat up Frank and started to cut him, but something stopped him."

"Yeah, it looks that way," Dante said. "Maybe a noise, or maybe it was Frank's dog, or it could have been Anna and me showing up. There's no way to tell what it was that sent him running out of here before he finished the job."

"He also changed the venue. Not the alley this time," Pohanski said.

"I don't think he could have gotten Frank to the alley where the first two murders occurred, since we've had it under surveillance," Roman said. "We've beefed up security there, with cameras, lights and patrol units putting in twenty-four-hour rotation."

"Well, that worked, but it didn't help Frank any." Pohanski shook his head. "This is a nightmare."

Dante couldn't disagree.

"Why Anna's father?" Pohanski asked.

Roman looked to Dante, who took point on this one. Good thing he was such a master at lying. "It has to be about Anna. The flowers, the notes, people she knows and is close to. Now her father."

"She wasn't close to or related to George Clemons."

"No, but we all were," Roman said. "And that got Anna involved with the case."

Pohanski nodded.

"And then the notes and flowers started. He was trying to get her attention. Now her father. My guess is he's either targeting Anna, or by killing her father the suspect wants her distracted, her attention diverted from the case."

"He's going to get his wish," Pohanski said. "With her father in the hospital there's no way she's going to be able to put a hundred-percent focus on working the case."

That's what Dante was afraid he'd do. "You pull her off this case it'll kill her."

Pohanski leveled his gaze on Dante. "Better than the suspect doing it. Tell her to spend time with her dad. She doesn't like it she can come see me. Right now she's on leave."

Fuck. Dante didn't want to be the one to deliver that news. "I'm heading to the hospital. You keep me informed if you find anything?"

Pohanski waved him off. Dante was torn between wanting to be on the crime scene every second and going over the area with a magnifying glass with the techs, and needing to be with Anna.

"I'll let you know what we find," Roman said. "You let me know about Anna's dad."

Dante nodded. "Thanks."

He drove to the hospital, found out that Frank had been moved up to the ICU.

At least he was still alive.

But when he walked into the room and saw Frank lying there, Dante's stomach sank.

His face was swollen and bruised and so were his arms. The parts of him that weren't battered were as white as the sheet he lay on. He was hooked up to bags of blood, lines running out of his body, plus a ventilator that looked to be doing the breathing for him.

Shit.

Anna sat at his bedside rubbing his arm. She didn't look in any better shape than her father, minus the bruises and wiring.

"Hey," Dante said as he stepped into the room.

Anna lifted her gaze to his. "Hey. Where's Rusty?"

"Your dad's next-door neighbor—the one with the black Lab—is taking care of him for now."

She nodded. "Good. Thank you."

Dante stayed in the doorway. "How is he?"

She stood, and they walked outside the curtained room

together and down the hall, pressing the button to leave the ICU.

Only then did Anna's shoulders slump.

"Need some coffee?" he asked, wrapping his arm around her.

She shook her head. "I'm fine."

He didn't take it personally; he understood the trauma and anger. "How's your dad?"

"It's not good. Massive internal bleeding, broken ribs, damage to his lungs, broken legs. The suspect kicked him in the head, so there's a brain injury, too."

Dante sucked in a breath and tried to tamp down the fury that welled up inside him.

"He never woke up. I never got to say anything to him." Her voice wavered as she lifted tear-filled eyes to him. "The doctors told me there's no brain-wave activity. He's not going to wake up, Dante."

His fury turned to pain that wrapped itself around his heart and squeezed tight. "I'm so sorry, Anna."

Despite the wall of brick her body presented, he pulled her into his arms anyway and held her. "We'll make him pay, baby."

She lay against him, unmoving. "I have to disconnect him. His organs are so damaged most of them aren't usable for donation, but they can use bone and tissue. Dad would have wanted that."

He smoothed his hand down her back. "You ready for that?"

She pushed away, her expression so cold it worried him. "It's not like letting him linger is going to bring him back. He'd be mad at me if I did that, and I'd only be doing it for me, not for him. He's gone."

"God, Anna. I'm sorry."

There was a fire in her eyes as she looked up at him. "So am I. He didn't deserve this. It's my fault."

"What? How can this be your fault? It's the killer's fault. Not yours."

"If I'd caught him, my dad would still be alive and wouldn't have had to endure the beating he got. No one deserves that. George didn't, Jeff didn't, and sure as hell my father didn't."

She wasn't thinking rationally. Dante knew it, and yet he wanted to shake some sense into her. "This isn't your responsibility to bear."

She waved her hand. "Whatever. I need to go sit with him."

"I'll go with you."

"No. I need to be alone with him if you don't mind."

"You shouldn't be alone, Anna. Not right now."

She pinned him with a hard stare. "Look, Dante, I appreciate you being here for me. But I can handle this. I'm fine."

"You're not fine."

"Don't think you know what's best for me. You don't."

She jammed the button and told the desk nurse her name. The door buzzed and she opened it. "Leave me alone for a while, okay? I need this."

She closed the door behind her and left Dante standing in the hallway by himself.

He'd never felt more useless.

Anna held her father's hand, letting her fingers linger on his pulse, his life force.

Even though he wasn't really in the shell of his body anymore. Not his brain anyway. Some monster had destroyed him, had taken the laughing, sweet, wonderful man she knew and killed him.

"I'm sorry I didn't find the killer in time to save you, Daddy," she said, squeezing his hand. "I'm sorry I failed."

She hated the tears that seemed to be falling endlessly. She grabbed another tissue and wiped them away.

"I know you wouldn't want me to cry. You'd tell me to stay strong, not to grieve and to get my ass back to work." She rubbed her fingers over his hand. "It'll be hard for me to do that, but I will. I'll make him pay for it, Dad."

No response. Logically she knew there wouldn't be one, but she couldn't help but hope for a miracle. A tiny movement of his fingers, a smile, anything that would give her hope that he was still in there, even though the sensible, adult part of her knew all hope was lost.

She shuddered in a breath, pushing away the child within her that just wanted her daddy to wake up.

"I'm going to take care of Rusty for you, so you won't have to worry about that. He's going to be my dog. I promise I'll look after him."

Her only link to her father would be that dog. She'd cherish Rusty as if he was her baby.

She rose and climbed onto the bed to lie next to her father. What would it hurt? She couldn't damage him. He was already gone, had a peaceful look on his face despite all the bruising from the beating.

She reached up to touch his face, willing him to open his eyes, to smile at her, to say it was all a joke.

But he didn't move, didn't open his eyes.

"What am I going to do without you, Daddy? I already miss you so much. Who am I going to go to for advice when I need it?"

The whir and beep of the machines that did his breathing for him reminded her that her father was, in essence, a machine now, kept alive by technology.

Still, he felt warm to her. His body against hers was her

last few minutes of comfort, just as he'd always comforted her with a hug or by sitting next to her whenever she was hurting.

And when the surgical team came in to prepare him for donation, she slid out of bed, kissed her dad's forehead and let them take him away. She sat in the chair in the empty room that felt so much emptier now without his presence.

"I love you, Dad. Say hi to Mom for me."

She bent her chin to her chest and sobbed.

Twenty

Anna managed to get through her father's funeral, through smiling and small talk with all the well-wishers who'd brought food and condolences the days before and after. She was polite, she made conversation, did all the things that would have made her father proud.

The guys were all there with her. Dante, Gabe and Roman stayed by her, bolstered her when she thought she wouldn't be able to do it. She'd tried to shake them off, tried to do this alone, but they refused to let her. She could go it alone if she wanted to, damn them all.

She loved them for it, because she wouldn't have been able to get through those grueling days without them.

Rusty had come home with her the day after the funeral, seemingly lost to be at her place instead of her dad's. He looked for her father in every room, and then finally seemed to realize that his master was gone and attached himself to her instead.

Two lost souls without their daddy. Rusty would look up at her with his soulful brown eyes, the saddest look on his face.

Yeah, she understood. That look broke her heart, and as she wandered aimlessly around the house, or did some

packing up around her dad's, one thing became clear—
she absolutely had to get back to work.

She thought endlessly of ways to get back on the case
so she could find the bastard who killed her father.

It was the only thing that compelled her to get up in
the morning, get in the shower and get through the day—
find the killer.

But Pohanski refused to relent, insisted she needed
more time to heal before she came back to the job.

Fuck the healing. She needed to work. She'd heal when
they caught the killer.

And she was already tired of babysitters. Roman had
come over this morning to have coffee with her. She
loved these guys, really she did, but she was tired of them
watching over her, staring at her as if they expected her
to snap at any moment.

Right now he sat at her kitchen table rolling his
coffee cup between his hands, his attempts at small talk
woefully pathetic. She wanted to talk about the case,
about the progress in finding her father's killer. They
wouldn't tell her anything.

"So Tess has a new client," Roman said.

She had to make an attempt to at least act interested.
"She does? That's great."

"Yeah. First Third Bank, their corporate branch, which
means she's going to be busy for the next few months
doing their books."

"I imagine she will be. How are the two of you doing?"

He smiled. "Pretty good, but you know how that goes.
Since this case began I've hardly had any personal time.
And now she's got this new client. So I'm busy, she's
busy. We don't get to see each other as much as either of
us would like."

"Yeah, I know how that goes." Really, she didn't, but

she was glad Roman had someone like Tess in his life. "If you like her, you'll make it work."

Then silence. Blissful silence. She glanced down at the display on her cell phone. "You on duty today?"

"Honey, we're all on duty until this killer is caught. Pohanski is on the rampage about it since—well, since your dad. He's got us all working double shifts. I just wanted to stop by to see if you're hanging in."

"I'm hanging in just fine, Roman. You really don't need to check up on me."

He slid his hand over hers. "I don't mind checking up on you. I know how hard this has been on you."

It would be a lot less hard if everyone stopped reminding her of it. "I'm doing all right. I've been clearing some of the junk from my dad's house. Figure I'll sell the place at some point."

Rusty came into the kitchen, rounded the table and sat by Anna. She rubbed his ears.

"How's the dog?" Roman asked.

"He's okay. Sad. Misses my dad, just like I do. I try to give him extra attention and love."

Roman nodded. "Same thing you need."

She laughed. "Is that why you're here?"

His expression went serious. "I care about you. You know that. And a little extra attention is exactly what you need right now. You never look after yourself."

"What I really want to do right now is get back on the job."

Roman frowned. "You sure that's a good idea so soon?"

"I think it's a great idea. I'm going crazy here."

He twined his fingers with hers. "I know you think you are, but it takes time to heal after losing someone."

She almost shot off that he wouldn't know anything

about that since he'd never had any family, but closed her mouth. Was she really that far on the ledge that she would hurt someone she loved? She had to get out of here before she burned bridges permanently. "It does. I know it does. But you know me, Roman. I don't idle well."

He smiled at that. "No, you don't. But I worry about you."

"You all worry too much about me. I'm happiest when I'm working."

And unhappiest when she had to lurk within her own thoughts and dark memories.

Dante stepped out of the bedroom, dragging her away from that darkness.

"Hey," Roman said, standing.

"What's up?" Dante asked.

"Just came by to say hi to Anna before I headed off to work." Roman put his cup in the sink and gave her a hug and kiss on the cheek.

"Thanks for coming over. I'm fine, really."

"You need anything, holler."

"Will do." She walked Roman to the door and opened it, smiling at him and hoping she could get him out the door.

She didn't understand when his smile died.

"What?"

She followed his gaze, going cold at the sight of the flowers just outside the door.

"No."

"Anna, let me take care of this," Roman said.

Dante came to the door, saw the flowers. "Fuck." He took Anna's arm, but she wrenched it away.

"Enough. Enough of this." She grabbed the flowers, not caring that she was ungloved, that they hadn't been tested for prints. She walked out to the trash can, opened the lid and dumped them and the card inside, then stalked back into the house.

Dante and Roman walked in after her.

"You think that was such a good idea?" Roman asked.

She whirled on him. "You know what? I don't care. I don't want to know what was in the note and I don't give a shit about the flowers. I don't care about fingerprints because I already know he didn't leave any. The son of a bitch killed my father. Goddammit, he killed my father." She fell onto the couch and lifted her chin, daring either of them with her glare to go out there and retrieve those flowers and the note.

Roman raised his hands. "Okay. I understand."

"I'll catch up with you," Dante said, then showed Roman to the door.

He closed the door and came into the room to sit down with her.

"I'm not going out there to get that note," she said.

"Okay."

Dante went into the kitchen. She followed him.

"You think I should."

He grabbed a cup of coffee. "I didn't say that."

"But you think I should."

He took a couple swallows. "I don't think you should do anything you're not comfortable with doing. You can leave the fucking flowers and the note in the trash if you want. I don't care."

"But there might be a lead in there."

He didn't say anything.

"He might have said something in the note that may tell us something."

He still didn't say anything.

"Goddammit." She went to her kit and grabbed gloves, evidence bags and tweezers, walked outside to the trash and grabbed the note. She bagged the flowers, then brought the note inside and into the kitchen. Dante's expression remained benign.

"What does it say?"

"Haven't opened it yet. I wanted to get it into the bag first."

She pulled the envelope open—it was unsealed, like the others—so she grabbed the end of the card with the tweezers and lifted it partially out of the envelope.

I did it for you, Anna.

Her stomach rolled and her hands shook.

Dante took the evidence bag with his gloved hands and laid it on the table, slipped the card back into the envelope with the tweezers and sealed it up.

All she could do was stare at it as her breathing increased.

Not for me. He didn't do it for me.

She closed her eyes and her father's smiling face swam before her. She felt the dizziness and pushed it away.

Not now. She wasn't going to wallow in grief anymore. This son of a bitch was going down.

"Anna."

She opened her eyes and glared at Dante, her teeth clenched so tightly it made her jaw hurt.

"Don't let him get to you. This is exactly the kind of reaction he wants from you."

"I'm fine. He's getting no reaction from me."

He didn't believe her and she knew it. "I'll take this in and drop it off, see if maybe this time he left a print."

"Whatever." She wanted to explode. At Dante. Wrong person to take it out on, but he was the only one here.

He reached for her, but she slapped his hand away. He walked out to finish getting ready to leave.

She'd hurt him, just as she'd been hurting him since her father died.

She'd been brutal to him the past couple weeks, had hardly said anything to him. And when she did speak to him it was in short, clipped replies, or she was a downright bitch.

Yet he was still here. He'd stayed with her, held her hand even when she didn't want him to. Despite cursing at him, screaming at him and telling him over and over again she wanted him out of her house and out of her life, he'd been a rock-solid presence, not once raising his voice to her in retaliation.

Maybe he liked abuse. Or maybe he realized she was grieving and he was letting her get it all out of her system at him.

He came back and filled one of the go cups with coffee.

"You're leaving?" she asked in that same angry tone she'd used on him every time she talked to him.

"Yeah. Going to follow up a lead."

Making a decision, she stood. "I'm going with you."

He arched a brow. "You're not cleared to go back to work."

"That's just a formality. Pohanski will clear me."

"You think so?"

"Of course." She picked up the phone and dialed Pohanski's desk. He picked up on the second ring, said he was happy to hear from her, asked her how she was doing.

"I'm ready to come back to work, sir."

"Are you sure? We can spare you if you need some extra time."

"You can't spare me. Roman told me you're working everyone on double shifts. You need me."

"That's true. We do. We need you to work some of the other cases while we have people on your father's case, and the related killings."

She paused. "Captain, I want back on this case."

He didn't pause. "Not gonna happen, Pallino. You're not going to work your father's murder, and it's directly related to the alley killings. You're off that case."

"Sir—"

"This isn't open to discussion. You want to come back to work, I have a shitload of it for you. But it won't be *that* case. Are we clear?"

"Yes, sir."

She hung up and turned to face Dante. His expression remained impassive.

"You can't work your father's case."

She grabbed her gun and holster. "And since when are you a stickler for the rules?"

He shrugged. "Fine with me. I don't report to your captain."

If glares could shoot bullets he'd be dead on the floor right now. "Fuck you, Dante. I've been ready since the day we buried my dad."

He turned and walked out the front door to his car. She followed, fuming silently as she slid into the passenger side.

"Shit. Give me a minute," she said, then hurried back into the house, ruffling her fingers over Rusty's fur as she let him out the back door and filled his water bowl out there.

"I'll be back later, Rusty. You be a good boy."

When she came back out and buckled her seat belt, Dante's lips quirked.

"What?" she asked.

"Forget you have a kid to take care of now?"

"You are so funny. Just drive."

He didn't say anything as they drove, which was probably a good thing considering she was teetering on the edge of another unreasonable outburst.

Then again, it wasn't his fault that she'd wandered around in a fog the first week after her dad died. And she'd had to get some papers from her father's house, and start figuring out what she was going to do with all his furniture, and then the house, too. So maybe she did have some stuff to deal with, and jumping right back into work wouldn't have been a great idea.

And now she couldn't work the case she'd been on since the beginning?

Damn Pohanski anyway. She was going to work it, even if she did it under the table.

He dropped off the evidence at Forensics first, then came back to the car. She was sitting there with her arms folded, still stewing.

"Done pouting over there yet?"

She shot him a look that he paid no attention to. "I'm not pouting."

"Good. When you're done not pouting we can strategize."

It was a good thing his balls weren't in kickable range. "About what?"

"Dr. Crey Robinson."

Robinson, the doctor they had been heading over to talk to the night they made the detour to her father's house first—the night her father had died. "Did you meet with him while I was off duty?"

"No. After…after that night he left town to attend a medical conference, then on vacation out of the country."

How convenient. And suspicious. "Is he back now?"

"Yeah. Got back two days ago and is working today. That's where we're headed."

"Okay."

Dante motioned with his head to the folder lying on the seat between them. "That's his file if you want to refresh."

She grabbed it, reviewed Robinson's school history and talked it over with Dante while they were driving. By the time they parked at the medical center, she was ready.

More than ready.

She didn't think she'd have to walk into a hospital again so soon after losing her dad. The stark whiteness of everything was so incongruous to the blackness of death she'd experienced within the walls of the hospital where she lost her father.

Her throat tightened and she stopped in the middle of the hall. Something wasn't right. The walls were moving. She blinked a couple times, then reached out for Dante as the overwhelming dizziness hit her.

Shit.

She vaguely heard the sound of Dante's voice, felt his arm around her as he led her to a nearby chair and gently pushed her head down. She rested her forearms on her knees.

"Anna, breathe. You forgot to breathe. Slow and easy."

His hand was cold and so was the corridor they sat in. She needed that. It helped.

"You can stop this before it starts. Remember, we have work to do."

She couldn't do it. She had to go home, wanted to forget all about hospitals and death and losing people she loved.

Sweat beaded and slid down her back. "It's hot in here. I can't breathe."

"It's not hot in here. It's cold. And you *can* breathe. You control it. Slow. Breathe slow. We have work to do, Anna. Stop this and let's get to work."

His words penetrated. Work. They had to talk to Dr. Robinson. If she went home and crawled into the fetal position, they'd never find out who killed her dad. And George and Jeff.

She wouldn't allow her weakness to win. She closed her mouth and controlled her breath.

"She okay?" she heard a female voice ask.

"She's fine. Just a panic attack. She hates hospitals."

Whoever it was laughed. "Me, too, and I work here."

"You're doing it. Bring yourself out of it," Dante said, not coddling her, his voice firm.

The haze began to clear and she finally began to feel the cool air surrounding her. The tightness in her chest loosened and the dizziness lifted enough that she could raise her head. She met Dante's gaze.

"You okay now?"

She nodded.

"Sit right here. I'll go get a bottle of water."

By the time Dante came back she felt in control again. "I'm okay."

"Sit here a minute anyway and take a couple sips."

She did, and then she stood, her legs not even wobbly. She capped the bottle and shoved it in her bag, then turned to Dante. "Thanks."

"No problem. Let's go find Robinson."

He never treated her as if she was weak or a hindrance. And she'd treated him like shit for almost two weeks.

She didn't deserve having someone like him in her life.

She grabbed his hand, pulled on it. "Dante, wait."

He stopped, frowned. "What?"

She drew him to her, wrapped her arms around him and laid her head on his chest. She tilted her head back and stared into his most gorgeous face. "I've been a bitch. You've been patient. *Sorry* seems like such an inept word. I can't thank you enough for being there for me."

He dragged his thumb over her jaw, then her bottom lip, making her quiver.

"You lost your dad. You were entitled to be as big a bitch as you wanted to be. You don't have to apologize for that." He bent and brushed his lips over hers.

She sighed against him, leaning her body into his chest.

He broke the kiss and stared down at her with a deeply sensual look. "You keep kissing me like that and I'm going to find a supply closet and we'll end up playing doctor instead of interviewing one."

Feeling better than she had in a long time, she said, "I like this playing-doctor idea."

He cocked her a grin. "Come on."

They found the neurology department, showed their badges and asked a woman at the desk to page Crey Robinson. She informed them he had just finished up a surgery, so there might be a short delay.

Short delay her ass. They waited two hours with no word on how soon it would be until Dr. Robinson would show.

And she really hated hospitals.

"You know I'm going to have to take the lead on this because you're not supposed to be on this case," Dante said.

Anna held back her irritation. It wasn't in her nature to be secondary to anyone, and she was so ready to sink her teeth into Crey Robinson.

She hated that it had to be like this. Damn Pohanski.

"I know," she said.

Finally, a tall, very handsome man with shaggy dark hair and black glasses sauntered down the hall toward them. With his striking good looks and air of supreme confidence, Anna was surprised women weren't swooning as he walked by.

She knew the type. He presented an air of I-am-a-god-and-you-should-worship-me. She'd seen it before in doctors she had to question in cases.

This should be fun.

He came to a halt in front of them. "I'm Dr. Creighton Robinson, chief resident of neurosurgery. You wanted to see me?"

Anna started forward, but Dante flipped his badge. "Special Agent Dante Renaldi of the FBI. This is my colleague from the St. Louis Police Department, Anna Pallino. Is there someplace we can talk?"

He frowned. "What's this about?"

"Someplace we can talk?" he asked again.

Since Dante wasn't swooning over him, and neither was she, the poor doctor didn't know how to react.

"Uh, yes, sure. Follow me."

Dr. Robinson led them into a conference room and shut the door, then stared at the clock. "I have a meeting in about ten minutes."

"Have a seat, Dr. Robinson," Dante said. "We'll try to be brief."

Obviously not used to being ordered around on his own turf, he said, "I'll stand."

"Fine. We're here to talk about Tony Maclin."

He paused for a second, then asked, "Who?"

"Tony Maclin. He went to the same high school as you did, but he was a few years behind you."

Robinson crossed his arms. "Then I wouldn't have known him."

"He was murdered in an alley off Lindell twelve years ago," Dante said. "Beaten to death."

"Really? Huh. I grew up in Kirkwood and I never heard about that murder. But since I don't know the guy, I wouldn't have known. I still have no idea why you're here."

"He was in the alley to either buy or sell drugs."

He gave them a blank look again. "Still no clue why you're asking me these questions."

"Were you ever involved in dealing drugs while you were in college?"

He laughed. A forced laugh. "No."

"Where were you on the nights of June twenty-third, June twenty-seventh and July tenth this year?" Anna asked.

He threw up his hands. "How the hell should I know?"

Defensive. Was that his normal demeanor, or did he have something to hide?

"Could you check?" Dante asked.

"Now?"

"That would be good."

He dragged out his phone and opened his calendar, scrolling through it. "June... What was the first date?"

Dante gave him the dates again.

He scrolled through his phone. "Working. All those dates. I was working. Here at the hospital. You can verify it with them."

"We will," Dante said.

Now the doctor was starting to look worried. "Do I need a lawyer?"

"I don't know, Dr. Robinson," Dante said. "Do you?"

"This is bullshit. I don't have anything else to say to you. I'm out of here." He opened the door and left.

Anna and Dante followed him and watched his long-legged stride eat up the hallway. He didn't once turn around to see if they followed or if they'd object to his departure.

They left the hospital and, as Dante pulled out of the parking lot, Anna said, "That was interesting."

"Understatement. He's hiding something."

She nodded. "I think so, too. For someone so cool when we first met him, his feathers were sure ruffled by the end of the interview."

"And it didn't take much to ruffle them. I think he knows something."

"We need to confirm if he was working the nights of all the murders. Let me call—shit."

Dante glanced over at her. "What?"

"I'm not supposed to be working. I can't call anyone. This sucks." She folded her arms.

"I'll make the calls. You can go into the precinct with me and work the other cases."

Dante knew Anna wasn't happy. But he only had so much power and influence, and in her precinct he had none.

Losing her father had taken its toll on her. He'd watched her cry, mope and lose the spark that made her who she was. The one thing he agreed with—she needed to get back to work, and he'd slide around Pohanski's edict to help her.

She'd gone into Pohanski's office when they'd returned to the precinct, had come out with a look on her face like she'd eaten something really bad.

He was at the desk next to hers.

"That bad?"

"He gave me bullshit cases, some open homicides to follow up on. Nothing new."

He slid his chair over. "Isn't that a good thing?"

She curled her lip. "In what way?"

"It'll give you some free time to work this one with me."

She shrugged. "I guess."

"Shake it off, Pallino. You're stuck with this until your captain decides otherwise."

"Doesn't mean I have to like it."

"You can 'not like it' while we're talking about Robinson."

"Fine."

Dante swiveled in his chair and looked toward Pohanski's office. Door was closed and so were his blinds. Great. He turned back to Anna.

"Robinson had definite fear or something to hide."

She leaned forward, shaking off her irritation. "I agree. My take on this is he was probably involved with selling drugs to Maclin, or getting Maclin to be part of his drug-selling network."

"And a prominent surgeon who once sold drugs? That'll ruin him."

Anna nodded. "Which means if he thinks we could possibly backtrack the Maclin case to him, or if he suspects any of us saw him with Maclin in the alley that night, he'd have a good reason for wanting to get rid of all of us."

Dante loved seeing the sparkle in Anna's eyes, the first light he'd seen in them since her dad was killed.

If Robinson was the killer, it would be hard for Dante to keep his hands off the bastard. But he also believed in justice and the law, something he hadn't believed in as a kid, which was why Maclin died in the alley that night.

He wouldn't make the same mistake twice. This time he'd let the law take care of him.

Dante's phone rang. He took the call, asked a few questions and wrote down the information, then hung up.

"Well, shit."

"What?" Anna asked.

"Hospital administrator confirms that Robinson was working on the nights the murders were committed."

"That's disappointing."

Dante shrugged. "So he has an alibi. Doesn't mean he didn't commit the murders."

She leaned back in her chair. "You think he hired them out?"

"It wouldn't surprise me. Pretty boy like that with his magic surgery hands. Wouldn't want to mess them up beating the hell out of someone."

She nodded. "You're right. He could have contracted someone to do the killings. It's a long shot, but we'll keep him on the list for now."

"Keep who on the list for now?" Roman asked as he walked in. "And nice to see you back at work, Anna."

"Thanks. It feels good to be back."

She filled Roman in on their interview with Crey Robinson and what they found out.

Roman slid into his chair and leaned back. "That's an interesting theory. Good one, though. There are a lot of cons out there who would do just about anything for money."

"But our killer is neat and tidy," Anna reminded them. "Cleans up the crime scene, leaves no evidence of himself and has access to drugs to disable the victims so he can take them to the alley."

"Which means he isn't your typical off-the-street

thug," Dante said. "I guess that would make sense, though. Robinson doesn't strike me as the type who would know your average street punk."

"That could work to our advantage," Anna said. "Someone more sophisticated than your average batterer is our target. That should narrow our search."

Anna swiveled in her chair to face Roman. "What did you find out about the morphine angle?"

"Several dealers have been busted recently for selling it. None of them are talking about who they sold to. You start giving up your clients, you lose business when you get back out on the street. I've got some leads on some dealers on the street I'm going to talk to next."

"Got names on the recent busts? Maybe I can get somewhere with them."

He punched up a list in his computer and hit the print button. "You're welcome to give it a try. I got nowhere with them."

"She thinks if she flirts with them she'll get somewhere," Dante said.

Roman laughed. "Give it your best shot, honey."

Anna grabbed the list off the printer and her keys. "Watch me work my magic. It's amazing how distracting breasts can be during an interview."

"So you're intending to flash them?" Dante asked.

"If you are, I'm coming along to watch," Roman added.

Anna shook her head as she came back to her desk to make a call. "You're both morons. No testosterone invited."

"In that case, I'm going to talk to Gabe," Dante said. He stood and grabbed his keys.

She lifted her head. "About what?"

"I want to know more about Robinson and the drug trade. I think Gabe can give me some insight."

"Okay."

He brushed her fingers with his. "You be careful and keep your shirt buttoned."

She laughed. "Will do my best."

Twenty-One

"I want you to tell me about the mob and the drug network you have going."

Gabe paused with the bottle of beer halfway lifted to his lips. He put it down on his kitchen counter. "You don't waste time, do you?"

Dante shrugged. "No time to waste, man. You know what we're up against. This is all connected somehow."

Gabe finally took a long swallow. "Yeah? How?"

"We interviewed Dr. Crey Robinson and think he was dealing drugs to Tony Maclin when Maclin was in high school and Robinson was a medical student."

Gabe hated this shit, hated that it involved kids. But that's where the money was, wasn't it? And you followed the money trail if you wanted to be in big business like Bertucci. "What do you want to know?"

"How big is this network? What's the organization?"

"The mob provides the product and recruits the sellers. The sellers go out and find the buyers, who in turn provide the money by buying the product."

"And who are the buyers?"

Gabe shrugged, trying to appear nonchalant, as though

he didn't give a shit. "Anyone and everyone. You know how it is. Rich people, poor people, young and old."

Dante nodded, his expression benign. He wasn't making judgments. "Let's keep it with the young for now. Who's tracking the high schoolers? You have a network of sellers in charge of getting the product to these kids?"

"Yes. There's a hierarchy. Bertucci's family took over that market about forty years ago. They have a stranglehold in the city and county. No one steps on his territory and gets away with it."

Dante took a drink and nodded. "I can imagine. The family's pretty powerful."

"They are."

"And how did you get wrapped up in all this?"

Now it was Gabe's turn to take a long pull of his beer, give himself time to come up with a suitable answer. "Just lucky, I guess."

"Is this really what you want to be doing with your life, Gabe?"

The truth this time. "I told you, I'm doing exactly what I always wanted to do."

Dante sighed, and Gabe felt his disappointment. He wished he could tell him the truth about what he was really doing, but he couldn't. That's how the game was played, and how he lived his life. Someday maybe he'd be able to tell his friends he was one of the good guys.

Then again, maybe not. And sometimes the people you cared the most about had to believe you were the scum of the earth. If that's how his job got done, that's what he'd live with.

"So a kid like Maclin back then… If he was buying drugs from Robinson, a college student…"

"Robinson would have worked for one of Bertucci's guys, a top-tier distributor who kept an eye on all the sellers. The distributors are given product and funnel it down, and the sellers get out there and push it to the kids. Then when they're out of product, which is usually in a hurry because these kids are greedy, they turn in their money, get their cut and get more product."

"Lucrative business?"

Sadly, yes. "Like you wouldn't believe. People like their drugs."

Dante slid him a sidelong glance. "How about you?"

"Me?" Gabe laughed. "I don't touch the shit. It's for business only, not pleasure. I've seen how whacked out people get on that stuff."

"Yeah. I've seen plenty of it, too. At least I don't have to worry about you OD'ing on me."

"No, you don't have to worry about that."

"I do worry about you staying alive, though."

Gabe took a swallow of beer. "You know what, Dante? I worry about that, too. Every goddamn day."

They both went silent then, and Gabe was glad for that. He needed to think about what he'd said, if there was anything he'd given away. He already gave away too much to his friends, and it threatened his job. But what could he do about that? Walk away from Anna? From Dante? No matter what his job, he still had his friends, and there were some people he'd never turn his back on.

He walked a fucking tightrope every day. And it was getting harder to remember what side he was on.

"Is there any way you could find out if Robinson was part of the network?"

Gabe figured that question was coming and shrugged. "I could try. It was a while back, though. There might not be a record of him, but I'll ask around. Sometimes they like to keep track of their old dealers, just in case they need favors."

"I guess that could come in handy."

"You never know. Drug dealer one day, politician the next. Blackmail is a handy thing in this business. And with Robinson having been a medical student…? They might have wanted to keep tabs on him in case they needed him later on."

"For impromptu bullet removal?"

Gabe quirked a half smile. "Something like that."

"I guess your job is never boring, is it, Gabe?"

He lifted his bottle to his lips. "Nope."

Dante called Anna after he left Gabe's condo late that night, figuring she'd still be working. Surprisingly, she said she was at home.

Maybe that was Rusty's influence. She couldn't abandon the dog all day long. Having someone other than herself to take care of might mean she had to take care of herself, too.

He walked in the front door and found her—and Rusty—curled up on the sofa watching a movie. Her hair was in a ponytail and she wore a tank top and very short cotton shorts. He tightened as he remembered the lack of intimacy between them the past couple weeks. The smile she gave him was encouraging.

He grabbed a soda, kicked off his shoes and climbed in next to her and Rusty.

"I made popcorn," she said, handing him the bowl.

He took a handful and focused his attention on the TV. "What are you watching?"

"Die Hard."

He turned to face her. "And here I expected to find you weeping over some chick flick, your tear-filled face buried in Rusty's fur."

She gave him a horrified look. "Do you not know me at all?"

He laughed and kissed the tip of her nose, then shoveled more popcorn into his mouth. "This is why you're perfect for me."

"Hmm," she said, then laid her head on his shoulder. "Maybe you want to watch a chick movie. Something weepy with a tragic ending, maybe?"

"Gag. I can go back to my own place, you know."

She moved the bowl to the table and climbed onto his lap, facing him. Rusty jumped to the floor, clearly annoyed by the two of them moving around on the sofa. "No, you can't go back to your own place."

He placed his hands on her hips, definitely more interested in her sitting on him than in any movie. "I'd rather be right here with you."

"You're just saying that because we haven't had sex in a while."

"You noticed. Finally." He lifted her tank top and slid his hands under. The softness of her skin and the heat of her turned his dick from semi to rock hard in the span of two-point-two seconds.

"Now you sound like a man who's been married for a long time."

He laughed and lifted her top off, sweeping his hands over the swell of her breasts. "And now you sound bitchy and wifey."

She arched a brow and pulled his shirt off, then raked her nails down his chest. "You're an asshole."

He unhooked her bra and removed it, tossing it to the floor. "I love when you whisper sweet words to me. Gets me all hot and hard."

She rocked against him, making him hiss.

"Why, yes...yes, it does." She slid back on his legs and

palmed his erection. "What are you going to do about that, Dante?"

He wrapped his hands around her butt and stood, marched them into the bedroom and threw her on the bed, being none too gentle about it.

She'd riled him up and he was long on passion and short on patience now.

He pulled her shorts down, then her panties, stood over her while he shed his clothes, anxious to remove any barriers between them. He was in a hurry, but not so much of one that he couldn't take a few seconds to stare down at her as she sprawled on top of the covers. Her body was beautiful, curved and lush, and he spotted several areas he wanted to take a long, slow journey across with his tongue.

God, the things her naked body did to his nervous system. She made him breathe faster, made his heart pound. He'd already started to sweat. And he was hard, tight and straining.

He sucked in a breath and leaned over her, mapping her hip with his tongue and moving along her rib cage, each harsh breath she took like a song to him. He moved up her body with his tongue, raked it across her neck and drew back to look at her, at the heat in her eyes that matched the inferno burning inside him.

He bent, kissed her, loving the taste of her, buttery and salty like popcorn as he slid his tongue between her lips and sucked. He was already out of control. This wasn't going to be slow and easy.

Anna wrapped her legs around him, her frenzy equaling his.

He didn't want to be gentle, not when he'd gone so long without her, and she gave him permission not to be. She scratched his arms, dug her heels into him, moaned against his lips and pressed her body against his, all clear signals that she was ready.

But he wanted her more than ready. With a gentle push, he moved her to the side and swept his hand over her sex. She was hot silk, tight and quivering as he tucked two fingers inside her and began to move. And the way she looked at him—there was no more fear or hesitation on her face. She was with him the whole way now as he brought her to the peak over and over again, held her there and then watched her fall.

There was nothing more beautiful or more arousing than watching his woman come, knowing he took her there, that she trusted him enough to let go like this. And when she opened her eyes and he saw such naked desire in them, he knew he'd reached the point of no return. He rolled over and took her mouth, kissing her as he slid inside her with one deep thrust.

She murmured his name on a gasp, and it made his balls tighten when she wrapped her legs around him, when she lifted against him to draw him in deeper. He buried his face in her neck and listened to her sighs, every breath as he ground against her and brought her with him again to the very edge.

He lifted his head and met her gaze, linked his fingers with hers, and this time when she cried out, he shuddered, going with her, letting her know he'd never let her fall without him.

After, he held her, both of them much more relaxed as they stroked each other's bodies.

This intimacy thing, even when they yelled at each other, was becoming scarily comfortable. Dante didn't know what was going to happen after the killer was found and he had to leave town.

"You're quiet," she said, her voice low and unsure.

"Was just thinking."

"About?"

"What happens when this case is over?"

"I guess you leave."

She made it sound so matter-of-fact, as though she didn't care. He knew she did, that she was as unsure as he was. But that was Anna. She wouldn't cling. And he wouldn't ask to stay. Which left them, essentially, nowhere.

"I guess I do."

His phone rang. They both sat up and looked at the clock. It was after midnight. Never a good thing when the phone rang that late.

"Yeah."

He listened, looked at Anna.

She already knew.

"Be right there."

He closed the phone, climbed out of bed to grab his pants.

"Tell me," she said, already out of bed and reaching for clothes.

"Roman was doing a drive-by in the alley to check security. Someone killed the uniform on patrol there, then attacked Roman and stabbed him."

She was eerily calm, on her knees listening as he spoke. "Is he dead?"

"No. He's alive. He managed to fight off the killer. They're taking him to the hospital. And he's conscious."

Roman survived. It was the first solid lead they had. Maybe they could identify the killer now. He grabbed his shoes and slid them on.

"Okay. He's alive."

He stood and turned to her. She still hadn't moved. He tipped his finger under her chin. "Yes, Anna, he made it."

She nodded and he saw the tears she refused to shed. "You're right, he did. Let's go to the hospital."

Anna was worried sick about Roman, but he didn't look too bad for being attacked. He had a stab wound in the right shoulder, had fought off the killer's attempt to carve and beat him. The suspect hadn't gotten around to getting the job done. He'd gotten punched a few times in the face and upper body, and he'd been kicked.

Roman had found an officer down, called it in, and he'd been attacked from behind, blindsided by the suspect who'd gotten him with the knife before he'd known what hit him. But Roman was strong and he'd fended off the attacker long enough for the black-and-whites to show up.

He was alive. It was all that mattered. She was so happy to see him alive when they got to the hospital she wanted to put her arms around him and not let go, but he was too banged up for that. As it was, she sat by his side and held his hand, at least until it was time to take his statement.

"Routine drive-by, like I've been doing lately, right?" he said. "I wanted to check to make sure the units were doing their job, that the surveillance equipment was in place and still working, right?"

He shifted, winced as he sat up straighter in the bed.

"Anyway, the unit was parked in the alley and the driver's-side door was open. Figured maybe Hannesey had gotten out of the car to do a walk through the alley. So I pulled up behind him and got out to go find him."

Dante was recording, Anna was listening.

"What time was this?" Dante asked.

"About ten-thirty or so. I was on my way home. Anyway, I get past the Dumpster and I see Hannesey down. I thought, shit. I crouched down, see that he's dead. But he's not beaten up like the other victims." Roman clenched his jaw. "He cut Hannesey's throat and just left him there to bleed to death."

Roman shoved his hand through his hair. His hand was shaking. Anna fought back tears, imagining what it must have been like for Roman to come up on that scene.

None of them wanted to lose one of their own, and a fellow officer being killed was like losing part of yourself. She felt responsible, as if she had started this chain of events. And now Hannesey was dead.

"I'm sorry, Roman."

"Anyway," Roman said, lifting his chin, "I called it in and stood up, ready to go hunting down the son of a bitch. That's when he jumped me from behind. I turned around and he stuck the knife in my upper shoulder. God, it hurt like hell. I turned around right away to face him, figuring he was going to kill me. I was trying to go for the knife in his hand, trying to wrestle it away from him, but I was down one arm. We fought and he hit me in the jaw, kicked my leg out from under me and I went down. That's when he kicked me in the ribs."

Anna could visualize the scene. Roman was lucky the same thing hadn't happened to him that happened to Hannesey. The killer could have taken the knife to his throat, too. "I'm glad you had fast reflexes."

"Me, too. I knew he was going to kill me, just like the others. I got mad. Mad for George, and your dad, and for Jeff. For Hannesey, too. I fought back. And then I heard the sirens. He must have, too, because he took off."

"I'm glad you made it."

"I can't believe the son of a bitch jumped me. I can't believe I didn't know he was there. How could I not know he was right goddamn behind me?"

Anna winced, knowing exactly what it was like to be taken by surprise in that alley. Images flooded her of that night so long ago, of what it felt like to have Maclin's arms go around her and drag her into the Dumpster.

This isn't about you. Snap out of it!

"Did you see his face?" Dante asked.

Roman shook his head. "He was dressed all in black, wore one of those biker skull masks that hide everything but your eyes. His eyes were dark brown. That's all I remember."

"How about build?" Anna asked.

"Pretty tall. At least six foot. Well built. Not like a bodybuilder, but good muscle. He wore thick gloves and shit-kicker boots."

Anna turned to Dante. "That explains the marks on the bodies."

Dante nodded. "But he stabbed Roman. That makes no sense."

"He didn't choose Roman as a victim. It was coincidence they were in the alley at the same time," Anna said. "I don't think he was prepared. Maybe he was setting the scene for his next victim."

"Or even revisiting the scene to relive the kills. Hannesey and then Roman surprised him," Dante suggested. "Maybe that's why there was a change in his method. Roman being there threw him off his game."

"I don't care what it was," Roman said. "I'm just damn glad I'm alive."

Anna leaned over and squeezed his hand. "So am I. Very glad."

Roman smiled up at her.

"Do you need me to call Tess for you?"

Roman shook his head. "Already did. She's out of town on an audit. Wanted to cancel it and come right back, but I told her no. They're going to spring me tomorrow anyway and she'll be back by the weekend, so I promised her she could wait on me hand and foot then."

Dante laughed. "Milk it for all it's worth, buddy."

"I intend to." Roman waggled his brows.

"You're terrible," Anna said.

"No, I'm not. And admit it. You're happy."

"I am," she said, fighting back tears.

He squeezed her hand. "Anna, stop that. I'm fine. Just some bruises and sore ribs, and the wound is superficial. A few stitches, is all."

Anna exhaled a sigh and nodded. "I can't tell you how relieved I am that you're all right. I don't think I can take losing anyone else. We have to catch this guy before anyone else dies."

"We have leads now that we didn't have before," Dante said. "He's losing his grip. I can feel it. He's going to fuck up and then he's ours."

For the first time since this whole thing started, Anna was beginning to believe it.

"It's also possible the suspect thinks Roman can identify him. That might make him desperate, and careless," Dante added. "He might come after Roman."

Roman laid his hands over his stomach. "Gee, thanks. Make me a target again."

Anna turned to Roman. "There are uniforms stationed outside your room, and when you're discharged there will be someone at the house."

Roman laughed, and then winced, grasping his side.

"I was teasing. I don't need protection at the house. A good night's sleep and I'll be fine once I go home."

"And we're not taking any chances on your life," Anna said. "You take the protection, understand?"

Roman looked to Dante, who just shrugged, so he said, "Yes, ma'am."

She stood, leaned over and kissed Roman's brow. "Rest."

He grabbed her hand. "He's going to keep doing this until we're all dead."

She nodded. "I know."

"You need to get them out of here."

"Them?"

"Dante and Gabe. They're next."

She closed her eyes, knowing Roman was right. "I know."

Roman looked worried, his normal bravado gone. "I don't want to lose anyone else, Anna."

She sucked in a breath and swept her hand over Roman's hair. "I don't want that, either. We're going to protect all of you. I promise. No one else is going to die."

Anna decided that testosterone made men stupid. What part of bodies dropping all around them could they not fathom? Even strong, capable men could be killed.

But no, they wouldn't listen, and now Dante was off meeting with Gabe about some lead he was working on. She was so irritated with him—with them both—she hoped he hung out with Gabe all night.

Dante had asked her to come with him, but she declined out of simple anger. And then he'd irritated her even more by telling her that whenever he wasn't with her, a uniform would be. She was a target, too.

She'd argued with him until they'd ended up shouting

at each other, but she couldn't argue with her captain, who'd insisted that either Dante would be there to provide protection or a uniformed officer would.

Dammit. She hated feeling as if she couldn't take care of herself.

She had agreed with Roman's statement in the hospital: Dante and Gabe were targets and they should leave. They both said no and neither of them were her favorite people right now. And she still couldn't convince Pohanski to put her back on the case.

Damn men.

The less she saw of any of them right now the better. The only male she liked at the moment was Rusty, and he had no balls, so he was an acceptable choice.

She and Rusty were curled up in bed and she was going to read every square inch of case files tonight if it took her the entire night. It wasn't as though she spent any time sleeping anyway.

They needed a break in the case. Surveillance equipment at the scene in the alley showed the suspect sneaking down the alley on foot and disappearing behind the Dumpster. He lingered there for a while, but their view was skewed, so no idea what he'd been doing back there. Then Hannesey had shown up and was taken down, and Roman came on the scene to find Hannesey and the suspect jumped him from behind. But Roman was right—it was hard to distinguish anything from the way the killer was dressed all in black, his face obscured by the skull mask.

So she was going to go through the entire case tonight, starting from the beginning—the very beginning—until she found something.

She grabbed Tony Maclin's file, wrinkling her nose as she did. She hated reliving the nightmare, hated Tony

Maclin with every fiber in her body, but she had to look over the case again, had to look over everything one more time.

This time she was determined to read every single damn word of this file and study every photograph until she had them committed to memory. She'd lost a best friend and her father, a uniform had died and she'd almost lost Roman. It was time to push her trauma behind her and focus on Maclin's case with an objective eye.

She opened the autopsy file and read from the beginning, taking her time. She wasn't squeamish. Hell, she attended plenty of autopsies. She could handle the written word, even if it brought back memories she found unpleasant. He'd shown her no mercy. She'd be equally as merciless as she read his autopsy.

Bruising to his chest and back. Three of his ribs had been broken. His nose had been shattered and two of his teeth had been knocked out. Blunt-force trauma to his head, and pieces of brick found in his scalp.

Wait. She stopped, read that section again.

Brick? What brick?

She flipped through the medical examiner's notes, read that blunt-force trauma to the head was listed as the cause of death, attributed to being struck by the brick.

Again, what brick?

She'd been dazed and in shock that night, but as she'd lain there against the wall and watched the guys pummel Tony Maclin, she sure as hell never saw any of them pick up a brick and hit him over the head. Sure, they'd struck him with their fists, but no one had used a brick on his head. Not that she remembered.

Maybe Dante or Gabe would, though.

Where had she left her phone? Kitchen, when she went in there to fix a soda. She slid out of bed to go get it, stopping cold when she heard a noise in the backyard. Something had either been bumped into or knocked over.

And it wasn't windy outside.

Rusty leaped off the bed on alert, the hairs on his back rising. He started to growl.

"Shh," she whispered. "Rusty, down. Stay."

Rusty did as ordered. She turned off the light in her bedroom, then reached for her gun. A round was already racked in the chamber, so she crept out of the bedroom, closed the door to keep Rusty in there and headed down the hall toward the back door.

She saw her phone on the kitchen counter, grabbed it and dialed Dante's number, holding the phone up to her ear.

He answered on the first ring.

"What's up?"

"Nothing, probably, but I heard something in the backyard."

"Where's the uniform?"

"I don't know. Out front, I guess."

"Go get him. We'll be right there."

"Don't. It's likely just a cat or the wind. The uniform and I can check it out."

"There's no wind and you're wasting my time talking. Don't go out there. We'll be there in ten minutes."

"Okay."

She clicked off and slid her phone in her pocket, went to look out the back door.

But she also wasn't stupid. She went to the front door and opened it.

No one was there. Uniform was supposed to stay at the front door at all times. She walked outside a few steps and didn't see him.

She shut the front door in a hurry, locked the dead

bolt and pulled the chain across, then turned to face the back door.

Shit.

She took a deep breath, let it out slowly, trying to calm the pounding of her heart.

Maybe the uniform went to take a leak. It was plausible enough, right?

Yeah, and it was going to snow in July.

She was going to try really hard not to conjure up the boogeyman where there wasn't one.

But then Rusty started barking in the bedroom, and she saw something move out back.

Dante said to wait for him. But dammit, she was a cop. She wasn't some untrained bimbo who needed a man to come save her. She was going to check it out.

She unlocked the slider, then pulled it open slow and easy.

It was muggy tonight, the air totally still. She couldn't hear anything but her own breathing. And Rusty, who was still barking in her bedroom.

She pulled the screen door back and stepped onto the patio. She made a quick glance over to the table and chairs, then over to the barbecue. Nothing looked out of place. She moved farther out into the yard and leaned out toward the back door by her bedroom, saw nothing and decided it had to be some kind of animal, but she'd do a thorough search.

She'd made one step into the grass when a body slammed into her.

Stunned, she was tossed into the grass and she lost her grip on her gun. It went flying a few feet out of her grasp.

Shit! Whoever knocked into her was big, heavy and definitely male, from the size of muscle mass and how hard he hit her. She tried to fight him off, but he was too big for her. He was a blur dressed all in black and she couldn't even see skin. He pinned her to the ground with the sheer size of his body, and memories of that night twelve years ago came flooding back.

"No!" she shouted. This wasn't twelve years ago, and she wasn't a scared sixteen-year-old anymore. He lay on top of her and she raised a leg up, effectively jamming it into his balls. She heard him grunt, and she used the advantage of his temporary pain to throw him off, then scramble away for her gun. But he grabbed her leg and jerked her back just before she could get her fingers on her gun, dragging her into the grass.

Then he slapped her across the face. He wore gloves, making the smack more painful.

Stunned at the impact, she lay there for a few seconds, trying to get the ringing out of her head as sharp pain sheared through her senses. He rose up and she saw the glint of a knife.

Oh, no. Not again. As he came for her she figured he probably thought she was scared and wouldn't move.

But this time she wasn't scared. She was angry.

That gave her the element of surprise this time. She bent her knees and shot them out, jamming her feet into his stomach and sending him flying backward. She scrambled and grabbed her gun, but by then he was on the run. She fired off a shot as he flew through the gate.

"Anna!"

She swiveled to see Dante and Gabe tear through the doorway, both of them with guns in their hands. She aimed the gun barrel toward the ground. "He just left through the gate," she said, panting and out of breath.

"Stay with her," Dante said, then tore out of the yard.

"You okay, honey?" Gabe asked, hooking one arm

around her and holding his gun in his other hand. He pointed it toward the gate, but backed them toward the house so they'd have a position of safety.

"Yeah, I'm fine. He knocked me around a little, but I'm okay. Where's the uniform?"

"In the bushes outside."

Dread made her stomach drop. "Is he dead?"

"No. Looks like someone slammed his head good into the side of your house. He's out cold. We already called for an ambulance and the cops."

She blew out a sigh of relief. "Thank God."

She followed him out front and they saw to the uniform, who was coming around. He had a bad gash on his forehead, but she was so damn happy he was conscious. When the ambulance and police cars screamed into her driveway, they stepped out of the way to let the paramedics deal with him.

"Let's go inside."

Gabe sat her down on one of the kitchen chairs, then turned on the light.

"You need some ice on your face. He walloped you," Gabe said, giving her a once-over and frowning.

She put her hand to her swelling cheek. "Yeah, the bastard slapped me a good one. I saw stars for a few seconds."

"What the fuck happened?"

"Hang on." She got up, winced a little as she limped down the hallway to let Rusty out, praising him for being such a good dog. He wagged his tail, went over to warily sniff Gabe, then laid his head in her lap when she sat again.

Gabe was already crushing ice and putting it in a bag.

"I heard a noise outside. So I went to investigate. The asshole football tackled me as soon as I cleared the patio."

"No sign of him," Dante said as he came through the slider and closed it.

He came over to her, lifted the ice pack away and winced. "Damn."

"I'm okay."

"You're lucky he didn't do more damage. Why didn't you stay in the house and wait for us, or call the cops?"

She tilted her head to the side and gave him a "duh" look. "I *am* the cops. I went out front to get the uniform but didn't see him."

Dante dragged his hand through his hair and paced. "So you go outside in the dark by yourself when you know a killer is after you? What the hell are you thinking, Anna?"

She shrugged and put the ice pack back on her cheek. "I'm thinking I was lucky you two showed up when you did, though he seemed to be on his way out of here as soon as I got hold of my gun and aimed it in his direction."

Dante kneeled in front of her. "Did he have a gun?"

"Not that I could tell. He had a knife, though. When he stood over me he pointed it at me."

Dante swept her hair away from her face. "That's not good."

"No, but the odd thing is, he had me at an advantage and didn't use it. He slapped me so hard I was dazed, and when I shook it off he was hovering over me with the knife. He could have stabbed me right then, or even when I was temporarily out of it, but he didn't."

Dante stood and pulled up a chair. Gabe handed him a beer and pulled out another chair. "Hesitation?" Gabe asked.

"Maybe. Or maybe he wanted to threaten me. I got the idea I wasn't really a target."

"Like he wanted to scare you more than hurt you?" Dante asked.

"Something like that. I could be wrong, though."

It took a couple hours to take statements and for Forensics to sweep her backyard. As Anna suspected, they didn't find much. With the battle between her and the assailant, and Gabe and Dante back there running after the suspect, the grass was a wreck and they couldn't get decent footprints.

Gabe called Roman, who rushed over. His arm was in a sling and he still had a limp and was bruised up, but he was starting to look a little better. He frowned when he saw her.

"Son of a bitch," he said, leaning over to brush her hair aside. "He hit you?"

"Yeah."

Roman sat next to her in the kitchen. "I'm so sorry. I should have been here."

She smiled. "I don't need a babysitter, Roman."

He lifted his arm and winced a little. "I doubt I could have offered much help anyway, goddammit."

"You could have shot the bastard."

Roman laughed. "I would have, too. I want him dead."

"We all want him dead." She filled him in on what happened while Gabe and Dante worked with the CSU team and the uniforms.

"Units have already been sent to find Sam Maclin. He's not at home." Dante said. "And his mother doesn't know where he is. He left the house about seven tonight, said he was going out, but didn't say where he was going."

"That makes him a viable suspect," she said. "What about Crey Robinson?"

"On duty, as usual. Which doesn't mean anything."

"No, it doesn't."

She was wiped out by the time the CSU team left. Dante was about to shuffle Roman and Gabe out the door when she remembered.

"Oh, wait. Maclin's file."

Roman and Gabe stopped at the front door. "What?" Gabe asked.

"I found something in Maclin's file."

They were in the living room now. Anna had drunk a couple beers, so she felt a lot better. Dante insisted she curl up with Rusty and rest. He sat next to her—really close. She couldn't say she minded all that much.

Roman slid into the recliner. "What about Maclin's file?"

"I finally read his autopsy report, front to back. I'd read it before, several times, but admittedly I skimmed because it was so unpleasant to relive the ordeal of that night. This time it finally sunk in. I think the connection wasn't there for me because it had been so long since I was in that alley."

"What?" Dante asked.

"Tony Maclin died of blunt-force trauma to the head. From a brick."

Dante frowned, then looked at Gabe and Roman. "A brick? Nobody hit him with a brick."

"I don't remember a brick," Roman said.

Gabe sat on the edge of the recliner and shook his head. "No, there wasn't a brick."

Anna nodded. "That's what I thought I remembered, too. I know you guys punched him, but there was no brick. But do you understand what I said? Cause of death was blunt-force trauma to his head—from the brick."

"Wait." Dante looked at the others, then switched back to Anna. "We didn't kill him?"

She smiled. "No. You didn't kill him. I think you all

hit him until he passed out, then when you helped me inside, someone else picked up a brick and hit him over the head. That's what killed him."

"Son of a bitch." Gabe sat there with an incredulous look on his face.

"Huh." Dante stared at her. "All these years, we thought we'd beat him to death."

"We didn't kill him." Roman looked at Dante and Gabe, then turned his attention to Anna. "Which means the suspect must have done the deed."

"That's a powerful secret. One he's been holding on to for years," Gabe said.

"But is it a good enough secret to want us all dead?" Anna asked. "Especially now, after all this time."

Dante nodded. "People have killed for way less than that. If he has something to lose, and he thinks we might know the truth about what happened that night, then yeah, I'd say he'd want to eliminate all of us."

Gabe stood. "Well, I'll leave the crime solving to all of you. All I know is that's one less death I'm responsible for."

Dante stood and slapped him on the back. "Makes you feel all good about yourself now, doesn't it?"

Gabe laughed. "Yeah. I might even go to church this weekend."

Roman stood, too, slowly made his way over to Anna. "This doesn't mean we're out of the woods yet." He kissed her cheek. "But it's good to know we didn't kill him. I've carried a lot of guilt over that all these years."

"I know. You watch yourself."

"I have been."

Dante walked Roman and Gabe to the door, closed and locked it, then returned to her.

He scooped Anna up in his arms and carried her to the bedroom.

"I'm capable of walking, you know."

He looked down at her. "And I could have lost you tonight. So let me indulge you."

He laid her in bed, helped her undress, then pulled the covers over her. He called Rusty, who lay down on the floor on her side of the bed. Then he undressed and climbed into bed next to her and turned out the lights.

"I could get used to having you here in my bed," she said.

"I could get used to being here."

That was all either of them said before she drifted off to sleep.

Twenty-Two

What Dante hadn't told Anna amidst all the chaos that had happened that night was that Gabe had come through with information about Crey Robinson's drug-dealing past. Robinson had worked for the Bertucci family as a dealer back when he was in college. Though it wasn't information that Anna would be able to verify through any legal channels.

But at least they knew now. Which meant Robinson stayed at the top of the suspect list, alibi or not.

She was back at work a couple days after the attack, ignoring the fatherly looks given to her by Pohanski. The swelling on her face had gone down and she was lucky not to end up with a black eye. She felt fine. A little stiff, but mobile and so ready to end this case and this killer she could taste it.

And still unable to work the case, which made her seethe.

So she worked the other homicides, which had generated very few leads, but they were still murders that needed follow-up. Roman helped her with those and they had interviewed a few suspects and got those out of the way. Unfortunately, the cases were so cold she was getting frostbite in July, so no luck on the newly assigned cases, which left her plenty of time to work on the one case they all wanted to close.

"So Crey Robinson has an alibi," she said to Dante as she leaned back in her chair. "Maybe he wasn't the only one in the alley that night. And maybe whoever was with him is doing the killings."

"It's a thought," Dante said.

"A pretty good one," Roman added.

He'd been back on duty longer than her, was recovering from his injuries. His arm was out of the sling and the knife wound was healing. He still walked with a limp but Pohanski put him back on active duty. Anna was just so damn happy Roman had escaped the killer she wanted to dance on top of her desk. They were winning. The killer had tried to take both Roman and her down and he hadn't succeeded.

It was only a matter of time and they'd have him.

They still hadn't found Sam Maclin, who'd seemingly gone missing after the night of her attack.

"Sam Maclin is still our strongest suspect," Dante said. "You're attacked and suddenly he can't be found. We have a BOLO out for him. His photo and license plate number has been sent out to all city and county LEs. We'll find him."

"Unless he skipped town before I was attacked, in which case he's not our suspect."

"We've alerted his mother and told her it's in his best interest to contact us and clear himself. If he gets in touch with her and he can come up with an alibi for the night of your attack, I can't imagine he wouldn't," Roman said.

"If he's innocent," Dante added, crossing his arms.

"Yeah. If he's innocent," Roman said.

Now that she'd discovered that the guys hadn't killed

Tony Maclin, the cloud of guilt had lifted. Where once she might have felt sorry about targeting another Maclin, now she didn't. If Sam Maclin was the one doing all the killings, he had to be stopped. And she wouldn't feel guilty about taking another son away from Susan Maclin.

"My bet is he's going to come home. His art is there, and that's his passion. I don't think he can stay away that long."

Dante nodded. "You may be right, but it's a big risk for him. He has to know we're watching."

"Maybe. But he thinks he's smarter than we are," she said.

"He is a smug bastard," Roman said. "He might think he can outsmart us."

"Or outwait us." Anna stood. "What if we pulled the surveillance crew outside his house? Everyone's supposed to be out there looking for the killer, anyway."

Dante's lips curled. "Good idea."

"Only we won't be outside waiting for him…"

Dante's eyes sparkled. "Sometimes you have devious ideas. Could have used someone like you out in the field."

She laughed. "No, thanks. This job is dangerous enough."

It had been difficult getting Susan Maclin's permission to allow them inside her home. She wasn't exactly happy to see them. In fact, her formerly gracious attitude toward them had changed to one of cool disregard. Almost hatred.

But Dante assured her they were only looking out for Sam's welfare and were trying to clear him off the suspect list, and the best way to do that was to bring him in. Hiding out from them only made him look bad.

She agreed with that, but she couldn't get him to

answer his phone. She told Dante she'd been trying several times a day and he wouldn't answer.

They'd tried hitting up his cell phone for a location, but got nothing.

They pulled the unmarked car off the street after doing a sweep of the neighborhood, including all the houses. Sam was nowhere in the vicinity.

Anna had stayed behind in the precinct after Dante and Roman left so Pohanski wouldn't think she was going with him. Pohanski was wandering the bull pen, so she got on the phone with a lead on one of her cases, tapping her pen against the desk and counting down every minute. As soon as Pohanski made himself scarce, she ended the call, grabbed her notebook and keys and left.

She met Dante at a convenience store a few miles from the precinct. They parked a block over and went in the back door of the Maclins' house.

Susan Maclin was already inside with Roman. He took her upstairs, out of sight, in case there was trouble. They wanted to make sure she was safe.

"I'll cover the living room and kitchen area," Dante said.

Anna nodded. "I'll take the art studio."

"Mic up so we can stay in contact in case anyone spots him," Dante said.

She took the earpiece and slid it in. "Everyone hear me?"

"Got you," Roman said.

She headed off into the studio. "Dante?"

"I hear you."

The cool air in the studio came as a relief, even with all the windows streaming in sunlight. The day had started blistering hot and had only gotten worse.

She wandered around to look at the art. What did

it take to have this kind of talent? The paintings, the sculptures—it was something that was beyond her. She loved art, loved going to the galleries to look at paintings and try to interpret the artists' messages. To have that level of talent left her in awe.

And to have an entire family with that kind of talent—she wondered how Tony would have ended up if he had lived. It was a shame he'd traded his talent for drugs and craziness. But they said some artists lived on the edge of madness. Was that what Tony had done? Had his talent driven him to the brink, and he'd dealt with it by turning to drugs?

And why had Maclin attacked her that night? Crime of opportunity, maybe. She'd been in the wrong place at the wrong time. And the attempted rape—that had come out of nowhere. She blamed his high for that. Or maybe he'd had the predilection for it all along. She supposed they'd never know.

She moved over to the sculpture in process, the one Sam had been working on when she and Dante had come to talk to him before. He'd made some progress on it. It was a bust, mostly finished now, of a young woman with flowing, wavy hair that cascaded over her shoulders. She wore a locket that dipped between her breasts.

The intricacy of the sculpture was amazing. How did he do something like that? The time it took to chip away at each piece, then mold it to make it look like an actual person must take hours of painstaking work.

She leaned in to examine the workmanship, and something caught her eye.

Her breath caught.

Above the breast, Sam had carved a heart.

Coincidence.

She backed away and moved to some of his finished pieces. They were all women, some full bodies.

And on each of them were carvings of a heart above the left breast, some so small they were barely noticeable. But they were there, on every piece.

"No."

"Anna?"

Dante's voice, concerned.

"Anna. Answer," he said again.

"I'm fine. Just checking something out."

"You see him?"

"No."

She examined the paintings, some done by Tony long ago, judging by his name written in the right-hand corner of the canvas. Most by his mother. In every one there were hearts. Some near the signature, some on the people.

How had she missed it before?

"You like the art?"

She whirled around and saw Sam facing her. He had a gun in his hand. She reached for hers.

"Don't."

She dropped her hand, but didn't relax, ready at any time to draw her weapon.

"How did you get in here?" she asked.

"I've been here the whole time."

"So your mother knew all along?"

He smiled. "No. She never knew about the hideaway."

"What hideaway?"

He cracked a smile. "Wall space in the house that connects rooms. Tony and I found it years ago. It was our secret. We never told Mom and Dad."

She swallowed, watched him casually hold the gun. He wasn't exactly pointing it at her. He was looking at all the art, zeroing in on his sculpture.

"I really need to get back to work."

"Then tell me everything. Did you kill all those people?"

His gaze shot to hers. Anger. "No."

"Did you come after me at my house the other night?" He frowned. "What? No."

"Then tell me how I'm supposed to believe you."

"Why didn't you ever tell anyone about what happened to my brother that night?"

A cold chill shivered down her spine. "You were there."

"Yeah. I was there." He lifted the gun. "I saw it all."

She wondered if he had really seen it all.

"Do you know what Tony did that night?"

His gaze didn't waver, not even when Sam and Roman came running in, guns drawn. She lifted her hand to stay them.

"Yeah. My brother died."

"Do you know what else he did that night?"

He cocked his head to the side. He didn't know.

Anna unbuttoned the top two buttons of her shirt and showed him the heart.

"Did you see him do this to me?"

Sam's gaze bored into the scar on her chest. His eyes filled with tears and he stepped forward, his hand out as if he wanted to touch her.

"Maclin, don't." Dante took a step forward.

"It's okay, Dante."

Sam didn't touch her, just drew closer. "Jesus Christ. I didn't know he cut you like that."

"You were there. You saw."

He started rocking back and forth on his heels, the gun still aimed at her, but his hand was more relaxed now. "We were home alone together and he told me he was going out. I told him I was old enough to go along. He said fine, so he took me with him, said we'd go play laser tag, but he had a stop to make first. He drove to the alley, told me to wait in the car for him, that he'd be right back. Said he had to buy some blow and I was supposed to stay in the car."

"You didn't stay in the car, did you?" Anna asked.

"No. I wanted to see. I was scared for him. I wanted to make sure he was gonna be okay, so I got out of the car and followed him into the alley, but I hid. He was waiting for the guy, then you...you showed up. He was already high. Really high. That's why I was worried about him, afraid he'd do something stupid. And he did. He jumped you and I didn't know what to do. I didn't know what to do."

Tears rolled down his cheeks.

"I was going to stop him, but I was scared. When we first got there he told me if the dealer found me he'd kill me, so I stayed where I was. And then your friends came and they beat up Tony, and I was even more scared that they'd find me and hurt me, too. So I just stayed hiding, trying not to make any noise."

"What happened after the guys left with me?"

"I was going to go get Tony and get the hell out of there, right? Because Tony was starting to get up. But then this guy came, and Tony asked for help, said some guys beat him up. And the guy was pissed, man. Really pissed. Said Tony blew it for him. And he took a brick and slammed it on Tony's head, hard."

Sam really started to cry then. Anna forced herself to stay composed, trying not to relive that night, the same night Sam had had to live through.

He could have stopped it, could have stopped it from the beginning. He chose not to.

"Then what happened?"

"I was afraid. I ran. I ran for blocks until I couldn't breathe anymore. I caught a taxi home and never told anyone what I saw. I saw my brother get killed and I never said anything to anyone. All these years I've felt weak and ashamed because I didn't do anything. I didn't stop him when he did…that…to you, and I didn't stop my brother from getting killed."

Sam lowered the gun and turned to face the sculpture. "All I could do was make beautiful things. The beautiful things to erase all that ugliness."

Dante rushed in and grabbed the gun from Sam. Roman cuffed him.

Susan Maclin had seen it all, heard it all, her eyes wide and tear filled as Anna walked by.

She stopped Anna. "My Tony did that to you?"

Anna nodded.

She lifted a fisted hand to her lips and began to sob. "I'm sorry. I'm so sorry."

They took Sam into the station. Dante got Pohanski and he led the interview.

In interrogation, Sam told him everything that went down twelve years ago, informed them that Tony told him his dealer was a medical student who'd gone to the same high school. Based on their suspicions about Crey Robinson, they gave Sam a photo lineup and he picked Robinson right away as the one who'd hit Tony with the brick.

It had given Anna a great sense of satisfaction when the arrogant Dr. Robinson was arrested for Tony Maclin's murder.

Now that their involvement in the Maclin case was out in the open, Pohanski called them all into the office.

"Jesus Christ," Pohanski said, pacing his office. "You didn't think to mention any of this to me before now?"

Anna didn't say a word. Neither did Dante or Roman.

"All this time. All these years. You were all involved in a murder and a cover-up. And Anna—your father?"

"Did what he thought was best, sir."

Pohanski rubbed his hand over his bald head. "What am I supposed to do about this now?"

She didn't think he was really asking any of them to answer that question.

"Son of a bitch. You were all kids then. And what Maclin did to you that night. Goddamn, Anna. I'm sorry about that. It's no wonder you decided to become a cop. And a damn good one."

"Thank you, sir."

He shot her a glare. "Don't thank me yet. I have to figure out what I'm going to do about this. About all of you."

"There's still a killer out there," Dante said.

"Don't remind me. My department's stretched thin as it is. And the fact the three of you were involved in solving a cold case is—shit, this is fucked up."

That was an understatement. "The guys saved my life that night, Captain. And everyone around me is dying because of it. Please let us figure out why and put a stop to it before everyone else around me dies."

He opened his mouth to speak, then shut it, continuing to pace and rub his head. "Give me a goddamn minute to think, Pallino."

She did, though it was difficult not to throw herself on his mercy and plead her case—all their cases. He had to see reason.

"You were all juveniles then, and Anna was a victim of a violent crime. And what was done to you, Anna, by

Maclin—whose killer has now been found—I don't think a prosecutor is going to want to mess with any of you. Robinson will be prosecuted for murder, he'll probably pull a plea deal and we'll be able to get out of this messy business with our skins intact."

"And the other murders?"

He gave her a straight look. "You can't investigate your father's murder, Anna."

"I can, though," Dante said.

Pohanski shrugged. "I have no jurisdiction over you, Dante. But you have to work within our guidelines. And if you happen to bring Anna or Roman along to assist in an unofficial capacity, that's up to you."

"But you'd better have another detective sign off on everything, and dot every *i* and cross every goddamn *t* so our asses are covered."

After Pohanski left them, Anna breathed a sigh of relief and the three of them regrouped to figure out the next steps. Sam was still a suspect in the other murders, but Anna didn't see it.

"He was focused on all of us, but afraid, mostly," she argued.

"He doesn't have alibis," Roman argued. "We can't clear him. He stays a suspect."

"Roman's right," Dante said. "You're letting your personal feelings get in the way."

She lifted her chin. "I don't have personal feelings. If he's guilty, he goes down. But other than him being a little dark and twisty, we don't have anything on him. He just has no alibis for the nights of the murders. And when he found out he was a suspect, he bolted and hid, which meant the night I was attacked he was hiding in his own house."

"So he claims," Dante said.

"The bad thing is we don't have him for anything, so he walks unless we can come up with some solid evidence," Roman said with a grimace.

Anna dragged her fingers through her hair. "Then we'll have to keep at him until we break him, or find the real killer."

"We'll take turns," Roman said. "He'll get so tired of talking he'll eventually give up."

Anna nodded. "Sounds like a plan."

"You look irritated," Dante said.

Anna slid on the sofa next to him. They'd worked well into the night and had finally gone home to take a break. They'd just finished a late dinner of take-out tacos. "I have no killer locked up, that's why I'm irritated."

They'd gotten nothing from Maclin. They'd leaned on him for hours. Besides that night in the alley twelve years ago, he claimed to have nothing to do with the current murders. And his attorney was locking him up tight.

"But at least you have Tony Maclin's killer."

"One down."

"There's still Crey Robinson to think about as a suspect in the other murders."

She leaned her head back and stared up at the ceiling. "I'm still considering it. Hard to prove."

"Not really. We investigate his money, look at cash withdrawals and when he made them, then track his movements, see if he met with any shady characters at the hospital, since that's where residents spend almost all their time anyway. Hospitals are notorious for gossip. The staff see everything that goes on."

She turned her head to face him. "You'd make a good cop. How do you do that?"

He laughed. "I don't just walk into an assignment without running background on the target. I need to know everything about a situation. I pay attention to the small details. Keeps me alive that way."

"Your life is dangerous."

"It can be. So can yours."

"Not like yours, I imagine." She swept her hand across his jaw. "Do you have to go back to it?"

The look he gave her was so intense it made her breath catch.

"Are you asking me not to?"

She paused, not sure how to answer him. She'd never ask anyone to give up the job they loved. She wouldn't ask it of Dante, not even if she wanted to keep him safe. If he loved what he did, just like she loved her job, she'd never ask him to walk away from it.

But the doorbell rang, followed by several fast knocks, and she couldn't answer his question.

"It's, like, two in the morning," she said.

Dante sprang off the sofa and peered through the peephole. "It's Roman."

He opened the door and Roman rushed in. He was drenched in sweat.

"What's wrong?" Anna rushed to him.

"Gabe took a shot at me."

Anna's eyes widened. "What? Are you hurt?" She didn't see any blood, but she ran her hands over him anyway.

He shook her off. "I'm fine. Pissed off, mainly because my goddamn brother tried to kill me and I don't know why."

"What the hell happened?" Dante asked as Anna led them into the living room to sit.

"I was on my way home from the station, about two

blocks from home. Suddenly the right-rear window on my car explodes. I knew right away it was a bullet, because another shot was fired into the car. So of course I'm shocked as hell and I duck down to avoid being shot at again and trying to get my bearings at the same time so I can get a six on the shooter.

"I swerved, pulled the car over to the side of the road and grabbed my gun. When I popped up to return fire, that's when I saw his bike speed away."

"Are you sure it was Gabe?" Dante asked.

Roman gave them a look. "I know his bike. I know Gabe. It was him."

Anna shook her head, unable to believe Gabe would do that. "Why would he shoot at you?"

"I don't know."

"Did you call it in?" Anna asked.

"No. I wanted to come here first, talk to the two of you. I don't know what to do, you know? It's Gabe."

Dante dialed Gabe's number and put the phone to his ear. "It goes to voice mail right away."

"This doesn't make any sense," Anna said. "Gabe would have no reason to shoot at you."

"That's what I thought, too. It doesn't make sense."

"What if it was a hit?" Anna asked.

Dante frowned. "On Roman? Why?"

She tilted her head. "Did you forget who Gabe works for?"

"No. I just don't think Gabe would do that. And why would he hit Roman? Is there something going on with his job that affects the local P.D.?"

Roman shook his head. "Nothing I know about."

Anna laid her chin in her hands. "You're right. There's nothing going on with Bertucci and the cops. And he'd never try to hurt one of you guys."

"Well, I hate to remind you," Roman said, "but he tried to tonight."

"Shit." Dante kicked the back of the chair. This didn't make sense. Why would Gabe take a hit out on Roman? Did Bertucci order it because of Robinson? And if so, why wouldn't Gabe give Anna or him a heads-up? It wasn't like him to blindly follow an order like that. He seemed loyal to his job and to Bertucci, but he wouldn't take down one of his own brothers.

Unless…

No. The possibility wasn't even fathomable.

"What are you thinking?" Anna asked him.

"I'm thinking I need to go find Gabe and have a talk with him."

She stood. "I'll go with you."

"No. You need to stay here. With Roman. We don't know where Gabe is or why he shot at Roman. For all we know he's out there somewhere looking to finish the job, or hunting the rest of us."

Anna frowned, then recognition dawned in her eyes. "You don't think…no, Dante. Not Gabe."

"I don't know what to think right now, and I won't know until I find him. Roman, you stay here with Anna. Make sure nobody gets in here but me."

Roman nodded. "You got it."

Anna went with Dante to the door. "You go out there alone, you're a target."

"He won't hurt me."

She let out a short laugh. "Yeah, I'm sure Roman thought that, too."

"He won't hurt me," he said again. "I'll find him and figure out what's going on."

She laid her palms on his chest. "If it's Gabe, if he's…

Then he's not thinking clearly. You don't know what he'll do."

"Then I'll take care of it."

"Just like that?"

The look he gave her was lethal. "This is what I do, Anna."

"I don't want him dead."

"He won't be unless it's necessary."

He knew from the look she gave him that she didn't like the situation. "I need to go with you."

"No. Someone's already made an attempt to kill you and Roman. I won't risk bringing both of you along. Enough of us have died already. This is what I'm good at. Let me do it. And if he comes here, then the two of you can handle him and call for backup. Either way we finish this tonight."

She hesitated for a few seconds, then nodded. "All right."

Dante loaded up ammo and an extra gun. Anna wrapped her arms around him and hugged him. He kissed her, pouring everything he had into that kiss. "I love you," he said, and her eyes widened. "I should have said it sooner, and now isn't the right goddamn time, but you never know and it needed to be said."

She swept her hand across his jaw and he memorized the feel of her touch. "I love you, too. And it won't be the last time you hear me say it."

He waited a heartbeat, memorizing her face, the way her eyes seemed to light up whenever she looked at him.

"Stay put. Lock the door." He kissed her again and slid out the door, listening for the lock, then got in his car and headed out, checking around the house before he left.

Everything was secure. Nothing looked out of place, so he slid into his car.

He tried Gabe's cell again, got nothing, figured he'd go to the condo first. If Gabe was really the killer, he wouldn't be there. He'd be hiding out, stalking them now that he'd missed his target.

When he pulled into the condo complex, Gabe's bike was parked out front.

Pretty ballsy considering Roman could have called in units to track him down. Another thing that made no sense. He pulled his gun out and knocked on the door. No answer. He rang the bell and knocked louder, several times.

Finally, a light came on and the door flew open. Gabe looked rumpled, as if he'd been asleep.

"What the fuck are you doing here so late?" he asked, then his eyes widened. "Did something happen?"

Dante pushed him inside and closed the door, then pointed the gun at him.

"Jesus Christ, Dante. What are you doing?"

"You took a shot at Roman tonight. I want to know why."

"A shot at…what? What the hell are you talking about? Someone shot at Roman?"

"On his way home. You shot at him twice, then took off."

Gabe held his hands up, still looking half-asleep. "I have no fucking idea what you're talking about."

"Where's your phone?"

Gabe blinked. "What?"

"Your phone. I tried to call you, but it went to voice mail."

"I know. Someone stole my goddamn phone when I was at the bar earlier tonight. Went to the bathroom to take a leak, when I came out it was gone."

"How long have you been home?"

"I don't know. What time is it?"

"Two-thirty or so."

"I got home around midnight. Bar was dead tonight."

"Get your pants on and come outside with me."

"What? Why?"

"Just do as I say." He held the gun up for emphasis.

"Yeah, gimme a minute."

Dante followed Gabe into the bedroom, where he slipped on a pair of jeans. Barefoot, he led Dante outside to his bike. Dante laid his hand on the motor of Gabe's Harley. It was cold.

Shit.

"Let's go back inside."

Dante closed the door again. Gabe turned to him.

"Want to tell me what the hell you're talking about? Someone took a shot at Roman?"

"Roman said you ambushed him a couple blocks from his house and took two shots at him while he was in his car."

"When?"

"Less than an hour ago."

Gabe crossed his arms. "Roman is full of shit. Why would I do that?"

"Contract hit?"

Gabe snorted. "Yeah, right. Bertucci has better things to do than kill cops. You think he wants that kind of attention? And Roman isn't even working us. He's not on mob stuff."

Dante dragged a hand through his hair, feeling as if he'd just been set up.

"Roman tell you all this?"

Dante shoved his gun in his holster. "Yeah. He showed up at Anna's tonight and told us you ambushed him."

"Where is he now?"

"With Anna at her place. I told him to watch over her."

Gabe frowned, then his shoulders dropped. "Fox got himself right into the henhouse."

Dante frowned. "What the fuck are you talking about?"

"Oh, come on, Dante. Are you blind? He's in love with her. He's been in love with her for years."

"He is not. He has a girlfriend. Tess somebody."

Gabe slid him a disbelieving look. "You ever meet Tess? You ever see her around anywhere?"

"No. But—"

"But nothing. I've been back for two damn years and *I've* never met the woman. I don't think she even exists."

"Anna knows her."

"When was the last time Anna saw them together? He might have been out with this Tess a few times, but not for a long time. She's a front, somebody he made up or went out with just to appease Anna because he doesn't want her to know he's sniffing around her like a lovesick puppy."

"Son of a bitch. I didn't know."

"He didn't want you to know."

Dante still didn't want to believe it. Not Roman. He'd always thought Roman the most innocent out of all the brothers. The straightest one, the one least likely to do anything bad. Maybe that had been his biggest mistake.

He grabbed his phone, punched Anna's number. It went right to voice mail.

"She's not answering. She'd answer. She'd want to know what was happening."

"Was Roman with you and Anna at any of the times the murders were committed?" Gabe asked.

"No, but neither were you."

"True enough. But I didn't bust in on you and Anna

tonight accusing Roman of taking a shot at me in order to get you out of the house."

"Fuck. And I fell for it."

Gabe grabbed the rest of his clothes and his gun. "Look, I don't know what kind of game Roman is playing, but we need to get to Anna."

"In a hurry."

They dashed out the door and into Dante's car.

"You don't have one of those siren-and-light thingies?"

"No."

"Should have taken Anna's car."

"No shit."

"Just speed, then. You know how to do that."

Dante hoped he could drive fast enough to get there, because Roman had wanted him out of the house and away from Anna for a reason. He just hoped it wasn't too late.

Anna paced back and forth, watching the phone on the table next to Roman and waiting for that call from Dante. She'd already made both of them coffee, but that had only made her more jittery.

Roman sat on the sofa watching her.

"You're making me dizzy," he said. "Come sit down."

She looked down at him and smiled. "Sorry. I'm nervous. And worried." She slid onto the sofa next to him.

He patted her hand. "Quit worrying. Dante's capable and you know he'll call as soon as he knows something."

"You're right."

"In the meantime, we should check to be sure everything's secure around here."

"I'm certain it's all shut tight. But I should take Rusty out, then lock up."

Roman stood. "Okay. I'll do a window-and-door check in all the rooms while you run him outside."

"Thanks." Gun in hand, she let Rusty out and stood guard over him. Once he finished his business, she brought the dog in and closed and locked the door, then came back to the sofa, laying her gun on the table next to her.

"Everything secure?" she asked Roman.

"Yup," he said, getting up from the sofa. "I'm going to get a soda. You want one?"

"Sure. The coffee didn't help anyway. Any call from Dante yet?"

"No, not yet."

She picked up her phone to check it, then frowned. "Hey, it's turned off. What the—"

Something sharp poked into her arm and she tried to jerk away, but hands held her down. She tried to jump off the sofa, but he held her firmly down as she kicked and flailed against his grip, propelling herself forward even as the drug started to take effect. She rolled onto the floor, him on top of her.

Rusty was barking. She heard the dog barking. She saw a blur of activity, then a whimper. Then silence.

Through her hazy, drug-addled vision, she saw Roman rolling her over, smoothing her hair away from her face.

Her entire body felt like a giant weight had been piled on top of it. She couldn't move, couldn't speak as her vision became warped. Roman's face looked like some kind of monster swimming in front of her.

She fought to stay awake, to move her limbs, her fingers, anything. But it was no use.

She couldn't even think straight anymore.

Why was she panicked? She couldn't remember. She was so tired. All she wanted to do was sleep.

She blacked out.

Twenty-Three

Dante had pushed the accelerator to one-twenty, and it still felt as if he wasn't going fast enough. When he screeched to a halt in front of the house, he already knew it was too late.

"Front door's ajar," Gabe said as they threw the car doors open and ran inside, guns drawn.

"Anna!" Dante yelled for her as he pushed the front door open, but he knew with a sinking depth in the pit of his stomach that Roman had taken her.

He heard Rusty barking and ran to the bedroom, opened the door. The dog bounded out, barking, searching the house for Anna, just the way they were.

They searched the entire house, but found nothing. No Anna.

"Roman won't be at his place. He'll know that's the first place we'll look."

"So where is he?"

"Fuck if I know."

Dante found Anna's cell under the sofa, along with the cap from a syringe.

"He drugged her. Fuck."

Gabe held up her cell. "Can't track her this way, and I imagine Roman's already ditched his."

Pushing his fear aside, Dante reminded himself to think like he was on a mission, not like a man in love and scared to death he was going to lose his woman. "He's knocked her out. Where is he going to take her? He has no other family, no other property that we know of. And it's not like he can just throw an unconscious woman over his shoulder and walk her into a hotel, so his choices are going to be limited."

Dante had to try to think like Roman, which was going to be hard. They used to be close as…brothers. He knew his every move. Now? Hell, the only person he'd really connected deeply with since he'd been back was Anna. "He has no close friends that I know of, but I've been gone."

Gabe shrugged. "He works. And he goes home. That's all I know about him. Anna would know more."

"That's not helpful."

"Sorry, man. But we'll find him."

"Wait. His car has a GPS unit. All the detectives' cars do."

"We couldn't be that lucky. He wouldn't be that sloppy or forgetful."

"Wouldn't he?" Dante grabbed Anna's laptop and logged onto the local system, waited for it to come up. "He's desperate right now. All his plans have gone to shit. He's not thinking clearly. If he's got Anna, he probably hasn't had time to change vehicles."

He entered Roman's unit number and waited for it to come up. When it did, he smiled. "Bingo. Who lives on the Hill?"

"No one I know," Gabe said. "Oh, wait. Anna told me once that Tess has a house there. Maybe she does exist."

"Do you think she's in on it with him?"

Gabe shot him a look of distaste. "God, I hope not."

"What's her last name?"

"Shit. I don't know. Let me think. Jameson, maybe? No. Jackson. That's it. She inherited the house from her parents."

"You know more about her than you thought."

Gabe shrugged. "Bits and pieces. Only because it was unusual for Roman to stick to any one woman for a long period of time."

Dante looked up the address. "Got it."

He didn't want to think about Roman being obsessed with Anna. Why hadn't she told him? Was she even aware of it?

"Let's go. We'll call Pohanski on the way and let him know where she is."

Anna batted away the cobwebs, trying hard to open her eyes. She was so tired, felt as if she'd had four or five tequila shots followed by several beers.

Had she partied last night? What time was it, anyway?

She tried to sit up, but she couldn't. Something restrained her.

She blinked to open her eyes. Seeing was a problem, and the room spun. She tried to get a grip, to focus on something, but it was all so blurry.

Whoa. Nausea rose up and she squeezed her eyes shut again, wishing she could roll over and bring her knees to her chest.

She did not feel good. At. All.

"The nausea will go away soon. Here, drink some water."

Her eyes shot open at the whisper in her ear.

Roman.

Instant clarity brought it all back to her, the haze disappearing like a sudden gust of wind blowing away the last of the fog.

Roman had come over, said Gabe had shot at him. Dante had gone after Gabe. Then Roman had—

She tried to speak, but her mouth was full of dry cotton.

"Drink."

She didn't want to drink anything he gave her.

He took a sip. "It's not drugged, honey. I promise. Now, drink." He put the glass to her lips.

She was so thirsty. She sipped, water spilling onto the sheets. She didn't care.

"Not too much or you'll get sick."

Now that her vision had cleared, she looked around. Her arms were over her head and she was tied to the iron bars of a bed. She glared at Roman.

"You drugged me."

He looked sad. Regretful. "I know. I'm sorry. I hadn't planned to do it this way, but things got out of control."

"I don't know what you're talking about. And I can't feel my hands. This hurts."

He looked pained. "They do? Let me untie you. Don't run."

"I'm not going to run, Roman. I just want to talk."

He took out a knife and she suppressed a shudder as he slit through the ropes at her wrists, releasing her from the bed. She rubbed her wrists, wincing as the circulation flowed back.

"You're going to be dizzy and weak for a while until the drug wears off. Don't try to get up."

She shifted to sit and scooted back against the pillows. "I just want to sit."

He backed away and crouched on the floor, rolling the knife around in his hands. He wielded the knife in and out through his fingers like an expert. She expected him to cut himself—the blade was sharp—but he obviously knew what he was doing as he watched her and played with the knife.

She focused on her surroundings. The bedroom was dark, so she couldn't make out much. She was in someone's house, but whose? This wasn't Roman's place.

"Where are we?" she asked.

"A house."

"Whose house?"

"That's not important. When you're feeling up to moving around, I'll show you. I want you to like it."

Why was it important to him that she like the house? "I need to know whose house this is, Roman."

The look he gave her was earnest, his expression that of a little boy eager to please. "It's our house."

Oh, shit. "Ours?"

"Or it will be as soon as you give your approval."

She wanted to object, to tell him it would never be their house, but she sensed how fragile his grasp on reality was, so she played along. "I'm sure it's going to be great if you picked it out for us."

"I've been planning this a long time."

"Have you? Tell me about it." She inched her feet to the side of the bed, letting her legs slide over the edge.

He watched her and frowned. "What are you doing?"

"I need to swing my legs back and forth so I can get some circulation going in them. Is that okay with you?"

He shrugged. "I guess so."

She moved her legs to show him what she was doing. "Tell me about the rest of the house."

"It's a two-bedroom. Not very big, but a nice place to start out. It's an older house—it's on the Hill—nice neighbors and a real friendly place. I'm sure you're going to like it a lot."

"I'm sure I will. I like the Hill a lot. Tess has a cute little house on the Hill, as I remember."

He frowned. "Yeah, she did."

Did? What did that mean? "What happened between you and Tess, Roman? You told me things were going well."

He lifted his gaze to hers. "She wasn't you. She was in the way."

Goose bumps broke out on her skin at the look he gave her. She shivered at the intensity of his gaze, at the way it bored into her, as if she was everything to him—everything he'd ever wanted.

He was insane. Totally and completely gone.

How had she not seen his obsession before? Had he really been that good at hiding it, or had she just not wanted to see it?

He functioned normally. He was a good detective. But she knew a lot of psychopaths functioned as normal productive members of society.

Until they killed.

"Roman, where's Tess?"

He wouldn't meet her gaze, just kept rolling the knife between his fingers.

"Roman," she said, her voice sharp in command. "Tell me where Tess is."

His gaze snapped to hers. "She's…gone."

The man looking at her now wasn't the Roman she thought she knew. His easygoing smile was gone, replaced instead by a heated passion she'd never seen before. And it was directed at her.

And now she knew. He'd killed George, Jeff and her father. She didn't understand why. And where was Tess? Poor Tess, who'd done nothing wrong except for not being Anna.

Hatred for Roman filled her. He'd beaten them all to death. Jeff. Her father, who had patiently worked with Roman and gotten him into the police academy. He'd killed a fellow police officer, too. And likely a sweet, innocent woman. He'd slaughtered them all, killed them all with his bare hands.

Just like she wanted to leap off the bed and kill Roman right now.

She tried not to think about any of that because she needed to get out of this alive.

Because if she got out of this alive, Roman would pay for what he'd done.

"When can we go see the rest of the house, Roman?"

He looked around. "You don't like this room?"

"I don't know. It's kind of dark in here, so I can't see much."

He grinned like a little boy. "Oh. Sorry. Let me turn on a light."

He stood and came toward her, the knife held out in front of him. It was the same one she'd seen held by her attacker in her backyard.

Her attacker had been Roman. The person who'd left her the flowers and the notes had been Roman.

It had all been Roman. Roman, who had played along with them, shocked and tearful when George and Jeff had died. Compassionate when her father had been killed. And all this time it had been him.

She'd never seen it coming.

It was going to take everything inside her not to leap at him and dig her fingers in his eyes, to try to wrestle the knife from him and stab him with it. Violent rage filled her, but she had to play it cool, had to keep her anger under control until the time was right.

He turned on the small lamp on the table next to the bed. It cast enough light in the room that she could see him. He crouched next to the bed.

"Better?"

She forced an easy smile. "Much better. Thanks."

"Need another drink?"

"No, I'm good right now."

"Okay."

He was quiet, so she sat and tried to get her bearings. With every minute that went by, the fuzziness in her head cleared. But she had no idea how she'd feel physically if she needed to run. She had to test it.

"Roman, I need to go to the bathroom."

He chewed on his lower lip, then motioned with his head toward the door at the other end of the room. "There's one in there. You can't get away. Window's too small."

"I'm not trying to get away. I just have to use the bathroom."

He stood, held the knife out. "Go ahead. Leave the door open."

Great. She'd at least be able to stand up and test her legs. "Okay, thanks."

She slid off the bed. A little wobbly at first, but not dizzy. She took slow steps toward the bathroom and went in, turned on the light. Small bathroom, one vanity. Very feminine.

She eased the shower curtain aside and smothered a gasp as she saw Tess lying in the tub, fully clothed and bloodied, a cut across her throat, her lifeless eyes staring up at Anna. She had ligature marks across her wrists and ankles, dried blood there as if she'd been tied up for a long time. There was bruising, too.

Jesus, how long had he kept her prisoner in her own home? Hadn't someone missed her?

How long had she been dead? Not long, from the looks of her.

Hands shaking, Anna realized she was going to have to keep up a normal front or Roman would likely slip into his delusion completely, and then she'd be in deep trouble. Her stomach clenched when she thought about Tess.

She came out of the bathroom, startled to find Roman leaning against the doorway just outside.

"Oh, hi," she said, skirting around him to head back toward the bed. His hand shot out and grabbed her wrist.

"Anna."

She closed her eyes for a brief second, praying Dante

and Gabe figured out in a hurry what had happened. They were smart. They'd find her.

She turned to face him. "Yes?"

"I'm in love with you."

She lifted her chin. "I love you, too, Roman. But I'm feeling a little dizzy right now. Is it okay if I sit down?"

He frowned, looked as if he didn't believe her. She let her body begin to shake and started to sag. He wrapped an arm around her. "Yeah, right. Forgot about the drug. Let's get you back to bed. Maybe you need to lay down again."

"I'm okay," she said as he got her to the edge and she sat. "I just need to sit for a few more minutes."

Long enough for the cops to come. For Dante to get here.

For someone to put a bullet in your head, you sick bastard.

Fortunately he sat her on the side of the bed facing the window, so he snuggled up against the wall underneath it. The shades were closed, but her position gave her a vantage point now. And with the light on, maybe someone would see her silhouette.

Maybe. Please.

"Roman."

He lifted a hopeful gaze at her. "Yes?"

"Why did you kill George?"

He shook his head back and forth. "George. He knew. He suspected something. He came to me, to talk to me, to tell me I needed help. I had to get rid of him. Too smart for his own good, dammit. He had to go before he told."

That's why he killed George. George found out something about Roman, and Roman killed him for it.

"Why did you kill Jeff and my dad?"

He frowned and looked away. "I don't want to talk about them."

"I do. It's important to me. I need to know."

"You're always thinking about them. About all of them. It was never about you and me and it needed to be about you and me. And then when I found out *he* was coming back I knew it was time. They all had to die."

"Is that why you killed them?"

He finally lifted his gaze to hers. "They all had to go so it would just be the two of us. You were always stuck in the past, too wrapped up in it. I had to make it go away. I have to make them all go away, so you'll focus on me. So you'll see me. Me!" He beat his chest.

"I'm the one you're supposed to be with, and you never saw it. All you saw was that night twelve years ago. And Dante. When he came back, he brought the past back with him. I saw it in your eyes. I saw the way you looked at him.

"I had to erase the past, which meant they all had to go. Then you'd be free to think about the future. Then you'd finally see me."

Roman was deeply screwed up. He was teetering so far on the edge of the cliff she could flick her finger at him and he'd fall off. She was going to have to tread very lightly. "I see you now. I'm sorry it took me so long."

He looked right through her as if he didn't even see her, as if he was looking at something else instead. "You still love Dante. I have to kill him so you'll forget him."

"Now that I know how you feel—"

He stood abruptly, anger turning his face red as he

pointed the knife at her. "No. They have to be gone or you won't forget. I have to make them disappear, or you'll keep thinking about them."

"Who told you that?"

He pointed the knife at her. "I know. If he's still alive you'll love him. Gabe has to go, too. They all have to go."

She stayed silent, pondering a way out. Dante would find her, and they'd both survive this. She had to believe that, had to stay strong and steady so when the time came she could make a move.

"Can I see the house now?"

He shook his head. "No."

"Roman, please? I'd really like to walk around. Maybe we can have a drink, sit in the living room and talk."

"You want to sit and talk?"

"Yes. Let's forget about everyone else and be just you and me."

His eyes gleamed with excitement. If she only had a sledgehammer...

"Okay. I'll come help you stand."

He moved toward her and she caught sight of a red dot hovering against the window shade.

Laser sight. Someone was outside. SWAT? God, she hoped so.

She stood as he came toward her and prayed like hell SWAT could tell the difference between Roman and her.

The window broke with the shot, but Roman hit the ground, pulling her down with him.

Shit. They'd missed. Roman rolled, scrambled to his knees and dragged her in front of him.

Everything happened so fast after that. Roman jerking

her out of the bedroom. Glass breaking as someone came busting through the window.

This wasn't going to end well for one of them.

Dante had Roman in his sights and he was going to take the shot, fuck Pohanski and his order to wait for SWAT.

"You sure about this?" Gabe had asked.

"I'm sure I'm not waiting."

"Then I'm right behind you."

Anna was in there and Roman was insane. He had one mission—get in there and get her away from him. The rest of Pohanski's team could stand around with their dicks in their hands when they got there, but he was going in.

As soon as he saw the silhouette and knew it was Roman, he sighted and took the shot. He saw the shadows moving after the shot and knew he'd missed. So he took off at a run and threw himself through the window, taking the chance that Roman wouldn't hurt Anna.

He rolled and came up, rifle aimed and ready to fire.

Roman was nowhere to be found. Bathroom was clear except for one dead woman in the tub that had to be Tess. He looked at Gabe and they both grimaced.

Dante moved out of the room at a careful pace, listening for sounds of breathing, looking for shadows in corners, anything that would give him a clue where they'd gone. He knew they wouldn't leave the house because by now Roman realized the place was surrounded.

Gabe was right behind him, moving in unison, with his back to him, checking to make sure they wouldn't be ambushed.

Dante stopped, listened, heard nothing and moved into the next bedroom. Empty, so they moved on.

Small house. There were only so many places Roman could hide. He heard a sound and stilled, his head turning in the direction of the noise. He made steps toward the door and turned the knob, opened it.

Stairs. Basement.

"I'm going down alone."

Dante turned to Gabe. "Halfway down and stop at the overhang. Cover me. If it goes bad, take him down and don't wait for SWAT."

"You got it."

Dante moved down the stairs, trying not to make noise, but it was an old house and wooden stairs creaked. Dammit.

He got to the bottom and hit the concrete floor. It was dark. His eyes were trained and he could see fine. He'd hit plenty of targets on a moonless night.

He scoped out the basement. It was littered with boxes and old furniture as he moved his way around. There was a storage room, but he already knew where they were. He stilled long enough to hear them breathing.

At least Anna was still breathing. If she was alive then there was hope he'd get her out of here.

He moved toward them, keeping himself covered by various beams and boxes because he knew damn well Roman had a weapon on him and wouldn't hesitate to take him out. He had his vest on, but he wasn't stupid.

"Roman, let her go."

Dante held the sniper rifle up against his shoulder, pivoted and pointed at Roman. He was backed into a corner, crouching, with Anna held against him, facing

Dante, Anna's body aligned perfectly with his. Roman wasn't stupid, either. He had to know they'd bring SWAT.

"I have a knife pointed at her, Dante. You so much as move one fucking hair, I kill her."

A knife? Why not his gun? Where was his gun?

The tip of the knife was positioned at her neck, right at her carotid artery. One sharp cut and she'd bleed out before medics could get to her.

So far Anna hadn't said a word. Maybe she was letting Roman play his game.

He kept his voice calm and level. "Why are you doing this?"

"You can't have her. She's mine. Why did you have to come back? She'd have been mine if you hadn't come back."

He heard the crack in Roman's voice, knew he was breaking down, but couldn't feel sorry for him.

"You tell him, Anna. Tell him how you're mine."

He saw her face. There was no fear there, only calm. She smiled at him.

A signal.

"I won't tell him that, Roman, because I don't love you. You're sick. You killed my father. You lied to me. All these years, you lied to me about who you really were. You killed Jeff and George and you beat my father to death. You killed Tess, too, for no reason. Do you really think I would allow someone like you to have me? If you think that, then cut my throat now, because I'd rather be dead than be with you."

"What? You said in there—"

She smiled at Dante. "I lied. I love Dante. I've always loved him and he's the only one I'll ever love."

Roman raised up and Dante saw the rage on Roman's face. He knew Anna was going to make her move. He raised his rifle and took aim, but Anna's head—her entire body—was in the way.

"You bitch!" Roman spun her around. Anna shoved him hard and Roman took a swing at her with the knife. She dropped to the floor.

Dante hit Roman with one shot to the chest. He flew back, the knife dropping out of his hands as he fell.

Dante ran toward Anna. All he saw was blood. Panic hit him with a gut punch. He couldn't lose her.

Anna grabbed onto her arm to stanch the flow of blood and stared at Roman's body on the ground.

His eyes were lifeless. He was gone.

She waited for a sense of triumph, of vindication. But all she felt was empty inside. It was over. Dante and Gabe were safe. It was all that mattered to her.

She lifted her gaze to Dante as he ran over to her, laid his rifle down and drew her against him. He pulled a handkerchief out of his pocket and wrapped it around the wound on her forearm.

"I'm okay," she said, laying her head against his chest. "Roman's dead. We're all alive. It can't get much better than that."

The tactical team burst in through the basement door. "Suspect is down," Dante said. "We need a medic in here. Anna's wounded."

Gabe came flying down the stairs, too, SWAT right on his heels. He skidded to a halt in front of them, then let out a long breath.

"Jesus Christ," Gabe said as he looked at Anna and frowned. "You're bleeding."

"I'm okay."

He nodded. "Then I'd say that battle came out on the right side."

Anna settled back against the wall, still trying to catch her breath as a medic started working on her arm.

Pohanski and his team came in, looked at her, at Roman.

"I'm all right," she said.

He looked at Roman. "Jesus Christ. This is a mess." He swept his hand over his head. "Roman…"

"I didn't know," Anna said to him.

Pohanski shrugged. "Who did? What kind of sick fuck was he? I guess we have some digging to do on him." He looked at Anna. "You get fixed up. You," he said to Dante, "did good."

He walked out. "The media is going to love this shit."

"I still can't believe it was Roman," Dante said.

"He was in love with me, deluded himself into thinking if he got rid of all of you, I'd forget you existed and the two of us could live happily ever after."

Dante stared incredulously at her. "I had no idea he was so screwed up."

"Neither did I. He fooled us all."

"How the hell did he pull it off? He was attacked in the alley. There was video, right?" Gabe asked.

Dante nodded. "He probably hired a guy to beat him up and stab him and kill Hannesey. Then gave him an escape car so he could hightail it out of there."

"I'd like to know who Roman hired," Anna said.

"We may never know that," Dante said.

"How can someone be that messed up?" Gabe asked. "How could he hurt the people he was supposed to care about?"

Anna's eyes welled up with tears. "I don't know. We'll never know."

"And how could none of us see it?" Gabe asked.

"We saw what he wanted us to see," Dante said.

"Serial killers and psychopaths are good at hiding who they really are. They can appear so normal," Anna said. "That's what's so scary about them."

"I guess." Gabe crouched and kissed the top of Anna's head. "I wouldn't want your job, honey. You deal with some fucked-up people."

Dante pulled her against him. "You did good. You kept him sane until we got here."

"I was a victim once," she said, feeling nothing as she stared down at Roman's body. "Never again."

She realized as the teams came in to work the scene that through it all she hadn't once had a panic attack.

Huh. Maybe she was getting tougher. Finally.

It was now or never. Decisions had to be made.

It had been a week since Roman's case had been wrapped up, and Dante had no reason to still be here. He'd given his statements. All the loose ends had been tied with a big, fat bow. Anna had ended up getting eight stitches in her arm. The cut hadn't been too deep. Thank God. Seeing Roman slash her with that knife had made his heart stop. He still relived that moment over and over again.

Damn, she'd been brave.

But now it was over.

He could go back to work. His work. His job. Wherever he wanted to go, because he had that level of freedom. Or not go, if he so chose, because he had that freedom, too. He'd put in his time. Death-defying time.

He could go back to it if he wanted. He'd always loved his job, as harrowing as it was sometimes.

Or he could stay here.

Only one person could help him make that decision, and they'd danced around talking about it for seven damn days now.

He was still staying at Anna's place and she seemed to be content with that, hadn't kicked him out, hadn't asked him to stay.

Actually, she hadn't said a goddamn thing at all. She'd done her job, filed her reports, been debriefed, given her interviews. At night she came home with him and they made love and talked about everything *except* the fact that he should probably be leaving.

For some reason by the time they came home, they were too tired to do anything other than eat and climb into bed.

And once in bed? Yeah, deep conversation was over. All they wanted was each other, and that required very few words.

So he decided he was going to talk to her at the precinct today. He'd corner her in the coffee room if he had to, but they were going to settle this once and for all.

Maybe she was tired of him and she wanted him to leave, and she didn't want to hurt his feelings, so she was waiting for him to grab a clue and get the fuck out of town. Maybe the bad memories would never go away for her, and he was part of the past she didn't want to relive over and over again.

Was he that dense he just couldn't see it?

And maybe he hadn't said anything himself because he didn't want to hear those words from her.

But she'd said she loved him.

And he said he loved her.

But sometimes that wasn't enough to build a foundation on.

Shit. *Quit being a pussy and just go get it over with.*

He marched into the office and saw her sitting at her desk, rubbing her brow. She was busy. He could come back later.

He hesitated. Then pushed his feet forward and stopped at her desk. "I need to talk to you."

She lifted her gaze to his. "I'm working on a case, Dante."

He hauled her out of her chair. "Now."

She glared at him, then her arm where he held her. "Are you out of your goddamn mind?"

"We're having a coffee break."

He led her into the coffee room and shut the door.

"First, do not ever manhandle me like that again."

"I love you."

She opened her mouth, then closed it, then opened it again. "I love you, too." Then she frowned. "What is this about?"

"It's time for me to leave."

"Oh." She crossed her arms and leaned against the counter. "So are you leaving?"

"I don't know. Am I?"

Her brows rose. "I'm not your mother."

"What the fuck is that supposed to mean?"

"It means I don't make the decisions for you. Last time I looked you were a grown-up. So are you leaving or aren't you?"

Damn, the woman infuriated him. "I guess not."

"Fine, then."

"Fine."

This wasn't going the way he'd planned. She seemed irritated. And he was pissed off.

Time to regroup. "Anna. Let's start over. I love you. I want to marry you. I want to have lots of babies with you. I don't want to leave. I want to stay. Do you want me to stay? Will you marry me and live with me and have kids with me?"

Her eyes looked as if they were going to pop right out of her head.

"Uh, what did you just say?"

He cocked his head to the side and crossed his arms. "You're going to make me repeat it?"

"Okay. No. Wait. You love me. I know you love me. But you want to do the whole marriage-and-babies thing?"

"Yes. Does that surprise you?"

"I don't know. Yes. No. I don't know. Everything about you surprises me, Dante."

He came over to her and put his hands on her hips. "I want a family, Anna. I never had one until you and the Clemonses and the guys. And I came back after twelve years and I had it again and almost lost all of you. I almost lost you. I don't want to leave. I don't want to lose you again. I want to have a place to call home. I want to have kids. I want to put down roots, not travel all over the world. And I want to do all of that with you."

Her lips quirked. "You do?"

"Yes, I do."

"What will you do for a living? Not much call for black ops in St. Louis."

He arched a brow. "Do you know that for sure?"

She punched his arm. "Seriously."

"Well, I hear the FBI is interested in hiring me for their local field office."

"Are you kidding?" She snorted.

"I'm not kidding. Based on my outstanding qualifications, I can pretty much write my own ticket."

"Your current…uh…employer will let you do that?"

"Yes. They'll let me go."

He'd been making inquiries. Plans. About their future together. Anna had never thought much about marriage and family. She'd figured she'd be married to her job as a detective for the rest of her life.

Until Dante had swept back into her life and turned it all upside down and sideways.

She'd gotten used to having him in her bed at night, and at her kitchen table for coffee and breakfast in the morning.

And she didn't intend to let him walk out of her life again.

She wound her arms around his neck and pressed her lips to his. "I love you. Let's get married and make babies."

"When?"

"I'm free this weekend and I've never been to Vegas."

He drew her against him and kissed her in a way she

would never tire of being kissed. Wholly, and with his entire heart. When he drew back, he said, "I like Vegas."

This time when her scar throbbed, it was because her heart was beating so damn fast she felt as if her chest would explode.

Now whenever she touched her heart, it would be because it was filled with love.

The past was dead. She was so ready for the future.

* * * * *

Acknowledgments

To Linda McFall, for believing in me enough to make this happen. Thank you for this.

To my editor, Krista Stroever, for your wonderful ideas, brilliant brainstorming and infinite patience in driving this book to its conclusion. Thank you!

To my agent, Kimberly Whalen, for getting me there, keeping me there and calming the waters along the way. I couldn't do this without you.

To my friends who are my rock every day—Shannon Stacey, Maya Banks and Angela James—thank you for letting me vent, throw things, cry and whine incessantly. Having friends I know I can count on means more to me than I can possibly say. You're the absolute best.

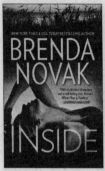

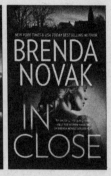

Check out all three *THE SEARCHERS* books
by *New York Times* and *USA TODAY* bestselling author

SHARON SALA

  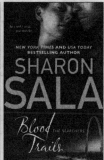

The truth will set you free—
if it doesn't get you killed.

Available wherever books are sold.

REQUEST YOUR FREE BOOKS!

2 FREE NOVELS
FROM THE SUSPENSE COLLECTION
PLUS 2 FREE GIFTS!

SUS11

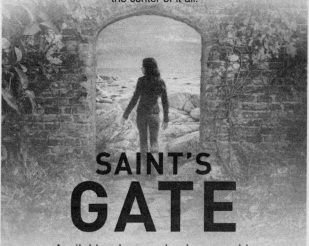